OXFORD WORLD'S CLASSICS

RUDIN · ON THE EVE

IVAN SERGEEVICH TURGENEV (1818–83) was brought up on the estate of his mother at Spasskoe-Lutovinovo and educated at the universities of Moscow and St Petersburg. In 1838 he went to study in Germany and became a convinced believer in the West, or a Westernist (*Zapadnik*). On returning to Russia he gradually turned to literature, first as a poet, then as the author of the famous *Sketches* (*Zapiski okhotnika*, 1847–52), in which he exposed the evils of serfdom. He also began to make a name for himself as a playwright (*A Month in the Country*, 1850), but his life had already become dominated by his devotion to the famous singer, Pauline Viardot. Arrested in 1852 and exiled to Spasskoe, he turned to the larger genre of the short novel, publishing *Rudin* (1856), *Home of the Gentry* (1859), *On the Eve* (1860), and *Fathers and Sons* (1862). The hostile critical reaction to the nihilist hero of this last novel, Bazarov, and his own desire to live close to Pauline Viardot made him choose to live abroad, first in Baden-Baden, then, after the Franco-Prussian War, in Paris. Two further novels (*Smoke*, 1867, and *Virgin Soil*, 1877) followed, in addition to many short stories. By the end of his life his reputation had become overshadowed by his great compatriots, Tolstoy and Dostoevsky, but as the first Russian writer to gain recognition in Europe and America and as a master of the short sociopolitical novel and the lyrical love story Turgenev still remains matchless among Russian writers.

DAVID MCDUFF has published a large number of translations of foreign verse and prose, including poems by Joseph Brodsky and Tomas Venclova, as well as contemporary Scandinavian work. He has translated a number of twentieth-century Russian novels including work by Dostoevsky, Tolstoy, and Leskov.

D1564551

OXFORD WORLD'S CLASSICS

*For almost 100 years Oxford World's Classics have brought
readers closer to the world's great literature. Now with over 700
titles—from the 4,000-year-old myths of Mesopotamia to the
twentieth century's greatest novels—the series makes available
lesser-known as well as celebrated writing.*

*The pocket-sized hardbacks of the early years contained
introductions by Virginia Woolf, T. S. Eliot, Graham Greene,
and other literary figures which enriched the experience of reading.
Today the series is recognized for its fine scholarship and
reliability in texts that span world literature, drama and poetry,
religion, philosophy and politics. Each edition includes perceptive
commentary and essential background information to meet the
changing needs of readers.*

OXFORD WORLD'S CLASSICS

IVAN TURGENEV

Rudin
On the Eve

Translated with an Introduction and Notes by
DAVID McDUFF

Oxford   New York
OXFORD UNIVERSITY PRESS
1999

East Baton Rouge Parish Library
Baton Rouge, Louisiana

Oxford University Press, Great Clarendon Street, Oxford OX2 6DP

Oxford New York

Athens Auckland Bangkok Bogotá Buenos Aires Calcutta
Cape Town Chennai Dar es Salaam Delhi Florence Hong Kong Istanbul
Karachi Kuala Lumpur Madrid Melbourne Mexico City Mumbai
Nairobi Paris São Paulo Singapore Taipei Tokyo Toronto Warsaw
and associated companies in Berlin Ibadan

Oxford is a registered trade mark of Oxford University Press

© David McDuff 1999

First published as an Oxford World's Classics paperback 1999

All rights reserved. No part of this publication may be reproduced,
stored in a retrieval system, or transmitted, in any form or by any means,
without the prior permission in writing of Oxford University Press.
Within the UK, exceptions are allowed in respect of any fair dealing for the
purpose of research or private study, or criticism or review, as permitted
under the Copyright, Designs and Patents Act, 1988, or in the case of
reprographic reproduction in accordance with the terms of the licences
issued by the Copyright Licensing Agency. Enquiries concerning
reproduction outside these terms and in other countries should be
sent to the Rights Department, Oxford University Press,
at the address above

This book is sold subject to the condition that it shall not, by way
of trade or otherwise, be lent, re-sold, hired out or otherwise circulated
without the publisher's prior consent in any form of binding or cover
other than that in which it is published and without a similar condition
including this condition being imposed on the subsequent purchaser

British Library Cataloguing in Publication Data

Data available

Library of Congress Cataloging in Publication Data
Turgenev, Ivan Sergeevich, 1818–1883.
[Rudin. English]
Rudin; On the eve / Ivan Turgenev; translated with an
introduction and notes by David McDuff.
(Oxford world's classics)
1. Turgenev, Ivan Sergeevich, 1818–1883—Translations into
English. I. McDuff, David, 1945– . II. Turgenev, Ivan
Sergeevich, 1818–1883. Nakanune. English. III. Title. IV. Title:
On the eve. V. Series. VI. Series: Oxford world's classics
(Oxford University Press)
PG3421.R8 1999 891.73'3—dc21 98–34399
ISBN 0–19–283333–2

1 3 5 7 9 10 8 6 4 2

Typeset by Graphicraft Limited, Hong Kong
Printed in Great Britain by
Cox & Wyman Ltd., Reading, Berkshire

East Baton Rouge Parish Library
Baton Rouge, Louisiana

CONTENTS

INTRODUCTION

In May 1850, having reached his early thirties, Turgenev faced the necessity of returning from France to Russia—for financial reasons. Having sent his *Diary of a Superfluous Man* to the journal *Notes of the Fatherland* and his play *The Student* (which was later to become *A Month in the Country*) to the eminent poet and critic Nekrasov at the *Contemporary* journal, he had received payments that were insufficient to cover his considerable debts. An appeal to the editor of the journal *Notes of the Fatherland*, Krayevsky, yielded only 200 roubles. At first, the idea of returning to Russia to seek help from his wealthy mother filled Turgenev with reluctance and foreboding. To his friend and mistress Pauline Viardot he wrote, in French, from Courtavenel, where he was staying during the singer's absence in London: 'Russia will wait; that immense, dark face, immobile and veiled, like the sphinx of Oedipus. She will swallow me later. I seem to see her heavy, inert gaze fix itself on me with gloomy attention, as befits eyes of stone. Rest easy, sphinx; I shall return to you, and you will be able to devour me at your leisure if I do not guess the riddle! Leave me in peace a little longer! I will return to your steppes!'

Given the biographical context of these words, the characterization of Russia as an enigmatic sphinx, a dark and brooding 'face' that was about to swallow the writer up, seems partly inspired by Turgenev's complex and tormented relationship with his mother, who made herself the source of his deep emotional ambiguity in matters of dependence, allegiance, and 'belonging'. Indeed, the writer's lifelong ambivalence towards Russia, his 'love–hate' relationship with it, can in many respects be traced in parallel with the divided nature of his own personal sense of himself as a son, stranded between the near-indifference of an emotionally cold and absent father, and the attentions of a possessive, sadistic mother.

Now, however, news suddenly came that the writer's mother, Varvara Petrovna, was seriously ill. She had sent him 6,000 roubles, and asked that he come to Russia at once. From Turgenev's point of view, and from that of his brother, Nikolai, the situation now appeared substantially altered. Finding Varvara Petrovna to some extent recovered, and delighted to have both her sons close at hand, they seized the opportunity at last to put an end to the financial insecurity that had dogged them both since early manhood. To their request that she grant them a regular income, she responded by offering them each a piece of property. In her lingering displeasure at their choice of career (Ivan, whom she had wanted to work in the civil service, persisted with his writing, and his protracted affair with Pauline Viardot, while Nikolai had resigned his commission in the army and was living a hand-to-mouth existence on the fringes of bohemia) she would not, however, notarize documentation of these gifts, or make them official—not only that, but she ordered the estate managers to sell off the year's harvest along with all the reserves of seed-grain in the barns. On learning of this, Turgenev was incensed: finally, after years of prevarication, he spoke his mind to his mother, telling her what he thought of the manipulative cruelty with which she had governed her sons' lives in her desire to exercise personal power over them. Pale with anger, Varvara Petrovna declared that she had no more children, and demanded that her sons leave immediately. When, the following day, Turgenev attempted to obtain an interview with her, she picked up a portrait of him, broke it in two, and smashed it on the floor. The serving-maid who was about to clear up the broken glass was told not to do so, and the broken pieces lay where they were for the next four months.

Although Turgenev was able to move with Nikolai to the small family estate at Turgenevo, and was thus spared being cast out completely, this traumatic event seems to have made an impression on the writer that lasted for the rest of his life. When, towards the end of 1850, Varvara Petrovna died of the dropsy that had been afflicting her for some time, Turgenev wrote to Pauline Viardot (again in French) on 24 November:

My mother died without having made any provisions at all; she left all this great swarm of lives that depended on her—one can say it—on the streets; we must do what she ought to have done. Her last days were very wretched. God preserve us from such a death! She sought only to shut out reality—on the eve of her death, when the rattle had already begun—an orchestra was playing polkas in the next room—at her ordering. One owes only respect and pity to the dead—so I shall say no more. And yet—as it is impossible for me not to tell you everything I feel and know—I shall add just one word—and that is that in her final moments—I am ashamed to say it—all my mother could think of was how to ruin us—my brother and me, and that the last letter she wrote to her steward contained exact and definite orders to sell everything for a pittance, to burn everything down if need be, so that nothing—Well—one has to forget—and I shall do it with all my heart, now that you know, you who are my confessor.—and make her loved and mourned by us all! Ah, yes—God preserve us from such a death!

The sense of shame, distaste, and outrage that is clearly expressed in the letter—mingled as it is with the remnants of a strong filial love and affection—cast a shadow over Turgenev's later life, and above all over his relation to his motherland, Russia. This shadow is at the root of Turgenev's writing: it was constantly to reveal itself, not only in his pronouncements about Russia (such as his remarks to the writer and publicist Alexander Herzen in 1862 about the Russian people being 'conservatives *par excellence*', bearers of 'a bourgeoisie in tanned sheepskins' whose vulgarity and coarseness were the result of a fundamental lack of moral education), but also in the heroes and other characters of his narrative prose. The enigma of the sphinx was gradually unravelled into the component strands of the answer to the riddle: that Russia, and Russians, must learn from the culture, history, and traditions of Western Europe, and put aside at least for a generation or two the Slavophile nationalism which, in the writer's view, was at present founded on a void of ignorance, prejudice, greed, and barbarism. Only when, with the help of Russia's educated class, the people had been rescued from this void, could a new Russia be built on civilized, humane, and rational principles derived from European enlightenment. But was Russia's educated class equal to the task demanded of it?

After their mother's death, the two brothers divided her inheritance between them. Turgenev received the large estate of Spasskoe—not without mixed feelings: for although he was now a rich man, he owed his good fortune to Varvara Petrovna, whom in life he had found unbearable. Now he moved between Spasskoe, Moscow, and St Petersburg, holding dinners, visiting salons and the theatre, and supervising performances of his plays and comedies. He worked on the final drafts of his dark portrayal of Russian provincial life, *A Sportsman's Sketches*, and on short stories. On the death of Gogol in 1852, Turgenev wrote an obituary of the great Russian writer, characterizing him as a defining force in Russian letters and as a 'national treasure'. These sentiments were not to the liking of the censor, however: in St Petersburg publication of the obituary was forbidden. Turgenev sent the manuscript to another censor in Moscow, who allowed it. The article appeared in print, but its author was summarily arrested and imprisoned in the Admiralty fortress. Here, in tolerable conditions, he continued to write—one work of this period of internment was the short story 'Mumu', in which the writer continued his meditation on his mother and the way in which he believed she had poisoned his boyhood—and was, at length, set free. The condition of his release was a kind of house arrest, or exile: he was to go to Spasskoe and remain there under police surveillance. This he did, and at the same time *A Sportsman's Sketches* was passed for publication by the censor—not without repercussions, which included the personal removal by Tsar Nicholas I of the Moscow censor's official concerned from his post—and at once became a literary sensation, both in Russia and in Europe.

Confined to Spasskoe, Turgenev began to reflect that it was time for him to achieve some really durable feat of literary creation: the novel he had long planned to write, but on which he had not yet started to work. Initially, this project centred on a novel called 'Two Generations'. In essence, it was another attempt to exorcise the baleful memory of his mother, and concerned a strong-willed woman, clearly based upon Varvara Petrovna, whose son falls in love with one of her female friends. Work on the book did not make much progress, however, and it was not until several years later, after the exile order had been lifted and the writer was able to travel to and from Moscow, that he returned to it. No sooner was he able to visit the literary salons and editorial offices again than, in 1855, the Crimean War broke out, and the author was once more confined to Spasskoe by the authorities. Nonetheless he began to plan a new novel, based in part on the personal experience of two inconclusive emotional involvements: one with Olga, the 18-year-old daughter of one of his cousins, and another with Lev Tolstoy's sister Marya. It seems possible that Olga may have served to some extent as a model for the character of Natalya in what would eventually become the new novel, *Rudin*.

Rudin

In late May and early June 1855 Turgenev entertained some of his friends and literary advisors, including Botkin, Grigorovich, and Druzhinin, at Spasskoe. On 2 June, after some three weeks, the guests left for Moscow, and the writer decided to resume work on 'Two

Generations'. A few days later, he again abandoned the project, and instead began work on the new project, which he initially called a 'long short story' (*bol'shaya povest'*). On 17 June he wrote to Botkin: 'This time I should like to justify at least a small part of the hopes that you have placed in me; have first written a detailed plan of the story, considered all the characters, and so on. Will something come of it? Perhaps—nonsense.' In spite of his doubts, Turgenev began to work on the story intensively. On 27 June he wrote to Panayev: 'I am writing the story energetically (have already completed 66 pages), and will deliver it to you by the date you desire,' and on 9 July to Botkin: 'I am working hard . . . with luck, the result will be something successful! At least I can say that I have never worked as conscientiously as this.' At last, on 24 July, Turgenev wrote to Marya Tolstaya: 'I have finished the story—and, if I am well, will bring it on Friday.'

Now that the 'story' was completed, Turgenev was anxious to try it out on his friends. As usual, their opinion counted for a great deal with him—he was almost always dependent on their judgement. Writing to Annenkov on 25 July, he asked him to call in at Spasskoe on his way back from Simbirsk in order to become acquainted with *Rudin*. 'For want of anything better to do,' Turgenev said in his letter, 'I have got down to work and completed a very long story on which I have worked as never before in all my life. I really do not know at all whether I have been successful with it. Its idea is a good one— but the execution—there is the rub. I shall read it to you—that is, if you do not cheat me in your usual way and arrive at my home in September.' On the same day he wrote to Botkin: 'I have taken advantage of being unable to go shooting, and yesterday finished a large story, some 7 printed sheets in length. I wrote it with love and deliberation—what has come of this, I do not know. I shall let it lie, then read it through, correct it, and having made a copy will send it to you—will you say something? Will Nekrasov?' A few days later, as he had promised, on Friday 29 July, Turgenev travelled to Pokrovskoe and read *Rudin* to Marya Tolstaya and her husband, Valery. According to Stakhovich, the reading made a favourable impression on the couple. Much later, in 1903, Marya recalled:

We were struck by the then unprecedented liveliness of the narrative and the pithiness of the arguments. The author was worried whether Rudin really stood out as being truly intelligent among the others, who merely indulge in sophistry. For all that, he considered it not only natural, but also inevitable that this 'man of the word' should find himself perplexed in his encounter with Natasha, who is stronger in spirit, and ready and able to achieve something in life.

What Turgenev had written was in essence a double portrait of two mutually attracted but conflicting personalities caught in a web composed not only of the social restrictions and conventions imposed by the 'polite society' of nineteenth-century Russia, but also of inherent character weaknesses emanating from that society. Natalya, the true rebel, in opposition to her family and social milieu, sees in the lordly, intellectual Rudin both the hope of marital fulfilment and of escape from a world she finds suffocating and sterile. Possessing true independence of character and inner strength, she finds herself involved with a man older than herself who, for reasons of background, education, and outlook, is unable to respond to her desire for a release into authenticity and the practical enactment of personal ideals. She finds herself bitterly disappointed. For Rudin, a typical, though gifted, representative of his generation, is only able to offer a shallow, romanticized infatuation, lacking in contact with his true emotions and deriving largely from his reading of German philosophy and nature poetry. Convinced that he is both personally and intellectually 'superfluous', and therefore doomed to exist on the margins of society, even in the experience of love he is unable to progress beyond the bounds of his own subjectivity. In this, he is an heir and successor to a line of characters in nineteenth-century fiction that begins with the hero—or anti-hero —of Pushkin's *Eugene Onegin*. His fate is a tragic one, but it is not merely a personal, individual fate—it represents the destiny of entire generations of Russian intellectuals, who found themselves drawn either towards a fashionable political leftism with its roots in France, and largely inapplicable to the backward social condition of Russia, or towards a Slavophile nationalism and conservatism of the type eventually espoused by Dostoevsky. Rudin chooses the former path —but in political action, as in love, he ultimately reveals himself as ineffectual and lacking in commitment. The only sacrifice he can make is that of himself—but in a cause that is alien to him, and which is really the sublimated form of a blind submission to superior powers— exemplified by the 'strong woman'.

According to Marya Tolstaya, Turgenev, even at this early stage, was concerned about the ambiguity of Rudin's character: after all, on the one hand he marks Rudin out from the rest of the people in his milieu as a man of unusual gifts and intelligence, while on the other he makes him submit to Natasha, by many years his junior, and even presents him as being inferior to her. Although Marya Tolstaya's letter containing her detailed opinion of the narrative's first draft has been lost, Turgenev's reply to it gives some idea of what it concerned. 'All your observations are correct,' he wrote, 'and I will take them into consideration and revise the whole of the final scene with the mother. If she and Rudin, as too often happens in life, exaggerated their feelings (perhaps unconsciously), then I would be right; but Natalya at any rate was sincere. Once again, thank you for your letter. In affairs of the heart women are infallible judges—and we men ought to obey them.'

With the aim of 'officially' presenting the manuscript to his literary advisors in October, Turgenev began a major revision of the work. This was in many ways a crucial period in his life as a writer. 'If the Pushkins and the Gogols,' he wrote to his correspondent S. T. Aksakov, 'worked and revised their things a dozen times, then we lesser men are commanded by God to do the same . . .' On 20 August he wrote to his friend and adviser, the writer Alexander Druzhinin: 'I keep having the sense that my literary career is really at an end. This story will decide the matter.' The reading took place in St Petersburg on 13 October. The audience was composed of the editorial board of the journal the *Contemporary*, and included the author's advisors: Botkin, Nekrasov, and Panayev. Its verdict on the work was positive, but the author decided to make further revisions, additions, and alterations in response to certain criticisms concerning points of detail. Work continued along these lines throughout November and December.

Rudin was originally published in two parts, the first of which contained Chapters 1–6, and the second Chapters VII–XII and the Epilogue (without the concluding scene). The first part of the novel appeared in the January 1856 issue of the *Contemporary*, to be followed by the second part, which appeared in the February issue. With each successive edition of the work, the author made minor corrections and adjustments, adding and removing small portions of text here and there. The final scene of the Epilogue, in which Rudin appears on the Paris barricades of 1848, was added in 1860, along with Rudin's comment to Lezhnev at the hotel: 'I am being sent back to live on my estate.' This sentence had originally read 'I am going back to live on my estate,' but Turgenev evidently altered it in order to give the reader

a hint of the increasingly 'political' direction of Rudin's activities, and
the consequent attention being paid to him by the Russian authorities. The fact that the sentence was allowed to appear in print may
also point to a certain relaxation of the government censorship of the
author's work.

   Towards the end of 1862 a volume containing French translations
of *Rudin*, *Diary of a Superfluous Man*, and *Three Meetings* was published in Paris, under the title *Dmitri Roudine, suivi du Journal d'un
homme de trop et de Trois rencontres*. According to the book's title-page,
translations were made by Louis Viardot (Pauline's husband) in col-
laboration with the author, but in fact Louis's knowledge of Russian
was so imperfect that the translations may fairly be said to be the work
of Turgenev himself. The French translation is for the most part fairly
close to the original Russian, but contains isolated passages that either
do not occur in the original, or are placed in different contexts. Thus,
for example, the description of Volyntsev in Chapter II: 'His facial
features strongly resembled those of his sister; but in their expression
there was less playfulness and liveliness, and his eyes, handsome and
tender, somehow had a melancholy look' is, in the French edition,
applied in slightly modified form to Natalya: 'Les traits de Natalie
rappelaient ceux de sa mère, mais leur expression était moins vive
et moins animée. Ses beaux yeux caressants avaient un regard triste.'
('Natalie's features recalled those of her mother, but their expression
was less lively and animated. Her beautiful, caressing eyes had a sad
expression'.) Pigasov's words about Rudin in Chapter XII: 'You'll see,
he'll end up dying somewhere in Tsarevokokshaisk or Chukhloma'
become, in Chapter XIII of the French edition: 'Il finira, croyez-moi,
par mourir n'importe où, soit en prison, soit en exil.' ('Believe me,
he'll end up dying somewhere or other, either in prison or exile.') In
the same chapter, Lezhnev's characterization of Rudin: 'there really
is no character in him', becomes 'ce que le manque, c'est la volonté,
c'est le nerf, la force' ('what is lacking is willpower, nerve, vigour')—
material that is added, and not found in the Russian version. In some
respects, therefore, the French translation of the novel deserves to be
considered as a separate literary work in its own right, distinct from,
yet closely associated with the original. The work's West European, non-
Russian dimension is an important one—for in this novel Turgenev
views his country, his generation, and his origins as it were from
the outside, as a 'foreigner'. Dostoevsky considered *Rudin* one of

Turgenev's most 'German' productions—but it is also one of his most 'French'. In fact, the French version of the novel may with some justification be considered as a work of French, not Russian literature, and demonstrates that, as a creative artist, Turgenev was equally at home in both literary traditions.

The main prototype of the novel's central character and hero, Rudin, was undoubtedly Turgenev's one-time friend and contemporary, the Russian revolutionary and anarchist Mikhail Aleksandrovich Bakunin (1814–76). Educated at a military school in St Petersburg, Bakunin was an officer of the Imperial Guard, but resigned and spent a number of years travelling in Europe before taking part in the revolutions of 1848–9 in Paris and Germany. In his written plan of the novel, Turgenev went so far as to write the initial letter 'B' instead of 'Rudin', making the association quite plain. At any rate, Turgenev did not deny the resemblance when discussing the novel with friends. 'What is Bakunin like as a man, you ask,' he wrote to Markovich on 16 September 1862. 'In Rudin I have presented a faithful portrait of him. Now he is a Rudin who was *not* slain on the barricade... I feel sorry for him: it is a heavy burden, the life of an obsolete and *démodé* agitator.' At the time Turgenev wrote the novel, Bakunin was imprisoned in the fortress of Schlüsselburg, having been denounced to the Russian authorities by the Austrian government.

Yet it would not do to suppose that Rudin is a straightforward copy of Bakunin. There are also differences, and what Turgenev created was a *type*, the type of the 'men of the 1840s', who included not only many of his intellectual contemporaries, but also himself. The radical polemicist, novelist, and literary critic N. G. Chernyshevsky pointed this out in an article that appeared in the *Contemporary* in 1860—a review of a book of short stories by the American author Nathaniel Hawthorne. In passing, Chernyshevsky discussed Turgenev's *Rudin*, of which he gave an undeservedly negative appraisal, phrasing his criticisms in terms acceptable to the censor. The novel's hero, Chernyshevsky wrote, 'was, to judge by all the evidence, supposed to be a man who had not written much in Russian, but had a very strong and beneficial influence on the development of our literary ideas, who eclipsed the greatest orators with the brilliance of his eloquence', and had become a kind of living legend. But Turgenev, Chernyshevsky went on, had allowed himself to be influenced by his 'friends and advisors', lost the thread of the narrative's 'lofty, tragic character', and instead of creating 'the portrait of a living man' had 'drawn a caricature; as though a lion were a suitable subject for caricature.'

Some of the novel's other characters, while drawn from life, also represent types and trends among the early nineteenth-century Russian intelligentsia. Such, for example, is the idealist Pokorsky, who is a composite of the radical Hegelian activist N. V. Stankevich and the young Belinsky (who later became Russia's great nineteenth-century literary critic). Lezhnev, like Rudin himself, is based on the type of the 'superfluous man'—in the novel, Lezhnev plays the part of Rudin's *alter ego*, an antagonist who, once the drama of the plot has been enacted and Rudin's character (or lack of it) has been focused and revealed, relaxes his antagonism and shows his spiritual brother understanding and compassion.

Although Turgenev's first novel was misunderstood by Slavophiles, who read it as the story of the tragic downfall of a man with noble aspirations who becomes ensnared in too much theory and abstraction, and treated with a certain degree of condescension by liberal and radical critics, who probably eyed the work uneasily, recognizing in its central figure character traits that all too clearly corresponded to their own, its initial critical reception was, nonetheless, on the whole balanced and perceptive. Above all, the author's intention that his hero should be seen as flawed and imperfect was generally understood and expressed. Zotov's review of March 1856 in the *St Petersburg Gazette* set the tone for many that followed. Zotov went so far as to consider the cynical Pigasov the most important character in the novel, while in his interpretation the first appearance of its hero, Rudin, 'places the reader in a state of bewilderment'. Zotov characterizes Rudin through the eyes of Lezhnev, and even more so through those of Pigasov, asserting that Rudin is 'no more than a windbag, covering up his unseemly actions with stentorian phrases'. By 'borrowing money from practically everyone and never repaying it', Rudin shows himself to be worse than 'the uneducated Khlestakov' (the principal character in Gogol's play *The Government Inspector*). In the February *Contemporary*, Nekrasov was equally at pains to highlight the negative characteristics of Rudin, even considering that the author might have overdone his criticism of 'these men' (the 'Rudins' of Russia). Nekrasov believed that in spite of all their weaknesses, it was from such men that Russia's future leaders would be born. Writing in the *St Petersburg Gazette* in June 1857, Druzhinin considered that Rudin, 'having taken from enlightenment that which seems to him radiant and fruitful . . . fulfils only the pre-liminary part of his task'. The 'task', in Druzhinin's view, is life itself: while Rudin has achieved a measure of reconciliation with life, he has not 'been able to rise to an understanding of *action*, to a possible and necessary harmony with the milieu that surrounds him'.

Thus, in many ways, Rudin fits into a long series of Russian literary heroes who, though they possess sensitivity, intelligence, and even a certain nobility of temperament, are unable to establish a relation to the real world of decision, commitment, and personal and practical achievement. From Pushkin's Onegin, through Lermontov's fatalistic Pechorin (*A Hero Of Our Time*, 1841), to Herzen's Beltov (in *Whose Fault?*, 1846–7), Rudin can trace his descent down a long line of 'Byronic' characters for whom the powers of negation and contradiction are more compelling than those of creation and synthesis. Rudin's flight from Natalya and death on the Paris barricade for the sake of a cause—revolutionary 'nonsense' in which, as he puts in his farewell letter to her, he does not even believe—are the expression of a lack of rootedness in life itself. How, Turgenev appears to be asking, can Russia build a modern, enlightened state on such shaky existential foundations? If the country's intellectual class, which ought to give practical, not merely theoretical, leadership, cannot fulfil its task, then what hope is there for the mass of ordinary Russians, who have no one whom they may follow, or from whom they may derive inspiration?

On the Eve

In his essay 'Hamlet and Don Quixote' (1860), Turgenev perceived the failure of the Russian intelligentsia in terms of two characteristic types: the 'Hamlets' are the analytical sceptics whose alienation from their fellow human beings leads them into idleness and inactivity, while the 'Quixotes' are those who, captivated by the *idea* of action, throw them-selves into enthusiastic but unproductive projects and exploits. While the plot and characterization of *Rudin* are obviously closely connected with the subject-matter of this essay, its juxtaposition of what Turgenev believed to be the two fundamental character-types of his age is reflected even more vividly in the novel *On the Eve*, which Turgenev had begun to plan even before *Rudin*, as early as 1853 or 1854. In a memoir of his year of exile he wrote: 'I was preparing to write *Rudin*; but the task I later attempted to perform in *On the Eve* from time to time arose before me. The figure of the principal heroine, Yelena, a type then new in Russian life, was taking shape fairly clearly in my imagination; but I lacked a hero, a man to whom Yelena, with her as yet vague, though powerful striving for freedom, could give herself.'

Help was at hand in the form of a manuscript written by a land-owning friend and neighbour of Turgenev's named Vasily Karateyev. In 1855 Karateyev left for the Crimea as an officer in the Orlov Volunteer Corps, and before his departure, fearing he might not return alive, gave Turgenev a small notebook, in which 'with fleeting strokes was sketched what later became the content of *On the Eve*.' Turgenev noted that

the story was . . . not completed, and broken off suddenly. During his time in Moscow, Karateyev had fallen in love with a girl who had responded to him with mutual affection; but who, having met the Bulgarian Katranov (a man, as I later found out, once quite famous and to this day not forgotten in his motherland), fell in love with him and went with him to Bulgaria, where he died soon after. The story of this love is conveyed sincerely, though clumsily . . . Only one scene, the excursion to Tsaritsyno, was sketched rather vividly—and in my novel I retained its principal features.

On reading Karateyev's manuscript, Turgenev is reported to have exclaimed: 'Here is the hero I have been looking for!' Nonetheless, he left the project lying for a while. Gradually, at occasional informal evening readings during the winter of 1858–9, according to Annenkov he began to 'try out' portions of 'a crumpled, clumsy, badly written manuscript story', surprising his listeners with 'his sympathy with a work that was undeserving of attention'. Turgenev evidently read directly from Karateyev's manuscript, though at the same time he was formulating the plan of his own novel. This preliminary work was finished by April 1859, and it was at around this time that Turgenev is supposed to have confided the contents of the plan to his friend and rival the writer Goncharov who, not for the first time, unjustifiably suspected Turgenev of having borrowed from one of his plots, on this occasion that of the novel *The Precipice* (not published until 1869)— Goncharov claimed to see resemblances to the love affair between two characters in his own novel. This incident merely convinced Turgenev of his friend's increasing hypersensitivity and abstraction from reality.

As the historical background for the narrative (a background which must already have been present in Karateyev's manuscript), Turgenev took the resolution of the so-called 'Eastern Question', and the events of the period from the summer of 1853 to the spring of 1854 which directly preceded the Crimean War. Ever since the late eighteenth century Russia had sought to take advantage of the decline of the Ottoman Empire and the problems it had caused in the balance of power in the region. To this end, it was anxious to increase its influence in the Balkans, and to take away from Turkey control of the narrow channel of water connecting the Black Sea and the Mediterranean. Russia's aim was to establish a unilateral protectorate over Turkey's empire, and this aspiration was viewed as a threat by Britain and France, who were determined that it should not succeed. By the early 1850s, under Tsar Nicholas I, Russia had grown emboldened to the point where it believed it would derive support in its aims from Austria, and (mistakenly) that Britain would collaborate in a partition of the Turkish-administered lands, which included Bulgaria. *On the Eve* has a strongly topical, contemporary flavour—the title suggests not only an impending personal catharsis, but also a political one—for it includes vivid references, not only to the Bulgarian conflict, but also to the occupation by Russian troops of the Turkish principalities of Moldavia and Walachia (now Romania), and the Russian fleet's sinking of a Turkish squadron in the Black Sea, an action that became known as the 'Sinope Massacre'.

Again, as in *Rudin*, for the central 'human interest' of the story Turgenev created a double portrait composed of an unusual, idealistic man—this time a Bulgarian revolutionary nationalist—and a 'strong woman' in rebellion against her family and the stifling social milieu it represented. Pre-emancipation Russia under Tsar Nicholas I was hardly an enlightened or enlightening place—Russia's serfs did not attain their freedom until 1861, after Nicholas's death and the ascendance to the throne of his son, Alexander—and the gentry among whom Yelena, the novel's heroine, was at home, though not a hereditary nobility in the Western sense, were nonetheless stuck firmly in their ways and seemingly impervious to change. In seizing on the human and intel-lectual background of the events that were now unfolding in the East, Turgenev was making his own contribution to what he hoped would become a process of social transformation in Russia. On a more personal note, however, his 'love stories' reflected his own somewhat stark and uncompromising view of love and matrimony—seen from his perspective, there existed only one possibility of fulfilment in life for a man, that of becoming happily married to a woman he loved. Anything short of this meant personal failure, loneliness, and an early death. The early death of Rudin, and the even earlier death of the Bulgarian Insarov, the hero of *On the Eve*, must be seen in the light of this conviction. In both cases, however, the ultimate villain is Russia itself, which is perceived as backward, oppressive, and inimical to human strivings for nobility and personal fulfilment.

First reactions to the finished manuscript of *On the Eve* were mixed. The pious Countess Yelizaveta Lambert, Turgenev's closest friend and the wife of an aide-de-camp to the Tsar, was one of the first to read it, and was horrified. The reason for her horror was the behaviour of the central female character, Yelena, who leaves her parents and runs away abroad with a political adventurer—though she marries him. Descriptions of such conduct were rare in the literature of the time, and on its publication in the *Russian Messenger* the book aroused a storm of controversy. In his memoirs the literary critic P. V. Annenkov charted its reception in the following terms:

In its appraisal of *On the Eve*, the public was divided into two camps and did not agree on the same interpretation of the work, as was the case with *A Nest of Gentlefolk*. The eulogistic section of the public was composed of the university youth, the class of scholars and writers, and the enthusiasts for the liberation of oppressed races—the novel's liberal, rousing tone was to their taste. Polite circles were, however, alarmed. Their life was a peaceful one, without much excitement, and passed in the expectancy of reforms, which in their opinion could not possibly be far-reaching or particularly serious in character—and they were horrified at the mood of the author, who in his novel raised frightening questions about the rights of nationalities and the lawfulness, in certain cases, of a belligerent opposition. To this section of the public, the inspired, enthusiastic Yelena seemed an anomaly in Russian society, which had never encountered such women. Among them—the members of this section—someone's saying went around: 'This *On the Eve* will not have a tomorrow.'

Several critics considered that the work could have little chance of public success. The publicist Nikolai Botkin wrote:

I read *On the Eve* with enjoyment. I do not know if there is another story by Turgenev that contains as many poetic details as are scattered throughout this one. It is as though he himself felt the looseness of the structure's principal lines, and in order to conceal that looseness, and also perhaps the vagueness of the fundamental lines, had enriched them with the most wonderful details, as the builders of Gothic cathedrals once did. For me, these poetic, truly artistic details make me forget the lack of clarity of the whole. What epithets, like unexpected rays of sunshine, suddenly revealing the inner perspectives of objects! To be sure, the unfortunate Bulgarian does not come off at all; his all-devouring love for his motherland is so feebly sketched that it rouses not the slightest sympathy, and as a result of this Yelena's love for him surprises rather than touches. This story cannot possibly have any success with the public, for the public reads in duck-like fashion and likes to swallow things whole. But I think there is scarcely a person with poetic feeling who will not pardon the story all its mathematical defects for those sweet sensations awoken within his soul by those tender, subtle and graceful details. Yes, I agree in advance with all that can be said about the defects of this story, and yet I consider it a charming one. It is true that it will not touch one, will not make one reflect, but it will breathe the aroma of life's finest flowers.

Lev Tolstoy, writing to the poet Afanasy Fet on 23 February 1860, was rather more dismissive:

I have read *On the Eve*. Here is my opinion: the writing of stories is in general a pointless activity, and all the more so for people who are depressed and do not really know what they want from life. As a matter of fact, *On the Eve* is much better than *A Nest of Gentlefolk*, and it contains some marvellous negative characters—the sculptor and the father. The others, however, not only fail as types, but are not even typical in their conception or situation—when, that is, they are not wholly trite and vulgar. Actually, this is an error Turgenev always makes. The girl is a real bad apple: 'Oh, how I love you' . . . 'she had long eyelashes . . .' In general I always find it surprising that Turgenev, with his intelligence and poetic sensitivity, cannot refrain from banality, even with regard to techniques. Most of this banality is to be found in his negative techniques, which are reminiscent of Gogol. There is no humanity or sympathy with the characters; instead, we are presented with monsters, which the author excoriates but does not pity. This sits somehow awkwardly with the tone and purport of the liberalism of all the rest of it . . .

In the periodical press, discussion of the work tended to centre on the character of Insarov, which was felt by many critics to be insufficiently delineated and lacking in substance. Another section of opinion condemned the actions of Yelena, considering them to be immoral—many of these commentaries were phrased in fairly sharp, abrasive terms. Some of the harshest criticism, however, came from the pen of the young radical publicist Dobrolyubov, whose complaints in the *Contemporary* were directed at questions not of morality but of artistic verisimilitude: Turgenev had not, he believed, made Insarov a credible human figure. 'Mr Turgenev,' he wrote, 'who has made such a thorough study of the better part of our society, has not found it possible to make him *ours*. It is not simply that he has imported him from Bulgaria, but that he has not brought this hero close enough to us simply as a human being.' The article was printed in spite of urgent protests by Turgenev to the *Contemporary*'s editor, Nekrasov, and set the tone for the general view of the novel among radical opinion, even though this was partially offset by some interventions from radical feminist critics, such as Yevgeniya Tur, who analysed the character of Yelena from the point of view of women's emancipation, praising Turgenev's heroine for her self-sacrifice and lack of egoism.

In retrospect, it seems clear that *On the Eve*, like *Rudin* before it, was misunderstood by many of Turgenev's contemporaries. In fact, the misunderstanding was one that stretched back to the very outset of Turgenev's literary career, and was connected with the public and critical interpretation of his artistic and philosophical aims and methods. Turgenev's first great public literary success, *A Sportsman's Sketches* (1852), was read either as a work of social criticism or—especially in Western Europe—as a series of exotic portraits of Russian country life. In fact, Turgenev had intended the book as a portrayal of Russia's soul, in the tradition of Gogol. The portrait was a sombre one, and had its roots not only in the author's personal experience of the Russian countryside, but also in the vision of the 'face, immobile and veiled' of the 'sphinx of Oedipus' that he described to Pauline Viardot in the letter quoted earlier. For Turgenev was concerned, not with the writing of works that exposed the social evils of Russia, or the quint-essence of the Russian countryside, but rather with the creation of a synthesis composed of the multiple and paralysing conflicts between nature and culture, stagnation and aspiration, reality and dream, which he perceived as central to Russia's spiritual and intellectual existence —conflicts and paradoxes that bordered on the universally human territory charted by Dante, Shakespeare, and Cervantes, and could be seen in terms of the concept of the tragic as developed by Schiller and Goethe. This was essentially a Western vision of Russia, its people, and destiny, yet seen through the eyes of a Russian who both loved and hated his own country. While Turgenev was greatly attached to the natural beauty of the Russian landscape, his attitude towards the

Russian people was a deeply ambivalent one. In the *Faust*-inspired
character of Rudin, Turgenev presents us with a man of European
education—perhaps, we are intended to suppose, one of the best minds
of his generation, a man who, because of the backward, stifling nature
of the social milieu that has created him and made him necessary, is
unable to make the leap into life and authenticity that is demanded
of him. Natalya, in Turgenev's view, is also a victim of this tragic
—and infernal—inertia. Yet, just like people of other nationalities,
Russians need their country. It is not their fault if it does not need
them. As Lezhnev puts it in Chapter XII:

Russia can manage without any of us, but none of us can manage without
Russia. Woe betide any man who thinks he can, and double woe betide any
man who really does manage without her! Cosmopolitanism is rubbish, and
the cosmopolitan is a nonentity, worse than a nonentity; outside of national
roots there is neither art, nor truth, nor life, nothing. Without physiognomy
there is not even such a thing as an ideal face; only a vulgar face is possible
without physiognomy. But again I say that this is not Rudin's fault: it is
his fate, a bitter and heavy fate for which the rest of us should not blame
him. It would take us a very long route to discover why the Rudins appear
in our land. (p. 108)

In *On the Eve*, Turgenev presents another view of largely the same
problem: Insarov, with his devout Bulgarian national feeling and
dedication to the cause of independence, has something few of his
Russian contemporaries can boast of: a sense of belonging, a focus and
purpose to individual existence. This, in the end, is what attracts Yelena
to him—yet she is uneasily aware that her own romantic dreams of
freedom sit awkwardly with her husband's plain, dogged, and prosaic
national radicalism. Yelena, one feels, would find it as impossible to
settle down in Insarov's milieu as Insarov would find it to become a
part of Yelena's Russia. Insarov's illness and death are the expression
of this tragic incompatibility, one that is founded on Russia's own self-
centredness and backwardness. As Shubin says to Uvar Ivanovich at
the end of Chapter XXX:

We have no one yet, there are no human beings, no matter where one looks.
It's all small fry, rodents, little Hamlets, samoyeds, or obscurity and the
subterranean backwoods, or arrivistes, pourers of emptiness into vacuity,
and sticks to beat drums with! Or else it's the other kind: studying themselves with shameful subtlety, constantly feeling the pulse of their every

sensation and reporting to themselves: that, they say, is what I feel, that is
what I think. A useful, practical occupation! No, if there were any worthwhile human beings among them, this girl, this sensitive soul, would not
be leaving us, would not be slipping away like a fish into water! What is
this, Uvar Ivanovich? When will our time come? When will some human
beings be born among us? (p. 260)

Strangely, perhaps, such an interpretation did not occur to the
radical and populist-minded intelligentsia of Turgenev's time, most
of whom ignored crucial passages like the one quoted above. In a
letter to Herzen of September 1862, Turgenev tried to steer his correspondent's attention towards the heart of the matter, writing:

The role of the *educated* class in Russia is to be the conveyor of civilization
to the people . . . The people before whom you bow is a conservative *par
excellence*—and even bears within it the germs of such a bourgeoisie in a
tanned sheepskin, a warm and dirty hut, with a belly eternally stuffed to
the point of heartburn and a revulsion towards any kind of civic responsibility or independent action that it will fairly claim all the true and accurate
features with which you have depicted the Western bourgeoisie.

In a further letter, written in October, he added: 'In the so often
repeated antithesis between the West: beauty without and ugliness
within—and the East: ugliness without and beauty within—lies
falseness.'

Some on the political right, including Konstantin Leontyev and
Dostoevsky, did perceive Turgenev's intention and thinking, and were
not pleased with what they saw: 'the moral triumph of the Insarovs
over the Bersenevs and the Shubins is unattractive to the Russian
soul (*it* is not blame!), and that is why you have remained cold to the
persons you respect, have not exalted them into the "pearl of consciousness" . . .' was Leontyev's reaction. Later, Dostoevsky wrote of
Turgenev in *A Writer's Diary*:

He poured abuse on Russia outrageously, horribly . . . Turgenev said that
we must crawl before the Germans, that there is one common road for
all—and an unavoidable one—civilization, and that all Russian attempts
at independence are swinishness and stupidity . . . I advised him, for con-
venience, to order a telescope from Paris. 'Why?' he asked. 'It's a long way
from here,' I replied. 'You can train your telescope on Russia and examine
us—otherwise it will really be rather hard to make us out.' He was dreadfully angry.

Turgenev's analyses of Russian rootlessness and despair were essentially modern in character—it is not far, one feels, from the psychological world of these two short novels to the moral and mental landscape of Baudelaire and French symbolism. Turgenev's own profound knowledge and understanding of French literature, and his personal friendships with Flaubert and Zola, make this analogy less distant than it might at first seem. Insarov's 'mignonette' found its way into the poetry of the French-inspired Russian pre-symbolist poet Innokenty Annensky (mentor of the poets Akhmatova, Gumilev, Pasternak, and Mandelstam), where it functions as one of the central lyrical motifs, along with other images and symbols derived from Turgenev's works. And beyond Russia, Turgenev's description of Insarov and Yelena's experience of Venice cannot, one feels, have been ignored by Thomas Mann in his own evocation of the city (in the novella *Death in Venice*). Above all, the conflicts of cultural loyalty and national self-perception that form the ideological, symbolic, and ethical core of *Rudin* and *On the Eve* are still actual in our own time. The manner in which Russia defines itself in relation to Europe and the rest of the Western world will be of crucial importance to the new world of the next century. In this process of definition Turgenev, like his peer and adversary Dostoevsky, still has much to contribute towards an understanding of the issues, and the struggles they involve.

NOTE ON THE TEXT AND TRANSLATION

THE text used in making the present translation is that contained in I. S. Turgenev, *Sochineniya*, Izdatel'stvo Nauka (Moscow–Leningrad, 1960). *Rudin* is in volume 6 (1963) and *On the Eve* (*Nakanune*) in volume 8 (1964). Reference has been made to the notes and textual commentaries in these volumes.

The translation attempts to follow Turgenev's language, style, and syntax as closely as possible, while remaining within an English stylistic framework. Some minor adjustments have been made in the punctuation, to allow for English conventions.

SELECT BIBLIOGRAPHY

Letters

Turgenev's Letters, trans. A. V. Knowles (London, 1983).
Turgenev: Letters, trans. David Lowe, 2 vols. (Ann Arbor, 1983).

Criticism and Biography

Costlow, Jane T., *Worlds Within Worlds: The Novels of Ivan Turgenev* (Princeton, 1990).

Dessaix, Robert, *Turgenev: The Quest for Faith* (Canberra, 1980).

Freeborn, Richard, *Turgenev: the Novelist's Novelist* (London, 1960).

Garnett, Edward, *Turgenev* (London, 1917).

Hershkowitz, Harry, *Democratic Ideas in Turgenev's Works* (New York, 1932).

Kagan-Kans, Eva, *Hamlet and Don Quixote: Turgenev's Ambivalent Vision* (The Hague–Paris, 1975).

Lloyd, J. A. T., *Ivan Turgenev* (London, 1942).

Lowe, David, *Turgenev's 'Fathers and Sons'* (Ann Arbor, 1983).

Magarshack, David, *Turgenev. A Life* (London–New York, 1954).

Nabokov, Vladimir V., *Lectures on Russian Literature* (San Diego, 1981).

Peterson, Dale, *The Clement Vision: Poetic Realism in Turgenev and James* (Port Washington, New York, 1975).

Pritchett, V. S., *The Gentle Barbarian: The Life and Work of Turgenev* (London–New York, 1977).

Ripp, Victor, *Turgenev's Russia: From 'Notes of a Hunter' to 'Fathers and Sons'* (Ithaca, New York, 1980).

Schapiro, Leonard, *Turgenev: His Life and Times* (New York, 1979).

Troyat, Henri, *Turgenev, A Biography*, trans. Nancy Amphoux (London, 1991).

Waddington, Patrick, *Turgenev and England* (London, 1980).

—— (ed.), *Ivan Sergeyvich Turgenev: 1818–1883–1983*, New Zealand Slavonic Journal (Wellington, 1983).

Worrall, Nick, *Nikolai Gogol and Ivan Turgenev* (New York, 1982).

Yachnin, Rissa and Stam, David, *Turgenev in English: A Checklist of Works By and About Him* (New York, 1962).

Yarmolinsky, Avrahm, *Turgenev: The Man—His Art—and His Age* (New York, 1926; London, 1927; revised edn., New York, 1959; London, 1960).

Zekulin, Nicholas: *Turgenev: A Bibliography of Books 1843–1982 By and About Ivan Turgenev* (Calgary, 1985).

Anthologies and Selections

Allen, Elizabeth Cheresh (ed. and introduction), *The Essential Turgenev* (Evanston, Illinois, 1994).

Magarshack, David (trans. and introduction), *Turgenev's Literary Reminiscences and Autobiographical Fragments, with an essay by Edmund Wilson* (London, 1959).

Further Reading in Oxford World's Classics

Gogol, Nikolai, *Dead Souls*, trans. and ed. Christopher English, with an Introduction by Robert A. Maguire.

Lermontov, Mikhail, *A Hero of Our Time*, trans. Vladimir and Dmitri Nabokov.

Herzen, Alexander, *Childhood, Youth, and Exile*, trans. J. D. Duff, with an Introduction by Sir Isaiah Berlin.

Turgenev, Ivan, *Fathers and Sons*, trans. and ed. Richard Freeborn.

—— *First Love and Other Stories*, trans. and ed. Richard Freeborn.

A CHRONOLOGY OF IVAN TURGENEV

1818   28 October: born in Orël, Russia, second son of Varvara Petrovna T. (*née* Lutovinova), six years older—and considerably wealthier—than Sergei Nikolaevich, his father.

1822–3   Turgenev family makes European tour. Ivan rescued from bear pit in Bern by his father.

1833   Enters Moscow University after summer spent in dacha near Moscow which provided the setting for his story 'First love' (1860).

1834   Transfers to St Petersburg University. 30 October: father dies.

1838–41   Studies at Berlin University and travels in Germany and Italy. Friendships with Granovsky, Stankevich, Herzen, and Bakunin.

1842   26 April: birth of illegitimate daughter. Writes master's dissertation, but fails to obtain professorship at St Petersburg University.

1843   Enters Ministry of Interior. Meets Belinsky. Long poem *Parasha* brings him literary fame. Meets Pauline Viardot.

1844   'Andrei Kolosov', first published short story.

1845   Resigns from Ministry of Interior. Meets Dostoevsky.

1847   First of *Sketches from a Hunter's Album*, 'Khor and Kalinych', published in newly revived journal *The Contemporary*.

1847–50   Lives in Paris or at Courtavenel, country house of the Viardots.

1850   'The Diary of a Superfluous Man.' Completes only major play, *A Month in the Country*. 16 November: mother dies. Inherits family estate of Spasskoe-Lutovinovo.

1852   *Sketches* published in separate edition. 16 April: arrested for obituary on Gogol, but really for publication of *Sketches*. Imprisoned for one month. Exiled to Spasskoe till November 1853.

1855   Meets Tolstoy.

1856   *Rudin*, first novel, published in *The Contemporary*. Travels widely, visiting Berlin, London and Paris. Till 1862 is abroad each summer.

1859   *Home of the Gentry*.

1860   *On the Eve*. 'First Love.' 12 August–2 September: Ventnor, Isle of Wight, and Bournemouth. Conceives figure of Bazarov.

1861   14 February: Emancipation of the serfs. Quarrels with Tolstoy, leading to a 17-year estrangement.

1862   *Fathers and Sons*.

1863   Beginning of his 'absenteeism' from Russia. Takes up permanent residence in Baden-Baden, close to Viardots.

1867   *Smoke*. Quarrels with Dostoevsky.

1870   'King Lear of the Steppes.' Resides for a time in London, driven from Baden-Baden by Franco-Prussian War.

1871   Moves to Paris, residing mostly at Bougival. Flaubert, George Sand, Zola, Daudet, Edmond de Goncourt, and Henry James among his friends.

1872   'Torrents of Spring.'

1877   *Virgin Soil*.

1878   Reconciliation with Tolstoy.

1879   Received in triumph on visit to Russia. 18 June: awarded honorary doctorate of civil law by University of Oxford.

1880   7 June: at celebrations to mark the unveiling of the Pushkin monument in Moscow, Turgenev's speech greeted coolly. 8 June: famous speech by Dostoevsky leads to public, but not private, reconciliation between the writers.

1883   3 September: dies at Bougival from misdiagnosed cancer of the spine after long illness. 27 September: buried at Volkovo cemetery in St Petersburg.

RUDIN

PRINCIPAL CHARACTERS

RUDIN, DMITRY NIKOLAICH (NIKOLAYEVICH)—familiar name:
  MITYA
LASUNSKAYA, NATALYA ALEXEYEVNA (daughter of Darya Lasunskaya)
  —familiar name: NATASHA
LASUNSKAYA, DARYA MIKHAILOVNA (mother of Natalya)
LIPINA, ALEXANDRA PAVLOVNA (sister of Volyntsev)—familiar name
  SASHA
LEZHNEV, MIKHAILO MIKHAILYCH—familiar name MISHA
PANDALEVSKY, KONSTANTIN DIOMIDYCH—in French CONSTANTIN
PIGASOV, AFRIKAN SEMYONYCH
VOLYNTSEV, SERGEI PAVLYCH (brother of Alexandra Lipina)—
  familiar name SERYOZHA

I

IT was a quiet summer morning. The sun was already quite high in the clear sky; but the fields still gleamed with dew, from the recently awoken valleys came a scented coolness, and in the woods, which were still damp and not yet astir, early songbirds were beginning to pipe cheerfully. On the crest of a gently sloping hill that was covered from top to bottom in newly blossomed rye, a small village could be seen. Towards this village, along a narrow country road, a young woman was walking; she wore a white muslin dress and a round straw hat, and held a parasol in her hand. A servant boy followed her at a distance.

She walked unhurriedly, and as though she were enjoying the walk. All around, through the tall, undulating rye, iridescent now with silvery-green, now with reddish ripples, long waves ran with a gentle rustle; in the upper air, skylarks chimed. The young woman was walking from her own village, situated no more than a verst* from the small village to which she was making her way; her name was Alexandra Pavlovna Lipina. She was a widow, childless and quite rich, and lived with her brother, Sergei Pavlych Volyntsev, a retired staff captain of cavalry. He was not married, and tended her estate.

Alexandra Pavlovna reached the small village, stopped at the first hut, which was extremely low and ramshackle, and, calling her servant boy, told him to go inside and inquire about the mistress's health. He soon returned, accompanied by a decrepit muzhik with a white beard.

'Well, then?' Alexandra Pavlovna asked.

'She's still alive...' the old man muttered.

'May one go inside?'

'Why not? Of course.'

Alexandra Pavlovna went inside the hut. It was poky, stuffy, and smoke-ridden. Someone began to move about and groan on the stove-bench. Alexandra Pavlovna looked around and in the semi-darkness saw the yellow and wrinkled head of an old woman, bound with a checked kerchief. Covered right up to the neck in a heavy *armyak*,* she was breathing with effort, feebly lifting her thin arms.

Alexandra Pavlovna approached the old woman, and put her fingers on the woman's forehead . . . It was well and truly on fire.

'How are you feeling, Matryona?' she asked, bending over the stove-bench.

'O-oh!' the old woman groaned, peering closely at Alexandra Pavlovna. 'Bad, bad, my dear! The hour of death is at hand, my little pigeon!'

'God is merciful, Matryona: perhaps you will get better. Have you taken the medicine I sent you?'

The old woman began to moan sadly and did not answer. She had not heard the question.

'Yes, she's taken it,' muttered the old man, who had stopped by the door.

Alexandra Pavlovna turned to face him.

'Is there no one with her apart from you?' she asked.

'There's a girl—her granddaughter, but she's away all the time. Never sits still: a fidgety one, she is. Can't be bothered even to give an old woman a drink of water. And as for me, I'm old myself—how am I to manage?'

'Couldn't she be taken to my hospital?'

'No! What's the good of hospital? She's going to die anyway. Lived enough, she has; anyone can see it's God's will. She can't get down from the stove-bench. What would she want with hospital? If they lift her, she'll die.'

'O-oh!' the sick woman began to moan. 'Pretty lady, don't leave my little orphan girl on her own; our masters are far away, but you...'

The old woman fell silent. Speaking had been a strain for her.

'Don't worry,' Alexandra Pavlovna said. 'Everything will be done. Look, I've brought you some tea and sugar. Have some if you feel like it... You do have a samovar, don't you?' she added, glancing at the old man.

'Samovar? No, we don't, but I could get one.'

'Then do, or I shall send my own. And tell your granddaughter not to be away all the time. Tell her she should be ashamed of herself.'

The old man made no reply, but took the packet of tea and sugar in both hands.

'Well, goodbye, Matryona!' said Alexandra Pavlovna. 'I shall come and see you again, don't give up, and take the medicine regularly...'

The old woman raised her head and stretched towards Alexandra Pavlovna.

'Give me your little hand, lady,' she murmured.

Instead of offering her hand, Alexandra Pavlovna leant down and kissed the old woman on the forehead.

'Now see to it', she said to the old man, as she left, 'that you give her the medicine exactly as it's prescribed... And let her have tea to drink.'

The old man again made no reply and merely bowed.

Once she was out in the fresh air, Alexandra Pavlovna took a deep breath. She unfurled her parasol and was about to go home when suddenly from round the corner of the hut, riding in a low racing droshky,* came a man of about thirty dressed in an old topcoat made of grey *kolomyanka*,* and a peaked cap of the same. Catching sight of Alexandra Pavlovna, he at once brought his horse to a standstill, and turned his face towards her. Broad and pale, with small, light-grey eyes and a whitish moustache, it matched the colour of his clothes.

'Good morning,' he said with a lazy, ironic smile. 'What are you doing here, may one inquire?'

'I've been visiting a woman who is ill... And where have you been, Mikhailo Mikhailych?'

The man who bore the name of Mikhailo Mikhailych looked her in the eye and smiled his ironic smile again.

'It's very good of you', he continued, 'to visit a woman who's ill; but wouldn't you do better to take her into your hospital?'

'She is too weak and can't be moved.'

'I say, you're not planning to close your hospital down, are you?'

'Close it down? Whatever for?'

'Oh, I just thought you might be.'

'What a strange idea! Whatever put it into your head?'

'Well, you spend so much time with Lasunskaya, and seem to be under her influence. And if she's to be believed, hospitals, schools, and so on are a lot of nonsense, superfluous inventions. Philanthropy should be individual, enlightenment too: it's all a matter of the soul... That is apparently how she talks. Who taught her those songs, I'd like to know?'

Alexandra Pavlovna laughed.

'Darya Mikhailovna is an intelligent woman, I have a great love and respect for her; but even she can be mistaken, and I do not believe her every word.'

'That's just as well,' Mikhailo Mikhailych retorted, still without dismounting from his droshky, 'for she herself does not believe her every word. But I'm very glad I met you.'

'What is that supposed to mean?'

'A good question! As though it were not always pleasant to meet you! Today you are as fresh and charming as this morning.'

Alexandra Pavlovna laughed again.

'What are you laughing at?'

'What am I laughing at? If you could only see the cold and languid expression with which you uttered your compliment! I'm surprised you didn't yawn afterwards.'

'A cold expression... You always want fire in everything; but fire serves no useful purpose. It flares up, smokes, and goes out.'

'And gives warmth,' Alexandra Pavlovna put in.

'Yes—and burns.'

'So what if it does? That isn't the end of the world. Anything is better than...'

'Well, I shall see if you say the same thing when you really do burn yourself properly,' Mikhailo Mikhailych interrupted her in annoyance, giving his horse a flick of the reins. 'Goodbye!'

'Mikhailo Mikhailych, wait!' Alexandra Pavlovna cried. 'When will you come to see us?'

'Tomorrow; give my greetings to your brother.'

And the droshky rolled off.

Alexandra Pavlovna watched Mikhailo Mikhailych go.

'What a *sack*!' she thought. Hunched, dusty, with his cap aslant on the back of his head, from which locks of yellow hair protruded, he really did look like a large sack of flour.

Alexandra Pavlovna slowly set off homewards along the road. She walked with lowered eyes. The sound of horse's hooves close to her made her stop and raise her head... Riding towards her along the road was her brother; beside him walked a young man, small in stature, in an unbuttoned summer frock-coat, a summer cravat, and a grey summer hat, with a small cane in his hand. He had already long been smiling towards Alexandra Pavlovna, even though he could see that she was walking in reflection, not noticing anything, and as soon as she stopped he went up to her and joyfully, almost tenderly, said:

'Good morning, Alexandra Pavlovna, good morning!'

'Ah! Konstantin Diomidych! Good morning!' she replied. 'Have you come from Darya Mikhailovna's?'

'Yes indeed, miss, yes indeed, miss,'* the young man chimed in, with a beaming face. 'I have come from Darya Mikhailovna's. Darya Mikhailovna sent me to you, miss; I preferred to come on foot... Such a wonderful morning, a distance of only four versts. I arrived, but did not find you in, miss. Your brother told me you had gone to Semyonovka, and his lordship was just preparing to set out himself; so I went with him, miss, to meet you. Yes, miss. How pleasant this is!'

The young man spoke a pure and correct Russian, but with a foreign pronunciation, though it was hard to determine what kind, exactly. In the features of his face there was something Asiatic. The long, hooked nose, the large, protruding, immobile eyes, the thick red lips, the jet-black hair—everything about him betrayed eastern descent; but the young man bore the surname Pandalevsky and called Odessa the home of his birth, though he had been brought up somewhere in Belorussia by a rich widow benefactress. Another widow had found him a place in the civil service. In general, ladies in their middle years were keen to provide patronage for Konstantin Diomidych: with them, he knew how to seek, knew how to find. Even now he was living in the home of a rich landowning woman, Darya Mikhailovna Lasunskaya, in the capacity of an adoptive son or boarder. He was very affectionate, obliging, sensitive, and secretly voluptuous, had a pleasant voice, played the piano rather well, and had a habit, when talking to someone, of truly fixing his eyes on them. He dressed very neatly and made his clothes last an exceedingly long time, kept his broad chin carefully shaven, and combed his hair meticulously.

Alexandra Pavlovna heard out his speech to the end, and turned to her brother:

'I keep meeting people today: only just now I was talking to Lezhnev.'

'Oh, indeed! Was he going somewhere?'

'Yes, and imagine, in a racing droshky, dressed in a kind of linen sack, all covered in dust... What an eccentric he is!'

'Yes, perhaps: but he is a wonderful man.'

'Who? Mr Lezhnev?' Pandalevsky asked, appearing surprised.

'Yes, Mikhailo Mikhailych Lezhnev,' Volyntsev retorted. 'But farewell, sister: it is time I was off to the fields; they're sowing buckwheat on your land. Mr Pandalevsky will take you home...'

And Volyntsev rode away on his horse at a trot.

'With the greatest of pleasure!' Konstantin Diomidych exclaimed, and offered Alexandra Pavlovna his arm.

She gave him hers, and both set off along the road to her estate.

*

It was evident that taking Alexandra Pavlovna by the arm afforded
Konstantin Diomidych much pleasure: he walked with small steps,
smiling, and his eastern eyes were even filmed with moisture, something that happened to them not infrequently, it should be said: it
cost Konstantin Diomidych no effort to be moved and shed a tear.
And who would not have found it pleasant to take a pretty, young,
and shapely woman by the arm? Of Alexandra Pavlovna the entire
province of —— said with one voice that she was lovely, and the
province of —— was not mistaken. Her small, straight, very slightly
upturned nose was enough to drive any mortal man out of his mind,
let alone her velvety chestnut-coloured eyes, her golden red hair, the
dimples on her small round cheeks, and other charms. Best of all in her
appearance, however, was the expression of her pretty face: trusting,
good-natured, and gentle, it both touched and attracted. Alexandra
Pavlovna looked and laughed like a child; the ladies found her a little
naive... Could one have wished for more?

'You say that Darya Mikhailovna sent you to me?' she asked
Pandalevsky.

'Yes, miss, she sent me,' he replied, pronouncing the letter 's'
like the English 'th'. 'Her ladyship earnestly wishes and instructed
me to pressingly ask you to be so kind as to dine with her today...
Her ladyship' (when speaking of a third person, especially a lady,
Pandalevsky strictly adhered to the plural form*) '—her ladyship is
expecting a new guest in her home, and she earnestly wishes you to
meet him.'

'Who is this?'

'A certain Muffel, a baron and gentleman of the royal bedchamber
from St Petersburg. Darya Mikhailovna met him at the house of Prince
Garin recently and speaks of him with high praise as being an amiable and progressively educated young man. The Baron also devotes
himself to literature, or rather... Ah, what a charming butterfly! Allow
me to direct your attention... or rather, to political economy. He has
written an article on some very interesting question—and wishes to
submit it to Darya Mikhailovna's judgement.'

'An article on political economy?'

'From the point of view of language, Alexandra Pavlovna, miss,
from the point of view of language. I think you know, miss, that
Darya Mikhailovna is a connoisseur of language. Zhukovsky* has
consulted with her ladyship, and my benefactor, the Elder Roxolan

Mediarovich Ksandryka*, who lives in Odessa... I expect you know that person's name?'

'Not at all, I've never heard of him.'

'You have not heard of that venerable man? Astonishing! I was going to say that even Roxolan Mediarovich had a very high opinion of Darya Mikhailovna's knowledge of the Russian language.'

'Isn't he a pedant, this baron?' asked Alexandra Pavlovna.

'Oh no, miss; Darya Mikhailovna relates that, on the contrary, it is at once plain he is man of the world. He talked about Beethoven with such eloquence that even the old Prince felt rapture... I must admit that I should have liked to hear it: it's in my field, you see... Permit me to offer you this beautiful wild flower.'

Alexandra Pavlovna took the flower and, after a few steps, dropped it on the road... To her house there remained some two hundred paces, no more. Recently built and whitewashed, it looked out in friendly fashion with its wide, bright windows from a thick leafwork of ancient limes and maples.

'Then what do you wish me to tell Darya Mikhailovna, miss?' Pandalevsky began, slightly offended by the fate of the flower he had presented. 'Will you come to dinner? Her ladyship also invites your brother.'

'Yes, we'll come, certainly. And how is Natasha?'

'Natalya Alexeyevna is well, thank the Lord, miss... But we have passed the turning to Darya Mikhailovna's estate now. Permit me to take my leave of you.'

Alexandra Pavlovna stopped.

'Are you really not going to come in and see us?' she asked in a hesitant voice.

'I should genuinely like to, miss, but I am afraid of being late. Darya Mikhailovna wishes to hear a new study by Thalberg:* so I must practise it and learn it. Moreover, I confess that I doubt that my conversation would afford you any pleasure.'

'But no... why...'

Pandalevsky sighed, and lowered his eyes expressively.

'Goodbye, Alexandra Pavlovna!' he said after a short silence, bowed, and took a step back.

Alexandra Pavlovna turned and walked home.

Konstantin Diomidych also set off back to his quarters. All the sugariness at once vanished from his face: a self-confident, almost severe expression appeared on it. Even Konstantin Diomidych's walk altered; now his stride grew broader and his step heavier. He walked some two versts, carelessly waving his small cane, and suddenly he showed his teeth in a grin again: by the side of the road he caught sight of a young, rather pretty peasant girl who was chasing calves out of the oats. Cautiously, like a tom-cat, Konstantin Diomidych approached the girl and began to talk to her. At first she said nothing, blushed and giggled, then covered her lips with her sleeve, turned away, and said:

'Really, *barin*,* please go away...'

Konstantin Diomidych wagged his finger at her and told her to bring him some cornflowers.

'What do you want cornflowers for? Making garlands, are you?' the girl rejoined. 'No, really, go away...'

'Listen, my pretty little thing...' Konstantin Diomidych began...

'No, go away,' the girl interrupted him. 'The young *barin*s are coming.'

Konstantin Diomidych looked round. Indeed: running along the road were Vanya and Petya, Darya Mikhailovna's sons; behind them walked their teacher, Basistov, a young man of twenty-two, who had just graduated from university. Basistov was a strapping fellow, with a simple face, a large nose, thick lips, and small, pig-like eyes, not good-looking and far from agile, but kindly, honest, and direct. He dressed carelessly, and neglected to have his hair cut—not out of foppishness, but laziness; was fond of eating, fond of sleeping, but also fond of a good book and a heated discussion, and hated Pandalevsky with all his soul.

Darya Mikhailovna's boys worshipped Basistov and were not at all afraid of him; he was on intimate terms with all the other people in the house, which did not entirely please the mistress, however much she might talk about how prejudice did not exist for her.

'Hello, my dear people!' Konstantin Diomidych began. 'You're out early for your walk! I', he added, turning to Basistov, 'have already been out for ages; the enjoyment of nature is a passion of mine.'

'We saw you enjoying nature,' Basistov muttered.

'You are a materialist: even at this moment, God knows what you are thinking. I know your sort.'

When talking to Basistov or people like him, Pandalevsky grew slightly exasperated and pronounced the letter 's' properly, even with a slight whistle.

'Come on, I suppose you were simply asking that wench the way?' Basistov said, moving his eyes both to right and to left.

He could feel that Pandalevsky was looking him straight in the face, and disliked this in the extreme.

'I repeat: you are a materialist and nothing more. You absolutely have to see only the prosaic side of everything.'

'Boys!' Basistov cried suddenly in a tone of command. 'You see that broom willow in the meadow? Let's see who can get to it first... Ready! Set! Go!'

And the boys rushed as fast as they could towards the willow. Basistov hurtled after them.

'Muzhik!'* Pandalevsky thought. 'He'll spoil those brats... A complete muzhik!'

And, casting a self-satisfied gaze over his own neat and elegant figure, Konstantin Diomidych tapped the sleeve of his frock coat a couple of times with splayed fingers, shook his collar, and continued on his way. Once back in his room, he put on a rather old dressing-gown* and, with an expression of concern, sat down at the piano.

II

DARYA MIKHAILOVNA LASUNSKAYA'S house was considered to be
very nearly the finest in the whole of the province of ——. Enormous,
stone-built, constructed according to drawings by Rastrelli,* in the
taste of the previous century, it rose majestically on top of a hill, at
the foot of which flowed one of the principal rivers of central Russia.
Darya Mikhailovna was herself a rich and aristocratic lady, a privy
councillor's widow. Although Pandalevsky said of her that she knew
all Europe, and that indeed Europe knew her, too!—the fact was that
Europe did not know her very well, and even in St Petersburg she
did not play an important role; though in Moscow, on the other
hand, everyone knew her and visited her. She belonged to the highest
society and was reputed to be a woman slightly strange, not entirely
good-natured, but exceedingly intelligent. In her girlhood she had been
very attractive. Poets had written verses to her, young men had fallen
in love with her, important gentlemen had chased after her. Since
then, however, some twenty-five or thirty years had passed, and of her
earlier charms there remained not a trace. 'Can it really be,' everyone
who saw her for the first time involuntarily asked themselves, 'can it
really be that this thin, sallow, sharp-nosed woman who is not yet old
was once a beauty? Can this really be her, the one about whom the lyres
resounded?...' And everyone inwardly wondered at the mutability of
all earthly things. Pandalevsky, it was true, considered that Darya
Mikhailovna's magnificent eyes had survived remarkably; but then it
was Pandalevsky who asserted that she was known throughout the
whole of Europe.

Every summer Darya Mikhailovna arrived at her country estate
with her children (she had three: her daughter Natalya, seventeen,
and her two sons, of ten and nine), and kept open house—in other
words, she received men, especially bachelors; the provincial ladies
she was unable to endure. On the other hand, what she had to put
up with from these ladies! Darya Mikhailovna was, if they were to
be believed, both proud and immoral and a dreadful tyrant; above
all, however, she permitted herself such liberties in conversation that
it was a matter for horror! Darya Mikhailovna was indeed fond, when
in the country, of living without hindrance, and in the free simplicity

of her manner one could observe a slight shade of contempt on the part of a lioness from the capital city for the rather ignorant and small-minded beings who surrounded her... With her city acquaintances, too, she adopted a very free-and-easy, even mocking manner; but it contained no shade of contempt.

Incidentally, reader, have you noticed that a person who is unusually indiscreet in a circle of subordinates is never indiscreet when superiors are present? Why should that be so? Though, as a matter of fact, such questions do not lead anywhere.

When at last, having memorized the Thalberg study, Konstantin Diomidych came down from his tidy and cheerful room to the drawing-room, he found the whole company of the house already gathered. The salon had already begun. Her legs tucked under her, twirling a new French pamphlet in her hands, the lady of the house was disposed on a wide couch; by the window at her needlework sat, on one side, Darya Mikhailovna's daughter, and on the other Mlle Boncourt—her governess, an old and wizened spinster of about 60, with a black hair-piece under a motley cap, and cotton-wool in her ears; Basistov had found a place in the corner, next to the door, and was reading a newspaper, while beside him Petya and Vanya played checkers and, leaning against the stove, his hands folded behind his back, a gentleman stood, small of stature, with tousled grey hair, a swarthy face, and small, black, darting eyes—a certain Afrikan Semyonych Pigasov.

This Mr Pigasov was a strange man. Embittered against everything and everyone—especially against women—he railed and cursed from morning till night, sometimes very pointedly, sometimes rather stupidly, but always with enjoyment. His irritability was of almost childish proportions; his laughter, the sound of his voice, the whole of his being seemed steeped in bile. Darya Mikhailovna was always glad to receive Pigasov: he entertained her with his *bien-trouvés*.* They really were rather amusing. He had a passion for exaggerating everything. For example: no matter what misfortune was being discussed in his presence—whether he was told that a village had been set on fire by lightning, that water had flooded a mill, or that a muzhik had severed his hand with an axe—he would always ask, with concentrated zeal: 'And what is her name?'—that is, what was the name of the woman who had caused the misfortune, since, by his assertion, the cause of every misfortune was a woman; one had only to examine the matter properly. On one occasion he hurled himself to his knees in front of a lady whom he scarcely knew, who was pressing some refreshment on him, and began tearfully, though with fury written on his face, to beseech her to have mercy on him, saying that he was guilty of no wrong in her regard and would never darken her doorstep in future again. Once a horse bolted down the hill with one of Darya Mikhailovna's laundry-maids, tossed her into the ditch, and very nearly killed her. From that day on, Pigasov unfailingly referred to this horse as a 'good, good little horsey', and considered the hill and the ditch exceedingly picturesque spots.

Pigasov had not been lucky in life—and so he affected this foolish behaviour. He had been born of poor parents. His father had occupied various minor posts, could scarcely read or write, and had no concern for his son's education; fed him, clothed him—and that was all. His mother spoiled him, but soon died. Pigasov educated himself, got himself into the district school, then into the gymnasium,* learned languages, French, German, and even Latin, and, leaving the gymnasium with an excellent certificate, set out for Dorpat,* where he waged a constant struggle with poverty, but saw the three-year course to its end. Pigasov's abilities were nothing out of the ordinary; he was notable for his patience and persistence, but especially strong in him was a sense of ambition, a wish to land in good society, not to fall behind the rest, in spite of fate. He studied diligently, and had entered Dorpat University out of ambition. Poverty made him angry and developed in him qualities of observation and cunning. He expressed himself distinctively; from youth onwards he assumed a special kind of bilious and irritable eloquence. His ideas did not rise above the common level; but he talked in such a manner that could make him appear not only an intelligent man, but even one who was very intelligent. Having obtained his candidate's degree,* Pigasov decided to devote himself to the vocation of scholar: he knew that in any other walk of life he could not possibly keep up with his companions (he endeavoured to select them from the highest social circle and knew how to ingratiate himself with them, even to the point of flattery, though continuing his vituperation). In this respect, however, he suffered, not to put too fine a point upon it, from a shortage of material. The essence of it was that Pigasov, an autodidact, but not out of love for science, knew too little. He cruelly failed his dissertation, while another student who lived in the same room with him, and at whom he continually poked fun, a man of great limitations but who had received a proper and sound education, was wholly triumphant. This failure drove Pigasov into a rabid fury: he threw all his books and notebooks in the fire and joined the civil service. At first things did not go badly: he could not have made a better official, not very active but extremely sharp and self-confident; but he wanted to break into society as soon as possible —he became entangled, got stuck, and was compelled to go into retirement. For some three years he stayed at home in a small village he had acquired, and then suddenly married a rich, semi-educated landowning girl, whom he had caught like a fish on a hook with his free-and-easy, mocking manner. But by now Pigasov's character had become too sour and irritable; he found family life a burden... His wife, having lived with him for a few years, secretly left for Moscow, selling her estate to a smart operator at the very moment when Pigasov had just built a farm on it. Shaken to the foundation of his being by this latest blow, Pigasov began legal proceedings against his wife, but emerged from them empty-handed... He lived out his days alone, making the rounds of his neighbours, whom he abused behind their backs and even to their faces, and who received him with a kind of forced half-laugh, though he scarcely inspired them with serious awe —and never took a book in his hand. He owned about a hundred souls; his muzhiks did not live in poverty.

'Ah! Constantin!' Darya Mikhailovna said, as soon as Pandalevsky entered the drawing-room. 'Will Alexandrine be coming?'

'Her ladyship Alexandra Pavlovna asked me to thank you and to say that it will afford her particular pleasure,' Konstantin Diomidych rejoined, bowing pleasantly in all directions and lightly touching his magnificently combed hair with a thick but white little hand, the nails of which were cut in the shape of triangles.

'And Volyntsev, too?'

'His lordship too, miss.'

'So tell me, Afrikan Semyonych,' Darya Mikhailovna went on, turning to Pigasov, 'in your opinion, all young ladies are affected?'

Pigasov's lips twisted to the side, and his elbow gave a nervous twitch.

'What I say,' he began in an unhurried voice—in his most intense fits of embitterment he spoke slowly and distinctly—'what I say is that young ladies in general—about those present, I am, of course silent...'

'But that does not prevent you from thinking about them, too,' Darya Mikhailovna interrupted.

'About them I am silent,' Pigasov reiterated. 'All young ladies are
in general affected in the highest degree—affected in the expression
of their emotions. If a young lady is frightened, for example, or happy
or sad about something, you can be sure that first she will give her
body a kind of elegant twist' (and Pigasov most unelegantly bent his
waist and spread wide his arms) 'and then cry: "Oh!" or burst out
laughing, or into tears. I did, however' (and here Pigasov smiled self-
contentedly) 'once succeed in obtaining a genuine, authentic expression of emotion from one remarkably unaffected young lady!'

'In what way?'

Pigasov's eyes flashed.

'I gave her a whack on the behind with an aspen stake. She fairly
squealed, and I said to her: "Bravo, bravo! There speaks the voice of
nature, that was an unaffected cry. You must always act like that in
future."'

Everyone in the room laughed

'What nonsense you do talk, Afrikan Semyonych!' Darya
Mikhailovna exclaimed. 'Am I to believe that you would strike a young
girl with a stake?'

'As I stand before God, a stake, an enormous stake, of the kind
that is used in the defence of fortresses.'

'*Mais c'est une horreur ce que vous dites là, monsieur,*'* cried Mlle
Boncourt, looking threateningly at the children, who had burst out
laughing.

'Oh, don't believe him,' Darya Mikhailovna said. 'After all, you know
what he is like, don't you?'

But it took the indignant Frenchwoman a long time to regain her
calm, and she kept muttering something to herself under her breath.

'You may not believe me,' Pigasov continued in a voice of composure, 'but I assure you that I have told you the exact truth. Who
should know it, if not I? I suppose that after this you will most likely
also not believe that our neighbour Chepuzova, Yelena Antonovna,
herself, observe, herself, told me how she caused the death of her own
nephew?'

'That's another of your inventions!'

'As you wish, as you wish! Hear the whole story and then judge for
yourselves. Observe that I have no wish to slander her, I am even fond
of her, that is, in so far as it's possible to be fond of a woman; there is
not a single book in her house, apart from the Saints' Calendar, and she

only knows how to read if she says the words out loud—experiences perspiration from the exercise and afterwards complains that her eyes are starting out of her head. In short, she's a good woman, and she has nice plump housemaids. Why would I slander her?'

'Well!' Darya Mikhailovna observed. 'Afrikan Semyonych is away on his hobby-horse again—he won't get off it until nighttime.'

'My hobby-horse... But women have no less than three of them, and they never get off them—except perhaps when they're asleep.'

'What three hobby-horses are those?'

'Reproach, Insinuation, and Rebuke.'

'Do you know something, Afrikan Semyonych?' Darya Mikhailovna began. 'It is not without reason that you bear such resentment towards women. Some woman must have...'

'Hurt me, you mean?' Pigasov interrupted her.

Darya Mikhailovna was slightly embarrassed; she remembered Pigasov's unhappy marriage... and merely nodded her head.

'It is true that there was one woman who hurt me,' said Pigasov, 'though she was kind, too, very kind...'

'And who was that?'

'My mother,' said Pigasov, lowering his voice.

'Your mother? How could she have hurt you?'

'By giving birth to me...'

Darya Mikhailovna frowned.

'I think', she began, 'our conversation is taking a less amusing turn... Constantin, play the new study by Thalberg for us... It may be that the sounds of music will tame Afrikan Semyonych. Orpheus tamed the wild beasts, after all.'

Konstantin Diomidych sat down at the piano and played the study very well. At first Natalya Alekseyevna listened with attention, but then resumed her work again.

'*Merci, c'est charmant*,' said Darya Mikhailovna. 'I like Thalberg. *Il est si distingué.** A penny for your thoughts, Afrikan Semyonych?'

'I think', Pigasov began slowly, 'that there are three kinds of egoist: egoists who live and let others live; egoists who live and don't let others live; and egoists who don't live and don't let others live... Women mostly belong to the third kind.'

'How charming! There is only one thing that surprises me, Afrikan Semyonych, and that is the self-assurance of your opinions: it is as though you never could be wrong!'

'Who says that? I, too, can be wrong: a man may also be mistaken. But do you know the difference between one of our mistakes and a mistake made by a woman? It is this: a man may, for example, say that twice two is not four but five or three and a half; but a woman will say that twice two is a stearin candle...'

'I think I have heard you say that before... But permit me to ask what relation your thought about the three kinds of egoist has to the music you have just heard?'

'None, and indeed I wasn't listening to the music.'

'Well, sir, I see you are incorrigible, no matter then,' Darya Mikhailovna retorted, slightly distorting Griboyedov's line.* 'What do you like, if music is not to your liking? Literature, possibly?'

'I like literature, but not the modern kind.'

'Why?'

'I will tell you why. I was recently crossing the Oka* on a ferry with some *barin* or other. The ferry put in at a steep place: the carriages had to be hauled ashore by hand. The *barin*'s carriage was very heavy. While the ferrymen strained themselves to the utmost trying to haul the carriage ashore, the *barin*, still on the ferry, kept groaning so much that one even felt sorry for him... There, I thought, is a new application of the system of division of labour! Modern literature is like that, too: others do the carrying and get on with the work, while it just groans.'

Darya Mikhailovna smiled.

'And this is called the representation of contemporary life,' the indefatigable Pigasov continued. 'Profound sympathy with social issues and so on... Oh, those loud words ringing in my ears!'

'But the women whom you attack so—they at least do not use loud words.'

Pigasov shrugged.

'They don't because they don't know how to...'

Darya Mikhailovna reddened slightly.

'You are beginning to be impertinent, Afrikan Semyonych!' she remarked, with a forced smile.

There was a general hush in the room.

'Where's Zolotonosha?' one of the boys suddenly asked Basistov.

'In Poltava Province, my dearest fellow,' Pigasov chipped in. 'In the very heart of Khokhol-land.* (He was glad of the opportunity to change the subject.) 'We were talking about literature just now,' he went on. 'If I had any money to spare I should at once become a Little Russian* poet.'

'What's this now? A fine poet, I'm sure!' Darya Mikhailovna retorted. 'Do you know the Little Russian language?'

'Not in the slightest; and anyway one doesn't need to.'

'How can that be?'

'Like this. All one needs to do is take a sheet of paper and write at the top: *Duma*; then start so: *Goy, ty dolya moya, dolya!* or: *Sede kazachino Nalivayko na kurgane!* and then: *Po-pid goroyu, po-pid zelenoyu, graye, graye voropaye, gop! gop!** or something of that sort. And the deed is done. Print it and publish it. The Little Russian will read it, prop his cheek in his hand, and quite certainly start to cry—such a sensitive soul he is!'

'For pity's sake!' Basistov exclaimed. 'What on earth are you talking about? That makes no sense at all. I've lived in Little Russia, I love it and I know its language... *graye, graye voropaye* is complete nonsense.'

'Perhaps it is, but the Khokhol will start to cry all the same. Language, you say... But is there really such a thing as a Little Russian language? I once asked a Khokhol to translate the following Russian sentence, which was the first to come into my head: *grammatika yest' iskusstvo pravil'no chitat'i pisat'* ('grammar is the art of reading and writing correctly'). Do you know how he translated it? *Khramatyka ye vyskus'tvo pravyl'no chytati y pysati...** Well, I ask you, is that a language? I'd sooner let my best friend be crushed in a mortar than agree to that.'

Basistov was about to object.

'Let him be,' said Darya Mikhailovna. 'I mean, you know that from him you will hear nothing but paradoxes.'

Pigasov smiled caustically. A lackey came in and announced the arrival of Alexandra Pavlovna and her brother.

Darya Mikhailovna rose to greet the visitors.

'Good evening, Alexandrine!' she said, going up to her. 'How clever of you to come... Hello, Sergei Pavlych!'

Volyntsev shook Darya Mikhailovna's hand and went over to Natalya Alexeyevna.

'What about the Baron, this new acquaintance of yours? Is he coming this evening?' Pigasov inquired.

'Yes, he is.'

'They say he's a great *philosophe*: fairly awash with Hegel.'*

Darya Mikhailovna made no reply, seated Alexandra Pavlovna on the couch, and found a place for herself beside her.

'Philosophy,' Pigasov went on, 'is the higher point of view! That's another thing that will be the death of me: those higher points of view. What can one see from up there? After all, if you're going to buy a horse, I don't think you want to look at it from a watchtower!'

'This Baron wanted to bring you an essay?' Alexandra Pavlovna asked.

'Yes, an article,' Darya Mikhailovna replied with exaggerated casualness. 'About the relations between trade and industry in Russia... But don't be afraid: we shall not read it here... that is not why I invited you. *Le baron est aussi aimable que savant*! And his Russian is so good! *C'est un vrai torrent... il vous entraîne*.'*

'His Russian is so good that it deserves praise in French!' Pigasov grumbled.

'Grumble away, Afrikan Semyonych, grumble away... It suits the rumpled look of your hair very well... But why is it taking him so long to get here? Do you know what, *messieurs et mesdames*,' Darya Mikhailovna added, with a glance around her. 'Let us go into the garden... There's still about an hour until dinner, and the weather is glorious...'

The whole company rose and set off into the garden.

Darya Mikhailovna's garden stretched all the way to the river. In it there were many old lime-tree avenues, golden-dark and fragrant, with emerald openings at the far end of them, many arbours of acacia and lilac.

Volyntsev, Natalya, and Mlle Boncourt found their way into the very remotest part of the garden. Volyntsev walked beside Natalya and said nothing. Mlle Boncourt followed at a slight distance.

'What have you been doing today?' Volyntsev inquired at last, tugging the ends of his magnificent dark-red moustache.

His facial features strongly resembled those of his sister; but in their expression there was less playfulness and liveliness, and his eyes, attractive and tender, somehow had a melancholy look.

'Oh, nothing,' Natalya replied. 'I've listened to Pigasov criticizing everything, done some embroidery on canvas, read.'

'And what have you been reading?'

'I've been reading... a history of the crusades,' Natalya said, with a slight hesitation.

Volyntsev looked at her.

'Ah!' he said at last. 'That must be interesting.'

He plucked a branch, and began to twirl it in the air. They walked another twenty paces or so.

'Who is this Baron your mother has made the acquaintance of?' Volyntsev went on inquiring.

'A gentleman of the royal bedchamber who is visiting the district; *maman* has a great deal of praise for him.'

'Your mother is capable of being carried away.'

'That proves she is still very young at heart,' Natalya observed.

'Yes. Soon I shall be sending your horse to you. It's almost completely broken in now. I want it to start at a gallop, and I'll see that it does.'

'*Merci...* But I feel ashamed. You are breaking it in yourself... they say that is very hard...'

'In order to afford you the slightest satisfaction, you know, Natalya Alekseyevna, I am ready... I... and not simply trifling matters like this...'

Volyntsev stopped short in confusion.

Natalya gave him an amicable glance and again said: '*Merci*.'

'You know,' Sergei Pavlych went on after a long silence, 'that there is not a thing... But why am I telling you this? For you know it all.'

At that moment a bell rang in the house.

'*Ah! la cloche du dîner!*' Mlle Boncourt exclaimed. '*Rentrons!*'*

'*Quel dommage,*' the old Frenchwoman thought to herself as she clambered up the steps of the balcony after Volyntsev and Natasha —*quel dommage que ce charmant garçon ait si peu de ressources dans la conversation...*'*—which could be translated into Russian as: 'You're good-looking, my dear fellow, but a bit on the feeble side.'

The Baron did not arrive for dinner. They waited for him for about half an hour.

At table the conversation was strained. Sergei Pavlych merely kept looking at Natalya, whom he was sitting beside, assiduously pouring water into her glass. In vain, Pandalevsky endeavoured to interest his neighbour, Alexandra Pavlovna: he bubbled all over with sweetness, but she was almost on the point of yawning.

Basistov rolled little balls of bread and did not have his mind on anything; even Pigasov was silent and, when Darya Mikhailovna commented to him that he was very ungracious today, sullenly replied:

'When am I ever gracious? That is not my business...' and, with a bitter smile, added: 'Have a little patience. After all, I am kvass, *du prostoï* Russian kvass,* while your gentleman of the bedchamber...'

'Bravo!' Darya Mikhailovna exclaimed. 'Pigasov is jealous, jealous in advance!'

But Pigasov made no reply to her, and merely glowered.

The clock struck seven, and they all gathered in the drawing-room again.

'He is obviously not coming,' said Darya Mikhailovna.

But then there was the sound of a carriage, a small tarantass* drove into the courtyard, and a few moments later a lackey came into the drawing-room and handed Darya Mikhailovna a letter on a silver saucer. She quickly read it through and, turning to the lackey, asked:

'And where is the gentleman who brought this letter?'

'He's sitting in the carriage, ma'am. Do you wish to receive him, ma'am?'

'Ask him to come in.'

The lackey went out.

'Imagine, what a nuisance,' Darya Mikhailovna went on. 'The Baron has received instructions to return at once to St Petersburg. He has sent me his article with a Mr Rudin, his friend. The Baron was going to introduce him to me—he thinks very highly of him. But what a nuisance! I had hoped the Baron would stay here for a while...'

'Dmitry Nikolayevich Rudin,' the lackey announced.

III

A MAN of about thirty-five came in, tall of stature, slightly stooping, curly-haired, swarthy, with a face that was irregular, but expressive and intelligent, a liquid brilliance in swift dark-blue eyes, a straight, broad nose, and handsomely profiled lips. The clothes he was wearing were not new, and too tight, as though he had grown out of them.

He walked swiftly up to Darya Mikhailovna and, bowing briefly, told her that he had long desired the honour of being introduced to her and that his friend, the Baron, had been very sorry to be unable to say goodbye in person.

The thin sound of Rudin's voice was at variance with his physical stature and his broad chest.

'Do sit down... very pleased,' said Darya Mikhailovna and, having introduced him to the entire company, asked if he was resident in the district or visiting from elsewhere.

'My estate is in T—— Province,' Rudin answered, 'and I have not been here long. I came on business, and am for the present staying in the town of your *uyezd*.'*

'With whom?'

'The doctor. He is an old university friend of mine.'

'Ah! the doctor... They speak highly of him. It's said that he knows his *métier* well. And the Baron, have you known him long?'

'I met him last winter in Moscow, and have just spent about a week with him.'

'He is a very clever man—the Baron.'

'Yes, ma'am.'

Darya Mikhailovna sniffed the corner of a handkerchief that had been drenched in eau-de-cologne.

'Are you in the civil service?' she asked.

'Who? I, ma'am?'

'Yes.'

'No... I am retired.'

There followed a brief silence. General conversation was renewed.

'Permit me to be curious,' Pigasov began, turning to Rudin, 'but are you familiar with the contents of the article that has been sent by the Herr Baron?'

'I am.'

'This article deals with the relations between commerce... or no, rather, between industry and commerce, in our fatherland... I think that is how you were so good as to express it, Darya Mikhailovna?'

'Yes, that is what it's about,' Darya Mikhailovna said, putting a hand to her forehead.

'I am a poor judge of such matters,' Pigasov continued, 'but I must admit that I find the very title of the article exceedingly... how shall I say it with a little tact?... exceedingly obscure and involved.'

'Why do you find it so?'

Pigasov gave an ironic smile, and cast a fleeting glance at Darya Mikhailovna.

'Is it clear to you, then?' he said, again turning his small, fox-like face towards Rudin.

'To me? Yes, it is.'

'Hm... You are better placed to know, of course.'

'Do you have a headache?' Alexandra Pavlovna asked Darya Mikhailovna.

'No. It's nothing... *C'est nerveux*.'

'Permit me to be curious,' Pigasov began again in his small, nasal voice, 'but your acquaintance, Herr Baron Muffel... that, I believe, is his name?'

'Yes indeed.'

'Does Herr Baron Muffel make a special study of political economy, or does he merely devote to that interesting science the hours of leisure that remain to him after his social diversions and civil service duties are over?'

Rudin looked fixedly at Pigasov.

'In this matter the Baron is a dilettante,' he answered, flushing slightly, 'but his article contains much that is true and interesting.'

'I cannot argue with you, without knowing the article... However, if I may dare to inquire, am I right in supposing that the work by your friend, Baron Muffel, probably confines itself more to general arguments than to facts?'

'It contains both facts and arguments based upon facts.'

'Indeed, sir, indeed. Let me tell you that in my opinion... and I can, after all, put a word in here; I spent three years at Dorpat... all these so-called general arguments, these hypotheses, systems... forgive me, I am a provincial, I cut the home truths straight... are simply no good for anything. They are all mere philosophizing—a way of deceiving people. Give us the facts, gentlemen, and they will suffice.'

'You don't say!' Rudin objected. 'And what about the meaning of the facts—shouldn't that also be given?'

'General arguments!' Pigasov continued. 'They will be the death of me, those general arguments, commentaries, conclusions! They are all founded on so-called convictions; each person talks about his convictions and, in addition, demands respect for them, makes a great fuss of them... Hah!'

And Pigasov shook his fist. Pandalevsky burst into laughter.

'Splendid!' Rudin said, quietly. 'So in your view there are no convictions?'

'No—they don't exist.'

'Is that your conviction?'

'Yes.'

'Then how can you say that there are none? There is one, at least, for a start.'

Everyone in the room smiled and exchanged looks.

'No, wait, wait a moment,' Pigasov began...

But Darya Mikhailovna clapped her hands and exclaimed: 'Bravo, bravo, Pigasov is beaten, is beaten!'—and stealthily removed Rudin's hat from his grasp.

'Be less hasty with your rejoicing, madam: you'll see!' Pigasov said with annoyance. 'It's not enough to crack a witticism with an air of superiority: one must prove, refute... We have strayed from the subject of the argument.'

'Wait,' Rudin observed coolly. 'The matter is very simple. You do not believe in the usefulness of general arguments, you do not believe in convictions...'

'That's right, that's right, I don't believe in anything...'

'Very well. You are a sceptic.'

'I don't see why it's necessary to use such a learned word. As a matter of fact...'

'But do not interrupt!' Darya Mikhailovna broke in.

'Bite, bite, bite!' Pandalevsky said to himself at that moment, smiling broadly all over his face.

'It is a word that expresses my thought,' Rudin continued. 'You understand it: so why not use it? You don't believe in anything... Why do you believe in facts, then?'

'Why? That's priceless! Facts are a matter of common knowledge, everyone knows what facts are... I judge them by experience, by my own feeling.'

'And I suppose your feeling cannot deceive you? Your feeling tells you that the sun moves round the earth... Perhaps you don't agree with Copernicus? You don't believe him either?'

A smile once more darted across every face, and all eyes were fixed on Rudin. 'Well, he's not a stupid fellow,' each person thought.

'It pleases you to go on joking,' Pigasov began. 'It's very original, of course, but not relevant to the matter in hand.'

'In what I have said up to now,' Rudin rejoined, 'there is, unfortunately, too little that is original. It has all long been known and a thousand times reiterated. The point does not lie there...'

'Where does it lie, then?' Pigasov asked, not without insolence.

In any argument he first made fun of his opponent, then became rude, and finally sulked and fell silent.

'In this,' Rudin went on. 'I confess that I can't help feeling sincere regret when, in my presence, intelligent people attack...'

'Systems?' Pigasov interrupted.

'Yes, if you like—systems. Why does that word frighten you so? All systems are founded on a knowledge of the fundamental laws, the principles of life...'

'But it's impossible to know them or discover them... for pity's sake!'

'Let me put it like this. They are of course not accessible to everyone, and to err is human. But you will probably agree with me that Newton, for example, discovered at least some of those fundamental laws. He was a genius, granted; but the discoveries of geniuses are great because they become the property of all. The striving to track down the general principles in particular phenomena is one of the basic characteristics of the human intelligence, and all our progressive education is...'

'So that is where you're headed, sir!' Pigasov interrupted in a drawn-out voice. 'I am a practical man and I have no time for all this metaphysical hair-splitting, nor do I want to...'

'Splendid! That is your privilege. Please observe, however, that your very desire to be exclusively practical man is also in its way a system, a theory...'

'Progressive education, you say!' Pigasov rejoined. 'There's another of your surprises! Very necessary it is, this much-vaunted progressive education! I do not give a brass farthing for your progressive education!'

'But how badly you argue, Afrikan Semyonych!' Darya Mikhailovna remarked, inwardly very pleased by the composure and elegant civility of her new acquaintance. '*C'est un homme comme il faut!*'* she thought, having taken a look into Rudin's face with benevolent attention. 'I must be nice to him.' These last words she mentally said to herself in Russian.

'I am not going to defend progressive education,' Rudin went on, after a short silence. 'It does not require my defence. You do not like it... every man to his own taste. Moreover, that would lead us too far astray. Just allow me to remind you of the old proverb: "Jupiter, you are angry: therefore you are wrong." What I meant was that all these attacks on systems, general arguments, and so on are particularly distressing because, along with systems, people repudiate knowledge itself, science, and faith in it, thus also faith in themselves, in their own powers. But people need that faith: they cannot live by impressions alone, it is a sin for them to fear thought and not trust it. Scepticism has always been characterized by sterility and impotence...'

'That's all just words!' Pigasov muttered.

'Perhaps. But allow me to observe to you that in saying: "That's all just words!", we often do so out of a wish to avoid saying something more serious than mere words.'

'Such as, sir?' Pigasov asked, narrowing his eyes.

'You know what I mean,' Rudin rejoined with involuntary impatience that was instantly brought under control. 'I repeat: if a man has no firm principle in which he believes, no soil on which he firmly stands, how can he be aware of the needs, the importance, and the future of his people? How can he know what he must do, if...'

'Please sit down!' Pigasov said curtly, bowed and moved aside, without looking at anyone.

Rudin looked at him, smiled a slight, wry smile, and fell silent.

'Aha! He has resorted to flight!' Darya Mikhailovna began. 'Do not let it trouble you, Dmitry... I'm sorry,' she added with a friendly smile, 'what is your patronymic?'

'Nikolaich.'

'Do not let it trouble you, dear Dmitry Nikolaich! He hasn't taken any of us in. He wishes to make it look as though he does not *want* to argue any more... He feels that he is *unable* to argue with you. Why don't you just sit down with us, and let us have a chat.'

Rudin moved up his chair.

'How is it that we have not met before?' Darya Mikhailovna continued. 'It astonishes me... Have you read this book? *C'est de Tocqueville, vous savez?*'*

And Darya Mikhailovna handed Rudin the French pamphlet.

Rudin took the thin little book, turned a few pages of it, and putting it back on the table, replied that he had not read this work of M. de Tocqueville, but often pondered the subject it touched upon. The conversation began to flow. At first Rudin seemed hesitant, unable to bring himself to express his opinion, could not find the words, but at last he warmed, and began to speak. After a quarter of an hour his voice alone resounded in the room. They all crowded round him in a circle.

Only Pigasov remained at a distance, in the corner, beside the fireplace. Rudin spoke intelligently, warmly, sensibly; displayed much knowledge and much reading. None of them had expected to find in him a man out of the ordinary... He was so mediocrely dressed, there was so little gossip about him. They all found it strange and incomprehensible that such a very clever man could suddenly appear in the middle of the country like this. All the more did this increase the surprise and, it may be said, charm with which he affected them all, starting with Darya Mikhailovna... She was proud of her find, and was already making advance plans about how she would introduce Rudin to society. In her first impressions there was much that was almost childish, in spite of her years. Alexandra Pavlovna, if truth be told, understood little of what Rudin had been saying, but was very astonished and pleased; her brother also marvelled; Pandalevsky kept an eye on Darya Mikhailovna, and felt envious; Pigasov thought: 'For five hundred roubles I could get you an even better nightingale!'... But most struck of all were Basistov and Natalya. Basistov was almost short of breath; he had sat all the time with his mouth open and his eyes a-goggle—and listening, listening as he had never listened to anyone in all his life, while Natalya's face was covered in a scarlet flush, and her gaze, motionlessly fixed on Rudin, darkened and shone at the same time.

'What wonderful eyes he has!' Volyntsev whispered to her.

'Yes, they are nice.'

'It's just a pity that his hands are too large and red.'

Natalya made no reply.

Tea was served. The conversation became more general, but by the very suddenness with which they all fell silent as soon as Rudin opened his mouth it was possible to judge the strength of the impression he had made. Darya Mikhailovna suddenly felt like teasing Pigasov. She went over to him and said under her breath: 'Why are you not saying anything and merely smiling in that caustic way? Have another try, engage him again'—and, without waiting for him to reply, she beckoned to Rudin.

'There is another thing you don't know about him,' she said, pointing at Pigasov. 'He is a dreadful hater of women, constantly attacking them; please, set him on the path of truth.'

Rudin looked at Pigasov... involuntarily from above: he was two heads taller than him. Pigasov was almost contorted with fury, and his irritable face had turned pale.

'Darya Mikhailovna is wrong,' he began in an unsteady voice. 'It is not only women whom I attack: I am not terribly fond of the entire human race.'

'What could have given you such a low opinion of it?' Rudin asked.

Pigasov looked him straight in the eye.

'Probably the study of my own heart, within which every day I discover more and more rottenness. I judge others by myself. Perhaps that is unfair, and I am far worse than others; but what can I do? It's a habit!'

'I understand you and have sympathy with you,' Rudin rejoined. 'What noble soul has not experienced the craving for self-abasement? But one ought not to linger in that exitless state.'

'I thank you most kindly for issuing my soul an attestation of nobility,' Pigasov retorted, 'but my state is all right, not too bad, so that even if there is an exit from it, no matter—I shall not seek it.'

'But that means—forgive the expression—preferring the satisfaction of your own personal vanity to the desire to live and exist in the truth...'

'You can say that again!' Pigasov exclaimed. 'Personal vanity—that even I understand, and so do you, and so does everyone; but truth— what is truth? Where is it, this truth?'

'You're repeating yourself, I warn you,' Darya Mikhailovna observed.

Pigasov shrugged his shoulders.

'So what's wrong with that? What I ask is: where is the truth? Not even the philosophers know what it is. Kant* says, this is what it is; while Hegel says, no, you're wrong, this is what it is.'

'And do you know what Hegel says about it?' Rudin asked, not raising his voice.

'I repeat', the excited Pigasov continued, 'that I cannot make out what the truth is. In my opinion it's not to be found anywhere in the world, or rather, the word exists but the thing itself does not.'

'Fie! Fie!' Darya Mikhailovna exclaimed. 'You ought to be ashamed to say such things, you old sinner! The truth doesn't exist? Why go on living, if that is so?'

'Well, Darya Mikhailovna,' Pigasov retorted in annoyance, 'I think that you, at any rate, would find it easier to live without truth than without your cook Stepan, who is such a master at preparing *bouillon*! And what would you need truth for, anyway, pray tell me? After all, one can't sew a nightcap out of it!'

'A joke is not an argument,' Darya Mikhailovna observed, 'especially when it is tantamount to slander...'

'I don't know about the truth, but a homely verity is evidently hard to swallow,' Pigasov muttered, and testily withdrew to one side.

Now Rudin began to talk about personal vanity, and said some very sensible things. He argued that a man without personal vanity was nothing, that personal vanity was the lever of Archimedes with which the earth could be moved from its place, but that at the same time only he who was able to master his personal vanity, like a rider his horse, and who sacrificed his individual self to the welfare of all, deserved the title of man...

'Egoism,' he concluded, 'is suicide. The egoist withers away like a lonely, barren tree; but personal vanity, as an active striving for perfection, is the source of all that is great... Yes! A man must break down the stubborn egoism of his personality in order to give it the right to express itself!'

'I wonder if you could lend me a pencil?' Pigasov said, turning to Basistov.

Basistov did not immediately understand what Pigasov wanted of him.

'What do you need a pencil for?' he asked, at last.

'I want to write down that last sentence of Mr Rudin's. If one doesn't write things down, one may forget them, for all one knows! And you will agree that a sentence like that is as good as a grand slam at *yeralash*.'*

'There are some things it is a sin to laugh at and make fun of, Afrikan Semyonych!' Basistov said with heat, and turned away from Pigasov.

Meanwhile Rudin had gone over to Natalya. She had risen: her face expressed embarrassment.

Volyntsev, who had been sitting beside her, was also on his feet.

'I see a piano,' Rudin began softly and kindly, like a prince on tour. 'Are you perhaps the one who plays it?'

'Yes, I do play,' said Natalya, 'but not very well. Konstantin Diomidych plays far better than I.'

Pandalevsky put his face forward, grinning.

'You shouldn't say that, Natalya Alexeyevna: you play not one whit worse than I.'

'Do you know Schubert's *Erlkönig*?'* Rudin asked.

'He does, he does!' Darya Mikhailovna said, joining in. 'Sit down, Constantin. You do like music, Dmitry Nikolaich, don't you?'

Rudin merely inclined his head a little and passed a hand through his hair, as though preparing to listen... Pandalevsky began to play.

Natalya stood beside the piano, directly opposite Rudin. With the first sound, his face assumed a beautiful expression. His dark blue eyes slowly strayed, from time to time pausing on Natalya. Pandalevsky finished playing.

Rudin said nothing, and went over to the open window. A fragrant haze lay over the garden like a soft shroud; nearby trees breathed a drowsy coolness. Stars glimmered quietly. The summer night both luxuriated and imparted luxury. Rudin cast a look into the dark garden —and turned round.

'This music and this night,' he began, 'have reminded me of my student days in Germany: our gatherings, our serenades...'

'Oh, so you have been in Germany, have you?' Darya Mikhailovna asked.

'I spent a year in Heidelberg and about a year in Berlin.'

'And did you dress like a student? They say that the students there dress in a special way.'

'In Heidelberg I wore large boots with spurs and a hussar's jacket with laces, and let my hair grow to my shoulders... In Berlin the students dress like everyone else.'

'Tell us something of your student life,' Alexandra Pavlovna said.

This Rudin began to do. He was not completely successful at it. For one thing, his descriptions lacked colour, and he did not know how to make his audience laugh. As a matter of fact, from stories about his foreign adventures he soon passed on to general arguments about the importance of enlightenment and science, about universities and university life as a whole. In broad, bold outlines he sketched an enormous tableau. They all listened to him with profound attention. He spoke in masterly fashion, enthrallingly, but not quite clearly... yet this very lack of clarity lent his discourse an especial charm.

An abundance of ideas prevented Rudin from expressing himself with definition and exactitude. Images were replaced by images; comparisons, now surprisingly bold, now startlingly correct, rose in the place of comparisons. His impatient improvisation exuded not the self-satisfied refinement of the experienced talker, but inspiration. He did not search for words: they came to his lips obediently and freely of their own accord, and every word seemed to flow straight from his soul, aflame with all the ardour of conviction. Rudin was in possession of what is almost the loftiest secret—the music of eloquence. He was able, by striking certain strings of the heart, to set all the others indistinctly chiming and trembling. His listener might not understand exactly what was being talked about; but that listener's chest would rise high, veils would part before his eyes, and something radiant would start to blaze ahead of him.

All of Rudin's ideas seemed turned towards the future; this lent them an impetuous and youthful quality... Standing by the window, not looking at anyone in particular, he spoke—and, inspired by the universal sympathy and attention, the proximity of young women, and the beauty of the night, carried away by the flow of his own sensations, he rose to eloquence, to poetry... The very sound of his voice, concentrated and quiet, augmented the fascination; some higher thing, surprising even to himself, appeared to be speaking through his mouth... Rudin spoke of that which lends eternal significance to the temporal life of man.

'I recall a Nordic legend,'* he said in conclusion. 'A king is sitting with his warriors in a long, dark storehouse, around a fire. The scene is at night, in winter. All of a sudden a little bird flies in through the open door at one end and flies out through one at the other. The king remarks that this little bird, like man in the world, has flown in out of the dark and flown away into the dark, and did not spend long in the warmth and the light... "King," the oldest of the warriors protests, "the little bird will not be lost even in the dark, and will find its nest..." Precisely: our lives are swift and insignificant; but all that is great is accomplished through human beings. The consciousness of being the instrument of those higher powers must come to stand in place of all man's other joys: in death itself he will find his life, his nest...'

Rudin stopped and lowered his eyes with a smile of involuntary confusion.

'*Vous êtes un poète*,' Darya Mikhailovna said under her breath.

And they all inwardly agreed with her—all, that is, except for Pigasov. Without waiting for the end of Rudin's long speech, he had quietly taken his hat and, as he left, whispered bitterly to Pandalevsky, who was standing near the door:

'No! I'm going away to join the ignoramuses!'

However, no one tried to detain him, and no one noticed his absence.

The servants brought in the supper and, half an hour later, everyone went their separate way by carriage or on foot. Darya Mikhailovna successfully entreated Rudin to stay overnight. Alexandra Pavlovna, as she returned home with her brother in their carriage, began several times to exclaim and marvel at Rudin's extraordinary intellect. Volyntsev agreed with her, but observed that Rudin sometimes expressed himself a little obscurely . . . in other words, not quite intelligibly, he added, doubtless wishing to give clarity to his thought: but his face grew dark, and his eyes, fixed on a corner of the carriage, seemed more melancholy than ever.

Pandalevsky, as he was preparing for bed and taking off his silk-embroidered braces, said out loud: 'A very smart fellow!'—and suddenly, giving his boy room-servant a stern glance, told him to go out. Basistov did not sleep all night and did not undress either, passing the time until dawn composing a letter to one of his friends in Moscow; while Natalya, though she did undress and go to bed, did not sleep for a single minute, and did not even close her eyes. Leaning her head on her hand, she stared fixedly into the dark; her veins pulsed feverishly and a heavy sigh frequently lifted her bosom.

IV

THE following morning, Rudin only just had time to get dressed when a servant from Darya Mikhailovna knocked at his door with an invitation to join her in her study for a cup of tea. Rudin found her alone. She greeted him most amiably, asked him if he had slept well, poured him a cup of tea herself, even asked him whether she had put enough sugar in it, offered him a Russian cigarette, and again repeated a couple of times her astonishment that she had not made his acquaintance earlier. Rudin was going to sit down at a slight distance; but Darya Mikhailovna beckoned him to a small soft seat next to her armchair, and, leaning forward a little in his direction, began to ask him questions about his family, his plans, and intentions. Darya Mikhailovna spoke casually, and listened absent-mindedly; but Rudin understood very well that she was courting him, almost fawning on him. Not in vain, after all, had she arranged this morning rendezvous, not in vain was she dressed simply but elegantly, *à la Madame Récamier*!* As a matter of fact, however, Darya Mikhailovna soon stopped asking him questions: she began to tell him about herself, about her girlhood, and the people with whom she had associated. Rudin listened to her effusions with interest, though—strangely enough!—no matter what person Darya Mikhailovna began to talk about, it was always she, she alone who remained in the foreground, while the other person somehow melted away and disappeared. On the other hand, Rudin learned in detail what Darya Mikhailovna had said to this or that well-known dignitary, and what influence she had had on this or that famous poet. To judge from Darya Mikhailovna's stories, one might have thought that all the remarkable men of the past quarter century had dreamed of nothing other than of how to get to see her and to earn her favour. She talked about them simply, without particular enthusiasm or praise, as if they were her friends and intimates, calling some of them eccentrics. She talked about them, and, like a splendid mounting around a precious stone, their names settled in a shining border around one central name —around Darya Mikhailovna...

But Rudin listened, took a puff of his cigarette from time to time, and kept quiet, only now and then inserting minor observations into the discourse of the lady, who had quite forgotten herself in talk. He was a good speaker, and loved to speak; the holding of a conversation was not his forte, but he also knew how to listen. Anyone whom he did not intimidate at the outset trustingly opened out in his presence: so willingly and approvingly did he follow the thread of what the other person had to say. There was in him a great deal of good nature—that special kind of good nature with which those who are used to feeling superior to others are filled. In arguments he seldom allowed his opponent to get a word in, and would crush him with his powerful and passionate dialectic.

Darya Mikhailovna expressed herself in Russian. She made a show of her knowledge of her native language, though Gallicisms and snippets of French turned up rather frequently when she spoke. She intentionally made use of simple, folk expressions, but not always with success. Rudin's ear was not offended by the strange heterogeneity of speech that flowed from Darya Mikhailovna's lips, and he hardly had an ear for this in any case.

Darya Mikhailovna grew tired at last and, leaning her head on the back of her cushioned armchair, fixed her eyes upon Rudin, and fell silent.

'Now I understand,' Rudin began in a slow voice, 'I understand why you come to the countryside each summer. You need this rest; the quiet of the countryside, after living in the capital, refreshes and strengthens you. I am sure that you must have a deep sympathy with the beauties of nature.'

Darya Mikhailovna looked at Rudin out of the corner of her eye.

'Nature... yes... yes, of course... I am terribly fond of it; but you know, Dmitry Nikolaich, even in the countryside one cannot live without people. And here there is almost no one. Pigasov is the most intelligent person here.'

'The angry old fellow who was here yesterday?' Rudin asked.

'Yes. As a matter of fact, even he is good enough for the countryside —though he makes one laugh at times.'

'He is not a stupid man,' Rudin retorted, 'but he is on the wrong path. I don't know if you would agree with me, Darya Mikhailovna, but from negation—complete and universal negation—there is no benefit to be had. Negate everything, and you may easily gain a reputation as a great intellect: that is a well-known ruse. Good-natured people will at once be ready to conclude that you are above what you negate. But this is often not so. For one thing, it is possible to find imperfection in everything, and for another, even if what you say is rational, it is all the worse for you: your mind, being directed solely at negation, will grow impoverished, and wither. In satisfying your personal pride, you deprive yourself of the true pleasures of contemplation: life—the essence of life—slips away from your petty and bilious observation, and you end up barking abuse and making others laugh. Only he has a right to censure and criticize, who also loves.'

'*Voilà Monsieur Pigassoff enterré*,'* said Darya Mikhailovna. 'What a master you are at defining a man! I dare say that Pigasov would probably not even understand you. For the only thing he loves is his own person.'

'And criticizes it only in order to have the right to criticize others,' Rudin chipped in.

Darya Mikhailovna began to laugh.

'From a sick head... how is it again... on to a healthy one.* By the way, what do you think of the Baron?'

'The Baron? He is a good man, with a kind heart, and erudite... but he has no character... and all his days he will remain half a scholar, half a man of the world, in other words, a dilettante, in other words, not to beat about the bush—a nothing. And what a pity!'

'I am of the same opinion,' Darya Mikhailovna rejoined. 'I have read his article... *Entre nous... cela a assez peu de fond.*'*

'Who else do you have here?' Rudin asked, after being silent for a while.

Darya Mikhailovna flicked the ash from her maize-leaf cigarette with her fifth finger.

'Oh, there almost isn't anyone else. There is Lipina, Alexandra Pavlovna, whom you saw yesterday: she is very nice, but that is all one can say of her. Her brother is also a splendid person, *un parfait honnête homme*.* Prince Garin you know. That's them all. There are also two or three neighbours, but they are really of no account at all. They either put on airs—dreadful pretensions—or shun society, or are quite unwelcomely familiar in their manners. I do not see ladies at all, you know. There is one other neighbour, a very educated man, even a scholar, they say, but he's a dreadful eccentric, a dreamer... Alexandrine knows him and, it appears, is not indifferent to him... You really ought to spend some time with her, Dmitry Nikolayevich: she is a charming creature; she just needs developing a little, yes, developing is what she requires!'

'She is very sympathetic,' Rudin observed.

'A complete child, Dmitry Nikolaich, a real baby. She was married, *mais c'est tout comme.** If I were a man, women like her are the only ones I would fall in love with.'

'Really?'

'Absolutely. Women like her are at least fresh, and freshness one cannot counterfeit.'

'But everything else one can?' Rudin asked, and laughed, which was something that happened very seldom with him. When he laughed his face took on a strange, almost senile expression, his eyes shrivelled to slits, his nose wrinkled...

'And who is this person you were talking about as being an eccentric, to whom Mme Lipina is not indifferent?'

'A certain Lezhnev, Mikhailo Mikhailych, a landowner from round here...'

Rudin lifted his head in amazement.

'Lezhnev, Mikhailo Mikhailych?' he asked. 'He is a neighbour of yours?'

'Yes. Do you know him?'

Rudin said nothing for a moment.

'I used to know him earlier... a long time ago. But he is a rich man, I believe?' he added, tweaking the fringe of the armchair.

'Yes, he is, though he dresses abominably and rides around in a racing droshky like the manager of an estate. I was going to get him to come here: he is clever, they say; and I have some business to discuss with him. I look after my estate by myself, you know.'

Rudin inclined his head.

'Yes, by myself,' Darya Mikhailovna continued. 'I don't introduce any foreign nonsense, but stick to what is Russian and our own, and, as you see, things are not going badly,' she added, moving her hand in a circle.

'I have always been convinced', Rudin observed politely, 'of the extreme injustice of those who would deny women the practical sense.'

Darya Mikhailovna smiled pleasantly.

'You are very broad-minded,' she said quietly. 'But now what was I about to say? What were we talking about? Yes! About Lezhnev. I have some business about demarcation of land to discuss with him. I have invited him here several times, and even today I am waiting for him; but, goodness knows why, he doesn't come... such an eccentric he is!

The curtain over the door softly opened, and a butler came in, a man tall of stature, grey-haired and going bald, in a black frock coat, white tie, and white waistcoat.

'What is it?' Darya Mikhailovna asked and, turning slightly towards Rudin, added under her breath: '*N'est-ce pas, comme il ressemble à Canning?*'*

'His honour Mikhailo Mikhailych Lezhnev is here,' the butler announced. 'Do you wish to receive him?'

'Oh, my goodness!' Darya Mikhailovna exclaimed. 'Speak of the devil! Ask him in!'

The butler went out.

'Such an eccentric man, he has arrived at last, and at the most inappropriate time: our conversation has been interrupted.'

Rudin got up from his seat, but Darya Mikhailovna stopped him.

'Where are you going? We can talk in your presence, too. And I should like you to define him, as you did Pigasov. When you speak, *vous gravez comme avec un burin.** Please stay.'

Rudin was about to say something, but thought for a moment, and stayed.

Mikhailo Mikhailych, with whom the reader is already acquainted, came into the study. He wore the same grey topcoat, and in his sunburned hands held the same old peaked cap. He calmly bowed to Darya Mikhailovna and went over to the tea table.

'At last you have come to visit us, Monsieur Lezhnev!' Darya Mikhailovna said. 'Please do sit down. You already know each other, I hear,' she went on, drawing his attention to Rudin.

Lezhnev glanced at Rudin and smiled rather strangely.

'I know Mr Rudin,' he said with a slight bow.

'We were at university together,' Rudin observed in an undertone, and lowered his eyes.

'We met later on, too,' Lezhnev said coldly.

Darya Mikhailovna looked at them both with some amazement, and asked Lezhnev to sit down. He did.

'You wished to see me', he began, 'about the demarcation?'

'Yes, that's right, but I also just wanted to see you. After all, we are near neighbours and almost related to each other.'

'I am most grateful to you,' Lezhnev retorted, 'but as far as the demarcation is concerned, I have completely settled that matter with your steward, and agree to all his proposals.'

'I already knew that.'

'The only thing is, he told me that without a personal meeting with you, the papers cannot be signed.'

'Yes; that is a custom I have established. By the way, I wonder if I may ask you, but all your muzhiks are rent-payers, are they not?'*

'Yes, indeed.'

'And you yourself are seeing to the demarcation? That is commendable.'

Lezhnev said nothing for a moment.

'Well, here I am, for a personal meeting,' he said.

Darya Mikhailovna smiled, wryly.

'I see that you are. You say it in such a tone... You must really not have wanted to come and see me.'

'I'm not in the habit of paying visits,' Lezhnev said phlegmatically.

'Not at all? But you visit Alexandra Pavlovna, do you not?'

'I'm an old friend of her brother's.'

'Her brother? As a matter of fact, I don't force anyone... But forgive me, Mikhailo Mikhailych, I am older than you and can take you to task: why are you so keen to live like a lone wolf? Or is it just *my* house you dislike? Do you dislike me?'

'I do not know you, Darya Mikhailovna, and so I cannot dislike you. You have a splendid house: but, I confess to you frankly, I am not fond of embarrassing myself. I don't even have a proper frock coat, I have no gloves; and I do not belong to your circle.'

'By birth, by education you belong to it, Mikhailo Mikhailych! *Vous êtes des nôtres!*'*

'Let us leave birth and education aside, Darya Mikhailovna! That is not the point...'

'A man must live with other people, Mikhailo Mikhailych! Why do you want to sit like Diogenes in his tub?'*

'For one thing, he did very well there; and for another, how do you know that I don't live with other people?'

Darya Mikhailovna bit her lip.

'That is another matter! It's simply that I regret not having been deemed worthy to be included among the people with whom you associate.'

'Monsieur Lezhnev', Rudin intervened, 'is, I think, exaggerating a most commendable emotion—the love of freedom.'

Lezhnev made no reply, and merely glanced at Rudin. A short silence ensued.

'So, madam,' Lezhnev began, getting to his feet, 'I may consider our business completed and can tell your steward to send me the papers.'

'Yes... though, I must admit, you are so discourteous... I ought to turn you down.'

'But, after all, the demarcation is far more advantageous to you than to myself.'

Darya Mikhailovna shrugged her shoulders.

'Will you not even have lunch in my house?' she asked.

'Thank you kindly, but I never eat lunch and I am in a hurry to get home.'

Darya Mikhailovna stood up.

'I shall not detain you,' she said quietly, going over to the window. 'I do not dare to detain you.'

Lezhnev began to take his leave.

'Farewell, Monsieur Lezhnev! Forgive me for troubling you.'

'It's all right, for heaven's sake,' Lezhnev retorted, and went out.

'How do you like that?' Darya Mikhailovna asked Rudin. 'I had heard he was an eccentric; but I mean, this is really too much!'

'He suffers from the same disease as Pigasov,' Rudin said. 'The desire to be original. The one pretends to be a Mephistopheles, the other—a cynic. In all of it there is much egoism, much personal pride and little truth, little love. In the end it is also a kind of calculation: a man puts on a mask of indifference and laziness, hoping that some-one will think: "look at that fellow, all that talent he has destroyed in himself?" But if one looks more closely—he has not even any talent!'

'*Et de deux!*'* Darya Mikhailovna said softly. 'You are a dreadful man for definitions. One cannot hide from you.'

'You think so?' Rudin said. 'As a matter of fact,' he continued, 'I ought not really to talk about Lezhnev; I love him, loved him as a friend... but later, as a result of various misunderstandings...'

'You quarrelled?'

'No. But we parted, and parted, I think, for good.'

'Yes, I must say I noticed that you did not feel quite yourself throughout the whole duration of his visit... But I am very grateful for this morning. I passed the time extremely pleasantly. But I must not abuse your kindness. I shall let you go until luncheon, and will go and attend to business. My secretary, you saw him—*Constantin, c'est* *lui qui est mon secrétaire**—must be waiting for me. I recommend him to you: he is a splendid, most helpful young man and is completely enthralled by you. *Au revoir, cher Dmitri Nikolaïch*! How grateful I am to the Baron for having introduced me to you!'

And Darya Mikhailovna extended her hand to Rudin. First he shook it, then raised it to his lips, then went out into the reception room, and from the reception room to the terrace. On the terrace he met Natalya.

DARYA MIKHAILOVNA's daughter, Natalya Alexeyevna, might not at first sight make a fetching impression. She had not yet had time to develop, was thin, dark-complexioned, and held herself in a slightly stooping posture. The features of her face were, however, beautiful and regular, though slightly too large for a seventeen-year-old girl. Especially pleasing was her pure and even forehead above delicate eyebrows that seemed as if fractured in the middle. She spoke little, listened and looked attentively, almost fixedly—as though she wanted to be aware of everything. She often remained motionless, her hands lowered, thinking; then the inner workings of her thoughts would be expressed in her face... A barely perceptible smile would suddenly appear on her lips and vanish; her large, dark eyes would quietly lift... '*Qu'avez vous?*'* Mlle Boncourt would ask her, and begin to scold her, saying that it was not done for a young girl to pass the time in reflection and assume an absent-minded air. But Natalya was not absent-minded: on the contrary, she studied diligently, liked reading and working. Her emotions were deep and strong, but secret; even as a child she had not cried much, and now she even sighed rarely, merely turning slightly pale if something upset her. Her mother considered her a well-behaved, sensible girl, and called her jokingly: '*mon honnête homme de fille*',* but did not have an excessively high opinion of her intellectual abilities. 'My Natasha fortunately has a cool temperament,' she would say. 'She's not like me... and it's just as well. She will be happy.' Darya Mikhailovna was wrong. As a matter of fact, it is a rare mother who understands her daughter.

Natalya loved Darya Mikhailovna and did not fully trust her.

'You have nothing to hide from me,' Darya Mikhailovna told her one day. 'But if you did you would keep quiet about it: you always have thoughts of your own...'

Natalya looked her mother in the face and thought: 'Why should one not have thoughts of one's own?'

When Rudin met her on the terrace, she was going to her room together with Mlle Boncourt, in order to put on her hat and set off into the garden. Her morning studies were already at an end. Natalya was no longer kept in submission, like a little girl, and Mlle Boncourt had long ago stopped giving her lessons on mythology and geography; but every morning Natalya had to read history books, travel books, and other edifying works—in Mlle Boncourt's presence. The books were chosen by Darya Mikhailovna, as though in adherence to some special system of her own. What actually happened was that she simply passed on to Natalya everything she was sent by a French bookseller from St Petersburg, everything, that is, except of course the novels of Dumas *fils** & Co. Those novels Darya Mikhailovna read herself. Mlle Boncourt would look over her spectacles with especial severity and acerbity when Natalya was reading history books: to the mind of the old Frenchwoman the whole of history was full of inadmissible things, though for some reason of the great men of antiquity she herself was familiar only with Cambyses,* and in more recent times Louis XIV and Napoleon, whom she could not abide. But Natalya also read books the very existence of which Mlle Boncourt did not suspect: she knew the whole of Pushkin by heart...

On meeting Rudin, Natalya blushed slightly.

'Are you going for a walk?' he asked her.

'Yes. We're going into the garden.'

'May I come with you?'

Natalya glanced at Mlle Boncourt.

'*Mais certainement, monsieur, avec plaisir,*' the old spinster said hurriedly.

Rudin took his hat and walked along with them.

At first Natalya found it awkward to walk beside Rudin on the same path; then she found it a little easier. He began to ask her about her studies, about how she liked the country. She replied not without timidity, but without that hurried diffidence that is so often both presented and accepted as modesty. Her heart was thumping.

'Don't you find it boring in the country?' Rudin asked, taking her in with a sideways look.

'How can one be bored in the country? I am very glad that we are here. I'm very happy here.'

'You are happy... That is a splendid remark. Though it is understandable: you are young.'

Rudin uttered this last word rather strangely: as though he were unsure whether he envied Natalya or felt sorry for her.

'Yes! Youth!' he added. 'The whole aim of learning is to attain by conscious means what is given to youth *gratis*.'

Natalya looked at Rudin attentively: she did not understand.

'I have spent all morning talking to your mother,' he continued. 'She is a remarkable woman. I understand why all our poets valued her friendship. Are you fond of verse?' he added, after a slight pause.

'He is examining me,' Natalya thought, and said quietly:

'Yes, I'm very fond of it.'

'Poetry is the language of the gods. I myself am fond of verse. But poetry does not consist of verse alone: it is suffused everywhere, it is around us... Look at these trees, at this sky—from everywhere there is a wafting of life and beauty; and where life and beauty are, there too is poetry.'

'Let us sit down here, on the bench,' he went on. 'There. I somehow feel that when you have got used to me' (and he looked her in the face with a smile) 'you and I shall be friends. What do you say?'

'He is treating me as if I were a little girl,' Natalya thought again and, not knowing what to say, asked him if he planned to stay long in the country.

'All the summer, all the autumn, and perhaps the winter, too. I'm a man of very modest means, you know; my affairs are in a sad condition, and I am also tired of dragging myself from one place to the next. It's time to take a rest.'

Natalya expressed astonishment.

'Do you really consider that it's time for you to take a rest?' she asked timidly.

Rudin turned his face towards Natalya.

'What do you mean?'

'I mean,' she rejoined with a certain embarrassment, 'that others may take a rest, but you... must work, try to be useful. Who will, if not you?...'

'I thank you for your flattering opinion,' Rudin interrupted her. 'To be useful... that is easy to say! (He passed his hand across his face.) To be useful!' he repeated. 'Even if there were in me a firm conviction as to how I could be useful—even if I had faith in my own powers—where would I find sincere, sympathetic souls?...'

And Rudin waved his hand so hopelessly and lowered his head so sadly that Natalya involuntarily wondered: could this really be the man whose enthusiastic, hope-filled words she had heard the evening before?

'But in fact, no,' he added, suddenly shaking his lion's mane, 'that is nonsense, and you are right. I thank you, Natalya Alekseyevna, I sincerely thank you.' (Natalya really did not know why he was thanking her.) 'A single remark from you has reminded me of my duty, has shown me my path... Yes, I must act. I must not hide my talent, if I have it; I must not waste my powers on mere chatter, empty, useless chatter, on mere words...'

And his words flowed like a river. He spoke beautifully, heatedly, convincingly—about the shame of cowardice and laziness, about the necessity for accomplishing real deeds. He showered himself with reproaches, arguing that to discuss in advance what one wanted to do was just as harmful as sticking a pin into a ripening fruit, that it was simply a wrongful waste of energies and essences. He asserted that there is not a noble thought that will not find sympathy, that the only people who remain uncomprehended are those who either do not know what they want or who do not deserve comprehension. He spoke for a long time and finished by thanking Natalya Alexeyevna again, quite unexpectedly squeezing her hand and saying: 'You are a beautiful, noble creature!'

This undue familiarity shocked Mlle Boncourt who, in spite of having spent forty years in Russia, understood Russian with difficulty and could only marvel at the attractive swiftness and fluency of the speech on Rudin's lips. Indeed, in her eyes he was something of the order of a virtuoso or artiste; and from that order of men, according to her ideas, it was impossible to demand the observance of decorum.

She stood up and, abruptly straightening her dress, declared to Natalya that it was time to go home, all the more so as *Monsieur Volinsoff* (as she called Volyntsev) was going to join them all for lunch.

'And here he is!' she added, glancing up one of the avenues that led to the house.

Indeed, Volyntsev could be seen not far off.

He approached with a hesitant step, bowed in greeting to them all from afar, and addressing Natalya with a painful expression on his face, said:

'Ah! You are out for a walk?'

'Yes,' Natalya replied, 'we're on our way back home.'

'Ah!' Volyntsev said. 'Well, let us go, then.'

And they all walked towards the house.

'How is your sister's health?' Rudin asked Volyntsev in a voice that was somehow especially affectionate. The evening before he had also been very amiable towards him.

'Thank you kindly. She is well. Perhaps today she will come here... I believe you were discussing something as I approached?'

'Yes, Natalya Alexeyevna and I were having a conversation. She made a remark that produced a great effect on me...'

Volyntsev did not ask what this remark was, and they all returned to Darya Mikhailovna's house in deep silence.

Before dinner another salon was arranged. Pigasov, however, did not come. Rudin was not at his best; he kept trying to make Pandalevsky play Beethoven. Volyntsev kept silent, and looked at the floor all the time. Natalya did not leave her mother's side, now lost in reflection, now setting to work. Basistov did not take his eyes off Rudin, waiting for him to say something clever. In this fashion some three hours passed rather monotonously. Alexandra Pavlovna did not come to dinner— and as soon as they had risen from table Volyntsev ordered his carriage to be harnessed, and slipped away without a word of farewell.

His spirits were heavy. He had loved Natalya for a long time, and was forever making ready to propose to her... She regarded him with favour—but her heart remained unmoved: he saw that clearly. He did not hold out any hopes of inspiring her with a more tender emotion, and was merely waiting for the moment when she would grow completely accustomed to him and become friends with him. What then was agitating him? What change had he noticed in these past two days? Natalya had treated him just as she had done before...

Whether it was that the idea had impressed itself upon his soul that perhaps he did not know Natalya's disposition at all, that she was even more alien to him than he had supposed, or whether it was that jealousy had awoken in him, or that he had a dim presentiment of something unpleasant... at any rate, he suffered, no matter how hard he tried to coax himself.

When he entered his sister's room, Lezhnev was sitting with her.

'Why have you come back so early?' Alexandra Pavlovna asked.

'I simply have. I got bored.'

'Is Rudin there?'

'Yes.'

Volyntsev threw his cap aside, and sat down.

Alexandra Pavlovna turned to him with animation.

'Seryozha, please help me to persuade this stubborn man' (she indicated Lezhnev) 'that Rudin is unusually clever and eloquent.'

Volyntsev muttered something.

'But I don't dispute it with you for one moment,' Lezhnev began. 'I do not doubt Mr Rudin's cleverness and eloquence; all I am saying is that I do not like him.'

'Have you seen him?' Volyntsev asked.

'I saw him this morning, at Darya Mikhailovna's. After all, it's *he* who is now her "grand vizier". The time will come when she will part with him, too—Pandalevsky is the only one she will never part with—but for the moment he is king. I saw him, how could I have failed to! He was sitting there—and she was showing me to him as if to say: "just look, my dear, at the eccentrics we have in Russia." I am not a stud-horse—I'm not used to being exercised in public. I upped and left.'

'But why were you at her house?'

'About the demarcation; but that's all rubbish: she simply wanted to take a look at my physiognomy. A lady—it's well-known!'

'You are insulted by his superiority—that's what it is!' Alexandra Pavlovna began, animatedly. 'That is what you are unable to forgive him. But I am certain that, in addition to a mind, he must also have an excellent heart. Just take a look at his eyes when he...'

'Of honour high and true doth speak...'* Lezhnev chipped in.

'You will make me angry, and I shall cry. I regret with all my heart and soul that I did not go to Darya Mikhailovna's, but stayed with you instead. You are not worth it. Stop teasing me,' she added in a plaintive voice. 'You would do better to tell me about his youth.'

'Rudin's youth?'

'Well, yes. After all, you told me that you know him well and have been acquainted with him for a long time.'

Lezhnev stood up and paced about the room.

'Yes,' he began, 'I know him well. You want me to describe his youth to you? Very well. He was born in T——v, the son of poor landowners. His father died when he was young. He was left alone with his mother. She was a woman of the kindest sort, and doted on him: lived on oatmeal and spent on him whatever other money she had. He received his education in Moscow, paid for at first by some uncle or other, and later, when he had grown up and become independent, by a wealthy prince with whom he had come to an understanding... well, forgive me, I shan't... with whom he became friends. Then he began university. At university I got to know him and became very close to him. I will tell you something of our day-to-day lives back then at some later date. Now I cannot. After that he went abroad...'

Lezhnev continued to pace about the room; Alexandra Pavlovna followed him with her gaze.

'From abroad,' he went on, 'Rudin wrote to his mother extremely seldom, and visited her only once, for about ten days... The old woman even died in his absence, in the hands of strangers, but until the very hour of her death she did not take her eyes off his portrait. I used to visit her when I was living in T——v. She was a kind woman and a most hospitable one, and was forever regaling me with cherry jam. She loved her Mitya to distraction. The gentlemen of the Pechorin* school will tell you that we always love those who are little capable of loving; but *I* think that all mothers love their children, especially the ones who are absent. Later I met Rudin abroad. There one of our Russian ladies had attached herself to him, some kind of bluestocking, no longer young or attractive, as befits a bluestocking. He spent a rather long time with her, and finally gave her up... or rather, no, my error: she gave him up. And then I gave him up. That is all.'

Lezhnev fell silent, passed his hand over his forehead and, as though he were tired, sank into an armchair.

'Do you know something, Mikhailo Mikhailych?' Alexandra Pavlovna began. 'I see that you are a malicious man; indeed, you are no better than Pigasov. I am sure that all you have said is true, that you have not made any of it up, and yet in what a hostile light you have presented it all! That poor old woman, her devotion, her lonely death, that lady... What was the purpose of all that?... Are you aware that one may depict the life of the very finest man on earth in such colours—and without adding anything, take note—that would inspire anyone with horror? Why, that is also in its way a kind of slander!'

Lezhnev stood up and paced about the room again.

'I had not the slightest wish to inspire you with horror, Alexandra Pavlovna,' he said at last. 'I am no slanderer. And in fact,' he added, after a moment's thought, 'there really is a certain amount of truth in what you have said. I was not slandering Rudin, but—who knows? —perhaps he has had time to change since those days—perhaps I am being unfair to him.'

'Ah! There, you see... Then promise me that you will renew your acquaintance with him, get to know him properly, and only then tell me your final opinion of him.'

'As you wish... But why are you so silent, Sergei Pavlych?

Volyntsev started, and raised his head, as though he had been woken.

'What am I to say? I don't know him. What's more, I have a headache today.'

'Indeed, you do look rather pale, today,' Alexandra Pavlovna said. 'Are you well?'

'I have a headache,' Volyntsev repeated, and left the room.

Alexandra Pavlovna and Lezhnev watched him go, and exchanged glances, but said nothing to each other. Neither for the one nor for the other was there any secret as to what was taking place in Volyntsev's heart.

VI

MORE than two months passed... During the whole of this time Rudin hardly ever left Darya Mikhailovna's. She could not manage without him. Telling him about herself and listening to his discourse had become a necessity for her. One day he wanted to leave, under the pretext that all his money had run out: she gave him 500 roubles. He also borrowed about 200 roubles from Volyntsev. Pigasov visited Darya Mikhailovna far less frequently than before: Rudin constrained him by his presence. The constraint was not experienced by Pigasov alone.

'I don't like this clever fellow,' he would say. 'He expresses himself affectedly, for all the world like a character out of a Russian story; he says "I", and then pauses with tender emotion... "I", he says, "I..." Then he always uses such long words. If you sneeze, he will at once start to explain to you why it was you sneezed, and did not cough... If he praises you, it's as if he were giving you promotion... If he starts to criticize himself, he sullies his own reputation—well, you think, now he won't dare to show his face again. Not at all! It even makes him more cheerful, as though he had treated himself to a gulp of vodka.'

Pandalevsky was rather afraid of Rudin, and cautiously sought his favour. Volyntsev was on strange terms with him. Rudin called Volyntsev a 'knight', praised him both to his face and behind his back; but Volyntsev could not bring himself to like him, and unfailingly felt an involuntary impatience and annoyance when Rudin in his presence began to analyse his virtues. 'He's laughing at me, isn't he?' he thought, and his heart was moved to anger. Volyntsev tried to restrain his feelings; but he was jealous of Natalya. And Rudin himself, though he always made a great fuss of Volyntsev when greeting him, though he called him a 'knight' and borrowed money from him, was hardly well disposed towards him. It would have been hard to define just what these two men felt when, gripping each other's hands in comradely fashion, they looked each other in the eye.

Basistov continued to revere Rudin, and hung on his every word. Rudin paid him little attention. Once he spent the whole morning with him, discussed with him the most important universal questions and problems, and awoke in him a most lively enthusiasm, but then turned his back on him... It appeared that only verbally did he seek pure and devoted souls. With Lezhnev, who had begun to visit Darya Mikhailovna, Rudin did not even enter into argument, and seemed to avoid him. Lezhnev also treated him coldly, though he did not express his final opinion of him, which put Darya Mikhailovna greatly out of countenance. She admired Rudin; but she also had confidence in Lezhnev. Everyone in Darya Mikhailovna's house submitted to Rudin's caprice: his slightest wishes were fulfilled. The order of the day's pursuits depended on him. No *partie de plaisir* was arranged without him. But he was no great lover of sudden excursions and undertakings and took part in them as adults do in children's games, with an affectionate and slightly bored goodwill. On the other hand, he entered into everything: talked with Darya Mikhailovna about the arrangements on her estate, the education of the children, her economy, and business matters in general; listened to her intentions, was not even burdened by trivial details, suggested reorganizations and innovations. Darya Mikhailovna admired them verbally—and that was all. Where matters of economy were concerned she adhered to the counsels of her steward, an elderly, one-eyed Little Russian, a good-natured and cunning rogue. 'Age is fat, youth is thin,' he would say, calmly smirking, and winking his sole and solitary eye.

After Darya Mikhailovna herself, Rudin conversed with no one as often or as long as he did with Natalya. He secretly gave her books, confided his plans to her, read her the first pages of articles and works he proposed to write. Their import often remained inaccessible to Natalya. Rudin did not, however, seem greatly concerned that she should understand—as long as she listened to him. His intimacy with Natalya was not entirely to Darya Mikhailovna's liking. 'But,' she thought, 'let her prattle to him in the country. She entertains him, like a little girl. There is no great harm in it, and she will learn a few things for all that... In St Petersburg I will change all this...'

Darya Mikhailovna was mistaken. It was not like a little girl that Natalya prattled to Rudin: she eagerly harkened to his words, she tried to penetrate their meaning, she submitted to his judgement her own thoughts, her own doubts; he was her preceptor, her leader. For the moment, only her head was a-boil... but a young head does not boil alone for long. What sweet moments Natalya experienced when, in the garden, on a bench, in the light, translucent shadow of an ash tree, Rudin would begin to read to her from Goethe's *Faust*, Hoffmann, the *Letters* of Bettina, or Novalis,* constantly stopping to explain the

things she found obscure! She spoke German badly, like almost all
our young ladies, but understood it well, while Rudin was completely
immersed in German poetry, the world of German romanticism and
philosophy, and allured her away with him into those secret lands.
Unfamiliar, beautiful, they opened before her attentive gaze; from the
pages of the book that Rudin held in his hands wondrous images, new,
radiant thoughts went pouring into her soul in chiming streams, and
in her heart, astounded by the noble joy of great sensations, the sacred
spark of enthusiasm quietly lit and flared...

'Tell me, Dmitry Nikolaich,' she began one day, as she sat by the
window, at her needlework, 'will you go back to St Petersburg for
the winter?'

'I don't know,' Rudin rejoined, lowering to his knee the book of
which he was turning the pages. 'If I have the means, I will go.'

He spoke languidly: he was feeling tired and had been inactive since
the morning.

'I think: why would you not be able to find the means?'

Rudin shook his head.

'That is what you think!'

And he looked meaningfully aside.

Natalya began to say something, and then held back.

'Look,' Rudin began, and pointed out of the window—you see that
apple tree: it has broken under the weight and plenty of its own fruit.
The true emblem of genius.'

'It broke because it had no support,' Natalya retorted.

'I know what you mean, Natalya Alexeyevna; but it is not so easy
for a person to find it, that support.'

'I think: the sympathy of others... at any rate, loneliness...'

Natalya became slightly confused, and blushed.

'And what will you do in the country in winter?' she added
hurriedly.

'What will I do? I'll finish my long article—you know—the one
about the tragic in life and art—I told you the plan of it the day before
yesterday—and send it to you.'

'And you'll publish it?'

'No.'

'Why not? Who will you have done it all for, then?'

'Preferably for you.'

Natalya lowered her eyes.

'That is beyond my powers, Dmitry Nikolaich!'

'What is your article about, may one ask?' Basistov, who was sitting some distance away, modestly inquired.

'The tragic in life and art,' Rudin repeated. 'Well then, Mr Basistov will read it. As a matter of fact, though, I haven't quite got the fundamental idea sorted out yet. Up to now I have not yet sufficiently assessed for myself the tragic significance of love.'

Rudin talked about love readily and often. At first, upon hearing the word 'love', Mlle Boncourt had started and pricked up her ears, like an old regimental steed at the sound of a bugle, but after a while she became used to it and would merely tighten her lips and take a pinch of snuff now and then.

'I think', Natalya timidly observed, 'that the tragic in love is unhappy love.'

'Not at all!' Rudin retorted. 'That is rather the comical aspect of love... This question needs to be put quite differently... One needs to delve somewhat more deeply... Love!' he continued. 'Everything in it is a mystery: how it arrives, how it develops, how it disappears. Now it appears suddenly, indisputable, joyful as the day; now it smoulders for a long time, like fire beneath ash, and breaks through like a flame within the soul, when all has been destroyed; now it creeps into the heart like a serpent, now suddenly slips away out of it again... Yes, yes; this is an important question. And indeed, who loves in our time? Who dares to love?'

And Rudin began to reflect.

'What has happened to Sergei Pavlych, why have we not seen him for such a long time?' he asked suddenly.

Natalya flushed, and bent her head towards her needlework.

'I don't know,' she whispered softly.

'What a most magnificent, most noble man he is!' Rudin said, standing up. 'He is one of the finest examples of the real Russian gentry...'

Mlle Boncourt gave him a sidelong glance with her small, French eyes.

Rudin paced about the room.

'Have you noticed,' he said, turning sharply on his heels, 'that the oak—and the oak is a strong tree—sheds its old leaves only when the young ones begin to break through?'

'Yes,' Natalya responded slowly. 'I have.'

'Precisely the same thing happens with an old love in a strong heart: it has died, but still clings on; only another, new love is capable of driving it out.'

Natalya made no reply.

'What does that mean?' she thought.

Rudin stood still for a moment, shook his hair, and walked away.

But Natalya went to her room. For a long time she sat on her bed in bewilderment, for a long time she reflected on Rudin's last words, and suddenly she clenched her fists and wept bitterly. What she was weeping about, God alone knew! She herself did not know why tears had suddenly come to her eyes. She wiped them away, but again they came coursing, like water from a spring that had long been amassing.

That very same day, at the home of Alexandra Pavlovna, a conversation took place between her and Lezhnev about Rudin. At first he persisted in saying nothing; but she was determined to attain her goal.

'I see', she said to him, 'that you still don't like Dmitry Nikolaich, just as always. I've purposely refrained from asking you questions so far; but now you have had a chance to find out if there has been a change in him, and I want to know why you don't like him.'

'Very well,' Lezhnev rejoined with his customary phlegm, 'if you are so impatient; only you must not be angry...'

'Well, begin, begin.'

'And you must allow me to say it all.'

'Yes, yes, begin.'

'Very well, madam,' Lezhnev began, sluggishly lowering himself on to the sofa, 'I will make no secret of it to you, I really do not like Rudin. He is a clever man...'

'Indeed he is!'

'He is a remarkably clever man, though in essence a superficial one...'

'That is easy to say!'

'Though in essence a superficial one,' Lezhnev repeated. 'But there's nothing so terrible about that: we are all superficial men. I don't even blame him for being a despot in his soul, lazy, not very knowledgeable...'

Alexandra Pavlovna threw up her hands.

'Not very knowledgeable? Rudin?' she exclaimed.

'Not very knowledgeable,' Lezhnev reiterated in exactly the same voice. 'He likes to live at other people's expense, performs a part, and so on... That is all in the order of things. But the bad thing is that he's as cold as ice.'

'He, that ardent soul, cold?' Alexandra Pavlovna broke in.

'Yes, cold as ice, and knows it and pretends to be ardent. The bad thing', Lezhnev continued, gradually becoming more animated, 'is that he plays a dangerous game—dangerous not for him, of course; he himself would not place so much as a copeck or a hair on a card—while others place their souls...'

'Whom or what are you talking about? I don't understand what you mean,' Alexandra Pavlovna said.

'The bad thing is that he isn't honest. I mean, he's a clever man: so he must know the value of his words—but he utters them as though they cost him something... There is no denying it, he is eloquent; but his eloquence is not Russian. And the other thing is that while it may be forgivable for a young fellow to speak eloquently, at his age it is shameful to amuse oneself with the sound of one's own words, it is shameful to put on airs!'

'I think, Mikhailo Mikhailych, that for the listener it does not matter whether one puts on airs or not...'

'I'm sorry, Alexandra Pavlovna, but it does matter. One person may make me a remark that strikes me to the core, while another may make the same remark and even more eloquently, but I won't budge an ear. Why is that?'

'Well, *you* may not,' Alexandra Pavlovna interrupted.

'No, I won't budge an ear,' Lezhnev retorted, 'even though it's possible that I have rather large ears. The point is that Rudin's words remain mere words and never become actions—and yet these same words may disturb and undo a young heart.'

'And who, who are you talking about, Mikhailo Mikhailych?'

Lezhnev paused.

'You want to know who I am talking about? About Natalya Alexeyevna.'

Alexandra Pavlovna was thrown off balance for a moment, but at once smiled, with irony.

'Really,' she began, 'what strange notions you always have! Natalya is still a child; and, in any case, even if there was something there, do you really suppose that Darya Mikhailovna...'

'For one thing, Darya Mikhailovna is an egoist and lives for herself; and for another, she is so confident of her ability to bring up children that it never enters her head to worry about them. Pah! How is it possible? One nod, one majestic look—and everything is back in place again. That's what she thinks to herself, that lady, who sees herself as a female Maecenas, as a brilliant intellect, and God knows what else, whereas really she is nothing more than an old society hag. But Natalya is not a child; believe me, she thinks more often and more deeply than you and I do. And now this honest, passionate, and ardent nature has to stumble across such an actor, such a coquette! Although, as a matter of fact, that too is in the order of things.'

'Coquette! You call him a coquette?'

'Yes, of course... Well, tell me yourself, Alexandra Pavlovna: what is his role in Darya Mikhailovna's home? To be an idol, an oracle in the house, to meddle in the household arrangements, the family squabbles and tittle-tattle—is that worthy of a man?'

Bewilderedly, Alexandra Pavlovna looked Lezhnev in the face.

'I do not recognize you, Mikhailo Mikhailych,' she said quietly. 'You are flushed, you are agitated. No, there must be something else lurking here...'

'Well, that's how it is! You talk to a woman straight, from conviction; but she won't rest content until she has thought up some petty, extraneous reason that has made you say precisely what you said, and not something else.'

Alexandra Pavlovna lost her temper.

'Really, Monsieur Lezhnev! You are starting to be no better than Mr Pigasov when it comes to victimizing women; but, as you please —though no matter how perspicacious you are, I find it hard to believe that you can have understood everyone and everything in such a short time. In my opinion you are wrong. You think that Rudin is some kind of Tartuffe.'*

'That's the whole point: he is not even a Tartuffe. At least Tartuffe knew what he wanted; while this fellow, for all his intellect...'

'Then what, what is he? Say what you want to say, unjust, wicked man!'

Lezhnev stood up.

'Now look here, Alexandra Pavlovna,' he began. 'It is you who are unfair, not I. You are cross with me because of my harsh judgements of Rudin; I have every right to speak harshly of him. It's possible that I have bought that right at rather a high price. I know him well: I lived together with him for a long time. You will recall that I promised to tell you some time about our daily life in Moscow. It appears that now I must do so. But will you have the patience to hear me out?'

'Go on, go on!'

'Very well.'

Lezhnev began to pace with slow strides about the room, pausing from time to time and inclining his head forward.

'Perhaps you know,' he began, 'or perhaps you do not know, that I was made an orphan early in life and by the time I was seventeen had no adult to supervise me. I lived in the house of an aunt in Moscow, and did as I pleased. I was a rather vain and touchy young fellow, who liked to put on airs and boast a bit. When I went up to university I behaved like a schoolboy, and soon ended up in a sorry episode. I shall not tell it to you: it does not deserve it. I lied, and lied rather atrociously... I was found out, unmasked, and put to shame... I lost my self-control and wept like a child. This happened at the lodgings of a friend, in the presence of my companions. They all began to roar with laughter at me, all except one student, the one who, let it be observed, was more indignant with me than the rest, the longer I persisted in admitting to my lie. Whether he felt sorry for me or not, I don't know, but he took me by the arm and brought me back to his quarters with him.'

'This was Rudin?' Alexandra Pavlovna asked...

'No, it was not Rudin... it was a person... he is dead now... an unusual person. His name was Pokorsky. To describe him in a few words is beyond my powers, but once one has started to talk about him, one does not want to talk about anyone else. He was a pure and lofty soul, with an intellect the like of which I have not encountered since. Pokorsky lived in a small, low room in the attic of an old wooden house. He was very poor, and somehow managed to get by through giving lessons. Sometimes he could not even offer his guest a cup of tea; and his only sofa had caved in so badly that it had begun to resemble a rowing-boat. But in spite of these inconveniences, large numbers of people visited him. Everyone liked him, he drew people's hearts towards him. You would not believe how sweet and cheerful it was to sit in his poor little room! It was at his place that I met Rudin. He had already dropped that prince of his by then.'

'What was so special about this Pokorsky?' Alexandra Pavlovna asked.

'How shall I say it? Poetry and truth—that was what drew everyone to him. With a clear and wide-ranging intellect, he was as charming and entertaining as a child. His radiant laughter still rings in my ears, and at the same time he

> Burned like a midnight lamp
> Before goodness' sacred shrine...*

That was how one half-insane and very charming poet of our circle expressed himself about him.'

'And what was it like when he spoke?' Alexandra Pavlovna asked again.

'He spoke well when he was in the mood, but not remarkably well. Even then, Rudin was twenty times more eloquent than him.'

Lezhnev paused and folded his arms.

'Pokorsky and Rudin were not like each other. In Rudin there was much more sound and fury, more making of fine phrases and, if you will, more enthusiasm. He seemed far more gifted than Pokorsky, but in reality he was a poor man compared to him. Rudin had a superb ability to develop an idea, any idea, and he was a master of argument; but his ideas were not born inside his own head: he took them from others, especially Pokorsky. Pokorsky looked quiet and gentle, even weak—and loved women to distraction, loved to carouse, and would never allow himself to become the target of insult. Rudin seemed full of fire, boldness, life, but in his soul was cold and almost timid, as long as his personal pride was not offended: then he would go into a frenzy. He tried by every means to make others submit to him, but did so in the name of general principles and ideas and really did have a powerful influence on many people. To be sure, no one liked him; I was possibly the only person who attached himself to him. People bore his yoke... Everyone surrendered to Pokorsky of their own accord. On the other hand, Rudin would never refuse to talk and argue with the first person he encountered... He had not read all that many books, but at least far more than Pokorsky or the rest of us; moreover, he had a systematic intellect and an enormous memory, and that has an effect on the young, after all! What they want are conclusions, results, even false ones, but results all the same! A completely honest man is not cut out for that. Try telling the young that you cannot give them the whole truth because you yourself are not in possession of it... the young will not listen to you. But you cannot deceive them, either. You yourself must at least half believe that you are in possession of the truth... That was why Rudin had such a powerful effect on us all. You see, I said to you just now that he hadn't read much, but he had read books of philosophy, and his head was ordered in such a way that from what he read he could instantly extract all the general substance, grasp the root of the matter, and then from it lead bright, straight threads of thought in all directions, opening up spiritual perspectives. Our circle consisted then, to tell you in all conscience, of boys—and half-educated boys at that. Philosophy, art, science, life itself—to us they were all merely words, or perhaps also concepts: alluring, beautiful, but scattered and disconnected. We were not aware of those concepts, perceived no common link between them, no common universal law, though vaguely we discussed it, made efforts to become aware of it... As we listened to Rudin, it seemed to us that at last we had grasped it, that common link, that the veil had at last been lifted! We knew that what he was saying was not his own idea—what did that matter?—but a harmonious order settled over everything we knew, all the scattered concepts suddenly united, fitted together, grew before us like a building, everything grew bright, a spirit wafted everywhere... Nothing remained meaningless or accidental: in everything a rational necessity and beauty were expressed, everything acquired a significance that was at once clear and mysterious, each individual phenomenon of life resounded like a chord, and we ourselves, with a kind of sacred reverential awe, a sweet quivering of our hearts, felt ourselves to be, as it were, the living vessels of eternal truth, its instruments, called to something great... You don't find all this absurd?'

'Not in the slightest!' Alexandra Pavlovna retorted slowly. 'Why do you think that? I don't quite understand all the things you are saying, but I do not find them absurd.'

'We have had time to learn a few things since those days, of course,' Lezhnev went on. 'All that may now appear to us like our child-hood... However, I repeat, at the time we were indebted to Rudin for many things. Pokorsky was incomparably superior to him, that is beyond dispute; Pokorsky breathed fire and strength into us all, but he sometimes felt enervated, and was silent. He was a nervous, unwell individual; yet when he spread his wings—Lord! where did he not fly! Into the very depths and azure of the heavens! But in Rudin, that handsome and elegant fellow, there was much that was trivial; he even gossiped; his passion was to take a hand in everything, to define and explain everything. His bustling activity never ceased... a political type, madam! I speak of him as I knew him at that time. As a matter of fact, alas, he has not changed... at the age of thirty-five!... Not every man can say that of himself.'

'Please sit down,' Alexandra Pavlovna said quietly. 'Why do you keep moving to and fro in the room, like a pendulum?'

'I feel better that way,' Lezhnev rejoined. 'Well, having landed in Pokorsky's circle, I must tell you, Alexandra Pavlovna, madam, that I underwent a complete regeneration: made my peace, asked questions, learned, rejoiced, revered—in a word, it was as if I had entered some temple. And indeed, when I remember our gatherings, well, I swear to God, there was much that was good, even moving, about them. Picture it if you will, five or six boys met together, one tallow candle burning, the tea that we drank a most foul brew, and the rusks we ate with it quite prehistoric; but if you had seen our faces, listened to what we said! In the eyes of each of us enthusiasm, our cheeks aflame, our hearts a-throb, as we talked about God, about truth, about the future of mankind, about poetry—sometimes it would be nonsense, we'd be carried away by trivialities; but what did it matter? Pokorsky would sit there cross-legged, propping his pale cheek in his hand, but his eyes would be fairly shining. Rudin would stand in the middle of the room and speak, speak beautifully, for all the world like a young Demosthenes* facing the roaring sea; the tousled poet Subbotin would from time to time, as if in his sleep, emit staccato exclamations; the forty-year-old *Bursch** Scheller, the son of a German pastor, who had a reputation among us for being a most profound thinker because of his perpetual silence, never broken on any account, would somehow air his silence with especial solemnity; the cheerful Shchitov himself, the Aristophanes of our gatherings, would go quiet and merely grin; two or three novices would listen with enthusiastic enjoyment... And the night would fly quietly and smoothly, as on wings. Then the dawn showed grey, and we would go our separate ways, moved, cheerful, honest, sober (none of us ever even mentioned liquor in those days), with a kind of pleasant weariness in our souls... Ah! It was a glorious time then, and I refuse to believe that it was all wasted! And it was not wasted—was not wasted even for those whom life made vulgar and insensitive later on... How many times I have chanced to meet such men, my former companions! The man might seem to have become an utter beast, yet one had only to utter the name of Pokorsky to him —and all the remnants of noble feeling would stir within him, as though in a dark and dirty room you had uncorked a forgotten phial of scent...'

Lezhnev fell silent; his colourless face reddened.

'But why did you quarrel with Rudin, when did it happen?' Alexandra Pavlovna said, looking at Lezhnev in bewilderment.

'I did not quarrel with him; I parted company with him, once I had thoroughly got to know him abroad. But even in Moscow I could have quarrelled with him. Even then he played an unkind trick on me.'

'What was it?'

'It was this. I... how shall I put it for you?... it does not go with my appearance... but I have always had a great capacity for falling in love.'

'You?'

'Yes. It's odd, isn't it? And yet it is so... Well, madam, back in those days I fell in love with a very charming young girl... But why are you looking at me like that? I could tell you something about myself that is far more astonishing than that.'

'What would that something be, may one inquire?'

'Something like this. During that time in Moscow I used to keep a nightly rendezvous with... whom do you suppose? A young lime tree at the far end of my garden. I'd embrace its delicate and slender trunk and it would seem to me that I was embracing the whole of nature, and my heart would expand and thrill as though indeed the whole of nature were flowing into it... That, madam, was what I was like!... But wait! Perhaps you think I didn't write poetry? Madam, I did, and I even composed an entire drama, in imitation of *Manfred*.* Among the dramatis personae was a ghost with blood on its chest, not its own blood, observe, but the blood of mankind as a whole... Yes, madam, yes, I pray you, do not be astonished... But I had begun to tell you about my love. I met a girl...'

'And stopped holding rendezvous with the lime tree?' Alexandra Pavlovna asked.

'Yes, indeed. This girl was a most kind and pretty creature, with cheerful, clear eyes and a silvery voice.'

'You describe her well,' Alexandra Pavlovna observed with an ironic smile.

'And you are a very stern critic,' Lezhnev retorted. 'Well, madam, this girl lived with her aged father... However, I won't enter into the details. I will only tell you that this girl really was extremely kind— she would always fill your tea-glass three-quarters full when you had only asked for half a glass! By three days, after my first meeting with her, I was already on fire, and by seven days I could restrain myself no more and admitted everything to Rudin. A young man who is in love cannot possibly refrain from blurting out his secret; and I usually confessed all of mine to Rudin. At the time, I was entirely under his influence, and that influence, I will say without beating about the bush, was beneficial in many ways. He was the first person not to treat me with disdain, the first who taught me some manners. I had a passionate fondness for Pokorsky and felt a certain awe of his spiritual purity; but I was closer to Rudin. Having learned of my love, he went into indescribable raptures: congratulated me, embraced me, and then at once proceeded to bring me to my senses and explain to me the full importance of my new situation. I listened open-mouthed... I mean, you know how well he can talk. His words had an extraordinary effect on me. I suddenly conceived a remarkable self-esteem, acquired a serious look and stopped laughing. I recall that at the time I even began to walk in a more cautious manner, as though within my breast there were a vessel full of precious liquid I was afraid of spilling... I was very happy, all the more so because everyone was so manifestly well-disposed towards me. Rudin wanted to meet the object of my affection; and I myself practically insisted on introducing him to her.'

'Well, now I can see, I can see what is wrong,' Alexandra Pavlovna interrupted. 'Rudin took your object away from you, and to this day you cannot forgive him... I'll wager that I'm not mistaken!'

'And you would lose the wager, Alexandra Pavlovna: you are mistaken. Rudin did not take my object away from me, nor did he want to take her away from me, but all the same he destroyed my happiness, although, having considered the matter with equanimity, I am now prepared to say "thank you" to him for that. At the time, however, I nearly lost my mind. In no way did Rudin wish to harm me—on the contrary! But as a consequence of his accursed habit of impaling each movement of life, both his own and that of others, with a word, like a butterfly on a pin, he proceeded to explain to both of us ourselves, our relationship, how we must behave, despotically compelling us to be aware of our feelings and thoughts, praising us, censuring us, even entering into a correspondence with us, imagine!... Well, he completely muddled and confused us! At the time, I would hardly have married my young lady (at least that much common sense was still left in me), but at any rate she and I might have spent a few months together in splendid fashion, like Paul and Virginie;* but then misunderstandings cropped up, tensions of all kinds—nonsense, in short. The end of it was that one fine morning Rudin persuaded himself into the conviction that it was his most sacred duty as a friend to inform the aged father of the whole matter—and indeed he did.'

'Really?' Alexandra Pavlovna exclaimed.

'Yes, and, mark you, he did it with my consent—that's what is strange!... I still remember to this day what chaos I carried around in my head at the time: everything simply went whirling round and became transposed, as in a camera obscura: white appeared as black, black as white, falsehood as truth, fantasy as duty... Ha! Even now my conscience hurts at the memory of it! Rudin—he didn't lose heart... not a bit of it! He would go darting about amidst all kinds of misunderstandings and muddle, like a swallow above a pond.'

'And so you parted from your fair maiden?' Alexandra Pavlovna asked, artlessly inclining her head to one side and raising her eyebrows.

'Yes... and did it badly, insultingly, awkwardly, in public, and unnecessarily so... I wept, and so did she, and the devil knows what happened... Some kind of Gordian knot had been tied—and it had to be cut, and that was painful! However, all is arranged for the best in this world. She married a good man and is now in clover...'

'But confess: you were still unable to forgive Rudin...' Alexandra Pavlovna began.

'What do you mean?' Lezhnev interrupted. 'I wept like a child when I saw him off on his departure abroad. Although, to tell the truth, a seed of doubt had been planted in my soul even then. And when I later met him abroad... well, by that time I'd grown a bit older... Rudin appeared to me in his true light.'

'What was it that you had discovered in him?'

'Oh, all the things I was telling you about an hour ago. However, enough of him. Perhaps it will all turn out all right in the end. I merely wanted to demonstrate to you that if I judge him sternly, it's not because I do not know him... As regards Natalya Alexeyevna, I will not waste words; but simply turn your attention to your brother.'

'My brother? Why?'

'Just take a look at him. Do you really not notice anything?'

Alexandra Pavlovna lowered her eyes.

'You are right,' she said quietly. 'It is true... my brother... for some time now I have not been able to recognize him... But do you really think...'

'Quiet! I think he's coming this way,' Lezhnev said in a whisper. 'But Natalya is not a child, believe me, though unfortunately she is as inexperienced as a child. You'll see, that little girl will surprise us all.'

'In what manner?'

'Like this... You know, it is little girls such as she who drown themselves, take poison, and so on. Do not let the fact that she is so quiet lead you astray: she has powerful passions within her, and character, too—oh my!'

'Well now I think you are venturing into poetry. To such a phlegmatic as you, I expect that even I would seem like a volcano.'

'No, not so!' Lezhnev said with a smile... 'And as for character—you have no character at all, thank God!'

'What sort of an insolent remark is that?'

'That? It's the greatest of compliments, for heaven's sake...'

Volyntsev entered, casting a suspicious look at Lezhnev and his sister. He had grown thinner of late. They both began to talk to him; but he scarcely smiled at their jokes and looked, as Pigasov had once put it, like a sad hare. Although, in fact, there was probably not a man on this earth who, at least once in his life, had not looked even worse. Volyntsev felt that Natalya was withdrawing from him, and that together with her the earth seemed to be slipping away from under his feet.

VII

THE next day was Sunday, and Natalya rose late. The day before she had been very quiet until evening, secretly ashamed of her tears, and had slept very badly. As she sat, half-dressed, at her small piano, she either played chords, barely audible ones, so as not to wake Mlle Boncourt, or else pressed her forehead against the cold keys and remained motionless for a long time. She kept thinking—not about Rudin himself, but about some remark he had made, and grew entirely immersed in her thought. From time to time Volyntsev came back to her memory. She knew that he loved her. But her thoughts instantly abandoned him... It was a strange excitement that she felt. That morning she dressed in a hurry, went downstairs, and after greeting her mother, seized the moment and went out alone into the garden... It was a hot, bright day, an effulgent day, in spite of showers that arrived now and then. Across the clear sky low, smoke-coloured clouds moved smoothly, not obscuring the sun, and from time to time dropping on the fields abundant torrents of a sudden and momentary downpour. The large, sparkling drops fell quickly, with a kind of dry rustle, like diamonds; the sun played through their gleaming mesh; the grass, only recently ruffled by the wind, did not move, greedily devouring the moisture; the drenched trees languorously quivered in all their leaves; the birds did not stop singing, and it was delightful to hear their garrulous chirruping against the fresh din and murmur of the passing rain. The dusty roads steamed and shone, slightly rainbow-like, beneath the sharp blows of steady spray. But then the cloud passed, a breeze fluttered up, the grass began to be suffused with emerald and gold... Clinging to one another, the leaves of the trees began to let the light show through... A powerful fragrance rose from everywhere...

The sky had almost completely cleared when Natalya went into the garden. From it breathed freshness and quiet, that gentle and happy quiet to which the human heart responds with a sweet languor of secret sympathy and undefined desires...

Natalya walked beside the pond, down a long avenue of silvery poplars; suddenly before her, as if he had emerged out of the ground, Rudin appeared.

She was embarrassed. He looked her in the face.

'Are you alone?' he asked.

'Yes, I am,' Natalya replied. 'But I only came out for a moment...
It is time I went back to the house.'

'I will accompany you.'

And he walked beside her.

'You seem sad,' he said quietly.

'Do I?... And I was about to point out to you that to me you seem
in low spirits.'

'Perhaps... I am like that sometimes. It is more excusable for me
than for you.'

'But why? Do you suppose that I have nothing to be sad about?'

'At your age one must enjoy life.'

Natalya walked several yards in silence.

'Dmitry Nikolayevich!' she said.

'What?'

'Do you remember... the comparison you made yesterday... do you
remember... with the oak tree?'

'Oh yes, I remember.'

Natalya stole a glance at Rudin.

'Why did you... what did you mean by that comparison?'

Rudin inclined his head and fixed his eyes on the distance.

'Natalya Alexeyevna!' he began with the restrained and meaningful
look that always made a listener think that Rudin was not expressing
even one tenth part of what was crowding into his soul, 'Natalya
Alexeyevna! You may have noticed that I talk little of my past. There
are certain strings I do not touch at all. My heart... who has any need
to know what has happened within it? To make a show of that has
always seemed to me a sacrilege. But with you I am open: you inspire
my trust... I cannot conceal from you that I have loved and suffered
like everyone... When and how? It is not worth talking about; but my
heart has experienced many joys and many sorrows...'

Rudin was silent for a while.

'What I told you yesterday', he continued, 'may to a certain extent
be applicable to me, and my present situation. But again, it is not
worth talking about. For me, that side of life has already vanished.
What is left for me is to drag myself along a hot and dusty road, from
post-house to post-house, in a jolting cart... When I will get there,
or whether I will get there—God knows... Let us rather talk of you
instead.'

'Is it really so, Dmitry Nikolayevich?' Natalya said, interrupting him. 'You expect nothing from life?'

'Oh, no! I expect many things, but not for myself... Activity, the bliss of activity, I shall never renounce, but I have renounced pleasure. My hopes, my dreams—and my own happiness have nothing in common. Love...' (at this word he gave a shrug) 'love is not for me; I... am not worthy of it; a woman who loves has the right to demand the whole of a man, but I am no longer capable of giving up the whole of myself. Moreover, to be appealing is a task for youths: I am too old. Why should I turn the heads of others? I only hope that God will let me keep my own on my shoulders!'

'I understand', Natalya said softly, 'that one who strives for a great goal must not think about himself; but is not a woman able to recognize the value of such a man? It seems to me that, on the contrary, a woman would be more likely to turn away from an egoist... All young men, these youths, in your opinion, they are all egoists, all merely preoccupied with themselves, even when they love. Believe me, a woman is not only capable of understanding self-sacrifice: she is also able to sacrifice herself.'

Natalya's cheeks had begun to blush slightly, and her eyes to glow. Before her acquaintance with Rudin she would never have uttered such a long discourse, and with such ardour.

'You have more than once heard my opinion on the calling of women,' Rudin rejoined with a condescending smile. 'You know, in my opinion, only Joan of Arc could save France... But that is not the point. I wanted to talk about you. You stand on the threshold of life... To discuss your future is both enlivening and not unproductive... Listen: you know, I am your friend; the interest I take in you is almost that of a close relative... And so I hope that you will not find my question immodest: tell me, is your heart so far still quite unmoved?'

Natalya flushed, and did not say anything. Rudin stopped, and so did she.

'You are not angry with me?' he asked.

'No,' she said, 'but I had in no way expected...'

'As a matter of fact,' he continued, 'you may refrain from answering me. I know your secret...'

Natalya glanced at him almost with alarm.

'Yes... yes; I know who appeals to you. And I must say—you could not have made a better choice. He is a splendid man; he will be able to recognize your worth; he has not been crushed by life—he is straightforward and serene of soul... he will compound your happiness.'

'Of whom do you speak, Dmitry Nikolaich?'

'As if you did not know! Volyntsev, of course. Well? It is true, is it not?'

Natalya turned away from Rudin slightly. She was utterly taken aback.

'He loves you, doesn't he? For heaven's sake! He can't take his eyes off you, follows your each and every movement; and ultimately, can love ever be concealed? You yourself are graciously disposed towards him, are you not? As far as I have been able to observe, your mother likes him too... The choice is yours...'

'Dmitry Nikolaich!' Natalya interrupted him, in her confusion stretching out a hand to a shrub that stood nearby. 'It is true that I find it awkward to speak of this, but I assure you... you are mistaken...'

'Mistaken?' Rudin echoed. 'I think not... I only made your acquaintance recently; but I already know you well. But what does the change I see in you, see clearly, signify? Are you really the same person that I found here six weeks ago?... No, Natalya Alexeyevna, your heart is not unmoved.'

'Perhaps,' Natalya replied barely audibly, 'but you are still mistaken.'

'How can that be?' Rudin asked.

'Leave me alone, do not question me!' Natalya retorted, and set off towards the house with rapid steps.

She herself had started to be afraid of all the things she suddenly felt within her.

Rudin caught up with her and stopped her.

'Natalya Alexeyevna!' he began, 'this conversation cannot end thus: it is too important for me, also... How am I to understand you?'

'Leave me alone!' Natalya repeated.

'Natalya Alexeyevna, for God's sake!'

Agitation was displayed in Rudin's face. He had turned pale.

'You understand everything, so you ought to understand me, too!' Natalya said, tore her arm away from him, and walked off, without looking round.

'Just one word!' Rudin cried after her.

She stopped, but did not turn round.

'You asked me what I meant by my comparison yesterday. I think you ought to know that I have no wish to deceive you. I was talking about myself, my past—and about you.'

'What? About me?'

'Yes, about you; I have, I repeat, no wish to deceive you... You know now what the new feeling was, the new feeling I spoke of then... Until today I would never have been able to bring myself to...'

Natalya suddenly hid her face in her hands and ran towards the house.

So shocked by the unexpected outcome of her conversation with Rudin was she that she did not even notice Volyntsev, past whom she ran. He stood motionless, leaning back against a tree. A quarter of an hour earlier he had arrived at Darya Mikhailovna's and had found her in the drawing-room, said a couple of words to her, withdrawn unobtrusively, and set off in search of Natalya. Guided by the intuition that is characteristic of people who are in love, he had gone straight into the garden and stumbled across her and Rudin at the very moment she had torn her arm away from him. In Volyntsev's eyes everything grew dark... Following Natalya with his gaze, he detached himself from the tree and took a few steps, not knowing where or why. Rudin caught sight of him, as he drew level with him. Both looked each other in the eye, bowed, and went their separate ways in silence.

'It will not end here,' both thought.

Volyntsev walked all the way to the far end of the garden. He felt bitter and sick; there was a leaden weight on his heart, and from time to time his blood rose with spite. The rain began again, in fitful drops, and Rudin went back to his room. He, too, was not at ease: the thoughts went spinning round within him like a whirlwind. The trusting, unexpected touch of a young and honest soul will confuse almost anyone.

At table everything somehow went wrong. Natalya, her face pale, could hardly sit upright in her chair, and did not raise her eyes. Volyntsev, according to custom, sat beside her and from time to time began to talk to her in a forced manner. It so happened that Pigasov was dining at Darya Mikhailovna's that day. He talked more than anyone else at the table. Among other things he began to argue that men, like dogs, could be divided into dock-tailed and long-tailed. 'Men may be dock-tailed,' he said, 'both by birth and by their own fault. Things go badly for the dock-tailed: they succeed at nothing—they have no self-confidence. But the man who has a long, fluffy tail is a lucky fellow. He may be both sicker and weaker than the dock-tailed chap, but he is sure of himself; when he wags his tail, everyone admires him. And that, after all, is what deserves our surprise: for the tail is a perfectly useless part of the body; what good is a tail? Yet everyone will judge your merits according to your tail.'

'I', he added with a sigh, 'am one of the dock-tailed sort, and, most vexingly of all, I cut off my own tail.'

'In other words,' Rudin observed casually, 'what you mean is something that La Rochefoucauld* actually said long before you: Have faith in yourself, and others will have faith in you. What tails have to do with it, I don't know.'

'Allow each person,' Volyntsev began sharply, and his eyes began to burn, 'allow each person to express himself as he chooses. They talk of despotism... In my opinion, there is no worse despotism than that of so-called clever men. May the devil take them!'

They were all amazed by Volyntsev's freakish behaviour, and they all fell silent. Rudin began to look at him, but could not withstand his gaze, turned away, smiled, and did not open his mouth.

'Aha! You're one of the dock-tailed ones, too!' thought Pigasov; but Natalya's heart shrank within her from fear. Darya Mikhailovna gave Volyntsev a long, bewildered look and, at last, reopened the conversation: she began to talk about an unusual dog that belonged to her friend the cabinet minister...

Volyntsev left soon after dinner. As he said goodbye to Natalya, he could not restrain himself, and said to her:

'Why are you so embarrassed, as though you were guilty? You cannot possibly be guilty in anyone's regard!...'

Natalya did not understand and merely watched him go. Before evening tea, Rudin approached her and, as he leant over the table, pretending to rearrange the newspapers, whispered:

'All this is like a dream, isn't it? I really must see you alone... just for a moment.' He turned to Mlle Boncourt. 'Here,' he said to her, 'this is the feuilleton* you were looking for,'—and, leaning towards Natalya again, added in a whisper: 'Try to be beside the terrace, in the lilac arbour, at about ten o'clock: I will be waiting for you...'

The hero of the evening was Pigasov. Rudin ceded the field of battle to him. He made Darya Mikhailovna laugh a great deal; first he told about a certain neighbour of his who, having spent some thirty years under his wife's heel, became so effeminate that one day, crossing a small puddle in Pigasov's presence, he lifted his hand behind him and drew the tails of his frock-coat sideways, as women do their skirts. After this, Pigasov addressed the subject of another landowner who began as a freemason, then became a melancholic, and finally expressed a wish to be a banker.

'How did you manage to become a freemason, Filipp Stepanych?' Pigasov asked him.

'Everyone knows how: I had a long fingernail on my little finger.'

But Darya Mikhailovna laughed most of all when Pigasov began to talk about love, and assured them that he, too, had been the object of sighs, and that one passionate German lady had even called him her 'appetizing little African and croaker'. Darya Mikhailovna laughed, but Pigasov was not making this up: he really did have a right to boast of his conquests. He asserted that there was nothing easier than to make any woman at all fall in love with one: all one had to do was repeat to her for ten days in a row that her lips were paradise, her eyes were bliss, and that all other women were mere floor-cloths by comparison, and on the eleventh day she herself would say that her lips were paradise and her eyes were bliss, and would fall in love with you. All kinds of things happen in the world. How can one tell? Perhaps Pigasov was right.

At half-past nine Rudin was already in the arbour. In the pale and remote depths of the sky tiny stars were just coming out; in the west there was still a reddish glow—there, too, the horizon seemed clearer and more pure; the semicircle of the moon gleamed golden through the black lacework of a weeping birch. The other trees either stood like morose giants, with thousands of luminous points resembling eyes, or fused together into solid, sombre masses. Not a single leaf moved; the upper branches of the lilacs and acacias seemed to be listening to something and stretching in the warm air. The house stood dark nearby; its long, illumined windows silhouetted against it in patches of reddish light. It was a gentle, quiet evening; but a suppressed and passionate sigh seemed to dwell in that quiet.

Rudin stood with folded arms, listening with strained attention. His heart beat violently, and he involuntarily held his breath. At last he heard light, hurried footsteps, and into the arbour came Natalya.

Rudin rushed up to her, and took her by the hands. Her hands were as cold as ice.

'Natalya Alexeyevna!' he began in an anxious whisper, 'I wanted to see you... I could not wait until tomorrow. I must tell you something that I did not suspect, that I was not even aware of until this morning: I love you.'

Natalya's hands gave a faint quiver in his.

'I love you,' he repeated, 'and how could I have deceived myself for so long, how did I not guess long ago that I love you?... But you?... Natalya Alexeyevna, tell me, do you?...'

Natalya scarcely paused for breath.

'You can see, I have come here,' she said quietly at last.

'No, tell me, do you love me?'

'I think... yes...' she whispered.

Rudin gripped her hands more tightly and moved to draw her towards him...

Natalya quickly looked round.

'Let me go, I'm frightened—I think that someone is eavesdropping on us... For God's sake, be cautious. Volyntsev is putting two and two together.'

'God be with him! You saw, I didn't even answer him today... Oh, Natalya Alexeyvna, how happy I am! Now nothing will disunite us!'

Natalya looked quickly into his eyes.

'Let me go,' she whispered. 'I must go.'

'One moment,' Rudin began...

'No, let me go, let me go...'

'You seem frightened of me?'

'No; but I must go...'

'Then at least repeat it once more...'

'You say you are happy?' Natalya asked.

'I? There is not a man in the world happier than I! Do you really doubt that?'

Natalya raised her head slightly. Her pale face was beautiful: noble, young, and stirred by emotion—in the mysterious shadow of the arbour, in the faint light that fell from the night sky.

'Know, then,' she said, 'I will be yours.'

'Oh, God!' Rudin exclaimed...

But Natalya slipped aside and walked away. Rudin stood there for a while, then slowly emerged from the arbour. The moon clearly illumined his face; on his lips a smile strayed.

'I am happy,' he said in an undertone. 'Yes, I am happy,' he repeated, as though wishing to convince himself.

He drew himself up straight, shook his curls, and walked nimbly into the garden, cheerfully swinging his arms.

But meanwhile in the lilac arbour the shrubs quietly moved apart, and Pandalevsky appeared. He looked cautiously around, shook his head, pressed his lips together, said meaningfully: 'So that's how it is, sir. This will have to be brought to the attention of Darya Mikhailovna,'—and disappeared.

VIII

RETURNING home, Volyntsev was so dejected and gloomy, answered his sister so reluctantly, and so quickly locked himself away in his study, that she decided to send a messenger for Lezhnev. She had recourse to him in all difficult situations. Lezhnev gave instructions to tell her that he would be there on the following day.

Volyntsev was no more cheerful by morning. After a glass of tea he had been about to set off in order to supervise the work of the estate, but instead remained behind, lay down on a sofa, and began to read a book, something that in his case did not happen very often. Volyntsev did not feel drawn to literature, and of poetry he was positively afraid. 'This is as incomprehensible as poetry,' he liked to say and, in confirmation of his words, would quote the following lines by the poet Aibulat:*

> And to the end of melancholy days
> Nor proud experience nor reason's thoughts
> Will crumple up within their hand
> Life's bloodstained forget-me-nots.

Alexandra Pavlovna looked at her brother in concern, but did not trouble him with questions. A carriage drove up to the front porch. 'Well,' she thought, 'thank goodness, Lezhnev...' A servant came in and announced that Rudin had arrived.

Volyntsev threw the book on the floor and raised his head.

'Who is it?' he asked.

'Rudin, Dmitry Nikolaich,' the servant repeated.

Volyntsev stood up.

'Ask him to come in,' he said quietly. 'But you, sister,' he added, turning to Alexandra Pavlovna, 'please leave us.'

'But why?' she began.

'I know why,' he interrupted with vehemence. 'Please, I beg you.'

Rudin came in. Volyntsev coldly bowed to him, standing in the middle of the room, and did not offer his hand.

'I think you will admit you were not expecting me,' Rudin began, and put his hat in the window.

His lips were twitching slightly. He felt awkward; but he was trying to conceal his embarrassment.

'No, I was not expecting you, it's true,' Volyntsev retorted. 'After yesterday, I would have expected someone else—with a message from you.'

'I understand what you mean,' Rudin said quietly, sitting down, 'and am very glad of your candour. It is far better this way. I myself have come to you as to a man of honour.'

'May we not do without the compliments?' Volyntsev remarked.

'I wish to explain to you why I have come.'

'You and I know each other: why should you not come and see me? What is more, this is not the first time you have favoured me with a visit.'

'I have come to you as one man of honour to another,' Rudin repeated, 'and now I want to call your own judgement as witness... I trust you completely...'

'But what is the matter?' said Volyntsev, who was still standing in his earlier position, and staring sullenly at Rudin, from time to time tugging the ends of his moustache.

'Permit me... I have, of course, come in order to have an explanation with you; yet that cannot be done at once.'

'Why not?'

'There is the involvement of a third person...'

'What third person?'

'Sergei Pavlych, you understand me.'

'Dmitry Nikolaich, I do not understand you at all.'

'As you wish...'

'What I wish is that you'd stop beating about the bush!' Volyntsev caught up.

He was beginning to grow seriously angry.

Rudin frowned.

'Very well... we are alone... I must tell you—as a matter of fact, you have probably already guessed' (Volyntsev shrugged his shoulders in impatience) '—I must tell you that I love Natalya Alexeyevna and have a right to suppose that she also loves me.'

Volyntsev turned pale but made no reply, walked over to the window, and turned away.

'You realize, Sergei Pavlych,' Rudin continued, 'that were I not certain...'

'For pity's sake!' Volyntsev broke in hurriedly. 'I do not doubt you in the slightest... Of course! May you prosper! I merely wonder what the devil put it into your head to come to me with this news... What have I got to do with it? What concern is it of mine whom you love and who loves you? I simply cannot imagine.'

Volyntsev continued to look out of the window. His voice sounded hollow.

Rudin got up.

'I will tell you, Sergei Pavlych, why I resolved to come and see you, why I did not even consider it within my rights to conceal from you our... our mutual inclination. I respect you too deeply—that is why I came; I did not want... neither of us wanted to put on an act in front of you. Your feelings for Natalya Alexeyevna were known to me... Believe me, I know my own value: I know how little worthy I am to replace you in her heart; but if this was fated to occur, would it really be better to employ subterfuge, to deceive, to pretend? Would it really be better to run the risk of misunderstandings or even the possibility of the kind of scene that took place at dinner yesterday? Sergei Pavlych, tell me.'

Volyntsev folded his arms on his chest, as though he were making an effort to tame himself.

'Sergei Pavlych!' Rudin continued, 'I have upset you, I can sense that... but try to see it from our point of view... try to see that we had no other means proving to you our respect, of proving that we are able to appreciate your straightforward nobility of soul. Candour, complete candour would be out of place with anyone else, but with you it becomes a duty. It is pleasant for us to think that our secret is in your hands...'

Volyntsev gave a forced laugh.

'I thank you for the power of attorney!' he exclaimed. 'Though, I pray you to observe, I did not want to know your secret, nor to betray my own, and you are dealing with it as though it were your own property. But then, of course, you speak as if for two persons. Am I therefore to suppose that Natalya Alexeyevna is privy to your visit and the purpose of that visit?'

Rudin became slightly embarrassed.

'No, I did not inform Natalya Alexeyevna of my intention; but, I know, she shares my manner of thinking.'

'That is all very fine,' Volyntsev began after a short silence, drumming his fingers on the windowpane. 'Though I must admit it would be far better if you respected me a little less. To tell you the truth, your respect is not worth the devil; but what is it that you want of me now?'

'I do not want anything... or no, rather, I want one thing: I want you not to view me as a man of perfidy and cunning, I want you to understand me... I hope that now you cannot be in any doubt of my sincerity... I want, Sergei Pavlych, for us to part as friends... for you to offer me your hand in the old way...'

And Rudin went over to Volyntsev.

'Forgive me, dear sir,' Volyntsev said quietly, turning round and taking a step back. 'I am prepared to render full justice to your intentions, that is all very fine, I will even say exalted, but we are simple people, do not gild our gingerbread, are not able to follow the flight of such great minds as yours... What to you appears sincere, to us seems importunate and lacking in modesty... What for you is plain and clear, for us is intricate and obscure... You make a boast of that which we conceal; how, then, are we to understand you? Forgive me: nor friend can I consider you, nor hand will I offer you... That is petty, perhaps; but then I myself am petty.'

Rudin took his hat from the window.

'Sergei Pavlych!' he said sadly, 'farewell; I was deceived in my expectations. My visit is indeed a rather strange one; but I hoped that you...' (Volyntsev made a motion of impatience) 'Forgive me, I shall say no more of this. When all's considered, I see that it is so: you are right, and could not have acted otherwise. Farewell, and let me at least once more, for the last time, assure you of the purity of my intentions... Of your modesty I am convinced...'

'This is too much!' Volyntsev exclaimed, shaking with anger. 'I in no way thrust myself upon your confidence, and so you have no right to count on my modesty!'

Rudin was about to say something, but merely spread his hands in the air, bowed, and walked out, while Volyntsev threw himself on the sofa and turned his face to the wall.

'May one come in to your study?' Alexandra Pavlovna's voice said, outside the door.

Volyntsev did not reply at once, and furtively passed his hand over his face.

'No, Sasha,' he said in a slightly altered voice. 'Wait a little longer.'

Half an hour later Alexandra Pavlovna again approached the door. 'Mikhailo Mikhailych is here,' she said. 'Do you want to see him?'

'Yes,' Volyntsev replied. 'Send him in.'

Lezhnev came in.

'What—are you unwell?' he asked, sitting down in the armchair beside the sofa.

Volyntsev raised himself slightly, supported himself on one elbow, gave his friend a long, long look in the face, and then told him the whole of his conversation with Rudin, word for word. Until now he had never even hinted to Lezhnev about his feelings for Natalya, though he had guessed that they were no secret to him.

'Well, brother, you've surprised me,' said Lezhnev, as soon as Volyntsev had finished his story. 'I've come to expect from him much that is strange and peculiar, but this... Though, as a matter of fact, I recognize him even here.'

'For pity's sake!' said the agitated Volyntsev. 'Why, it's simply brazen insolence! I mean, I very nearly threw him out of the window! What was he up to? Was he trying to brag in front of me, or was he in a blue funk? And what was the point of it? How can one decide to go and see someone...'

Volyntsev threw his hands behind his head and was silent.

'No, brother, you are wrong,' Lezhnev retorted with calm. 'You will not believe me, but you see, he did it from a good motive. Really... By his lights, you see, he was acting nobly and with candour, and he got the chance to talk a bit, to put some eloquence into play; for that's what our fellow needs, without it he cannot live... Oh, his tongue is his own enemy... Well, but it is also his servant.'

'The solemnity with which he came in and spoke, you cannot imagine!...'

'Indeed, but that is all part of it. He does up his frock coat as though he were fulfilling a sacred duty. I should like to cast him away on a desert island and watch on the sly how he dealt with the situation. Why, he never stops talking about simplicity!'

'But tell me, brother, for the love of God,' Volyntsev asked, 'what on earth is it—philosophy, or what?'

'How can I put it? On the one hand, yes, perhaps, it is philosophy —but on the other, it is not that at all. One should not dump all kinds of rubbish on philosophy, either.'

Volyntsev glanced at him.

'Do you think he might have been lying?'

'No, my son, he was not lying. And in any case, do you know something? Enough of this subject. Come along, my good fellow, let us smoke our pipes and ask Alexandra Pavlovna to come in... With her here, our talk will be better and our silence easier. She'll give us some tea.'

'If you wish,' Volyntsev rejoined. 'Sasha, come in!' he cried.

Alexandra Pavlovna came in. He caught her hand, and firmly pressed it to his lips.

Rudin arrived home in a strange and troubled state of mind. He was annoyed with himself, reproaching himself for unforgivable impulsiveness and childishness. Not without reason did someone say: there is nothing more painful than the consciousness of a stupid action one has just committed.

Remorse nagged at Rudin.

'The devil must have made me visit that landowner!' he whispered through his teeth. 'What an idea to have! Simply asking for insolence!...'

Meanwhile, at Darya Mikhailovna's house something unusual was taking place. The mistress had not shown herself all morning, and did not come down to dinner: according to Pandalevsky, the only person who had been allowed in to see her, she had a headache. Rudin had also seen little sign of Natalya: she stayed in her room with Mlle Boncourt... Encountering him in the dining-room, she looked at him so sadly that his heart quivered. Her face had altered, as though a misfortune had descended on her since the day before. An anguish of vague forebodings began to torment Rudin. In order to obtain at least some diversion, he occupied himself with Basistov, talked with him for a long time, and found him to be a mettlesome and lively fellow with enthusiastic hopes and a faith as yet unsullied. Towards evening Darya Mikhailovna appeared for an hour or two in the drawing-room. She was courteous to Rudin, but kept herself rather remote, now tittering, now frowning, speaking with an affected twang, and increasingly in hints... There was about her undeniably an air of the court lady. Recently she had seemed to grow slightly cool towards Rudin. 'What riddle is this?' he thought, taking a side view of her small, back-tilted head.

His wait for the solution of the riddle was not a long one. On the way back to his room at around midnight, he passed along a dark corridor. Suddenly someone thrust a note into his hand. He looked round: retreating from him was a girl, Natalya's maid, he thought. Arriving in his room, he sent his manservant away, unfolded the note, and read the following lines, inscribed in Natalya's hand:

Come tomorrow morning between six and seven, no later, to Avdyukhin Pond, on the other side of the oak wood. Any other time is impossible. This will be our last meeting, and it will all be over if... Come. A decision must be made...

PS. If I do not come, it means that we shall not see each other any more: then I will let you know...

Rudin began to reflect, turned the note in his hands, put it under his pillow, undressed, lay down, but took a long time to fall asleep, slept a fragile slumber, and it was not yet five when he awoke.

IX

AVDYUKHIN POND, beside which Natalya had arranged to meet Rudin, had long ago ceased to be a pond. Some thirty years earlier it had burst its dam, and since that time had been abandoned. Only from the smooth, flat bed of the ravine, which had once been covered by fertile silt, and from the remains of the dam could one guess that here there had been a pond. In this same place there had also existed a country estate. It had long ago disappeared. Two enormous pine trees recalled its memory; the wind eternally sighed and gloomily droned in their high, scraggy greenness... Among the common folk passed mysterious rumours of a terrible crime that was supposed to have been committed at their foot; it was also said that neither of them would fall without causing someone's death; that here a third pine tree had once stood, which had come down in a storm and crushed a girl to death. The whole locality around the old pond was considered to be haunted by evil spirits; empty and bare, but lonely and dismal, even on a sunny day, it was made even more dismal and lonely by the vicinity of a decrepit oak wood, which had long ago died and withered. The sparse, grey skeletons of the massive trees towered like mournful spectres above a low undergrowth of bushes. They made an uncanny sight: as though evil old men had gathered together and were planning something unpleasant. A narrow, scarcely trodden path wound around the side. No one ever walked past Avdyukhin Pond unless they had a special need to do so. It was with a purpose that Natalya had chosen such an isolated spot. From it to Darya Mikhailovna's house was a distance of no more than half a verst.

The sun had long ago risen when Rudin arrived at Avdyukhin Pond; but the morning was not a cheerful one. Unbroken clouds of a milky colour covered the whole sky; the wind chased them at speed, whistling and whining. Rudin began to walk to and fro along the dam that was covered with clinging burdock and blackened nettles. He was not at ease. These rendezvous, these new sensations diverted him, but also troubled him, especially after the note he had received the day before. He could see that matters were coming to a head, and was secretly losing courage, although no one would have thought it, watching the concentrated determination with which he folded his arms on his chest and cast his gaze about him. Not in vain had Pigasov once said of him that his head, like that of a Chinese tumbler-doll, constantly outweighed the rest of him. But with his head alone, no matter how powerful it was, a man would find it hard even to know what was happening within himself... Rudin, the clever, perspicacious Rudin, was not able to say for certain whether he loved Natalya, whether he was suffering, or whether he would suffer when he parted from her. Then why, not even pretending to be a Lovelace*—that degree of justice must be accorded to him—had he confused the poor girl? Why did he await her with such secret trepidation? To this there is but one answer: no one is so easily infatuated as a man without passion.

As he walked to and fro along the dam, Natalya came hurrying to him across the fields, through the wet grass.

'Young lady, young lady, you'll get your feet wet!' her maidservant Masha was saying to her, barely managing to keep up with her.

Natalya did not listen to her and ran on without looking round.

'Oh, I do hope they haven't spotted us!' Masha kept saying. 'It's a miracle we managed to get out of the house. I hope the Mademoiselle hasn't woken up... Thank goodness it's not far to go... And there's his honour waiting for us, ma'am,' she added, suddenly catching sight of the stately figure of Rudin, standing picturesquely on the dam, 'only he shouldn't be standing in full view like that—he ought to go down into the dell.'

Natalya stopped.

'You wait here, Masha, by the pine trees,' she said quietly, and went down towards the pond.

Rudin approached her, and stopped in amazement. He had never before observed such an expression on her face. Her eyebrows were drawn together, her lips pressed tight, and her gaze was stern and straight.

'Dmitry Nikolaich,' she began, 'we have no time to waste. I have only come here for five minutes. I must tell you that my mother knows everything. Mr Pandalevsky spied on us the day before yesterday and told her of our meeting. He has always been my mother's spy. Yesterday she summoned me to see her.'

'Oh God!' Rudin exclaimed. 'This is dreadful... And what did your mother say?'

'She was not angry with me, did not scold me, merely reproached me for light-mindedness.'

'Only that?'

'Yes, and she told me that she would rather consent to see me dead than as your wife.'

'Did she really say that?'

'Yes; and she also added that you yourself have not the slightest desire to marry me, that you have merely flirted with me, out of boredom, and that she had not expected it of you; that, as a matter of fact, she herself was to blame: for having allowed me to meet with you so often... that she is relying on my common sense, that I have caused her great surprise... and I cannot even remember all the other things she said to me.'

Natalya said all this in a voice that seemed steady, almost soundless.

'And you, Natalya Alexeyevna, what did you reply to her?' Rudin asked.

'What did I reply to her?' Natalya echoed. 'What do *you* intend to do now?'

'Oh God! God!' Rudin rejoined. 'This is cruel! So soon!... such a sudden blow!... And your mother was so indignant?'

'Yes... yes, she does not want to hear mention of your name.'

'That is dreadful! So there is no hope?'

'None.'

'Why are we so unlucky? That infamous Pandalevsky!... You ask me, Natalya Alexeyevna, what I intend to do? My head is spinning round—I cannot put two and two together... All I can feel is my un-happiness... I am surprised that you can maintain your composure!...'

'Do you think it is easy for me?'

Rudin began to walk along the dam. Natalya kept her eyes fixed on him.

'Did your mother ask you any questions?' he said quietly, at last.

'She asked me if I loved you.'

'Well... and what did you say?'

Natalya was silent for a moment.

'I did not lie.'

Rudin took her by the hand.

'Always, in everything, noble and magnanimous! O, the heart of a girl is pure gold! But did your mother really so emphatically declare her will regarding the impossibility of our marriage?'

'Yes, emphatically. I already told you, she is convinced that you yourself do not intend to marry me.'

'So she considers me a deceiver! How have I deserved that?'
And Rudin clutched at his head.

'Dmitry Nikolaich!' Natalya said quietly, 'we are wasting time.
Remember, this is the last time I shall see you. I did not come here
in order to cry, to complain—you can see, I am not crying—I came
for advice.'

'But what advice can I give you, Natalya Alexeyevna?'

'What advice? You are a man; I am used to trusting you, and shall
trust you to the end. Tell me, what are your intentions?'

'My intentions? Your mother will probably ban me from the
house.'

'Perhaps. She told me yesterday that she would have to break off
her friendship with you... But you are not answering my question.'

'What question?'

'What do you think, what should we do now?'

'What should we do?' Rudin answered. 'Submit, of course.'

'Submit,' Natalya slowly repeated, and her lips turned pale.

'Submit to fortune,' Rudin continued. 'What else can we do? I
know too well how bitter, painful, intolerable it is; but judge for yourself, Natalya Alexeyevna, I am poor... To be sure, I can work; but
even if I were a rich man, in a position to endure a forced separation
from your family, your mother's anger?... No, Natalya Alexeyevna,
there is no point even in thinking about it. Obviously, we are not
fated to live together, and the happiness of which I dreamed is not
for me!'

Natalya suddenly covered her face with her hands and began to cry.
Rudin drew closer to her.

'Natalya Alexeyevna! Dear Natalya!' he began with ardour, 'do not
cry, for God's sake, do not torment me, console yourself...'

Natalya lifted her head.

'You tell me to console myself,' she began, and her eyes flashed
through her tears. 'I am not crying about what you think I am crying... That is not what hurts me: what hurts me is that I have been
deceived in you... What? I come to you for advice, and at a moment
such as this, and your first word is: submit... Submit! So that is how
you put into practice your theories about freedom, sacrifices that...'

Her voice failed.

'But Natalya Alexeyevna,' Rudin began, embarrassed, 'remember...
I do not retract my words... but...'

'You asked me', she continued with renewed strength, 'what I replied to my mother when she told me that she would sooner consent to my death than to my marrying you: I replied to her that I would rather die than marry someone else... And you say: submit! So she was right: you really were playing with me, from idleness, out of boredom...'

'I swear to you, Natalya Alexeyevna... I assure you...' Rudin kept saying.

But she did not listen to him.

'Why did you not stop me? Why did you yourself... Or did you not count on any obstacles? I feel ashamed to talk about it... but in any case, it is all finished now.'

'You must calm yourself, Natalya Alexeyevna,' Rudin began, 'we must think together, the two of us, what practical measures...'

'You have so often spoken of self-sacrifice,' she interrupted, 'but do you know that if you had said to me today, at once: "I love you, but I cannot marry you, I am not responsible for the future, give me your hand and come with me,"—do you know that I would have gone with you, that I would have ventured everything? But it seems that it's a long way from word to deed, and you have turned cowardly now, just as you turned cowardly the day before yesterday at dinner, in front of Volyntsev!'

The colour rushed to Rudin's face. Natalya's unexpected willingness had shocked him; but her last words wounded his self-esteem.

'You are too excited now, Natalya Alexeyevna,' he began. 'You cannot know how cruelly you insult me. I hope that in time you will render me justice; you will realize what it has cost me to give up a happiness which, as you yourself say, has imposed no obligations on me. Your tranquillity is more precious to me than anything in the world, and I would be the basest of men, were I to decide to take advantage of...'

'Perhaps, perhaps,' Natalya interrupted, 'perhaps you are right; and I don't know what I am saying. But until now I have believed you, have believed your every word... In future, please, consider your words, do not speak at random. When I told you that I love you, I knew what that word means: I was prepared for anything... Now all that is left for me is to thank you for the lesson, and to say farewell.'

'Stop, in the name of God, Natalya Alexeyevna, I implore you. I do not deserve your contempt, I swear to you. Try to see it from my position. I am responsible for both you and for myself. If I did not love you with the most devoted love—then, by almighty God, I would instantly have proposed to you that you elope with me... Sooner or later, your mother would forgive us... and then... But before thinking about my own happiness...'

He paused. Natalya's gaze, fixed directly on him, embarrassed him.

'You are trying to prove to me that you are an honourable man, Dmitry Nikolaich,' she said softly. 'I have no doubt of that. You are not capable of acting from calculation; but it was not that I wanted to make sure of, not for that I came here...'

'I did not expect, Natalya Alexeyevna...'

'Ah! Now you have let it slip! No, you did not expect all this— you did not know me. Don't worry... you do not love me, and I do not impose myself on anyone...'

'I love you!' Rudin exclaimed.

Natalya straightened up.

'Perhaps; but in what way do you love me? I remember everything you say, Dmitry Nikolaich. Do you remember, you told me that without complete equality there is no love... You are too high-principled for me, you are not a good match for me... I am justly punished. Ahead of you lie tasks that are more worthy of you. I shall not forget this day... Farewell...'

'Natalya Alexeyevna, are you leaving? Are we really to part from each other like this?'

He stretched out his arms to her. She paused. His imploring voice, it seemed, made her hesitate.

'No,' she said softly, at last, 'I feel that something in me has broken... I came here, I spoke with you as in a fever; I must come to my senses. It is not proper that this should be, you yourself have said it, it shall not be. Oh Lord, as I came here, in my thoughts I said farewell to my home, to the whole of my past—and what? Whom did I encounter here? A cowardly man... And how do you know that I am not capable of enduring a separation from my family? "Your mother does not give her consent... That is dreadful!" That is all I have heard from you. Is it you, is it you, Rudin? No! Farewell... Oh! If you loved me, I would feel it now, at this moment... No, no, farewell!'

She quickly turned and ran to Masha, who had long ago begun to grow concerned and make signs to her.

'*You* are being cowardly, not I!' Rudin cried after Natalya.

She had already ceased to pay attention to him, and was hurrying home across the fields. She arrived safely back to her bedroom; but only just managed to cross the threshold when her strength failed her, and she fell, unconscious, into Masha's arms.

But Rudin continued to stand on the dam for a long time after. At last he roused himself, with slow steps reached the path, and quietly walked along it. He was very ashamed... and grieved. 'How can it be?' he thought. 'At eighteen years of age!... No, I did not know her. She is a remarkable girl. What strength of will!... She is right; she is worthy of a love different from the one I felt for her... Felt?' he asked himself. 'Perhaps I no longer feel love any more? So now it has all ended as it ought to have done! How pathetic and contemptible I was before her!'

The light clip-clop of a racing droshky made Rudin lift his eyes. In it, drawn by his faithful trotter, rode Lezhnev. Rudin silently exchanged bows with him and, as if struck by a sudden thought, turned off the road and quickly walked in the direction of Darya Mikhailovna's house.

Lezhnev gave him time to get away, watched him as he went, and after a short pause for thought, also turned his horse around—and drove back to Volyntsev, at whose house he had spent the night. He found Volyntsev asleep, did not ask for him to be woken, and in the expectation of tea, sat down on the balcony and lit his pipe.

X

VOLYNTSEV rose at about ten and, having discovered that Lezhnev was sitting on his balcony, was most astonished and asked him to be invited inside.

'What happened?' he asked. 'I mean, you were intending to go home.'

'Yes, I was, but I met Rudin... Striding through the fields alone, looking dejected. So I turned round and came back again.'

'You came back because you met Rudin?'

'Well, to tell you the truth, I don't know why I came back; probably because I remembered you: I felt like sitting with you for a while, and there would be plenty of time for me to get back home again.'

Volyntsev smiled bitterly.

'Yes, one can't even think about Rudin now without also thinking of me... Servant!' he cried loudly. 'Bring us tea!'

The friends set about drinking their tea. Lezhnev began to talk of farming, a new method of thatching barns with cotton...

Suddenly Volyntsev leapt up from his armchair, and brought his fist down on the table with such force that the cups and saucers rattled.

'No!' he exclaimed. 'I can take this no longer! I shall challenge this clever fellow to a duel, and either he can shoot me, or I can try to put a bullet through his learned skull!'

'Tut-tut, man, for pity's sake!' Lezhnev muttered. 'Shouting like that, indeed! I've dropped my chibouk...* What's the matter with you?'

'The matter is that I can't hear his name with indifference: it sets all my blood racing.'

'Enough, brother, enough! You ought to know better!' Lezhnev retorted, fishing his pipe up off the floor. 'Give it up! To hell with him!'

'He's insulted me,' Volyntsev continued, pacing about the room ... 'Yes! He's insulted me. You must be able to see for yourself that. I didn't find the right tactic at the beginning: he puzzled me; and in any case, who could have expected such a thing? But I shall show him that no one plays around with me... I'll shoot him like a partridge, the damned philosopher.'

'A lot of good that will do you! Not to speak of your sister. I know, you're in the grip of passion... why should you think of your sister? And as regards the other female person involved, do you really think you would put matters in order by killing the philosopher?'

Volyntsev threw himself into his armchair.

'Then I'll go away somewhere! Otherwise the misery here will simply crush my heart; I simply won't know where to turn.'

'Going away... that's a different matter! Now, to that I agree. And do you know what I propose to you? Let us go together—to the Caucasus, or possibly just to Little Russia, and eat *galushki*.* A fine thing to do, brother!'

'Yes; but who would we leave my sister with?'

'But why doesn't Alexandra Pavlovna come with us? As God is my witness, it would turn out splendidly. Looking after her—I'd do that! She won't want for anything; if she feels like it I'll arrange for a serenade to be sung under her window every night; I'll spray the yamshchiks* with eau-de-cologne and strew flowers along the roads. And you and I, brother, we shall quite simply be new men; we shall have such a marvellous time, and come back with such great big bellies, that no love will ever get hold of us again!'

'You're just joking, Misha!'

'I'm not joking at all. That was a brilliant idea you had just now.'

'No! Rubbish!' Volyntsev exclaimed again. 'I want to fight, to fight him!'

'There you go again! What a fury you're in today, brother!...'

The servant came in, holding a letter.

'Who is it from?' Lezhnev asked.

'It's from Rudin, Dmitry Nikolayevich. A servant brought it from the Lasunskys'.'

'From Rudin?' Volyntsev echoed. 'For whom?'

'For you, sir...'

'For me... Give it here.'

Volyntsev grabbed the letter, quickly unsealed it, and began to read. Lezhnev watched him closely: a strange, almost joyful amazement appeared on Volyntsev's face; he lowered his hands.

'What is it?' Lezhnev asked.

'Read,' Volyntsev said in an undertone, and held out the letter.

Lezhnev began to read. This is what Rudin had written:

Esteemed Sergei Pavlovich!

I am leaving Darya Mikhailovna's house today, and am leaving forever. This will no doubt surprise you, particularly after what took place yesterday. I cannot explain to you just what it is that compels me to act in this fashion; but it none the less seems to me that I am duty-bound to inform you of my departure. You do not like me, and even consider me a bad person. I do not intend to justify myself: time will justify me. In my opinion it is both unworthy of a man and futile to try to demonstrate to someone who is prejudiced the unfairness of his prejudices. Whoever wishes to understand me will forgive me, but whoever does not want to understand or is unable to—the accusations of that person do not touch me. I was mistaken in you. In my eyes you remain, as before, a noble and honourable man; but I supposed that you would be able to stand above the milieu in which you developed... I was mistaken. What can one do? It is not the first time, and will not be the last. I repeat to you: I am leaving. I wish you happiness. You must admit that that is a wholly disinterested wish, and I hope that you will now be happy. Perhaps in time you will alter your opinion of me. I do not know if we shall ever meet again, but at any rate I remain, in sincere respect, yours,

D.R.

PS. The two hundred roubles I owe you I will send to you as soon as I have returned to my estate in the province of T——. I also request you not to speak of this letter in Darya Mikhailovna's presence.

PPS. Yet one more final but important request: as I am now leaving, I hope that you will not mention my visit to you when Natalya Alexeyevna is present...

'Well, what do you say?' asked Volyntsev, as soon as Lezhnev had finished the letter.

'What is there to say?' retorted Lezhnev. 'Exclaim in Eastern manner: "Allah! Allah!"—and put into one's mouth the finger of wonder—that is all one can do. He is leaving... Well, good riddance. But here's the interesting part: he considered it his *duty* to write this letter, and he presented himself to you out of a sense of duty, also... For these gentlemen there is a duty at every step, and everything is duty—and debts,' Lezhnev added, pointing to the postscript with a sarcastic smile.

'And the fine phrases he fires off!' Volyntsev exclaimed. 'He was mistaken in me: he expected I would stand above my milieu... Lord, what a lot of rot! Worse than poetry!'

Lezhnev made no reply; but his eyes had a smile in them.

Volyntsev stood up.

'I want to go and see Darya Mikhailovna,' he said quietly. 'I want to find out the meaning of all this...'

'Wait, brother: let him get away first. You don't want to go bumping into him again, do you? After all, he is leaving the scene—what more do you want? You'd do better to go to bed and take a nap; why, I'll wager you tossed around from side to side all night. But now your affairs are sorting themselves out...'

'From what do you deduce that?'

'It just seems to me that way. Really, take a nap, and I will go to your sister—I'll sit with her for a while.'

'I have absolutely no desire to take a nap. Why should I do that?... I'd do better to ride off and inspect the fields,' said Volyntsev, tugging at the skirts of his coat.

'That is not such a bad plan, either! Off you go, brother, go and inspect the fields...'

And Lezhnev made his way to Alexandra Pavlovna's part of the house.

He found her in the drawing-room. She greeted him affectionately. She was always pleased when he arrived; but her face remained sad. Rudin's visit of the previous day had troubled her.

'Have you come from my brother?' she asked Lezhnev. 'How is he today?'

'He is all right, he has gone to inspect the fields.'

Alexandra Pavlovna was silent for a while.

'Please, tell me,' she began, closely examining the border of her handkerchief. 'Do you know why...'

'Why Rudin came here?' Lezhnev caught up. 'Yes, I know why: he came here to say goodbye.'

Alexandra Pavlovna lifted her head.

'What? To say goodbye?'

'Yes. Have you not heard? He is leaving Darya Mikhailovna's.'

'Leaving?'

'For good; at least, that is what he says.'

'But for heaven's sake, how is one to understand that, after all that has...'

'Well, that is another matter! It defies understanding, but it is so. Something must have happened between them. A string was drawn too taut—and it broke.'

'Mikhailo Mikhailych!' Alexandra Pavlovna said. 'I don't understand any of this; I think you are merely laughing at me.'

'I swear to God I am not... It is true what they say, he is leaving, and is even writing letters to his friends to tell them of it. It is, if you like, not a bad thing to happen from a certain point of view; but his departure has prevented the realization of a certain most marvellous undertaking that your brother and I had begun to discuss.'

'What on earth? What undertaking?'

'This. I proposed to your brother that we should go travelling for relaxation, and take you along with us. I would take the responsibility of looking after you personally...'

'How wonderful!' Alexandra Pavlovna exclaimed. 'I can just picture to myself how you would look after me. Why, you would let me die of hunger.'

'You say that, Alexandra Pavlovna, because you do not know me. You think I am a blockhead, a complete blockhead, some kind of wooden stick; but do you know, I am capable of melting like sugar, and kneeling for days on end?'

'That I should like to see, I must admit!'

Lezhnev suddenly rose.

'Then marry me, Alexandra Pavlovna, and you shall see it.'

Alexandra Pavlovna blushed to her ears.

'What did you say, Mikhailo Mikhailych?' she repeated in embarrassment.

'What I said,' Lezhnev replied, 'was something that has for a long time, and a thousand times, been on the tip of my tongue. I have finally let it slip, and you may do as you think best. But so as not to hinder you in any way, I shall now go outside. If you want to be my wife... I shall be out there. If it does not go against the grain, you have only to send for me: then I will know...'

Alexandra Pavlovna was about to tell Lezhnev to remain, but he briskly walked away, stepped into the garden without his hat, leaned on the gate, and began to stare off into space.

'Mikhailo Mikhailych!' the voice of the housemaid rang out behind him. 'Please come and see the *barynya*.* She's sent for you.'

Mikhailo Mikhailych turned round, put both hands round the maid's head, much to her astonishment, kissed her on the face, and went to Alexandra Pavlovna.

XI

On returning to the house, immediately after his meeting with Lezhnev, Rudin locked himself in his room and wrote two letters: one to Volyntsev (the reader is already familiar with it) and the other to Natalya. He sat for a very long time over this second letter, crossed out and altered much of it and, having painstakingly transcribed it on to a thin sheet of notepaper, folded it as small as possible and put it in his pocket. With sadness on his face, he paced the room a few times, sat down in the armchair in front of the window, and leaned his head on his hand; a tear gently sprang to his eyelashes . . . He stood up, fastened all the buttons of his coat, called the servant, and told him to ask Darya Mikhailovna if she would see him.

The servant soon came back and announced that Darya Mikhailovna had asked him to come in. Rudin went to her.

She received him in her study, as on the first occasion, two months earlier. But now she was not alone: with her sat Pandalevsky —unassuming, fresh, well-groomed, and complaisant, as always.

Darya Mikhailovna greeted Rudin courteously, and Rudin courteously bowed to her, but at a first sight of their smiling faces any experienced person would have realized that, even though it was not spoken out loud, some discord had taken place between them. Rudin was aware that Darya Mikhailovna was angry with him. Darya Mikhailovna suspected that he already knew everything.

Pandalevsky's report had greatly upset her. Her worldly *hauteur* had been stirred. Rudin, a poor man, lacking in rank and so far an unknown quantity, had had the insolence to make an assignation with her daughter—the daughter of Darya Mikhailovna Lasunskaya!

'Let us admit, he is clever, he is a genius!' she said. 'But what does that prove? That after this any man can hope to be my son-in-law?'

'For a long time I could not believe my eyes,' Pandalevsky chimed in. 'How could a man not know his place? It astonishes me!'

Darya Mikhailovna was very agitated, and Natalya caught the brunt of it.

She asked Rudin to be seated. He sat down, but it was no longer the former Rudin, who had almost been a master in the house; now he appeared not even as a good friend, but as a guest, and not an intimate guest at that. All this was accomplished in a single moment. Thus is water suddenly transformed into solid ice.

'I have come to you, Darya Mikhailovna,' Rudin began, 'to thank you for your hospitality. Today I received some news from my small estate, and have no option but to go there this very day.'

Darya Mikhailovna gave Rudin a fixed look.

'He has forestalled me, so he must have guessed,' she thought. 'He is saving me the need for a painful explanation; so much the better. Thank goodness for clever men!'

'Really?' she said loudly. 'Oh, what a nuisance! Well, what can one do? I hope to see you in Moscow this winter. We shall be leaving here soon ourselves.'

'I am not sure, Darya Mikhailovna, whether I will manage to visit Moscow; but if I can gather the means to do so, I shall consider it my duty to pay you a call.'

'Aha, brother!' Pandalevsky thought in his turn. 'For a long time you've been the *barin* round here, and now look at the way you've had to express yourself!'

'It would appear you have received some unsatisfactory news from your estate?' he articulated in his usual measured tones.

'Yes,' Rudin retorted stiffly.

'A bad harvest, perhaps?'

'No... something else... Believe me, Darya Mikhailovna,' Rudin added, 'I shall never forget the time that I have spent in your house.'

'And I, Dmitry Nikolaich, shall always remember our acquaintance with pleasure... When are you going?'

'Today, after dinner.'

'So soon!... Well, I wish you a good journey. Though if your business does not detain you, it may be that you will still find us here.'

'I shall hardly have the time,' Rudin retorted, and got up. 'Forgive me,' he added, 'I am at present unable to pay back the debt I owe you; but as soon as I reach my estate...'

'Enough, Dmitry Nikolaich!' Darya Mikhailovna interrupted him. 'You ought to be ashamed of yourself!... But what is the time?' she asked.

Pandalevsky took from his waistcoat pocket a gold enamel watch and looked at it, carefully leaning a pink cheek on his firm, white collar.

'Thirty-three minutes after two o'clock,' he said softly.

'Time to dress,' Darya Mikhailovna observed. '*Au revoir*, Dmitry Nikolaich!'

Rudin stood up. The whole conversation between him and Darya Mikhailovna had carried a peculiar imprint. Thus do actors rehearse their roles, thus do diplomats at conferences exchange fine phrases that have been agreed in advance...

Rudin went out. By now he knew from experience that people of high society do not even give up someone who is no longer necessary to them, but simply drop him: like a glove after a ball, like the wrapper of a piece of candy, like a lottery ticket that has not won.

He hurriedly packed and began, with impatience, to await the moment of departure. Everyone in the house was very astonished to learn of his intention; even the servants stared at him in bewilderment. Basistov did not conceal his sorrow. Natalya manifestly avoided Rudin. She tried not to meet his gaze; he did, however, succeed in thrusting his letter into her hand. At dinner Darya Mikhailovna once again repeated that she hoped to see him before they left for Moscow, but Rudin made no reply to her. Pandalevsky tried to engage him in conversation more frequently than any of the others. Rudin several times felt an urge to hurl himself upon him and give his blooming, rosy face a sound battering. Mlle Boncourt quite often glanced at Rudin with a sly and strange expression in her eyes: a similar expression may sometimes be observed in old, very intelligent gun-dogs... 'Ehe!' she seemed to be saying to herself. 'That's settled *your* hash!'

At last it struck six, and Rudin's tarantass was ready. He began hurriedly to say farewell to them all. Inside he felt very bad. Never had he expected that he would leave this house in such a fashion: it was as though he were being turned out... 'How did this happen? And what is all the hurry for? Even so, the end is the same,'—that was what he thought as he bowed to all sides with a forced smile. For the last time he looked at Natalya, and his heart missed a beat: her eyes were fixed on him with a sad, parting reproach.

He swiftly ran down the steps and sprang into the tarantass. Basistov offered to accompany him to the first post-house, and got in beside him.

'Do you remember,' Rudin began, as soon as the tarantass had driven out of the courtyard on to the broad road that was planted with fir trees, 'do you remember what Don Quixote says to his sword-bearer as he leaves the duchess's palace? "Freedom," he says, "my friend Sancho, is one of a man's most precious possessions, and happy is the man to whom heaven has given a crust of bread, and who does not need to be obliged to someone else for it!"* What Don Quixote felt then, I feel now... My good Basistov, may God grant that one day you too experience that feeling!'

Basistov squeezed Rudin's hand, and the young man's heart beat powerfully within his stirred breast. All the way to the post-house, Rudin spoke of the dignity of man and the meaning of true freedom —spoke ardently, nobly, and with veracity—and when the moment of parting arrived, Basistov could not restrain himself, but threw himself on Rudin's neck and began to sob. As for Rudin, he shed a few tears; but he wept about something other than parting from Basistov, and his tears were the tears of personal vanity.

Natalya went to her room and read Rudin's letter.

'Dear Natalya Alexeyevna,' he had written to her,

I have decided to leave. There is no other way out for me. I have decided to leave before I am told in so many words to remove myself. With my departure, all misunderstanding will be brought to an end; and it is hardly likely that anyone will be sorry to see me go. Then what is the point of waiting?... All is as it is; so why write to you?

I am parting from you probably for ever, and to leave you with a memory of me that is even worse than I deserve would be too bitter. That is why I am writing to you. I want neither to make excuses for myself, nor to accuse anyone at all but myself: I want, in so far as is possible, to explain myself... The events of recent days were so unexpected, so sudden...

Our meeting of today will serve me as a memorable lesson. Yes, you are right: I did not know you, but I thought I did! During my life I have had to do with people of all kinds, and I have formed close friendships with many women and girls; but when I met you, for the first time I met a soul that is *wholly* honest and sincere. This was something outside my customary experience, and I was unable to appreciate you. I felt an attraction towards you from the first day of our acquaintance—you may have noticed this. I spent hour after hour with you, and I did not get to know you... and I was able to imagine that I loved you! For this sin I am now punished.

There was also another time, in my earlier life, when I loved a woman, and she loved me... My feeling for her was a complicated one, as was hers for me; but since she herself was not ordinary, it suited her. The truth did not dawn on me at the time: I did not perceive it even now, when it appeared before me... In the end I did perceive it, but too late... The past cannot be returned... Our lives might have fused together—and will never fuse together. How can I prove to you that I could have loved you with a genuine love—a love of the heart, not of the imagination—when I myself do not know if I am capable of such a love!

Nature has given me many things—I know that, and will not be over-modest before you out of false shame, especially now, at such bitter moments, such moments of real shame for myself... Yes, nature has given me many things; but I will die without having done anything worthy of my powers, without leaving behind me any beneficial trace. All my riches will be wasted: I shall not see the fruits of my seeds. I lack... I myself cannot say just what it is I lack... I probably lack that without which one cannot set the hearts of men in motion, nor take possession of a woman's heart; and dominion over minds alone is both precarious and useless. Strange, almost comic is my fate: I aspire to give the whole of myself, eagerly, in full—and cannot give myself. I will end by sacrificing myself for some non-sense in which I will not even believe... My God! To still be preparing to do something at the age of 35!...

Never before have I spoken out like this to anyone—this is my confession. But enough about myself. I want to talk about you, and give you some advice: more than that I am unfit to do... You are still young; but no matter how long you live, always follow the promptings of your heart, and do not submit to your own mind or anyone else's. Believe me, the simpler and more intimate the circle round which life is focused, the better; the point is not to seek new aspects of life, but rather to make sure that all its transitions are accomplished in proper time. 'Blessed is he who in his youth was young...'* But I am aware that this advice has far more relation to myself than to you.

I will confess to you, Natalya Alexeyevna, that I feel very wretched. I was never under any illusions as to the nature of the emotion I inspired in Darya Mikhailovna; but I hoped that I had found at least a temporary mooring... Now I must wander the world once more. What will ever replace your conversation, your presence, your attentive and intelligent gaze?... I am myself to blame; but please try to see that fate has mocked us, as if on purpose. A week ago I myself would hardly have guessed that I loved you. Two days ago, at evening, in the garden, for the first time I heard you say... but what is the point in reminding you of what you said on that occasion—and so now, today, I am leaving, leaving in disgrace, after a cruel explanation with you, taking with me no hope at all... And you do not yet know the degree to which I am guilty before you... There is in me a kind of stupid candour, a kind of indiscretion... But what is the point of talking about it? I am leaving for ever.

[Here Rudin had been about to tell Natalya about his visit to Volyntsev, but thought the better of it and struck out this whole passage, while in his letter to Volyntsev he added the second postscript.]

I remain alone upon the earth in order to devote myself, as you told me this morning with a cruel smile, to other tasks more suited to me. Alas! If only I could devote myself to those tasks, finally conquer my laziness... But no! I shall remain the same unfinished creature that I have been hitherto... The first hindrance—and I go to pieces entirely; what happened with you proved that to me. If at least I had sacrificed my love to my future cause, my vocation; but I was simply afraid of the responsibility that fell on me, and so it is true, I really am unworthy of you. I am not worth it, that you should tear yourself away from your natural sphere... However, perhaps it is all for the best. From this ordeal I shall perhaps emerge purer and stronger.

I wish you complete happiness. Farewell! Remember me sometimes. I hope that you will hear more of me.

Rudin

Natalya lowered Rudin's letter to her knee and for a long time sat motionless, her eyes fixed on the floor. This letter, more clearly than any arguments, demonstrated to her that she had been right when that morning, parting from Rudin, she had involuntarily exclaimed that he did not love her! But this did not bring her any ease. She sat without moving; it seemed to her that dark waves closed above her head without a ripple, and she fell to the bottom, growing cold and numb. All find their first disillusionment painful; but for a sincere soul that has had no desire to deceive itself, and to which light-mindedness and exaggeration are foreign, it is almost intolerable. Natalya remembered her childhood when, out walking in the evening, she had always tried to go in the direction of the bright rim of the sky, where the sunset burned, and not towards the darkness. Dark, life stood before her now, and she had turned her back to the light...

Tears welled in Natalya's eyes. Tears are not always beneficial. They are comforting and healing when, having long swollen within the breast, they at last come flowing—at first with effort, then ever more easily, ever more sweetly; the speechless languor of melancholy is resolved by them. But there are also cold tears, tears that flow meagrely: the grief that has settled on the heart like a heavy and unmoving burden squeezes them from the heart drop by drop; they are joyless and bring no respite. Distress weeps with such tears, and whoever has not shed them has not yet been unhappy. Natalya came to know them on that day.

Some two hours passed. Natalya plucked up her spirits, wiped her eyes, lit a candle, burned Rudin's letter on it to the end, and threw the ash out of the window. Then she opened Pushkin at random and read the first lines that met her eye (she often told her fortune with him in this way). This is what met her eyes:

> Whoe'er has felt shall be disturbed
> By phantom of irrevocable days...
> For him no more of fascination,
> For him the snake of recollection,
> As by repentance he is gnawed...*

She stood for a moment, looked at herself in the mirror with a cold smile and, with a small, up-down movement of her head, went downstairs to the drawing-room.

Darya Mikhailovna, as soon as she caught sight of her, led her to the study, sat her down beside her, gave her an affectionate pat on the cheek, all the while looking closely, almost with curiosity, into her eyes. Darya Mikhailovna felt secretly bewildered: for the first time the thought had come into her head that she did not really know her daughter. On hearing from Pandalevsky of Natalya's rendezvous with Rudin, she had not so much been angry as astonished that the sensible Natalya could determine on such an action. But when she had summoned her and begun to scold her—not at all in the way that might have been expected of a woman of European education, but rather loudly and inelegantly—Natalya's firm replies, the determination in her gaze and movements, embarrassed, even frightened Darya Mikhailovna.

Rudin's sudden and also not entirely comprehensible departure had lifted a great weight from her heart; but she had expected tears, hysterical fits... Natalya's outward calm again confused her.

'Well now, child,' Darya Mikhailovna began. 'How are you today?'

Natalya gave her mother a look.

'I mean, he has left... the object of your feelings. Do you know why he went on his way so quickly?'

'Mamma!' Natalya said in a quiet voice. 'I give you my word that if you yourself do not mention him, you shall never hear anything from me either.'

'So you admit, then, that you were guilty in my regard?'

Natalya lowered her head and repeated:

'You shall never hear anything from me.'

'Now, look!' Darya Mikhailovna retorted with a smile. 'I believe you. But the day before yesterday, if you remember, you... Well, I shan't go into it. It's finished, dead and buried. Isn't it? There, I recognize you again; for a while you had me quite at a loss. Well, then, kiss me, my clever one!...'

Natalya brought Darya Mikhailovna's hand to her lips, and Darya Mikhailovna kissed her on her tilted head.

'Always listen to my advice, don't forget that you are a Lasunsky and my daughter,' she added, 'and you will be happy. And now off you go.'

Natalya went out of the room in silence. Darya Mikhailovna watched her go and thought: 'She is like me—she too will fall in love: *mais elle aura moins d'abandon.*'* And Darya Mikhailovna immersed herself in memories of the past... the distant past...

Then she gave instructions for Mlle Boncourt to be called, and sat with her for a long time, in *tête-à-tête* behind locked doors. Having let her go, she summoned Pandalevsky. She demanded to know the real reason for Rudin's departure... but Pandalevsky completely put her mind at rest. This was something at which he was skilled.

Next day Volyntsev and his sister came to dinner. Darya Mikhailovna was always very amiable to him, and on this occasion she treated him with particular affection. Natalya was intolerably unhappy; but Volyntsev was so deferential, and talked with her so timidly, that within her soul she could not but thank him.

The day passed quietly, in rather tedious fashion, but as they left and went their separate ways, they all felt that they had fallen back into their old routine; and that means a great deal, a very great deal.

Yes, they had all fallen back into their old routine... all, that is, except Natalya. Alone at last, it was with effort that she dragged herself to her bed and, weary, drained of energy, fell with her face on the pillow. So bitter, repugnant, and vulgar did living seem to her, so ashamed was she of herself, her love and her sadness, that at that moment she would probably have agreed to die... Many were the wretched days, the nights of sleepless, tormenting emotions that still lay before her; but she was young—life was only just beginning for her, and sooner or later life will claim its own. No matter what the blow that may strike a person, if that day he will take something to—you must forgive the crudity of the expression—eat, and more the next, there already is your first consolation...

Natalya suffered intensely, she suffered for the first time... But one's first sufferings, like one's first love, are not repeated—and thank God!

XII

ABOUT two years had gone by. The first days of May were at hand. On the balcony of her house sat Alexandra Pavlovna, not Lipina now, but Lezhneva; it was more than a year since she had married Mikhailo Mikhailych. She was charming as ever, though she had put on a little weight recently. In front of the balcony, from which steps led down into the garden, a wet-nurse was walking to and fro, holding a red-cheeked baby in a little white coat, with a white pompom on his hat. Alexandra Pavlovna looked at him now and then. The baby did not cry, sucked his finger solemnly, and gazed tranquilly around him. One could already tell that this was a son worthy of Mikhailo Mikhailych.

Beside Alexandra Pavlovna on the balcony sat our old friend Pigasov. His hair had turned noticeably greyer since we parted from him last, he had grown thinner, and spoke with a hissing sound: one of his front teeth had fallen out; the hissing lent even more venom to his discourses... His bitterness was not decreasing with the years, but his witticisms were losing their sharp edge, and he repeated himself more often. Mikhailo Mikhailych was not at home; he was expected back in time for evening tea. The sun had already set. In the place where it had gone down, a band of pale-gold, lemon colour extended along the horizon; on the side opposite there were two: the lower one azure, the other, higher up, red-and-lilac. Small, gauzy clouds were fading in the upper sky. It all promised settled weather.

Suddenly Pigasov began to laugh.

'What is it, Afrikan Semyonych?' asked Alexandra Pavlovna.

'Oh, nothing... Yesterday I heard a muzhik say to his wife—she'd been chattering away—"Stop that squawking!"... That appealed to me greatly. "Stop that squawking!" And indeed, what can a woman put up by way of rational argument? You know, I never talk about people who are present. Our ancestors were more intelligent than us. In their fairy tales the beautiful woman always sits by a window, a star on her forehead, but she never says a word. Now, that is how it ought to be. Yet, judge for yourself: the day before yesterday our marshal's wife more or less took a pot-shot at my forehead, as with a pistol; she told me that she didn't like my *tendency*! Tendency! Well, would it not have been better for her and for everyone if through some benign disposition of nature she had suddenly been deprived of the use of her tongue?'

'Well, you have not changed, Afrikan Semyonych: still attacking us poor creatures... You know, it's really a kind of misfortune, truly it is. I feel sorry for you.'

'Misfortune? What, with respect, are you talking about? First, there are in my opinion only three misfortunes in the world: to spend the winter in cold lodgings, to wear tight boots in summer, and to sleep in a room where there's a crying infant one's not allowed to spray with insect powder; and secondly, for pity's sake, I am now the most gentle of men. You could make fair copies of me! That's how moral my conduct is.'

'Your conduct is splendid, I'm sure! Though Yelena Antonovna was complaining to me about you yesterday.'

'Indeed, ma'am! And what did she tell you, may one enquire?'

'She told me that for the course of an entire morning the only answer you would give to all her questions was: "What's the use?", "What's the use?", and in such a squeaky voice, too.'

Pigasov laughed.

'Well, it was a good idea, you'll agree, Alexandra Pavlovna... eh?'

'An astonishing one! Is it really permissible to be so impolite to a woman, Afrikan Semyonych?'

'What? Yelena Antonovna is a woman, in your view?'

'But what is she, in yours?'

'A drum, for pity's sake, a regular drum, of the kind that one beats with sticks...'

'Ah, yes!' Alexandra Pavlovna interrupted, wishing to change the subject of conversation. 'They say you may be congratulated?'

'What on?'

'The conclusion of your lawsuit. Glinov Meadows are yours.'

'Yes, they are,' Pigasov rejoined, gloomily.

'You have been trying to attain this for so many years, and now you seem dissatisfied.'

'Let me tell you, Alexandra Pavlovna,' Pigasov said quietly and slowly. 'Nothing can be worse or more vexing than a happiness that arrives too late. It can afford one no satisfaction, and it deprives one of one's right, one's most precious right—to scold and curse at fate. Yes, madam, it is a bitter and a vexing thing—belated happiness.'

Alexandra Pavlovna merely shrugged her shoulders.

'Nurse,' she began, 'I think it is Misha's bedtime now. Give him here.'

And Alexandra Pavlovna attended to her son, while Pigasov went off, growling, to the other end of the balcony.

Suddenly, not far away, passing alongside the garden, Mikhailo Mikhailych appeared in his racing droshky. In front of his horses two enormous watchdogs ran: one yellow, the other grey; he had recently bought them. They never stopped scrapping with each other, and lived in inseparable friendship. An old, hairy mongrel came out of the gateway to meet them, opened his mouth as if preparing to bark, but in the end simply yawned and set off back inside, wagging his tail in friendly fashion.

'Look, Sasha,' Lezhnev shouted to his wife from afar, 'look who I'm bringing to see you...'

Alexandra Pavlovna did not immediately recognize the man who was sitting behind her husband's back.

'Ah! Mr Basistov!' she exclaimed at last.

'The very man,' Lezhnev replied, 'and what wonderful news he has brought. Just wait a moment, and you'll find out.'

And he drove into the courtyard.

A few moments later he appeared with Basistov on the balcony.

'Hurrah!' he exclaimed, embracing his wife. 'Seryozha is to marry!'

'Whom?' Alexandra Pavlovna asked with excitement.

'Natalya, of course... My friend here brought this news from Moscow, and there is a letter for you... Do you hear, Mishuk?' he added, picking his son up in his arms. 'Your uncle is to marry!... What a phlegmatic villain! All he can do is blink!'

'The young master wants to sleep,' the nurse observed.

'Yes, ma'am,' Basistov said quietly, going over to Alexandra Pavlovna. 'I arrived today from Moscow, on Darya Mikhailovna's instructions—to audit the accounts of the estate. And here is a letter.'

Alexandra Pavlovna hurriedly unsealed the letter from her brother. It consisted of only a few lines. In the first flush of joy he informed his sister that he had proposed to Natalya, received her consent and Darya Mikhailovna's, promised to write more with the first post, and embraced and kissed them all in his absence. It was obvious that he had written the letter in a kind of daze.

Tea was served, and they made Basistov sit down. The questions showered on him like hail. Everyone, even Pigasov, was delighted by the news he had brought.

'Please tell us one thing,' Lezhnev said, in passing. 'We received rumours about a certain Mr Korchagin. That was all nonsense, then?'

(Korchagin was a handsome young man—a social lion, exceedingly stuck-up and pompous; he comported himself in an extraordinarily solemn and majestic manner, as though he were not a real human being at all, but rather a statue of himself erected by public subscription.)

'Well, no, not quite nonsense,' Basistov rejoined with a smile. 'Darya Mikhailovna was very well disposed towards him; but Natalya Alexeyevna would not even hear of him.'

'But you see, I know him,' Pigasov caught up. 'And he's a double-dyed numbskull, an ignominious numbskull... for pity's sake! Why, if all men were like him, it would take big money to persuade one to live at all... for pity's sake!'

'Perhaps...' Basistov rejoined. 'But in society he plays a far from insignificant role...'

'Well, anyway, it doesn't matter!' Alexandra Pavlovna exclaimed. 'Who cares about him? Oh, how glad I am for my brother!... And Natalya—is she cheerful and happy?'

'Yes, ma'am. She is quiet, as always—I mean, you know her—but I think she is content.'

The evening went by in pleasant and lively conversation. They sat down to supper.

'And by the way,' Lezhnev asked Basistov, as he poured him some Château Lafite, 'do you know where Rudin is?'

'At present I do not know for certain. He arrived in Moscow last winter for a short visit, and then set off for Simbirsk with a family; he and I corresponded for a while: in his last letter he told me he was leaving Simbirsk—didn't say where for—and since then I've heard no more about him.'

'He'll not perish!' Pigasov chipped in. 'He'll be sitting somewhere delivering his sermons. That gentleman will always find himself two or three admirers who'll listen to him open-mouthed and lend him money. You'll see, he'll end up dying somewhere in Tsarevokokshaisk or Chukhloma*—in the arms of an aged spinster in a wig, who will consider him the greatest genius on earth...'

'You speak very harshly of him,' Basistov observed in an under-tone, and with displeasure.

'Not harshly at all,' retorted Pigasov, 'but quite fairly. In my opinion he is simply nothing but a lickspittle. I forgot to tell you,' he continued, addressing Lezhnev, 'you know, I made the acquaintance of that fellow Terlakhov, with whom Rudin travelled abroad. My goodness, my goodness! The things he told me about him, you cannot imagine —it would make you die laughing! It's a notable fact that all Rudin's friends and followers eventually becomes his enemies.'

'I ask to be excluded from the ranks of such friends!' Basistov interrupted, heatedly.

'Well, *you* are another matter! No one is talking about you.'

'But what did Terlakhov tell you?' Alexandra Pavlovna inquired.

'Oh, many things: I cannot remember them all. But the best one was this anecdote about what happened to Rudin. In the course of his constant development—these gentlemen are forever developing: for example, other men merely eat and sleep, but *they* are in a "developmental process" of sleeping and eating; is it not so, Mr Basistov?' Basistov made no reply—'Well then, in the course of his constant development, by the path of philosophy Rudin reached the conclusion that he ought to fall in love. He began to search for an object of love that would be worthy of such an astonishing conclusion. Fortune smiled on him. He made the acquaintance of a French girl, a very pretty milliner. It all happened in a certain German town, on the Rhine, observe. He began to pay her visits, take her various books, talk to her about nature and Hegel. Can you imagine the milliner's predicament? She thought he was an astronomer. But you know him, he always lands on his feet; well, he was a foreigner, a Russian—she liked him. So, in the end he arranged a rendezvous, and a very poetic rendezvous it was: in a gondola on the river. The French girl consented: put on her best clothes and went off in the gondola with him. They were out on the river for about two hours. And what do you think he did all that time? Patted the French girl on the head, looked meditatively at the sky, and repeated several times that he felt a fatherly tenderness for her. The French girl returned home in a fury, and later told Terlakhov everything. That's the kind of gentleman Rudin is!'

And Pigasov began to laugh.

'You are an old cynic!' Alexandra Pavlovna observed, vexedly. 'But I am increasingly of the conviction that even those who criticize Rudin can find nothing bad to say of him.'

'Nothing bad? For pity's sake! What about his eternal living at others' expense, his borrowing... Mikhailo Mikhailych! Why, I expect he borrowed from you, didn't he?'

'Listen, Afrikan Semyonych!' Lezhnev began, and his face assumed a serious expression. 'Listen: you know, and my wife knows, that of late I have not been very favourably disposed towards Rudin and have even frequently condemned him. Be that as it may,' (Lezhnev poured champagne into the goblets) 'here is what I propose to you: just now we drank a toast to the health of our dear brother and his bride-to-be; I now propose to you a toast to the health of Dmitry Rudin!'

Alexandra Pavlovna and Pigasov looked at Lezhnev in amazement, and Basistov sat up straight as a rod, grew flushed with joy, and goggled for all he was worth.

'I know him well,' Lezhnev continued. 'His defects are well known to me. They are made all the more clearly apparent because he is not a petty man.'

'Rudin is a character of genius!' Basistov caught up.

'There may perhaps be genius in him,' Lezhnev retorted, 'but character... That is the whole of his misfortune, that there really is no character in him... But that is not important. I want to speak of what is good and rare in him. There is enthusiasm in him; and believe me, that to me, as a phlegmatic man, is a most precious quality in our age. We have all grown intolerably sober-minded, indifferent, and inert; we have fallen asleep, we have frozen, and therefore we should thank the man who even for a moment can stir us and warm us! It's time for that! Do you remember, Sasha, I once spoke to you of him and reproached him for coldness. I was both right and wrong then. The coldness is in his blood—that is not his fault—and not in his head. He is not an actor, as I called him, not a trickster, not a cheat; he lives at others' expense, not like an *arriviste* but like a child... Yes, he will indeed die somewhere in destitution and poverty; but is that in itself any reason for us to cast a stone at him? He will achieve nothing precisely because there is no character, no blood in him; but who is within his rights to say that he will not bring, has not already brought benefit? That his words have not dropped many a good seed into young souls, whom nature has not denied, as it has him, the power of activity, the ability to fulfil their own intentions? And I myself, I was the first to experience all this upon my own person... Sasha knows what Rudin meant to me when I was young. I remember that I also used to claim that Rudin's words could not possibly have any effect on people; but then I was talking about people like myself, at the age I am now, about people who have already lived and been broken

down by life. One false note in any discourse—and all its harmony
has vanished for us; but fortunately, in a young man the sense of
hearing is not so developed, not so spoilt. If the essence of what he
hears seems beautiful to him, what does he care about the tone? He
will find the tone within himself.'

'Bravo! Bravo!' Basistov exclaimed. 'How well you put it! And
as for Rudin's influence, I swear to you, not only was that man able to
astound one, he could also get one moving, he wouldn't let one stand
still, he would churn up the foundations of one's being, set one alight!'

'Do you hear?' Lezhnev continued, addressing Pigasov. 'What further proof do you need? You attack philosophy; when you speak of
it, you cannot find words that are contemptuous enough. I myself am
not that fond of it, and do not really understand it; but our principal
adversities come not from philosophy! Philosophical stratagems and
ravings will never take root in the Russian; he has too much common
sense for that; but one cannot allow every honourable aspiration for truth
and awareness to be attacked as "philosophy". Rudin's misfortune is
that he does not know Russia, and that is indeed a great misfortune.
Russia can manage without any of us, but none of us can manage without Russia. Woe betide any man who thinks he can, and double woe
betide any man who really does manage without her! Cosmopolitanism is rubbish, and the cosmopolitan is a nonentity, worse than a
nonentity; outside of national roots there is neither art, nor truth, nor
life, nothing. Without physiognomy there is not even such a thing as
an ideal face; only a vulgar face is possible without physiognomy. But
again I say that this is not Rudin's fault: it is his fate, a bitter and
heavy fate for which the rest of us should not blame him. It would
take us a very long route to discover why the Rudins appear in our
land. But for the good that is in him, let us be grateful to him. That
is easier than being unfair to him, and we have been unfair to him.
To punish him is not our task, and is in any case unnecessary: he has
punished himself far more cruelly than he deserved... And may God
grant that misfortune will remove all the bad from him and leave only
the good in him! I drink to Rudin's health! I drink to the health of
the companion of my best years, I drink to youth, to its hopes, to its
aspirations, to its trustfulness and honesty, to all the things that made
our hearts pulse at the age of twenty, and which was better than anything we had ever known or will ever again know in life... I drink to
you, golden time, I drink to the health of Rudin!'

They all clinked glasses with Lezhnev. In his fervour, Basistov very nearly broke his, and drained it instantly, while Alexandra Pavlovna shook Lezhnev's hand.

'I had no idea that you were such an eloquent speaker, Mikhailo Mikhailych,' Pigasov observed. 'A match for Mr Rudin himself; you even set me going.'

'I'm not an eloquent speaker at all,' Lezhnev retorted, not without annoyance. 'And you, I think, are not hard to set going. However, enough of Rudin; let us talk of something else... Tell me... what is his name, again?... Pandalevsky, is he still living at Darya Mikhailovna's?' he added, turning to Basistov.

'Of course he is! She has gone to great lengths to secure him a very good position.'

Lezhnev smiled dryly.

'Well, there's a man who won't die in poverty, one may bank on that.'

Supper was ended. The guests went their separate ways. Remaining alone with her husband, Alexandra Pavlovna looked him in the face with a smile.

'What good form you were in this evening, Misha!' she said softly, stroking his forehead with her hand. 'How cleverly and nobly you spoke! But you must admit that you got slightly carried away in Rudin's favour, just as you used to get carried away in opposition to him...'

'One does not kick a man when he's down... but then I was afraid he might turn your head.'

'No,' Alexandra Pavlovna retorted, straightforwardly. 'He always struck me as being too learned, I was afraid of him and did not know what to say in his presence. But Pigasov poked some rather cruel fun at him today, didn't he?'

'Pigasov?' Lezhnev said. 'I intervened so warmly on Rudin's behalf precisely because Pigasov was here. He has the audacity to call Rudin a lickspittle! Well, in my opinion, his role, Pigasov's, that is, is a hundred times worse. He has an independent income, mocks at everything, yet how he ingratiates himself with the aristocratic and the rich! Do you know that this Pigasov, who criticizes everything and everyone with such animosity, who assails philosophy and women—do you know that when he worked in the civil service he used to take bribes, and big ones, too! Hah! There is something to think about!'

'Really?' Alexandra Pavlovna exclaimed. 'I would never have expected it!... Listen, Misha,' she added, after a short pause. 'There is something I want to ask you...'

'What?'

'What do you think—will my brother be happy with Natalya?'

'How can I put it?... There is every probability... She will be the one who gives the orders—between ourselves there's no reason to make any secret of it—she is more intelligent than he; but he's a fine man and loves her with all his soul. What more do you want? I mean, we love each other and are happy, are we not?'

Alexandra Pavlovna smiled, and gave Mikhailo Mikhailych's hand a firm squeeze.

On the same day on which all that has been described by us was taking place in the house of Alexandra Pavlovna, in one of the far-flung guberniyas* of Russia, at the hottest hour, a rickety little hooded basswood cart harnessed to a troika* of hired horses was trundling along a main road. On the coachman's seat, digging his heels aslant into the swingle-tree, protruded a short, grey-haired muzhik in a tattered heavy coat, from time to time giving the reins a tug and brandishing a small knout; while in the cart itself, seated on a meagre trunk, was a man tall of stature, in a peaked cap and an old, dusty cloak. This was Rudin. He sat with his head lowered and the peak of the cap pulled down over his eyes. The cart's uneven jolting threw him from side to side, and he seemed quite insensible, as though he were drowsing. At last, he straightened up.

'When are we going to reach the post-house?' he asked the muzhik who sat on the coachman's seat.

'Well, you see, sir,' the muzhik said, tugging the reins even more violently, 'when we get up to the brow of the hill it will be a couple more versts, no more... All right, you! Mind out... Or I'll mind out for you,' he added in a reedy little voice, beginning to lash the right-hand horse with his knout.

'You seem to be making very little headway,' Rudin observed. 'We've been trundling along since this morning and can't seem to get anywhere. You might at least sing something.'

'But what can a man do, sir! You can see for yourself that the horses are worn out... it's the heat again. And the likes of us can't sing: we're not yamshchiks... Sheep-brain, sheep-brain!' the little muzhik suddenly

exclaimed, addressing a passer-by in a wretched brown *svita** and
down-at-heel bast sandals, 'Step aside, sheep-brain!'

'Look at you... coachman!' the passer-by muttered after him, and
stopped. 'Moscow type!' he added in a voice full of reproach, shook
his head, and began to hobble off.

'Where are you going, then?' the muzhik resumed unhurriedly,
tugging at the wheel-horse. 'Oh, you sly one, truly you're a sly one!'

The worn-out little horses somehow at last managed to drag themselves to the post-house. Rudin got out of the cart, paid the muzhik
(who did not bow to him, and tossed the money about in the palm of
his hand for a long time—as if to say: you didn't give a big enough
tip) and carried his trunk into the post-room by himself.

A friend of mine who travelled around Russia a great deal in his
day once made the observation that if on the walls of a post-room there
hang pictures portraying scenes from *A Prisoner of the Caucasus** or
Russian generals, then horses will be quickly available; but if the pictures show the life of the renowned gambler Georges de Germany,*
then the traveller can have no hope of a swift departure; he will
have time to admire the twisted quiff, the white pleated waistcoat,
and exceedingly tight and short breeches of the gambler in his youth,
his frenzied physiognomy as, now an old man, brandishing aloft a
chair in a shack with a steep-sloping roof, he murders his son. In the
room that Rudin had entered hung precisely these scenes from
Thirty Years, or the Life of a Gambler. In response to his cry the postmaster appeared, sleepy-looking (incidentally—has anyone ever seen
a postmaster who was not sleepy-looking?), and, not even waiting
for Rudin to ask the question, in a languid voice declared that there
were no horses.

'How can you tell me there are no horses,' Rudin said quietly, 'when
you don't even know where I'm bound for? I arrived here with hired
ones.'

'We have no horses for any destination,' the postmaster replied.
'And where are you bound for?'

'——sk.'

'There are no horses,' the postmaster said again, and went away.

Rudin drew near to the window in vexation and threw his peaked
cap on the table. He had not altered much, but had grown sallower
in the last two years; strands of silver gleamed here and there in his
curls, and his eyes, still beautiful, seemed to have lost their lustre;

small wrinkles, the marks of bitter and anxious feelings, had settled around his lips, his cheeks, and temples.

The clothes he was wearing were shabby and old, and no white linen was visible anywhere about his person. The time of his flowering was evidently over: he had, as the gardeners say, run to seed.

He began to read the inscriptions on the walls... a well-known diversion of bored travellers... Suddenly the door began to creak, and the postmaster entered.

'There are no horses for ——sk, and there won't be any for a long time,' he began, 'but there are return horses for ——ov.'

'——ov?' Rudin said quietly. 'But for pity's sake! That is not at all on my route. I am headed for Penza, and ——ov is on the way to Tambov, I think.'

'So what? You can travel on from Tambov, or otherwise you can make a turning when you get to ——ov.'

Rudin thought for a moment.

'Well, you may be right,' he said at last. 'Tell them to harness the horses. It's all the same to me: I'll go to Tambov.'

The horses were soon brought. Rudin carried out his small trunk, got into the cart, and sat down, with lowered head, as before. There was something helpless and sadly submissive about his bowed figure... And the troika went trundling off at a leisurely trot, its bells fitfully jingling.

EPILOGUE

A FEW more years went by.

It was a cold autumn day. Up to the front entrance of the main hotel of the provincial town of S—— drove a four-wheeled carriage; out of it, stretching, and groaning slightly, climbed a gentleman not yet elderly but already possessed of that ample corporation it is usual to call 'considerable'. Ascending the staircase to the first floor, he stopped at the entrance to a wide corridor and, not seeing anyone about, in a loud voice asked for a room. Somewhere a door banged, and from behind low screens leapt a tall lackey who walked forward with a nimble, rolling gait, his shiny back and rolled-up sleeves gleaming in the corridor's semi-darkness. Entering his room, the traveller at once threw off his overcoat and scarf, sat down on the sofa, and leaning on his knees with his fists, first looked around him, as though only half-awake, and then asked for his servant to be called. The lackey made an evasive movement and disappeared. This traveller was none other than Lezhnev. Military recruitment work had called him from the country to the town of S——.

Lezhnev's servant, a young fellow with curly hair and red cheeks, in a grey overcoat belted with a blue sash, and soft felt boots, came into the room.

'Well, then, brother, we're here,' Lezhnev said quietly. 'And there were you worrying that the tyre was going to come off that wheel.'

'Yes, we're here!' the servant rejoined, trying to smile through the raised collar of his overcoat. 'But it's a miracle the tyre didn't come off...'

'Is there no one here?' a voice rang out in the corridor.

Lezhnev gave a start, and began to listen.

'Hallo! Who's there?' the voice said again.

Lezhnev got up, went over to the door, and quickly opened it.

Before him stood a man tall of stature, hunched-up and almost completely grey-haired, in an old velveteen frock-coat with bronze buttons. Lezhnev recognized him immediately.

'Rudin!' he exclaimed with excitement.

Rudin turned round. He could not make out the features of Lezhnev, who stood with his back to the light, and peered at him in bewilderment.

'Do you not recognize me?' Lezhnev began.

'Mikhailo Mikhailych!' Rudin exclaimed, and proffered a hand, but became embarrassed and started to withdraw it...

Lezhnev hurriedly seized it in both of his.

'Come in, come into my room!' he said to Rudin, and led him inside.

'How you have changed!' Lezhnev pronounced, after a short pause, and involuntarily lowering his voice.

'Yes, so they tell me!' Rudin rejoined, letting his gaze wander round the room. 'The years... But you are just the same. How is Alexandra... your wife?'

'Thank you, well. But what on earth brings you here?'

'Me—here? That is a long story. Actually, I came here by chance. I was looking for a friend of mine. However, I'm very pleased...'

'Where are you going to dine?'

'I? I don't know. At an inn somewhere. For I must leave here today.'

'Must?'

Rudin smiled meaningfully.

'Yes, sir, must. I am being sent back to live on my estate.'

'Dine with me.'

For the first time, Rudin looked Lezhnev straight in the eye.

'You are asking me to dine with you?' he said.

'Yes, Rudin, for old times' sake, as companions. Are you willing? I was not expecting to meet you, and God knows when we shall see each other again. You and I cannot simply part like this!'

'Very well, I agree.'

Lezhnev shook Rudin's hand, called his servant, ordered the dinner, and asked for a bottle of champagne to be placed upon ice.

During the dinner Lezhnev and Rudin, as if by agreement, spent the time talking about their student days, remembering many things and many people—dead and living. At first Rudin spoke reluctantly, but he drank a few glasses of wine, and the blood flamed up in him. At last the lackey took away the final course. Lezhnev got up, locked the door, and returning to the table, sat down directly opposite Rudin, and quietly supported his chin in both hands.

'Well,' he began, 'now you must tell me everything that has happened to you since I last saw you.'

Rudin looked at Lezhnev.

'My God!' Lezhnev thought again. 'How he has changed, poor fellow!'

Rudin's features had changed little, especially since the time we saw him at the post-house, though the imprint of approaching age had already set itself upon them; but their expression was now altered. The gaze of his eyes was different; in his whole being, in his movements, now delayed, now incoherently jerky, in his cold, almost broken speech there was a final weariness, a secret and silent sorrow, far distinct from that half-simulated melancholy which once he had flaunted, as youth in general flaunts it, filled with hopes and trustful personal vanity.

'Tell you everything that has happened to me?' he began. 'To tell you everything is impossible, and is not worth it... I have suffered a great deal, wandered not only in body—but also in soul. With what and with whom have I not been disillusioned, my God! Whom have I not befriended! Yes, whom!' Rudin repeated, having noticed that Lezhnev was looking him in the face with a kind of special concern. 'How many times have my own words become repugnant to me—not in my own mouth, I mean, but in the mouths of people who shared my opinions! How many times have I passed from the irritability of a child to the vacant insensibility of a horse that does not even flick its tail under the knout... How many times have I rejoiced, hoped, fought at loggerheads, and then abased myself for nothing! How many times have I flown forth as a falcon—and returned on my hands and knees, like a snail with a broken shell!... Where have I not been, what roads have I not walked!... And roads are often muddy,' Rudin added, turning away slightly. 'You know...' he continued...

'Listen,' Lezhnev said, interrupting him. 'We used to be on familiar terms with each other... Are you willing? Let us bring back the old days... Let's drink to each other, on familiar terms!'*

Rudin roused himself, got to his feet, and in his eyes fleeted something that a word cannot express.

'Let's drink,' he said. 'Thank thee, brother, let us drink.'

Lezhnev and Rudin each drained a goblet.

'You know,' Rudin began again, continuing the familiar mode of address, with a smile, 'There is some kind of worm inside me that nibbles me and gnaws me and will not let me fully rest. It impels me out towards people—at first they submit to my influence, but then...'

Rudin moved his hand through the air.

'Since I parted from you... from thee, I have relived and re-experienced many things... I began to live, twenty times I turned over a new leaf—and you see the result!'

'You had not the endurance,' Lezhnev said quietly, as if to himself.

'As you say, I had not the endurance!... I was never able to build anything; and is there much sense in building, brother, when there is not even any soil beneath one's feet, when one needs to create one's own foundation first? I shall not describe to you all my adventures, or rather, that's to say, all my failures. I will tell you two or three instances... those instances in my life when, it seemed, success already smiled on me, or rather, when I began to hope for success—which is not quite the same thing...'

Rudin threw back his grey and now thinning hair with the same motion of his hand he had once used to throw back his thick, dark curls.

'Well then, listen,' he began. 'In Moscow I became friendly with a rather strange gentleman. He was very rich and owned vast estates; he was not in the civil service. His main, his only passion was a love of science, of science in general. To this day I still cannot comprehend why this passion manifested itself in him! It suited him about as well as a saddle does a cow. He could only keep up with things of the mind with an effort, and was almost incapable of speaking, merely moved his eyes about expressively and nodded his head meaningfully. I have never, brother, encountered a nature more ungifted and poorer than his... In the province of Smolensk there are places like that—sand and nothing else, or occasionally grass that no creature would ever eat. Nothing came easily to him—everything simply unravelled away from him, as far away as possible; and he was also mad about making everything easy difficult. If it had depended on his instructions, his servants would have eaten with their heels, I swear it. He worked, wrote, and read incessantly. He courted knowledge with a kind of stubborn persistence, a terrible patience; there was enormous self-pride in him, and he possessed an iron character. He lived alone and had a reputation as an eccentric. I made his acquaintance... well, and he liked me. I took his measure fairly soon, I will admit, but his fervour touched me. What was more, he had the kind of means that made it possible to do good through him, bring positive advantage... I moved into his house and finally went off with him to his estate in the country. Brother, I had enormous plans: I dreamt of various improvements, innovations...'

'As at Lasunskaya's, remember?' Lezhnev observed with a good-natured smile.

'Oh no! There I knew, within my soul, that nothing would come of my words; but here... here a completely different sphere opened before me... I had brought some books on agronomy with me... to be sure, I had not read a single one of them... well, and so got down to business... At first I didn't get anywhere, as I had expected, but later I did get somewhere. My new friend did not say anything, merely watched, did not interfere, or rather did not interfere up to a certain point. He accepted my suggestions and carried them out, but with doggedness, slowly, with secret mistrust, and kept doing things his own way. He attached an exceedingly high value to each single one of his thoughts. He would clamber up it with effort, like a ladybird on the end of a blade of grass, and sit there, sit on it, as though he were preparing to spread his wings and fly—and then suddenly would topple to the ground, and start to climb again... Do not be astonished by all these comparisons. Even back then they seethed within my soul. I struggled like this for about two years. The work made little progress, in spite of all the trouble I had taken. I began to grow weary, I was sick of my friend, I began to say sarcastic things to him, he weighed on me like a featherbed; his mistrust gave way to a sullen irritability, we were both seized by a feeling of hostility, we could no longer talk about anything; he surreptitiously but constantly tried to prove to me that he was not subject to my influence; my instructions were either distorted, or cancelled altogether... I noticed, at last, that I was living in the home of my gentleman landowner in the capacity of a retainer whose task it was to provide some intellectual exercise. I felt bitter about wasting my time and efforts to no purpose, bitter about feeling deceived in my expectations time and time again. I was very well aware what I stood to lose by leaving: but I could not manage myself, and one day, after a painful and disgraceful scene, of which I was a witness and which showed me my friend in a now all too disadvantageous light, I quarrelled with him finally and left, abandoned my fine, pedantic gentleman who was made from the flour of the steppes with a dash of German treacle...'

'In other words, you abandoned your daily crust of bread,' Lezhnev said quietly, and put both hands on Rudin's shoulders.

'Yes, and ended up again light and naked in empty space. Fly, as they say, whither thou wilt. *Ekh*, let us drink!'

'To your health,' Lezhnev said softly, got up, and kissed Rudin on the forehead. 'To your health and in memory of Pokorsky... He also knew how to remain destitute.'

'So there is number one of my adventures for you,' Rudin began, after a short while. 'Shall I continue?'

'Continue, please do.'

'*Ekh*! But I don't feel like talking. I am weary of talking, brother... Well, never mind, so be it. Having called at various other places... Incidentally, I could tell you the story of how I became the secretary of a well-meaning man of exalted rank and what the outcome of it was; but that would take us too far... Having called at various other places, I resolved at last to become... do not laugh, if you please... a man of business, of practical endeavour. What happened was this: I became friendly with a certain... you may have heard of him, perhaps... a certain Kurbeyev... no?'

'No, I have not. But for pity's sake, Rudin, how could you, with your intellect, have failed to surmise that it was none of your business to be a... forgive the pun... a man of business?'

'I know, brother, that it was not; though, when one comes to think of it, what is my business, then?... But if you had seen Kurbeyev! Please don't imagine that he was some kind of empty windbag. They say I used to be eloquent once upon a time. Compared to him, I am of no account whatsoever. He was an amazingly learned man, brother, who knew a great deal, a brain, brother, a creative brain in matters of industry and commercial enterprise. The boldest, the most unexpected projects fairly boiled within his mind. He and I joined forces and resolved to employ our energies for a cause of general utility...'

'What kind of cause, permit me to inquire?'

Rudin lowered his eyes.

'You will laugh.'

'But why? No, I shan't laugh.'

'We resolved to turn a river in the province of K—— into a navigable channel,' Rudin said with an awkward smile.

'Indeed! This Kurbeyev must be a capitalist, then?'

'He was poorer than I was,' Rudin retorted, and quietly hung his grey head.

Lezhnev began to laugh, but suddenly stopped and took Rudin by the hand.

'Forgive me, brother, please,' he began, 'but I simply was not expecting such a thing. Well and so what happened—did this enterprise of yours remain on paper?'

'Not entirely. There was the beginning of an implementation. We hired workmen... well, and we set about the task. But then various obstacles cropped up. For one thing, the owners of the water-mills had no time for us at all, and on top of that we could not handle the water without an engine, and there wasn't enough money for an engine. We spent six months living in dugout shelters. Kurbeyev subsisted on bread alone, and I, too, was undernourished. As a matter of fact, I do not regret it: the nature there is wonderful. We struggled and struggled, tried to persuade the merchants, wrote letters, circulars. In the end I sank my last half-copeck into that project.'

'Well,' Lezhnev observed, 'I think it was not hard to sink your last half-copeck in it.'

'No, it was not hard, precisely.'

Rudin looked out of the window.

'But I swear to God, it was not a bad project, and it could have brought enormous gains.'

'Then where did this Kurbeyev get to?' Lezhnev asked.

'Him? He is in Siberia now, a gold-mine proprietor. And you'll see, he'll make his fortune; he won't perish.'

'Maybe; but I don't think you will make yours, will you?'

'I? What is there to do about that? However, I know that in your eyes I've always been an empty man.'

'You? Enough of that, brother... There was a time, it's true, when only the dark sides of you met my eyes; but now, believe me, I have learned to value you. You won't make your fortune... And I love you for that... for pity's sake!'

Rudin smiled faintly.

'Really?'

'I respect you for it!' Lezhnev said again. 'Do you understand?'

Both were silent.

'Well, shall I go on to number three?' asked Rudin.

'You'll be doing me a favour!'

'As you wish. Number the third, and last. I have only now managed to have done with this one. But have I not bored you?'

'Continue, continue.'

'Well, you see,' Rudin began, 'one day I thought, in my leisure... I have always had a great deal of leisure... I thought: I have plenty of knowledge, my intentions are good... I mean, you would not deny that my intentions are good, would you?'

'Certainly not!'

'On all the other points I had more or less failed... Why should I not become a pedagogue, or, to put it more plainly, a teacher... rather than live, to no purpose...'

Rudin stopped and sighed.

'Rather than live to no purpose, would it not be better to make an attempt to hand on to others what I knew: perhaps they would be able to derive at least some benefit from my knowledge. After all, my abilities are not exactly run-of-the-mill, and I am able to use my tongue... So I decided to devote myself to this new undertaking. I had some trouble in obtaining a post; I did not want to give private lessons; the elementary schools were not the right place for me. At last I suc- ceeded in obtaining a post as a teacher in the local gymnasium.'

'A teacher—of what?' Lezhnev asked.

'A teacher of Russian philology.* I will tell you that never did I undertake a task with such fervour as I did that one. The thought that I might influence the young filled me with inspiration. For three weeks I sat preparing my introductory lecture.'

'Do you have it with you?'

'No: it got lost somewhere. It turned out not badly, and met with approval. I can see the faces of my listeners as if it were now—young, good-natured faces, with an expression of open-hearted attention, concern, even amazement. I mounted the dais and read my lecture in a state of fever; I had thought it would be enough for an hour or more, but I finished it in twenty minutes. The inspector was sitting there—a wizened old man with silver spectacles and a short wig —and every so often he would incline his head towards me. When I got to the end and jumped down from the chair he said to me: "Good, sir, only a bit high-flown, and rather obscure, and not much said about the subject itself." But the gymnasium students followed me with respectful looks... truly. Why, that is what makes youth so precious! I brought my second lecture in written form, and the third, too... then I began to improvise.'

'And were you successful?' Lezhnev asked.

'I was very successful. The listeners came in multitudes. I told them everything that was in my soul. Among them there were three or four boys who were really outstanding; the others understood me but little. Though, as a matter of fact, I must admit that even those who understood me sometimes embarrassed me with their questions. But

I did not lose heart. They all liked me a great deal; in their lessons I gave them all full marks. But then an intrigue was started against me... or rather, no! There was no intrigue, but I had simply entered the wrong sphere. I was encroaching on others, and they made things awkward for me. To the gymnasium students I gave lectures of a kind not always given to students; my listeners received little from my lectures... I myself had a poor grasp of the facts. What was more, I was not satisfied by the round of activities that was assigned to me... and that, as you know, is my weakness. I wanted to make fundamental reforms, and, I swear to you, those reforms were both sensible and easy to make. I hoped to bring them in via the headmaster, a good and honest man on whom at first I had influence. His wife helped me. Brother, I have not met many such women in my life. She was by then nearly forty; but she had faith in goodness, like a fifteen-year-old girl loved all that was beautiful, and was not afraid to advance her convictions in front of anyone at all. I shall never forget her noble enthusiasm and purity. On her advice I started to draw up a plan... But then I found myself undermined, slurs were cast upon me in her presence. I was done particular harm by the teacher of mathematics, a small man, sharp, splenetic, and with no belief in anything, like Pigasov, but far more able than he... Incidentally, how is Pigasov, is he still alive?'

'Yes he is, and, imagine, married to a woman from the petty bourgeoisie, who beats him, they say.'

'It serves him right! Well, and is Natalya Alexeyevna in good health?'

'Yes.'

'Is she happy?'

'Yes.'

Rudin was silent for a while.

'Now what was I talking about?... Yes! the mathematics teacher. He conceived a hatred of me, compared my lectures to firework displays, was quick to seize on every not-quite-clear expression of mine, once even caught me out over some sixteenth-century monument or other... but mainly, he suspected my intentions; my last soap bubble collided with him, as with a pin, and burst. The inspector, with whom I did not get along right away, set the headmaster against me; there was a scene, I was unwilling to yield, got angry, the matter reached the ears of the authorities; I was compelled to resign. I would not let things rest there, I wanted to show that it was out of the question for me to be dealt with in this way... but I could be dealt with in any way they thought fit... Now I must leave here.'

Silence ensued. Both friends sat with heads lowered.

Rudin was first to speak.

'Yes, brother,' he began, 'I can say with Koltsov:* "To what, my youth, have you brought me now, fenced me in so tight that I've nowhere to go?..." And meanwhile, was I really good for nothing, was it really true that there was no work for me on this earth? I often asked myself that question, and no matter how much I have tried to abase myself in my own eyes, I have not but been able to feel within myself the presence of powers that are not given to all men! Why do those powers remain sterile? And there is something else, too. Do you remember when you and I were abroad, how conceited and false I was then?... As though back in those days I had no clear perception of what I wanted, I grew intoxicated on words and believed in phantoms; but now, I swear to you, I can speak out loudly, in front of everyone, about what I want. I really have nothing at all to hide: I am wholly, and in the most essential meaning of the word, a man who is loyal;* I resign myself, want to adapt myself to circumstances, want little, want to attain a goal that is near, bring at least some benefit, even though it is insignificant. No! I don't succeed! What does it mean? What prevents me from living and acting like others?... That is all I dream about now. But no sooner have I managed to enter a particular situation, to stop at a certain point, than fate whisks me away from it again... I have come to fear it—my fate... What is the reason for all that? Solve this enigma for me!'

'Enigma!' Lezhnev echoed. 'Yes, it is true. You have always been an enigma to me. Even in your youth, when, after some trivial escapade, you would suddenly begin to talk in such a way that one's heart trembled, and then again you'd begin... well, you know what I mean... even back then I did not understand you: that is why I ceased to like you... There are so many powers in you, such a tireless striving for the ideal...'

'Words, all words! There were no deeds!' Rudin interrupted.

'Deeds! But what kind of deeds...'

'What kind of deeds? Providing for a blind woman and her entire family by one's labour, as Pryazhentsev did, you remember... There is a deed for you.'

'Yes; but a kind word is also a deed.'

Rudin looked at Lezhnev without saying anything and quietly shook his head.

Lezhnev was on the point of saying something, and passed his hand across his face.

'So you are going to your estate, then?' he asked at last.

'Yes.'

'And do you have an estate remaining to you?'

'There is still something left there. Two and a half souls. There is a corner to die in. At this moment you are probably thinking: "Even now he cannot get by without a fine phrase!" Fine phrases, it is true, have been my ruin, they have worn me out, and to the end I have not been able to shake them off. But what I said was not a fine phrase. They're not fine phrases, brother, this white hair, these wrinkles; these ragged elbows are not a fine phrase. You have always been strict with me, and you were right; but there is no place for strictness now, when it is at last all over, and there is no oil in the lamp, and the lamp itself is broken, and in a moment or two the wick will burn out... Death, brother, must reconcile at last...'

Lezhnev leapt to his feet.

'Rudin!' he exclaimed. 'Why are you telling me this! What have I done to deserve this from you? What kind of judge am I, and what sort of man would I be if, at the sight of your hollow cheeks and wrinkles, the expression "fine phrases" could enter my head? Do you want to know what I think of you? By all means! What I think is: here is a man... with his abilities, what might he not have attained, what earthly advantages might he not possess now, if he had willed it!... but instead I find him hungry, without a refuge...'

'I arouse your compassion,' Rudin said in a toneless voice.

'No, you are mistaken. You inspire me with respect—that's what. Who prevented you from spending year after year with that landowner, your friend, who, I am quite certain, had you simply been willing to humour him, would have secured your fortune? Why were you unable to get along at the gymnasium, why, every time—strange fellow that you are!—no matter with what intentions you began an undertaking, did you invariably end it by sacrificing your personal advantage, by refusing to put down roots in unkind soil, no matter how fertile it was?'

'I was born a rolling stone,' Rudin continued with a melancholy smile. 'I am not able to stand still.'

'That is true; but that inability is not caused by there being a worm inside you, as you began by telling me... It's not a worm that lives inside you, not a spirit of idle restlessness: the fire of love burns in you and, evidently, in spite of all your petty troubles, it burns in you more powerfully than in many who do not even consider themselves egoists, and who would probably call you an intriguer. In your place I would have begun long ago by silencing that worm within me and reconciling myself with everything; but in you there has not even been an increase of spleen, and I am certain that today, at this very moment, you are again ready to tackle fresh work, like a young man.'

'No, brother, I am weary now,' Rudin said quietly. 'I have had enough.'

'Weary! Another man would have died long ago. Death, you say, brings reconciliation, but don't you think that life does, too? Whoever has lived and not become tolerant towards others does not deserve tolerance himself. And which of us can say that he is not in need of tolerance? You have done what you could, struggled while you could... What more is there? Our roads diverged...'

'You, brother, are quite a different man from me,' Rudin interrupted with a sigh.

'Our roads diverged,' Lezhnev continued, 'perhaps precisely because, thanks to my financial fortune, my sang-froid, and other happy circumstances, nothing prevented me from staying where I was and being a spectator, with folded arms, while you had to go out into the fields, roll up your sleeves, and labour, toil. Our paths diverged... but look how close we are to each other. Why, you and I practically speak the same language, we understand each other on only half a hint, we grew up on the same feelings. Why, there are only a few of us left, brother; you and I are the last of the Mohicans! We were able to diverge, even to quarrel in those old years when we still had a lot of life ahead of us; but now, when the crowd is thinning around us, when new generations are moving past us, towards goals that are not ours, we must hold on firmly to each other. Let us clink glasses, brother, and sing for old times' sake: *Gaudeamus igitur!*'*

The friends clinked glasses, and in emotional, out-of-tune, utterly Russian voices sang the old student song.

'Now you are going to your estate,' Lezhnev began again. 'I do not think you will stay there long, and cannot imagine what you will end up as, or where, or how... But remember: whatever happens to you,

you will always have a place to go, a nest where you can find shelter. It is my house... do you hear, old man? Thought also has its invalids: they also need a refuge.'

Rudin got up.

'Thank you, brother,' he continued. 'Thank you! I shall not forget you for this. The only thing is, I am not worthy of a refuge. I have spoiled my life, and have not served thought as I ought to have done...'

'Silence!' Lezhnev continued. 'Each of us remains what nature has made him, and one may demand no more of him than that! You called yourself the Wandering Jew... But how do you know, perhaps what you ought to do is to wander eternally, perhaps by doing that you fulfil a higher destiny: not for nothing does Russian folk wisdom say that we all walk under God. You are going,' Lezhnev continued, seeing that Rudin was picking up his cap. 'Will you not stay the night?'

'I am going! Goodbye. Thank you... But I shall end badly.'

'Only God can know that... Are you really going?'

'Yes. Goodbye. Do not remember me unkindly.'

'Well, don't remember me unkindly, either... and do not forget what I told you. Goodbye...'

The friends embraced. Rudin quickly went out.

For a long time Lezhnev paced to and fro about his room, stopped in front of the window, thought, said in a low voice: 'poor fellow!'— and, sitting down at the table, began to write a letter to his wife.

Outside the wind got up and began a sinister howling, heavily and maliciously striking the tinkling panes. A long autumn night set in. Happy the man who on such nights sits beneath the roof of a house, who has a warm corner... And may the Lord help all wanderers without shelter!

On the sultry noon of 26 June 1848, in Paris, when the rising of the 'national workshops' had almost been crushed, in one of the narrow side-streets of the Faubourg St Antoine a battalion of the regular army was taking a barricade. Several cannon-shots had already broken through it; those of its defenders who were still alive were abandoning it and thinking only of their own salvation when suddenly, right at its summit, on the knocked-in body of an upturned omnibus, there appeared a tall man in an old frock-coat with a red scarf tied about his waist, and a straw hat over grey, dishevelled hair. In one hand he held a red banner, in the other a blunt and crooked sabre, and was shouting something in a strained, thin voice and waving both banner and sabre. A Vincennes rifleman took aim at him—and fired... The tall man dropped the banner—and, like a sack, went toppling down face first, as though he were bowing at someone's feet... The bullet had passed right through his heart.

'*Tiens!*' said one of the fleeing *insurgés* to another, '*on vient de tuer le Polonais.*'*

'*Bigre!*'* the other replied, and both rushed into the cellar of a house, all of whose shutters were closed and whose walls were brightly scarred with the marks of bullets and shot.

This *Polonais* was—Dmitry Rudin.

ON THE EVE

PRINCIPAL CHARACTERS

INSAROV, DMITRY NIKANOROVICH
STAKHOVA, YELENA NIKOLAYEVNA (daughter of the Stakhovs)—
   familiar name LENOCHKA, in French Hélène
STAKHOV, NIKOLAI ARTEMYEVICH (Yelena's father)
STAKHOVA, ANNA VASILYEVNA (Yelena's mother)
STAKHOV, UVAR IVANOVICH (a distant uncle of Nikolai Artemyevich)
SHUBIN, PAVEL YAKOVLEVICH—in French PAUL
BERSENEV, ANDREI PETROVICH
MÜLLER, ZOYA NIKITISHNA—in French ZOË
KURNATOVSKY, YEGOR ANDREYEVICH
AVGUSTINA KHRISTIANOVNA (mistress of Nikolai Artemyevich)

IN the shade of a tall lime tree, on the bank of the Moscow River, not far from Kuntsevo, on one of the hottest summer days of 1853, two young men lay on the grass. One of them looked about twenty-three, tall of stature, swarthy, with a pointed and slightly crooked nose, a high forehead, and a discreet smile on his broad lips, and lay on his back, reflectively gazing into the distance and slightly narrowing his small grey eyes; the other lay on his front, propping his blond, curly head with both hands, and also looking somewhere into the distance. He was three years older than his companion, but seemed far younger; his moustache had scarcely begun to grow, and a light down curled on his chin. There was something childishly pretty, something attractively elegant in the small features of his fresh, round face, in his sweet, dark-brown eyes, handsome, prominent lips, and small white hands. Everything about him breathed the happy cheerfulness of good health, everything about him breathed youth—the unconcern, the self-confidence, the spoiledness, the charm of youth. He moved his eyes, and smiled, and propped up his head as young boys do who know that people like to gaze on them. He wore a loose white coat like a smock; a light blue kerchief enveloped his slender neck, and a crumpled straw hat lay in the grass beside him.

By comparison, his companion seemed an old man, and no one would have thought, looking at his angular figure, that he too was enjoying himself, that he too felt comfortable. He lay in an awkward position; his large head, broad above and angular below, sat awkwardly on his long neck; awkwardness could be detected in the very posture of his arms, of his torso, tightly enveloped as it was by a short black frock-coat, of his long legs with their raised knees, like the rear legs of a dragonfly. In spite of all this, it was impossible not to recognize in him a man of good breeding; the mark of 'decency' was observable in all his ungainly being, and his face, plain and even rather ridiculous though it was, displayed the habit of thinking, and kindness. His name was Andrei Petrovich Bersenev; his companion, the blond-haired young man, went by the name of Shubin, Pavel Yakovlevich.

'Why don't you lie on your front, like me?' Shubin began. 'It's much better this way. Especially when one raises one's legs and knocks one's heels together—like this. One has the grass under one's nose: if one gets tired of staring at the landscape, one can watch some big-bellied insect crawling along a blade of grass, or an ant bustling about. It really is better like this. You, on the other hand, have adopted a kind of pseudo-classical pose now, for all the world like a ballerina in a theatre, leaning her elbows on a pasteboard rock. You should bear in mind that you now have a perfect right to relax. It's not so easy, becoming a third candidate.* Relax, sir; stop exerting yourself, stretch your limbs!'

Shubin delivered this entire speech through his nose, half indolently, half in jest (spoilt children talk like this with friends of the family who bring them sweets), and, not waiting for a reply, went on:

'What strikes me most of all about ants, beetles, and other gentlemen of the insect kingdom is their remarkable earnestness: they run to and fro with such grand and solemn physiognomies, as though their lives really had some significance! For pity's sake—man, the lord of creation, a higher being, is gazing upon them, but they care nothing for him; not only that, but some mosquito will sit on the lord of creation's nose and start to consume it as food for itself. That is insulting. Yet, on the other hand, how are their lives in any way inferior to ours? And why should they not put on grand airs, if we allow ourselves to put on grand airs? Right then, philosopher, solve that riddle for me! What, you're not going to say anything? Eh?'

'What?' Bersenev said quietly, rousing himself.

'What!' Shubin echoed. 'Your friend expounds deep thoughts in your presence, but you don't listen to him.'

'I was admiring the view. Look how warmly those fields are gleaming in the sun!' (Bersenev spoke with a slight lisp.)

'A nice splash of colour,' Shubin said quietly. 'In a word, nature!'

Bersenev shook his head.

'All this ought to mean far more to you than it does to me. It's in your line: you're an artist.'

'No, sir; it is not in my line, sir,' Shubin retorted, putting his hat on the back of his head. 'I am a butcher, sir; my business is flesh, the shaping of flesh, shoulders, legs, arms, but in this there is no form, no finish, it has collapsed in all directions... Go, try to catch it!'

'But after all, there is beauty here, too,' Bersenev observed. 'Incidentally, have you finished your bas-relief?'

'Which one?'

'The child with the goat.'

'To the devil! The devil! The devil!' Shubin exclaimed in a singing voice. 'I looked at the real ones, the old ones, the ancients, and I dashed my own rubbish to pieces. You point out nature to me and say: "There is beauty here, too." Of course, there is beauty in everything, even in your nose there is beauty, but one can't go chasing after every kind of beauty. The old masters—they didn't chase after it; it descended into their creations of its own accord, Lord knows from where, heaven, most likely. The whole world belonged to them; we don't have the possibility of spreading ourselves so wide: our arms are too short. We throw out our line to a single small point, and we keep watch. If the fish bite— bravo! But if they don't...' Shubin stuck out his tongue.

'Wait, wait,' Bersenev retorted. 'That is a paradox. If you don't empathize with beauty, love it everywhere you encounter it, then it will not come into your art, either. If a beautiful view, beautiful music say nothing to your soul, I mean, if you do not empathize with them...'

'Oh you—empathizer!' Shubin blurted out, laughing at the newly invented word, while Bersenev fell into reflection. 'No, brother,' Shubin went on, 'you are a clever fellow, a philosopher, a third candidate of Moscow University, it makes a chap frightened to argue with you, especially me, a student who hasn't finished his studies; but I will tell you this: besides my art, I love beauty only in women... in girls, and that only recently...'

He turned over on to his back and put his hands behind his head.

A few moments passed in silence. The silence of the midday heat weighed on the radiant and sleeping land.

'Incidentally, speaking of women...' Shubin began again. 'Why does no one take Stakhov in hand? Did you see him in Moscow?'

'No.'

'The old chap has gone completely mad. Spends whole days sitting with his Avgustina Khristianovna, bored out of his wits, but goes on sitting there. They gape at each other so stupidly... It's actually unpleasant to watch. Just imagine! What a family God blessed that man with: but no, give him Avgustina Khristianovna! I know nothing more loathsome than her duck-like physiognomy! The other day I modelled a caricature of her in the style of Dantan.* It came out not badly. I'll show you it.'

'And the bust of Yelena Nikolayevna?' Bersenev asked. 'Is it making any progress?'

'No, brother, it is not making any progress. That face could drive one to despair. One looks: the lines are pure, severe, straight; it seems that it would not be hard to catch the likeness. Not on your life... It evades one's grasp, like hidden treasure. Have you ever watched her listening? Not a single feature moves, only the expression of her gaze changes constantly, and that makes her entire appearance change. What would you have a sculptor do, and a bad one at that? A remarkable creature... a strange creature,' he added after a short silence.

'Yes; she's a remarkable girl,' Bersenev repeated after him.

'And the daughter of Nikolai Artemyevich Stakhov! Don't talk to me about blood and breeding after that. And you know, the funny thing is that she really is his daughter, she resembles both him and her mother, Anna Vasilyevna. I respect Anna Vasilyevna with all my heart, after all, she is my benefactress; but I mean, she's an old hen! Where did Yelena get that soul? Who ignited that fire? There is another riddle for you, philosopher!'

As before, however, the 'philosopher' made no reply. Verbosity was in general not one of Bersenev's faults, and when he spoke he expressed himself awkwardly, with hesitations, gesticulating unnecessarily with his arms; on this occasion, however, a special kind of silence had settled on his soul—a silence that resembled weariness and sadness. He had recently moved away from the city after long and difficult labours that had taken up hours of each day. Inactivity, comfort, and the purity of the air, the consciousness of a goal attained, whimsical and casual conversation with a friend, the suddenly evoked image of a beloved being—all these varied yet at the same time somehow similar impressions fused within him to a single general emotion, which calmed him and agitated him and enfeebled him in equal measure... He was a very nerve-ridden young man.

Beneath the lime tree it was cool and tranquil; the flies and bees that flew into the sphere of its shade seemed to buzz more quietly; the pure, thin grass of emerald colour, with no admixture of gold, did not sway; the tall stems stood motionless, as if enchanted; as if enchanted, as if dead, the small clusters of yellow flowers hung on the lower branches of the lime. With each breath one took, a sweet odour forced its way into the very depths of one's chest, but one's chest breathed it willingly. In the distance, on the other side of the river, all the way to the horizon everything sparkled, everything burned; from time to time a breeze passed there, scattering and intensifying the sparkling; a radiant vapour undulated above the land. No birds were audible: they do not sing in the hours of heat; but crickets chattered everywhere, and it was pleasant to listen to that ardent sound of life as one sat in the coolness, at peace: it inclined one to sleep, and awoke dreams.

'Have you observed', Bersenev suddenly began, helping his words along with gestures, 'what a strange emotion nature arouses in us? Everything in it is so complete, so clear, I mean, so satisfied with itself, and we understand that and admire it, and at the same time, in me at least, it always provokes a kind of unease, a kind of anxiety, sorrow, even. What does this mean? Is it that, before it, faced with it, we are made more powerfully aware of our incompleteness, our indistinctness, or do we have too little of the kind of satisfaction with which it contents itself, while the other kind—that's to say, the kind of satisfaction *we* require—it does not possess?'

'Hm,' Shubin retorted. 'I will tell you the reason for it all, Andrei Petrovich. You have described the feelings of a solitary person, who does not live, but merely looks and is entranced. What good does looking do? Do some living, and then you will be up to scratch. No matter how much you go knocking on nature's door, it won't reply in words that are comprehensible, for it does not have the power of speech. It will resonate and throb like a string, but don't expect a song from it. A living soul—and above all a female soul—*that* will respond... And so, my noble friend, I advise you to provide yourself with a consort of the heart, and all your dreary sensations will instantly vanish. That is what we "require", as you put it. You see, this unease, this sorrow, those sensations are merely a kind of hunger. Give your stomach real food, and everything will come right again. Occupy your place in space, be a body, my good fellow. And for goodness' sake, what do you need nature for? Just listen for yourself: love... such a powerful, ardent word! Nature... such a cold, scholastic expression! And so' (Shubin broke into song): ' "Long live Marya Petrovna!"*— or then again', he added, 'not Marya Petrovna—why, it's all the same! *Vous me comprenez.*'*

Bersenev sat up and leaned his chin on folded hands.

'Why do you mock?' he said, not looking at his companion. 'Why do you jeer? Yes, you are right: love is a big word, a big emotion... But what kind of love are you talking about?'

Shubin also sat up.

'What kind of love? Any kind you wish, as long as it's there. I will confess to you that in my opinion there really are no different kinds of love. If one falls in love...'

'With all one's soul,' Bersenev chipped in.

'Oh yes, that goes without saying, the soul is not an apple: it can't be shared out in portions. If one falls in love, one cannot be wrong... And I had no thought of jeering. There is such tenderness in my heart just now, it has melted so... I simply wanted to explain why nature, in your opinion, has such an effect on us. Because it wakens in us the need for love and is not able to satisfy it. It quietly drives us into other, living embraces, but we don't understand it and expect something from nature itself. Oh, Andrei, Andrei, it's beautiful, this sun, this sky, every-thing, everything around us is beautiful, but you are full of sorrow; yet if at this moment you held the hand of a woman you loved, if that hand and the whole of that woman were yours, if you even saw with *her* eyes, felt not with your own, solitary emotions, but with hers —nature would not awaken sorrow and anxiety in you, Andrei, and you would not merely observe its beauty; nature itself would rejoice and sing, it would echo your own hymn, for then you would have imparted a tongue to it, bereft of speech as it is!'

Shubin leapt to his feet and paced to and fro a couple of times, but Bersenev lowered his head, and his face covered with a slight blush.

'I do not quite agree with you,' he began. 'Nature does not always hint to us of... love.' (He was slow to utter this word.) 'It also threatens us; it reminds us of terrible... yes, of inaccessible secrets. Is not nature destined to devour us, does it not constantly devour us? In nature there is both life and death; and death speaks just as loudly in nature as does life.'

'In love, too, are life and death,' Shubin interrupted.

'And then,' Bersenev went on, 'when, for example, I stand in the forest in springtime, in a green thicket, when I seem to hear the romantic sounds of Oberon's horn'* (Bersenev felt slightly ashamed as he spoke these words) '—is that not also...'

'The longing for love, the longing for happiness, that is all it is!' Shubin interposed. 'I too know those sounds, I too know the tender emotion and the expectancy that visit one's soul beneath the canopy of the forest, in its depths, or at evening, in the open fields, when the sun is setting and the river is filling with mist beyond the bushes. But from forest, and river, and earth and sky, from every little cloud, from every blade of grass I expect, I want happiness, in everything I sense its approach, I hear its call! "My God is a light and cheerful God!" I started a poem like that once; you must admit, it's a wonderful first line, but I could not find a second line to go with it. Happiness! Happiness! For as long as life has not passed, for as long as we have power over our limbs, for as long as we are not going downhill but up! The devil take it!' Shubin continued, on a sudden impulse, 'We are young, not ugly, not stupid: we shall conquer happiness for ourselves!'

He gave his curls a shake, and self-confidently, almost with defiance, looked up at the sky. Bersenev raised his eyes to him.

'So is there nothing superior to happiness?' he said quietly.

'Like what, for example?' Shubin asked, and stopped.

'Well, for example, you and I, as you say, are young, we are good people, let us assume; each of us wants happiness for himself... But is this word "happiness" really the kind of word that could unite us, set us both afire, make us give each other our hands? What I mean is, is not the word "happiness" an egotistical one that tends to disunite?'

'Well, do you know any that unite?'

'Yes; and there are not a few of them; you also know them.'

'Oh? What are these words?'

'How about art—since you are an artist—and motherland, learning, freedom, justice.'

'And love?' Shubin asked.

'Love is also a word that unites; but not the kind of love you yearn for now: not love as pleasure, but love as sacrifice.'

Shubin frowned.

'That is all very well for Germans; but I want to love for myself; I want to be number one.'

'Number one,' Bersenev repeated. 'Whereas I think that making oneself number two is the whole point of our lives.'

'If everyone were to act as you advise,' Shubin said softly with a plaintive grimace, 'no one on earth would ever eat pineapples: they would always be giving them to someone else.'

'Which means that pineapples are not necessary; though, as a matter of fact, one need not worry: there will always be those who are fond of taking the bread from other people's mouths.'

Both friends were silent.

'I met Insarov again the other day,' Bersenev began. 'I invited him to come and see me; I should really like to introduce him to you... and to the Stakhovs.'

'What Insarov is this? Oh yes, that Serb or Bulgarian you were telling me about! The patriot fellow? Is it he that's been filling your head with all these philosophical ideas?'

'Perhaps.'

'An unusual individual, is he?'

'Yes.'

'Clever? Gifted?'

'Clever?... Yes. Gifted? I don't know, I don't think so.'

'No? Then what is remarkable about him?'

'You will see. And now I think it's time for us to go. I expect Anna Vasilyevna is waiting for us. What time is it?'

'After two. Let's go. It's stifling here! This conversation has set my blood alight. There was a moment when you, too... I'm not an artist for nothing: I have an eye for everything. Confess, there's a woman in your thoughts, isn't there?...'

Shubin was about to look Bersenev in the face, but Bersenev turned away and walked out from under the lime tree. Shubin set off after him, stepping along in a casual, graceful way with his small feet. Bersenev moved clumsily, raising his shoulders high as he walked, craning his neck; and yet he seemed a more decent man than Shubin, more of a gentleman, we should say, had not that word been so vulgarly trivialized among us.

II

THE young men walked down to the Moscow River and strolled along its banks. From the water coolness breathed, and the quiet splashing of small waves caressed the ear.

'I'd like to go in for another bathe,' Shubin began, 'but I'm afraid it would make us late. Look at the river. It's as if it were enticing us. The ancient Greeks would have seen a nymph in it. But we are not Greeks, O nymph! We are thick-skinned Scythians.'

'We do have rusalkas,'* Bersenev observed.

'You and your rusalkas! What use to me, a sculptor, are those emanations of a frightened, cold imagination, those images born in the stuffy air of a peasant cottage, in the gloom of winter nights? I require light, space... When, O Lord, shall I go to Italy? When...'

'In other words, to Little Russia, you mean?'

'Shame on you, Andrei Petrovich, for reproaching me for an act of thoughtless stupidity, of which in any case I bitterly repent. Well, yes, I behaved like a fool: the most kind Anna Vasilyevna gave me money to travel to Italy, but instead I set off for the khokhols,* to eat dumplings, and...'

'Spare me the whole of it, please,' Bersenev interrupted.

'Yet all the same I will say that the money was not wasted. I saw such types there, especially female ones... Of course, I know it: outside Italy there is no salvation!'

'You'll go to Italy,' Bersenev said quietly, without turning round to him, 'and you will do nothing. You will simply flap your wings, and won't fly. We know your sort!'

'Stavasser* flew, though... And he wasn't the only one. Well, if I don't fly, that means I'm a penguin, and have no wings. I am stifled here, I want to go to Italy,' Shubin went on. 'The sun is there, beauty is there.'

A young girl in a wide-brimmed straw hat, with a pink parasol on her shoulder, appeared at this moment on the path along which the friends were walking.

'But what do I see? Here too beauty comes to meet us! Greetings from a humble artist to the charming Zoya!' Shubin cried suddenly, with a theatrical flourish of his hat.

The young girl to whom this exclamation referred stopped, wagged her finger at him, and allowing the two friends to draw near to her, said in a small, resonant voice that had a slightly guttural quality:

'What is wrong, gentlemen, are you not coming to dinner? The table is set.'

'What do I hear?' Shubin said, throwing up his hands. 'Ravishing Zoya, have you really taken it upon yourself to come and look for us in this heat? Is that how I am to understand the import of your words? Tell me, is it really so? Or rather, no, you had better not utter that word: the remorse would kill me instantly.'

'Oh, do stop it, Pavel Yakovlevich,' the girl retorted, not without vexation. 'Why do you never talk seriously to me? I shall lose my temper,' she added with a coquettish grimace, and blew out her lips.

'Do not lose your temper with me, ideal Zoya Nikitishna; you would not wish to plunge me into the dark abyss of frenzied despair. I cannot speak seriously, because I am not a serious person.'

The girl gave a shrug of her shoulder and turned to Bersenev.

'He's always like this: treats me as though I were a child: yet I'm eighteen. I'm grown-up now.'

'O Lord!' Shubin groaned, and turned up his eyes, while Bersenev smiled ironically, without saying anything.

The girl stamped her foot.

'Pavel Yakovlevich! I shall lose my temper! Hélène was going to come with me,' she went on, 'but she stayed in the garden. The heat frightened her, but I'm not afraid of the heat. Come along.'

She set off ahead down the path, slightly swaying her slender figure at each step, and throwing back her long, soft ringlets from her face with a pretty hand clad in a black mitt.

The friends followed her (Shubin now pressed his hands silently to his heart, now raised them above his head), and a few moments later they found themselves in front of one of the numerous dachas that surround Kuntsevo. The small wooden cottage with a mezzanine floor, painted pink, stood amidst a garden, and looked out, almost naively, from the leaves and branches of the trees. Zoya was the first to open the wicket gate, ran into the garden, and shouted:

'I have brought the wanderers home!'

A young girl with a pale and expressive face rose from a bench near the path, and in the doorway of the house there appeared a lady in a lilac silk dress who, raising an embroidered batiste shawl above her head as protection from the sun, gave a languid, listless smile.

III

ANNA VASILYEVNA STAKHOVA, née Shubina, had been left both
fatherless and motherless at the age of seven, and the heiress to a rather
considerable estate. She had both very rich relatives and very poor ones
—the poor ones on her father's side, the rich ones on her mother's:
Senator Volgin and the Princes Chikurasov. Prince Ardalion Chikurasov,
who was appointed her guardian, found her a place at the best Moscow
boarding-school, and upon her leaving the boarding-school took her
to live in his own home. He kept open house, and in winter gave balls.
Anna Vasilyevna's future husband, Nikolai Artemyevich Stakhov, won
her at one of these balls, at which she wore 'a charming pink dress with
a coiffure of small roses'. She had preserved that coiffure... Nikolai
Artemyevich Stakhov, the son of a retired captain who had been
wounded in 1812 and obtained a remunerative post in St Petersburg,
entered military school at the age of sixteen, and enlisted with the
Guards. He was a handsome man, well built, and considered to be
very nearly the best cavalier at the middle-ranking evening parties
he mostly attended: he had no entrance to the *grand monde*. From his
youth onwards, he was preoccupied by two dreams: to become an
aide-de-camp to the Tsar and to make an advantageous marriage; with
the first dream he parted soon enough, but held on to the second one
all the more tenaciously. In consequence of this, he travelled to Moscow
each winter. Nikolai Artemyevich spoke French quite well and had
a reputation as a philosopher, as he did not carouse. While yet only
an ensign, he had liked to argue insistently, for example, about whether
it was possible for a man to travel all over the entire terrestrial globe
in his lifetime, or to know what takes place at the bottom of the sea
—and always held to the view that it was impossible.

Nikolai Artemyevich was twenty-five when he 'landed' Anna
Vasilyevna; he retired from the army and went off to the country to
be master of his estate. He soon got fed up with country life, for the
estate was run on a quit-rent basis;* he settled in Moscow, in his wife's
house. As a young man he had not played any games at all, but now
he suddenly acquired a passion for lotto, and when lotto was banned,
for *yeralash*.* At home he found life tedious, began a liaison with a
widow of German origin, and spent nearly all his time with her. In
the summer of '53 he did not travel down to Kuntsevo: he remained

in Moscow, pretending it was so that he could enjoy the mineral waters; in reality, he did not want to part from his widow. As a matter of fact, he did not spend much time in conversation with her, either, but spent most of the time arguing in his usual way about whether it was possible to predict the weather, et cetera. On one occasion some-one called him a *frondeur*;* this title pleased him no end. 'Yes,' he thought, smugly turning down the corners of his mouth and swaying to and fro, 'it is not easy to satisfy me; you won't pull the wool over my eyes.' Nikolai Artemyevich's '*frondeur*ism' consisted in his hearing, for example, the word 'nerves' and saying: 'And what are nerves?'— or someone would mention in his presence the advances in astronomy, and he would say: 'Do you believe in astronomy, then?' When, how-ever, he wanted finally to rout his opponent, he would say: 'That is all merely fine phrases.' It must be admitted that to many individuals, objections of this kind seemed (and still seem to this day) irrefutable; but Nikolai Artemyevich had not the slightest inkling that Avgustina Khristianovna, in letters to her cousin, Feodolinda Peterzilius, called him: *Mein Pinselchen*.*

Nikolai Artemyevich's wife, Anna Vasilyevna, was a small, thin woman with delicate features, inclined to agitation and melancholy. At her boarding-school she had studied music and read novels, but had then given it all up: had begun to dress smartly, and lost interest in that, too; started to involve herself in her daughter's education, but then become infirm, and entrusted her to the care of a governess; in the end, all she did was to be melancholy and quietly agitated. The birth of Yelena Nikolayevna had ruined her health, and she could have no more children; Nikolai Artemyevich would allude to this circumstance when justifying his acquaintance with Avgustina Khristianovna. Her husband's infidelity caused Anna Vasilyevna great distress; she found it particularly painful that on one occasion he made a present to the German woman of a pair of grey horses from her, Anna Vasilyevna's, own stud farm. She would never reproach him to his face, but furtively complained about him to everyone in the house in turn, even her daughter. Anna Vasilyevna did not like to go out visiting; she enjoyed it if a guest sat with her and told her some news or other; left on her own, she began to fall ill at once. She had a very loving, gentle heart: life soon ground her down.

Pavel Yakovlevich Shubin was her nephew thrice removed. His father had been in the civil service in Moscow. His brothers had entered the cadet corps; he had been the youngest, his mother's favourite, of delicate constitution: he had remained at home. He had been earmarked for university, and kept on at the gymnasium with difficulty. From early years he had begun to show a propensity for sculpture; one day, the ponderous Senator Volgin caught sight of one of his statuettes at the home of his aunt (he was about sixteen at the time) and declared that he intended to be the young talent's patron. The sudden death of Shubin's father very nearly altered the young man's entire future. The senator, a patron of talents, made him a present of a plaster bust of Homer—and that was all; but Anna Vasilyevna helped him with money, and, by the skin of his teeth, at the age of nineteen, he just managed to get into the medical faculty of the university. Pavel felt no disposition whatsoever for medicine, but, as a result of the quota of students that existed at the time, it was impossible for him to enter any other faculty; what was more, he hoped to study anatomy. But he did not finish studying anatomy; he did not pass on to the second year of the course and, without waiting for the examination, left the university in order to devote himself exclusively to his calling. He worked hard, but in snatches; wandered about the environs of Moscow, modelled and drew the portraits of peasant girls, took up with various persons, young and old, of lofty and lowly station, with Italian moulders and Russian artists, would not hear of the Academy, and did not acknowledge a single professor as his master. He possessed definite talent—his name began to be known in Moscow. His mother, a Parisienne by birth, of good family, a kind and intelligent woman, taught him French, fussed over him and looked after him day and night, was proud of him and, dying young of consumption, asked Anna Vasilyevna to take him in hand. By that time he was already twenty-one. Anna Vasilyevna fulfilled her last wish: he occupied a small room in an outbuilding of the dacha.

IV

'COME along then, come along, let us have dinner,' said the mistress of the house in a plaintive voice, and they all directed their steps to the dining room. 'You sit next to me, Zoë,' Anna Vasilyevna said quietly. 'And you, Hélène, entertain our guest, and you, Paul, please behave and do not tease Zoë. I have a headache today.'

Shubin again raised his eyes to heaven; Zoë replied to him with a half-smile. This Zoë, or, to be more precise, Zoya Nikitishna Müller, was a pretty, slightly squinting Russian-German girl, fair-haired and plump, with a nose that doubled at the tip, and tiny red lips. She sang Russian romances not at all badly, and could play various pieces of a cheerful or sentimental nature on the piano without making too many mistakes; dressed with taste, but in a way that was somehow childish, and also too neat. Anna Vasilyevna had taken her on as a female companion for her daughter and had then constantly kept her to herself. Yelena did not complain about this: she really had no idea what to talk about with Zoya whenever she happened to find herself alone with her.

The dinner lasted rather a long time; Bersenev talked to Yelena about university life, his intentions and hopes. Shubin listened and said nothing, and ate with exaggerated eagerness, from time to time casting comically mournful glances at Zoya, who invariably replied to him with the same phlegmatic little smile. After dinner, Yelena, Bersenev, and Shubin set off to the garden; Zoya watched them go and, with a slight shrug of her little shoulders, sat down at the piano. Anna Vasilyevna started to say: 'Why don't you go for a walk, too?'— but, not waiting for an answer, added: 'Play something sad for me...'

'*La dernière pensée de Weber*?'* Zoya asked.

'Oh yes, Weber,' Anna Vasilyevna said quietly, sank into an armchair, and let a tear well on to her eyelash.

Meanwhile Yelena had taken the two friends to the acacia arbour, in the midst of which stood a small wooden table with benches round it. Shubin looked round, skipped up and down a few times, and saying 'Wait!' in a whisper, ran off to his room, fetched a piece of clay, and began to model a figure of Zoya, swaying his head, muttering, and chuckling.

'Those same old jokes again,' said Yelena, glancing at his work, and turning to Bersenev, with whom she continued the conversation that had been begun at dinner.

'The same old jokes,' echoed Shubin. 'A truly inexhaustible subject! Today in particular I have no patience with her.'

'And why is that?' Yelena asked. 'One might think you were talking about some nasty, disagreeable old woman. A young, pretty girl...'

'Of course,' Shubin broke in, 'she is pretty, very pretty; I am certain that anyone passing by who took a look at her could not help thinking: "there's someone it would be nice to... dance the polka with"; I am also certain that she knows this and that she finds it pleasant... Then why these bashful faces, this modesty? Well, but you know what I mean,' he added through clenched teeth. 'Anyway, you're busy with something else just now.'

And, breaking the figure of Zoya, Shubin hurriedly, and as if in annoyance, set about remoulding and kneading the clay.

'So you would like to be a professor, would you?' Yelena asked Bersenev.

'Yes,' he replied, pressing his red hands between his knees. 'That is my cherished dream. Of course, I am very well aware of all that I lack in order to be worthy of such a lofty... What I mean is that I am not sufficiently trained, but I hope to obtain permission to go abroad; I shall stay there for three or four years, if necessary, and then...'

He stopped, lowered his eyes, then quickly brought them up and, awkwardly smiling, straightened his hair. When Bersenev spoke to a woman, his speech grew even slower, and he lisped even more than usual.

'Do you want to be a professor of history?' Yelena asked.

'Yes, or philosophy,' he added, lowering his voice, 'if that will be possible.'

'He's already as strong as the devil in philosophy,' Shubin observed, drawing deep lines on the clay with his fingernail. 'What does he need to go abroad for?'

'And you would be quite satisfied with your position?' Yelena asked, propping her head on her elbow, and looking him directly in the face.

'Yes, I would, Yelena Nikolayevna, I would. After all, what better calling could there be? My goodness, to follow in Timofei Nikolaye-vich's* footsteps... The mere thought of such a career fills me with joy and confusion, and... the confusion, which... which stems from my awareness of my insufficient abilities. My dear dead father gave me his blessing in this matter... I shall never forget his last words.'

'Your father died last winter?'

'Yes, Yelena Nikolayevna, in February.'

'They say,' Yelena continued, 'that he left a remarkable work in manuscript; is that true?'

'Yes, he did. He was a wonderful man. You would have liked him, Yelena Nikolayevna.'

'I am sure that I would. And what was the content of this work?'

'The content of the work, Yelena Nikolayevna, is not easy to describe to you in only a few words. My father was a very learned man, a Schellingian.* Sometimes he used expressions that are not always clear...'

'Andrei Petrovich,' Yelena interrupted him, 'forgive my ignorance, but what does that mean: a Schellingian?'

Bersenev smiled slightly.

'A Schellingian is a follower of Schelling, the German philosopher, and as for the teaching of Schelling, it...'

'Andrei Petrovich!' Shubin suddenly exclaimed, 'in the name of the Almighty! You're not going to give Yelena Nikolayevna a lecture on Schelling, are you? Spare her!'

'No, I'm not, not at all,' Bersenev muttered, and blushed. 'I was going to...'

'And why shouldn't he give a lecture,' Yelena chimed in. 'You and I could really do with a few lectures, Pavel Yakovlevich.'

Shubin stared at her, and suddenly burst into laughter.

'What are you laughing at?' she asked coldly and almost sharply.

Shubin fell silent.

'Oh enough, don't be angry,' he said quietly after a moment or two. 'I am to blame. But really, for pity's sake, what is the attraction, in weather like this, under these trees, of talking about philosophy? Let us rather talk about nightingales, roses, or young smiling eyes...'

'Yes; and about French novels, and women's clothes,' Yelena continued.

'Clothes, too, perhaps,' Shubin rejoined, 'if they are pretty.'

'Perhaps. But what if we don't feel like talking about clothes? You like to call yourself a free artist—then why do you infringe on the freedom of others? And why, may one ask, if your manner of thought is such, do you attack Zoya? She is particularly apt at holding conversations about both clothes and roses.'

Shubin suddenly flushed, and got up from the bench.

'Oh, so it's like that, is it?' he began in an uncertain voice. 'I understand your allusion; you are sending me away to her, Yelena Nikolayevna. In other words, I am not wanted here?'

'I had no thought of sending you away.'

'What you mean,' Shubin continued, heatedly, 'is that I am not worthy of other company, that she and I are a pair, that I am as empty and trivial and petty as that sugar-sweet German girl? Is that it, ma'm?'

Yelena knit her brow.

'You have not always talked like that about her, Pavel Yakovlevich,' she observed.

'Ah! A reproach! A reproach now!' Shubin exclaimed. 'Oh very well, I will not conceal it, there was a moment, just a moment, mind you, when those fresh, vulgar little cheeks... But if I wanted to pay you back for your reproach and remind you... Goodbye, ma'm,' he added suddenly, 'or I shall think the better of my words.'

And, striking the clay, which was shaped in the form of a head, with his hand, he rushed out of the arbour and went off to his room.

'A child,' Yelena said softy, watching him go.

'An artist,' Bersenev said with a quiet smile. 'All artists are like that. One must forgive them their whims. It is their right.'

'Yes,' Yelena replied, 'but so far Pavel has done nothing to earn that right. What has he achieved up till now? Give me your arm and let us walk along the avenue. He disturbed us. We were talking about your father's work.'

Bersenev took Yelena's arm and walked about the garden with her, but the conversation that had been initiated, broken off too soon, did not recommence: Bersenev again set about giving an account of his views on the vocation of professor, and on his own future career. He moved quietly at Yelena's side, stepping along awkwardly, awkwardly holding her arm, from time to time pushing her with his shoulder, and never looking at her; but his words flowed lightly, if not entirely fluently, he expressed himself simply and truly, while in his eyes, as they wandered slowly over the trunks of the trees, the gravel of the path, the grass, shone the quiet pathos of noble feelings, and in his calmed voice there was the joy of someone who knows that he is succeeding in expressing his thoughts to another person who is dear to him. Yelena listened to him attentively and, turning half towards him, fixed her gaze on his now slightly pale face, on his eyes, friendly and gentle, though avoiding an encounter with hers. Her soul opened, and something of tenderness, justice, and goodness both flowed into her heart and grew within it.

SHUBIN had still not come out of his room by night time. It was already quite dark, the moon, not yet full, was high in the sky, the Milky Way had begun to gleam white and the stars to shimmer when Bersenev, having said goodnight to Anna Vasilyevna, Yelena, and Zoya, walked up to his friend's door. He found it locked, and tapped on it.

'Who's there?' said Shubin's voice.

'It's me,' Bersenev replied.

'What do you want?'

'Let me in, Pavel, that's enough of this capricious behaviour; are you not ashamed?'

'I'm not behaving capriciously, I'm sleeping and dreaming of Zoya.'

'Please stop this. You are not a child. Let me in. I need to talk to you.'

'Haven't you had enough of talking to Yelena?'

'Enough, I say; let me in!'

Shubin replied with a pretended snore. Bersenev shrugged his shoulders and set off home.

The night was warm and somehow peculiarly quiet, as though everything around was listening and keeping watch; and Bersenev, enveloped in the motionless shadows, involuntarily stopped, and also listened and kept watch. A light whisper, like the rustle of a woman's dress, rose from time to time in the crowns of the nearby trees, and awoke in Bersenev a sweet and uncanny sensation, a sensation of semi-fear. A shiver passed over his cheeks, his eyes grew cold with momentary tears—he wanted to move with measured, quite inaudible steps, to hide, to steal. A sudden breeze assailed him from the side: he started imperceptibly and froze on the spot; a drowsy beetle fell from a branch and struck the road; Bersenev quietly exclaimed: 'Oh!'— and once again stopped. But he began to think about Yelena, and all these passing sensations vanished instantly: there remained only the vivifying impression of nocturnal coolness and his nocturnal walk; his entire soul was occupied by the young girl's image. Bersenev walked with his head lowered, and remembered her words, her questions. He fancied he heard the sound of rapid footsteps behind him. He listened: someone was running, someone was trying to catch up with him; there was the sound of gasping breath, and suddenly before him, out of the black circle of shadow that fell from a great tree, without a hat to cover his dishevelled hair, his face pale in the light of the moon, Shubin emerged.

'I'm glad you came this way,' he said with effort. 'I wouldn't have been able to get to sleep all night if I hadn't caught you up. Give me your arm. You are going home, aren't you?'

'I will come with you.'

'But how is it you are out with no hat on?'

'It doesn't matter. I took my necktie off as well. It's warm.'

The friends took a few paces.

'It's true isn't it? I was very stupid today?' Shubin asked, suddenly.

'If you want my honest opinion, yes, you were. I couldn't understand what you were up to. I've never seen you like that before. And why did you lose your temper, for heaven's sake? For what trivial reason?'

'Hm,' Shubin mumbled. 'It's all very well for you to put it that way, but trivial reasons are not involved here. You see,' he added, 'I'm bound to inform you, that I... that... you may think of me what you will... I... well, there it is! I am in love with Yelena!'

'You're in love with Yelena!' Bersenev repeated, and stood still.

'Yes,' Shubin went on, with forced nonchalance. 'Does it surprise you? I will tell you more. Until this evening I might have hoped that with time she would return my love. But today I became convinced that there is no point in my hoping. She loves someone else!'

'Someone else? Who?'

'Who? You!' Shubin exclaimed, and slapped Bersenev on the shoulder.

'Me?'

'You,' Shubin repeated.

Bersenev took a step backwards, and remained motionless. Shubin looked at him, vigilantly.

'And that surprises you? You are a modest young man. But she loves you. On that account you may put your mind at rest.'

'What rot you're talking!' Bersenev said, at last, in vexation.

'No, it isn't rot. But why are we standing still? Let's go on. It's easier on the move. I've known her for a long time, and know her well. It's impossible that I am wrong. You appealed to her heart. There was a time when she fancied me; but, for one thing, I'm too frivolous a young man for her, while you are a serious chap, you are a morally and physically irreproachable person, you... wait, I haven't finished, you are an honest, moderate enthusiast, a genuine representative of those priests of science, of whom—no, no, that's not right—*of whose persons and merits* the class of our middle Russian nobility are so justly proud! And, for another, Yelena found me kissing Zoya's hand the other day!'

'Zoya's?'

'Yes, Zoya's. What else do you expect me to do? She has such pretty shoulders.'

'Shoulders?'

'Yes, well, hands, shoulders, isn't it all the same? Yelena caught me in the midst of those recreational pursuits after dinner, while before dinner I had been railing against Zoya. Yelena unfortunately does not understand the completely natural quality of such contradictions. Then *you* turned up: you are an idealist, you believe in... well, what do you believe in?... You blush, get embarrassed, talk about Schiller,* about Schelling (and after all, she is always looking for remarkable men), well, and so you've been victorious, while I, unhappy fellow, try to make light of it... and... and... meanwhile...'

Shubin suddenly burst into tears, stepped to one side, sat down on the ground, and clutched at his hair.

Bersenev went over to him.

'Pavel,' he began, 'what sort of childish behaviour is this? For pity's sake! What's wrong with you today? Lord knows what nonsense you've taken into your head, and you're crying. You know, I really think you are pretending.'

Shubin raised his head. Tears glistened on his cheeks in the rays of the moon, but his face was smiling.

'Andrei Petrovich,' he began, 'you may think of me what you will. I am even ready to agree that I was being hysterical just now, but I swear to God, I am in love with Yelena, and Yelena loves you. As a matter of fact, I promised to accompany you home and I will keep my promise.'

He stood up.

'What a night! Silvery, dark, young! How wonderful it is now for those who are loved! How happy they are not to sleep! Will you sleep, Andrei Petrovich?'

Bersenev made no reply, and quickened his step.

'Where are you hurrying to?' Shubin went on. 'Believe me, there will never be another night like this in your life, but at home Schelling awaits you. True, he stood you in good stead today; but still you should not hurry. Sing, and if you know how to sing, sing even more loudly; if you can't sing, take your hat off and throw your head back and smile to the stars. They are all looking at you, at you alone: all the stars do is look at people in love—that is why they are so charming. After all, you are in love, are you not, Andrei Petrovich?... You don't reply to me... Why don't you reply?' Shubin began again. 'Oh, if you feel happy, say nothing, say nothing! I am prattling on because I'm a poor, hapless creature, I am unloved, I'm a conjuror, an artist, a clown; but what speechless ecstasies I should drink from these nocturnal airs, beneath these stars, these diamonds, if I knew that I was loved!... Bersenev, are you happy?'

As before, Bersenev said nothing and quickly walked along the level road. Ahead, between the trees, the lights of the village in which he lived began to glimmer; it consisted of only a dozen small dachas. At its very beginning, on the right-hand side of the road, beneath two spreading birches, was a little shop; all its windows were now closed up, but a broad strip of light fell like a fan from the open door on to the trampled grass and flowed upwards through the trees, sharply illumining the whitish inner sides of the dense leaves. A girl, a housemaid by the look of her, stood in the shop with her back to the doorway and was arguing with the owner over some purchase: beneath the red shawl she had thrown over her head and was holding under her chin with her bare hand, her small round cheek and slender neck were only just visible. The young men stepped into the strip of light, Shubin looked into the interior of the shop, stopped, and cried: 'Annushka!' The girl peered at him, took fright, became embarrassed and, without finishing her purchase, descended the front steps, slipped nimbly past and, with a slight look back, walked across the road, to the left. The shopkeeper, a chubby man, indifferent to everything in the world, like all out-of-town small tradesmen, grunted and yawned as he watched her go, while Shubin turned to Bersenev with the words: 'That... that, you see... there's a family I know here... and that's their... now don't go thinking...'—and, not finishing his sentence, he ran off after the departing girl.

'At least dry your tears!' Bersenev shouted to him, and could not keep from laughing. But when he had returned home again, his face no longer had its cheerful expression; he was not laughing any more. Not for one moment did he believe what Shubin had told him, but the words he had spoken imprinted themselves deeply on his soul. 'Pavel was pulling my leg,' he thought... 'but some day she will fall in love... Who will she fall in love with?'

In Bersenev's room there was a piano, a small and not very new one, but with a soft and pleasant though not quite faultless tone. Bersenev sat down at it and began to play some chords. Like all Russian gentry, in his youth he had studied music and, like almost all Russian gentry, played very badly; but he loved music passionately. Strictly speaking, what he loved about it was not the art, the forms in which it is expressed (symphonies and sonatas, even operas made him feel melancholy), but its raw element: he loved the vague and sweet, aimless and all-embracing sensations that are aroused within the soul by the combination and modulation of sounds. He stayed at the piano for more than an hour, repeating the same chords many times, awkwardly searching for new ones, pausing in rapture over diminished sevenths. His heart ached within him, and his eyes more than once filled with tears. He was not ashamed of them: he shed them in darkness. 'Pavel is right,' he thought. 'I have a premonition: this night will not be repeated.' At last he stood up, lit a candle, put on his dressing-gown, fetched the second volume of Raumer's *History of the Hohenstaufens**—and, sighing once or twice, settled down to some diligent reading.

VI

YELENA, meanwhile, returned to her room, sat down before the open window, and leaned her head in her hands. To spend about quarter of an hour each evening by the window of her room had become a habit with her. She would commune with herself at this time, reflecting on the events of the day that had passed. It was not long since her twentieth birthday. She was tall of stature, had a pale and dark-complexioned face, large grey eyes beneath curved eyebrows surrounded by tiny freckles, a forehead and nose that were completely straight, a compressed mouth, and a rather pointed chin. Her dark brown tress of hair descended low on her slender neck. In all her being, in the expression of her face, attentive and slightly fearful, in her clear, but changeable gaze, in her smile, which seemed strained, in her voice, which was quiet and uneven, there was something nervous, electric, something impetuous and hurried, in a word, something that might not appeal to everyone, that even put some people off. Her hands were narrow and pink, with long fingers, and her feet were also narrow: she walked quickly, almost impulsively, leaning slightly forward. She had grown up very strangely; to begin with she had worshipped her father, formed a passionate attachment to her mother, and then cooled towards both of them, especially her father. Of late she had treated her mother like an ailing grandmother; while her father, who had been proud of her while she had the reputation of being an unusual child, began to be afraid of her when she had grown up, describing her as 'some kind of zealous female republican, God only knows in whose image!' Weakness exasperated her, stupidity made her angry, falsehood she would not forgive 'until the end of time'; her demands made no concessions to anyone, and even her prayers were repeatedly mingled with reproach. A person had only to lose her respect—for she pronounced her verdict quickly, often too quickly—and he ceased to exist for her. Every impression settled harshly on her soul; life did not come easily to her.

The governess to whom Anna Vasilyevna had entrusted the task of completing her daughter's education—an education, let us observe in parenthesis, that had not even been begun by the depressed mother —was of Russian lineage, the daughter of a ruined bribe-taker, a boarding-school girl, and a very sensitive, kindly, and deceitful creature; she would now and then fall in love, and ended, in 1850 (when Yelena was seventeen), by marrying some officer or other who at once walked out on her. This governess was very fond of literature and herself wrote verses of a sort; she gave Yelena a taste for reading, but reading alone did not satisfy her: from childhood on Yelena yearned for action, for active goodness; the poor, the hungry, and the sick concerned, troubled, tormented her; she dreamed about them, made enquiries with all her friends about them; charity she gave solicitously, with involuntary solemnity, almost with excitement. Every maltreated animal, every emaciated yard dog, every kitten condemned to death, every fledgling fallen from the nest, even insects and reptiles, found protection and shelter with Yelena: she fed them herself and felt no repugnance for them. Her mother did not try to stop her; her father, on the other hand, was very indignant with his daughter for her, as he expressed it, 'vulgar mollycoddling', and claimed that one could hardly move about the house for all the dogs and cats in it. 'Lenochka,' he would shout to her, 'come quickly, a spider is trapping a fly, set the poor thing free!' And Lenochka, in a state of utter alarm, would come running, set the fly free, and unglue its legs. 'Why don't you just let it bite you, if you're so kind,' her father would comment ironically; but she paid no attention. In her tenth year Yelena made friends with a beggar girl, Katya, and held secret rendezvous with her in the garden, brought her delicacies, gave her presents of kerchiefs and ten-copeck pieces—Katya would not take toys. She would sit down beside Yelena on the dry ground, in an out of the way place, behind a clump of nettles; with a feeling of joyful humility she would eat Yelena's coarse bread, listen to her stories. Katya had an aunt, a nasty old woman who often beat her. Katya hated her and forever spoke of how she would run away from her aunt, how she would live in *all God's freedom*; with secret respect and fear, Yelena listened to these new, unfamiliar words, stared fixedly at Katya, and everything about Katya—her black, swift, almost animal-like eyes, her sunburnt arms, her hollow little voice, even her ragged dress, then seemed to Yelena something special, almost holy. Yelena would go home, and for a long time afterwards think about beggars, and God's freedom; think about how she would cut herself a stick of hazel, and put on a satchel, and run away with Katya, how she would wander the roads wearing a garland of cornflowers: she had once seen Katya wearing

such a garland. If one of her parents came into the room at such times
she would avoid them and sulk. On one occasion she ran off for a
meeting with Katya and got mud on her dress; her father espied her
and called her a slattern, a peasant girl. She flushed all over—and a
sense of fear and strangeness assailed her heart. Katya often sang a
half-savage little soldiers' song; Yelena learned the song from her by
heart... Anna Vasilyevna overheard her singing it, and was indignant.

'Where did you learn that loathsome thing?' she asked her daughter.

Yelena merely looked at her mother and did not say a word: she
felt she would rather allow her mother to tear her to pieces than give
up her secret, and again a mingling of fear and sweetness passed
through her heart. As a matter of fact, however, her acquaintance with
Katya did not continue for long: the poor little girl fell ill with a fever,
and died a few days later.

Yelena grieved very much and for a long time could not sleep at
nights, when she learned of Katya's death. The beggar girl's last words
constantly rang in her ears, and it seemed to her, that she was being
called...

And the years passed and passed: quickly and silently, like torrents
beneath fallen snow, Yelena's girlhood flowed away, in outer inactivity,
but inner struggle and unease. She had no female companions: of all
the girls who visited the Stakhovs' house she did not make friends with
one. Parental authority never weighed on Yelena, and from the age
of sixteen she was almost completely independent; she began to live
her own life, though it was a lonely one. Her soul both flared and
flickered in solitude, she struggled like a bird in a cage, but there was
no cage: no one placed restraints on her, no one tried to hold her back,
but she strained and languished. She sometimes did not understand
herself, was even afraid of herself. All that surrounded her seemed
to her either meaningless or incomprehensible. 'How can one live without love? But there is no one to love!' she would think, and became
intensely afraid of these thoughts, these sensations. At the age of
eighteen she almost died of a malignant fever; shaken to its foundation, her whole organism, by nature healthy and strong, for a long
time could not recover. The last traces of the illness vanished at last,
but Yelena Nikolayevna's father still continued to talk, not without
asperity, of her 'nerves'. Sometimes it entered her head that she wanted
something no one in the whole of Russia wanted or had any idea of.
Then she would grow calm, even laugh at herself, pass day after day

in unconcern, but then suddenly some strong, nameless thing she could not master would begin to seethe within her, crying out to break to the surface. The storm would pass, and the tired wings that had not flown would be lowered again; but these outbursts took their toll. No matter how hard she tried not to betray the nature of what was taking place within her, the anguish of her troubled soul could be detected even in her outward calm, and her parents would often, with good reason, shrug their shoulders, express astonishment, and fail to comprehend her 'oddities'.

On the day that our story began, Yelena remained longer by the window than usual. She spent much thought on Bersenev, and on her conversation with him. He appealed to her; she believed in the warmth of his emotions, the purity of his intentions. He had never previously spoken to her as he had that evening. She remembered the expression of his timid eyes, of his smile—and smiled herself, and fell to reflection, though not about him now. She began to gaze into the night through the open window. For a long time she gazed at the dark, lowering sky; then she rose, tossed her hair back from her face with a movement of her head, and herself not knowing why, stretched out to it, that sky, her bare, now colder arms; then she brought them down, got down onto her knees before her bed, pressed her face against the pillow, and in spite of all her efforts not to yield to the emotion that had come welling over her, began to cry, with strange, perplexed, but burning tears.

VII

NEXT morning at about twelve, Bersenev set off in a return cab for Moscow. He needed to get money from the post office, buy some books, and at the same time he wanted to see Insarov and talk things over with him. During his recent talk with Shubin, Bersenev had had the idea of inviting Insarov to stay at his dacha. But it took him some time to track him down: from his previous lodgings he had moved to new ones, which were not easy to get to: they were situated in the rear courtyard of an ugly stone tenement house, built in the St Petersburg manner, between the Arbat and Povarskaya Street. In vain did Bersenev wander from one dirty entrance to another, in vain did he call for a yardkeeper or for 'anyone'. Even in St Petersburg the yardkeepers try to avoid the gaze of visitors, and in Moscow all the more so: no one responded to Bersenev; only an inquisitive tailor, in his waistcoat and with a hank of grey thread over his shoulder, thrust his wan and unshaven face, which had a black eye, from a high-up ventilation window, and a black goat with no horns, which had clambered up onto a dunghill, turned round, bleated plaintively, and began to chew its cud more rapidly. A woman in an old coat and down-at-heel shoes at last took pity on Bersenev and pointed out Insarov's lodgings to him. Bersenev found him in. He rented a room from the same tailor who had so indifferently gazed from the ventilation window on the difficulties of someone who had got lost—a large, almost completely empty room with dark green walls, three quadrangular windows, a tiny bed in one corner, a small leather sofa in another, and an enormous cage that hung right up near the ceiling; in this cage a nightingale had once lived. Insarov came to greet Bersenev as soon as he crossed the threshold, but did not exclaim: 'Oh, it's you!' or 'Oh, good Lord! What stroke of fortune brings you here?', did not even say: 'Hello', but simply shook his hand and led him to the room's sole existing chair.

'Sit down,' he said, himself sitting down on the edge of the chair.

'My place is still in a mess, as you can see,' Insarov added, pointing to the pile of papers and books on the floor. 'I haven't got it properly organized yet. There's been no time yet.'

Insarov spoke Russian altogether correctly, pronouncing each word firmly and clearly; but his guttural, though in fact pleasant, voice did not really sound very Russian. Insarov's foreign origins (he was Bulgarian by birth) were also clearly detectable in his appearance: he was a young man of about twenty-five, lean and sinewy, with a hollow chest and gnarled hands; the features of his face were sharp, his nose hooked, his hair straight and raven-black, his forehead low, his eyes small, with a fixed look and sunken, his eyebrows thick; when he smiled, handsome white teeth showed for a moment from behind thin, hard, too clearly marked lips. He wore an old but neat little frock-coat, buttoned up to the top.

'Why did you move out of your old lodgings?' Bersenev asked him.

'This place is less expensive; it's closer to the university.'

'But it's the vacation now... And what do you want to live in the city in summer for? You should have rented a dacha if you'd decided to move.'

Insarov made no reply to this observation and offered Bersenev a pipe, muttering: 'I'm sorry, I have no cigars or cigarettes.'

Bersenev lit the pipe.

'Well, for example,' he went on, 'I have rented a cottage near Kuntsevo. Very inexpensive and very comfortable. There's even a spare room at the top.'

Once more Insarov made no reply.

Bersenev drew in some smoke.

'It even occurred to me,' he began again, letting out the smoke in a thin stream, 'that if, for example, there were someone... you, for example, it occurred to me... who might like... who might agree to lodge there, at the top of the house... how good that would be! What do you think, Dmitry Nikanorych?'

Insarov raised his small eyes to him.

'You are proposing that I come and live in your dacha?'

'Yes; I have a spare room up at the top there.'

'I'm very grateful to you, Andrei Petrovich; but I do not think that my means would allow that.'

'In what way would they not allow it?'

'They would not allow me to live in a dacha. It is out of the question for me to keep two sets of lodgings.'

'But you see, I...' Bersenev began, and paused. 'You would incur no extra expense from it,' he continued. 'Your lodgings here would, let's assume, continue to be at your disposal, what's more, everything costs very little over there; we could even make arrangements for us to dine together, for example.'

Insarov said nothing. Bersenev began to feel awkward.

'At least come and visit me some time,' he began, after a short pause. 'Just a few steps away from me lives a family I should very much like to introduce you to. What a wonderful girl there is there, if only you knew, Insarov! A close friend of mine also lives there, a man of great talent; I am sure that you would get along with him.' (The Russian likes to regale one—if with nothing else, then with his friends.) 'I mean it, come and see us. Or even better, come and live with us, I really do mean it. We could work together, read together... I am studying history and philosophy, you know. All that would interest you, and I have lots of books.'

Insarov got up and paced about the room.

'Allow me to enquire,' he asked at last, 'how much do you pay for your dacha?'

'A hundred silver roubles.'

'And how many rooms are there in it?'

'Five.'

'So, if I were to pay my full share, it would amount to twenty-five roubles for one room?'

'Your full share... But for pity's sake, I really don't need the room. It just stands empty.'

'Perhaps; but listen,' Insarov added with a determined and at the same time artless movement of his head. 'I could only take advantage of your proposal if you would agree to take money from me according to my full share. I am able to pay twenty-five roubles, especially since, in the light of what you say, I shall be able to economize on everything else.'

'Of course; but really, it gives me a bad conscience.'

'Otherwise it is out of the question, Andrei Petrovich.'

'Well, as you wish; but what a stubborn fellow you are!'

Again Insarov made no reply.

The young men made an agreement about the day on which Insarov was to move in. They summoned the landlord; but at first he merely sent his daughter, a little girl of about seven, with an enormous multi-coloured kerchief on her head; she attentively, almost with terror, listened to all that Insarov told her, and left without saying anything; next her mother appeared, heavily pregnant, and also wearing a kerchief on her head, but a tiny one. Insarov explained to her that he was moving to a dacha near Kuntsevo, but was keeping his room and entrusting all his things to her care; the tailor's wife also seemed frightened, and withdrew. At last the landlord arrived; at first he seemed to understand everything and merely said, reflectively: 'Near Kuntsevo?'—but then opened the door and shouted: 'So are you going to keep the room, or not?' Insarov reassured him. 'Because I need to know,' the tailor repeated, and slipped away.

Bersenev set off home, very pleased with the success of his proposal. Insarov saw him to the door with an amiable politeness little used in Russia and, remaining alone, carefully took off his frock-coat and busied himself with the unpacking of his papers.

VIII

ON the evening of that same day, Anna Vasilyevna sat in her drawing-room and prepared to cry. Also in the room were her husband and a certain Uvar Ivanovich Stakhov, Nikolai Artemyevich's cousin thrice-removed, a retired cornet of about sixty, a man corpulent to the point of immobility, with sleepy yellow eyes and thick colourless lips in a puffy, yellow face. Ever since his retirement he had taken up permanent residence in Moscow, living on the interest from a small principal left to him by his wife, who had come from a merchant's family. He did nothing, and hardly even thought, or if he did think, then kept his thoughts to himself. Only once in his life had he become emotional and shown some activity: that was when he read in the newspapers about a new musical instrument at the London World Exhibition —the 'contrabombardon'*—and wished to order this instrument for himself, even enquiring where to send the money and through which agency. Uvar Ivanovich wore a capacious frock-coat the colour of tobacco and a white cravat at his neck, ate frequently and abundantly, and only in difficult situations, that is to say, each time he needed to express some opinion or other, convulsively moved the fingers of his right hand in the air, first from thumb to little finger and then from little finger to thumb, repeating over and over again, with difficulty: 'One ought to... somehow, that is...'

Uvar Ivanovich sat in an armchair beside the window, breathing with effort. Nikolai Artemyevich paced about the room with large strides, his hands thrust in his pockets; his face expressed displeasure.

He stopped at last, and shook his head.

'Yes,' he began, 'in our day young people were raised differently. Young people did not permit themselves to *mankirovat'** (be dis-respectful to) their elders. (He pronounced the Russian word with a nasal *man*, in the French manner.) But now I can only look and be astonished. Perhaps *I* am not right, but *they* are. I, however, still have my own view of things: for I was not born an idiot. What are your thoughts on the subject, Uvar Ivanovich?'

Uvar Ivanovich merely looked at him and twiddled his fingers a little.

'Yelena Nikolayevna, for example,' Nikolai Artemyevich went on. 'I don't understand Yelena Nikolayevna, really I don't. I am not sufficiently exalted for her. Her heart is so vast that it embraces the whole of nature, to the last cockroach or frog, in a word, everything except her own father. Well, that's fine: I know this and don't go poking my nose in any more. For here there are nerves, and erudition, and soaring to the skies, and all that is a line that is foreign to us. But Mr Shubin... he is, let us assume, a remarkable, an extraordinary artist, about that I will not argue; but to be disrespectful to an elder, to someone to whom he is, no matter what one says, obliged for many things—that, I confess, *dans mon gros bon sens,** I cannot tolerate. I am not by nature someone who places high demands; but everything has its limits.'

Anna Vasilyevna rang the bell nervously. A boy servant came in.

'Why doesn't Pavel Yakovlevich come?' she said quietly. 'Why does he not come when I call him?'

Nikolai Artemyevich shrugged his shoulders.

'Why on earth do you want to call him, anyway? I don't require it at all, don't wish it, in fact.'

'Why, Nikolai Artemyevich? He has upset you; perhaps he has disturbed the course of your treatment. I want him to explain himself. I want to know what he may have done to anger you.'

'I tell you again, I do not require it. And what makes you say these things... *devant les domestiques*...'*

Anna Vasilyevna blushed slightly.

'You should not say that, Nikolai Artemyevich. I never say anything... *devant les domestiques*... Now off you go, Fedushka, and see that you bring Pavel Yakovlevich here without delay.'

The servant boy went out.

'And none of this is in any way necessary,' Nikolai Artemyevich said through his teeth, and again began to stride about the room. 'That was not at all what I had in mind.'

'For mercy's sake, Paul must apologize to you.'

'For mercy's sake, what do I need his apologies for? And what are apologies, anyway? All that is just fine phrases.'

'What do you need his apologies for? He must be made to see reason.'

'Make him see reason yourself. He's more likely to listen to you. I bear no grudge against him.'

'No, Nikolai Artemyevich, you have been in a bad mood ever since you arrived today. You have even grown thinner of late, it seems to me. I fear that your course of treatment is not benefiting you.'

'I cannot do without my course of treatment,' Nikolai Artemyevich observed. 'There is something wrong with my liver.'

At that moment, Shubin came in. He seemed tired. A mild, slightly mocking smile played on his lips.

'You asked for me, Anna Vasilyevna?' he said quietly.

'Yes, of course I did. For mercy's sake, Paul, this is dreadful. I am very unhappy with you. How can you be disrespectful to Nikolai Artemyevich?'

'Nikolai Artemyevich has complained to you about me?' Shubin asked, glancing at Stakhov with the same ironic smile on his lips.

Stakhov turned away and lowered his eyes.

'Yes, she did. I don't know what you made yourself guilty of in his regard, but you must apologize at once, as his health is very fragile just now and, when it comes down to it, we must all of us respect our benefactors when we are young.'

'Ah, what logic!' Shubin thought, and turned to Stakhov:

'I am ready to apologize to you, Nikolai Artemyevich,' he said with a polite half-bow, 'if I have indeed offended you in any way.'

'That is not at all... what I meant,' Nikolai Artemyevich retorted, avoiding Shubin's gaze as before. 'As a matter of fact, I willingly forgive you, because, as you know, I am not a man who places high demands.'

'Oh, of that there is not the slightest doubt!' Shubin said quietly. 'But permit me to be curious: does Anna Vasilyevna know what my guilt consists in?'

'No, I don't know anything,' Anna Vasilyevna observed, craning her neck.

'Oh good Lord!' Nikolai Artemyevich exclaimed hurriedly. 'How many times have I asked, implored, how many times have I told you how loathsome I find all these explanations and scenes! Once in an age one comes home, wants to have a rest—go to the family circle, they say, *l'intérieur*, the life of a family man—but all I ever find here are scenes and trouble. Not a moment's peace. In spite of oneself, one ends up at the club... or... or somewhere. A man is a living creature, he has a physical constitution, it has its own requirements, but here...'

And, without finishing the speech he had begun, Nikolai Artemyevich quickly went out, slamming the door behind him. Anna Vasilyevna watched him go.

'The club?' she whispered bitterly. 'It is not the club you are off to, you fickle man! At the club there is no one for you to give presents of horses to, horses from my own stud farm—and the grey ones, too! My favourite colour. No, no, frivolous man,' she added, raising her voice, 'it is not the club you are off to. And you, Paul,' she went on, getting to her feet, 'are you not ashamed of yourself? You're not a little boy any more, are you? Oh, now I have started to have a headache. Where is Zoya, do you know?'

'I think she's upstairs in her room. That sensible little vixen always hides in her lair in this kind of weather.'

'Oh, please, please!' Anna Vasilyevna looked around her. 'Have you seen my liqueur glass of grated horseradish anywhere? Paul, do me a favour, don't make me angry in future.'

'What would I want to make you angry for, dear aunt? Let me kiss your sweet hand. As for your horseradish, I saw it in the study, on the small table.'

'Darya is always putting it in places where I can't find it,' Anna Vasilyevna said, and withdrew, her silk dress rustling.

Shubin was about to go after her, but stopped, hearing the leisurely voice of Uvar Ivanovich behind him.

'That is not how you ought to be dealt with... milksop,' said the retired cornet, in alternating tones.

Shubin went over to him.

'And why should I be "dealt with", venerable Uvar Ivanovich?'

'Why? You are young, so show some respect. Yes.'

'Respect for whom?'

'For whom? You know for whom. That's right—grin away.'

Shubin folded his arms.

'O representative of the primeval chorus,' he exclaimed, 'power of the black earth, foundation of the social edifice!'

Uvar Ivanovich began to twiddle his fingers.

'That will do, brother, do not tempt me.'

'Here', Shubin went on, 'we have a nobleman no longer young, it appears, yet how much that is happy and childlike is still concealed in him! Respect! And do you know, primordial man, why I have incurred Nikolai Artemyevich's wrath? You see, he and I spent the whole of this morning with his German lady; the three of us sang "Do Not Leave Me", you should have heard us. You would find it touching, I think. We sang, my good sir, we sang—well, and I got bored; I could see that something was wrong, there was too much love and affection going on. And I began to tease them both. It had the right effect. At first she got angry with me, and then with him; and then he got angry with her and told her that he was only happy at home and that it was heaven there; and she told him that he had no morals, and I said "*Ach!*" to her in German; he left, but I stayed; he came here, to paradise, that is, but paradise made him feel wretched. So he began to get peevish. Well sir, who is to blame now, in your opinion?'

'You are, of course,' Uvar Ivanovich retorted.

Shubin stared at him fixedly.

'May I have the boldness to ask, respected warrior,' he began in a servile voice, 'did it please you to utter those mysterious words in consequence of some emanation of your power of abstract thought, or was it under the inspiration of a momentary need to produce the concussion of the air that is called sound?'

'Do not tempt me, I say!' Uvar Ivanovich groaned.

Shubin began to laugh, and ran off.

'Hey!' Uvar Ivanovich exclaimed a quarter of an hour later. 'I should like... a glass of vodka.'

The boy servant brought vodka and snacks on a tray. Uvar Ivanovich slowly took the glass from the tray and for a long time, with strained attention, gazed at it as though he did not quite understand what it was he was holding. Then he looked at the servant boy and asked if his name was Vaska. Then he assumed a vexed expression, drank the vodka, took a snack and groped to fish his handkerchief from his pocket. But the servant boy had already long ago taken the tray and decanter back to their places, eaten what was left of the salt herring, and begun a nap, nestling down on his master's overcoat, while Uvar Ivanovich continued to hold his handkerchief in front of him on outspread fingers, looking with the same strained attention, now at the window, and now at the floor and walls.

IX

SHUBIN had gone back to his quarters in the outhouse, and was on the point of opening a book. Nikolai Artemyevich's valet came warily into his room and handed him a small, triangular note sealed with a large official stamp. 'I hope,' the note said, 'that you, as an honourable man, will not allow yourself to refer by even a single word to a certain promissory note that has been the subject of conversation today. My attitudes and principles, the paltriness of the sum itself, and the other circumstances are known to you; when all is said and done, there are family secrets that must be respected, and family peace is such a sacred thing that only *êtres sans cœur*,* among whom I have no cause to reckon you, reject it. (Please return this note.) N. S.'

Shubin traced underneath, in pencil: 'Don't worry—I don't steal handkerchiefs from pockets yet'; returned the note to the valet, and again settled down with his book. But it soon slipped out of his hands. He looked out at the sky, which had begun to turn red, at the two young, mighty pine trees that stood on their own, apart from the other trees, and thought: 'In the daytime the pines are bluish, but how magnificently green they are in the evening!'—and set off into the garden, in the secret hope of meeting Yelena there. He was not disappointed. Ahead of him, on the road between the bushes, her dress appeared for a moment. He caught her up and, drawing level with her, said quietly:

'Don't look at me, I don't deserve it.'

She looked at him fleetingly, fleetingly smiled, and walked on, into the depths of the garden. Shubin set off after her.

'I ask you not to look at me,' he began, 'yet I start talking to you: a manifest contradiction! But that doesn't matter, it's not as if it hadn't happened to me before. I just remembered that I have not yet asked you to forgive me for my stupid behaviour yesterday. You are not angry with me, Yelena Nikolayevna?'

She stopped, and did not reply to him at once—not for any anger she might have felt, but her thoughts were far away.

'No,' she said at last. 'I am not angry in the slightest.'

Shubin bit his lip.

'What an anxious... and what an indifferent face!' he muttered. 'Yelena Nikolayevna,' he continued, raising his voice, 'permit me to tell you a small anecdote. I had a friend, and this friend also had a friend, who at first conducted himself as befits a decent man, but then took to drink. So then, early one morning, my friend encountered him in the street (and please observe, by this time they had already severed their acquaintance), encountered him, and saw that he was drunk. My friend simply turned away from him. But the fellow approached him and said: "I would not have been angry, if you had not greeted me, but why did you turn away? It may be my drinking comes of sorrow. Peace to my ashes!"'

Shubin fell silent.

'And that was all?' Yelena asked.

'Yes.'

'I don't understand. What are you hinting at? Just now you told me not to look in your direction.'

'Yes, and now I have told you how wrong it is to turn away.'

'But did I really...' Yelena began.

'Did you not?'

Yelena blushed slightly and extended her hand towards Shubin. He firmly pressed it.

'Now it is as if you had caught me in the act of bad feeling,' Yelena said. 'But your suspicion is not just. I never even thought of avoiding you.'

'Granted, granted. But I think you will admit that at this moment you have a thousand thoughts in your head, of which you will not entrust even one to me. Well? Do I not speak the truth?'

'Perhaps.'

'Then what is the reason for this? What is it?'

'My thoughts are not clear even to myself,' Yelena said quietly.

'All the more reason to confide them to someone else,' Shubin chimed in. 'But I will tell you what the matter is. You have a poor opinion of me.'

'I?'

'Yes, you. You imagine that everything in me is semi-artificial, because I am an artist; that not only am I not capable of any practical activity—in that you are probably right—but am not even capable of any genuine, deep emotion: that I cannot even cry sincerely, that I'm a windbag and gossip—and all because I'm an artist. What kind of unhappy, godforsaken people are we, then? For example, I am ready to swear that you do not believe in my remorse.'

'No, Pavel Yakovlevich, I do believe in your remorse, and I also believe in your tears. But it seems to me that even your remorse amuses you, as do your tears.'

Shubin gave a start.

'Well, I can see that this is, as the doctors put it, an incurable case, a *casus incurabilis*. Now all one can do is bow one's head and submit. Yet, good Lord! Is this really true, can I really go on consorting with myself when beside me there exists a soul such as this? And to know that one will never gain entry to that soul, never know why it is sad, why it rejoices, what ferments in it, what it wants, where it is going... Tell me,' he said quietly after a short silence, 'could you never, not in any circumstances, love an artist?'

Yelena looked him straight in the eye.

'I do not think so, Pavel Yakovlevich; no.'

'*Quod erat demonstrandum*,' Shubin said with comic dejection. 'Henceforth I suppose it will be more fitting for me not to disturb your solitary walks. A professor would ask you: on the basis of what facts do you say no? But I am not a professor, I am a child, according to your conceptions; but one does not turn away from children, remember that. Goodbye. Peace to my ashes!'

Yelena was about to stop him, but thought for a moment and also said:

'Goodbye.'

Shubin emerged from the courtyard. A short distance away from the Stakhovs' dacha, he encountered Bersenev. He was walking with brisk steps, his head down and his hat on the back of his neck.

'Andrei Petrovich!' Shubin cried.

Bersenev halted.

'On you go, on you go,' Shubin continued, 'I was simply saying hello, I don't want to detain you—and make your way straight into the garden; there you will find Yelena. I think she is waiting for you... she is waiting for someone, at any rate. Do you realize the power of those words: she is waiting! And do you know, brother, what a remarkable thing happened? Imagine, I've been living in the same house as her for two years now, I am in love with her, and only now, at this very moment, I not so much understood her as *saw* her. Saw her and threw up my hands. Do not gaze on me, please, with that falsely caustic smile,

which little suits your measured features. Well yes, I know, you are
going to remind me about Annushka. What of it? I won't say no.
Annushkas are a good match for fellows such as I. Long live the
Annushkas and the Zoyas and even the Avgustina Khristianovnas
of this world! Now in you go and see Yelena, while I set off for...
Annushka's, you suppose? No, brother, worse than that: Prince
Chikurasov's. He's a patron of the arts, a Kazan Tartar, like Volgin.
Do you see this letter of invitation, these characters: RSVP? Not even
in the country is there any peace for me. *Addio!*'

    Bersenev listened to Shubin's tirade without saying anything, and
as if he were slightly embarrassed on his account; then he entered the
courtyard of the Stakhovs' dacha. As for Shubin, he really did go to see
Prince Chikurasov, to whom with a most amiable appearance he said
the most bitingly insolent things. The Kazan Tartar patron of the arts
guffawed loudly, the patron's guests laughed, but no one had any enjoyment, and on parting all were in a bad temper. Thus, two unfamiliar
gentlemen meeting on the Nevsky Prospect* will suddenly grin at each
other, crinkle eyes, nose, and mouth in a saccharine manner, and at
once, having passed each other, adopt their previous indifferent or
morose, for the most part haemorrhoidal, expressions.

X

YELENA greeted Bersenev cordially, not in the garden now but in the drawing-room, and at once, almost impatiently, resumed their conversation of the day before. She was alone: Nikolai Artemyevich had quietly slipped off somewhere, while Anna Vasilyevna lay upstairs with a wet bandage on her head. Zoya sat beside her, having neatly straightened her skirt and folded her arms on her knees; Uvar Ivanovich was drowsing in the mezzanine room on a wide and comfortable sofa which had received the nickname 'Self-Sleeper'.* Bersenev again mentioned his father, whose memory he held sacred. Let us also say a few words about him.

The owner of eighty-two souls, whom he had emancipated before his death, an Illuminatus,* a former student at Göttingen, the author of a manuscript work on 'The Emanations or Manifestations of the Spirit on Earth', a work in which Schellingianism, Swedenborgianism and Republicanism were mixed together in a most original fashion, Bersenev's father had brought him to Moscow while he was still a boy, immediately after the decease of his mother, and had himself taken care of the boy's education. He had prepared for each lesson, toiled with extraordinary conscientiousness but with a complete absence of success: he was a dreamer, a bibliophile, a mystic, spoke with a stammer, in a hollow voice, expressed himself obscurely and ornately, mostly in analogies, was shy even of his son, whom he loved passionately. It was no wonder that after the lessons his son merely looked blank, and made not a hair's breadth of progress. The old man (he was approaching fifty, and had married very late) guessed at last that things were not going right, and put his Andryusha into a boarding-school. Andryusha began to learn, but remained under parental supervision: his father visited him constantly, making the headmaster's life a misery with his admonitions and homilies; the form-masters also found the uninvited guest burdensome: every so often he would bring them, as they put it, 'peculiar' books on education. Even the schoolboys felt awkward at the sight of the old man's swarthy, pockmarked face, of his emaciated figure, perpetually enveloped in a kind of sharp-tailed frock-coat. The schoolboys did not suspect at the time that this morose, never-smiling gentleman, with his spindly gait and long nose, rent his heart and grieved over each one of them almost as if they were his own sons. On one occasion he conceived the idea of talking to them about George Washington. 'Young alumni!' he began, but at the first sound of his strange voice the young alumni scattered. Life for the esteemed former student at Göttingen was not a bed of roses: he was constantly overwhelmed by the course of history, by all manner of questions and considerations. When young Bersenev went up to university, his father attended the lectures with him; but his health had by now begun to fail him. The events of '48 shook him to the foundations (he had to rewrite the whole of his book), and he died in the winter of '53 without waiting for his son to leave university, but congratulating him on his degree in advance, and blessing him for his service to learning. 'I hand on the torch to you,' he said to him two hours before he died. 'I have held it as long as I could; you too must not let it fall until the end.'

Bersenev talked to Yelena about his father for a long time. The awkwardness he felt in her presence disappeared, and his lisp was less pronounced. The conversation moved to the university.

'Tell me,' Yelena asked him, 'were there any remarkable men among your companions?'

Bersenev remembered Shubin's words.

'No, Yelena Nikolayevna, to tell you the truth there was not a single remarkable fellow among us. And indeed, how could there have been? They say that Moscow University once had its day! Only that day is not now. Now it is merely a school, not a university. I found my companions something of a burden,' he added, lowering his voice.

'A burden?' Yelena whispered.

'Though as a matter of fact,' Bersenev went on, 'I must qualify that remark. I know one of the students—to be sure, he was not in my course—and he is a truly remarkable man.'

'What is his name?' Yelena asked.

'Insarov, Dmitry Nikanorovich. He's a Bulgarian.'

'Not a Russian?'

'No.'

'Then why does he live in Moscow?'

'He came here in order to study. And do you know what the purpose of his study is? He has but one thought: the liberation of his motherland.* His life has also been an extraordinary one. His father was a rather well-to-do merchant, a native of Tirnovo. Tirnovo is a small town now, but in former times it was the capital of Bulgaria, when Bulgaria was still an independent monarchy. He did business in Sofia, had dealings with Russia; his sister, Insarov's aunt, still lives in Kiev, where she is married to the senior history teacher at the gymnasium there. In 1835, eighteen years ago, that is, a horrible crime took place: Insarov's mother suddenly vanished without trace; a week later she was found with her throat cut.' Yelena gave a shudder. Bersenev paused.

'Continue, continue,' she said quietly.

'There were rumours that she had been abducted and murdered by a Turkish Aga; her husband, Insarov's father, discovered that this was true, and wanted to take his revenge, but he only wounded the Aga with a dagger... He was shot.'

'Shot? Without a trial?'

'Yes. At that time Insarov was in his eighth year. He remained in the care of neighbours. The sister learned of the fate of her brother's family and wanted to have her nephew in her own home. He was conveyed to Odessa, and from there to Kiev. In Kiev he spent no less than twelve years. That is why he speaks Russian so well.'

'He speaks Russian?'

'As you and I do. When he was twenty (this was at the beginning of '48) he wanted to return to his motherland. He visited Sofia and Tirnovo, traversed the length and breadth of Bulgaria on foot, spent two years there, and learned his native language again. The Turkish government pursued him, and it is probable that during those two years he was subject to great danger; I once saw a broad scar on his neck, which must have been the mark of a wound; but he does not like to talk about it. He is also a silent fellow, in his way. I tried to ask him questions—nothing came of it. He replies in general phrases. He is dreadfully stubborn. In '50 he came back to Russia, to Moscow, with the intention of completing his education, forming close contacts with Russians, and then, when he leaves the university...'

'Then what?' Yelena interrupted.

'Whatever God may grant. It is hard to guess the future.'

For a long time Yelena did not remove her gaze from Bersenev.

'Your story is of great interest to me,' she said quietly. 'What is he like to look at, this... what did you call him... Insarov of yours?'

'How shall I put it? In my opinion, rather handsome. In any case, you will see him for yourself.'

'How will that be possible?'

'I shall bring him here, to see you. He is moving to our village the day after tomorrow, and will be living in the same quarters with me.'

'Really? And will he want to come and see us?'

'Of course he will! He'll be very pleased to.'

'He is not proud?'

'He? Not in the slightest. Or rather, if you like, he is proud, but not in the sense in which you mean it. For example, he will not borrow money from anyone.'

'And he is poor?'

'Yes, he is not rich. On his trip to Bulgaria he gathered one or two crumbs that survived from his father's possessions, and his aunt helps him; but all that is a trifle.'

'He must have a great deal of character,' Yelena observed.

'Yes. He is a man of iron. And at the same time, you will see, there is something childlike and sincere about him, for all his concentration, secretiveness, even. To be sure, his sincerity is not our worthless kind, the sincerity of people who decidedly have nothing to conceal... But I shall bring him to see you, only wait.'

'And he is not shy?' Yelena asked again.

'No, he isn't shy. Only proud men are shy.'

'Are you a proud man, then?'

Bersenev was embarrassed, and threw up his hands.

'You stir my curiosity,' Yelena continued. 'Well, and tell me, did he obtain his revenge on that Turkish Aga?'

Bersenev smiled.

'It's only in novels that people obtain their revenge, Yelena Nikolayevna; and what is more, in the space of twelve years that Aga could have died.'

'But Mr Insarov told you nothing of that?'

'No.'

'Why did he visit Sofia?'

'His father lived there.'

Yelena began to reflect.

'To liberate one's motherland!' she said quietly. 'It is terrible even to say those words, they are so immense...'

At that moment Anna Vasilyevna entered the room, and the conversation came to an end.

Strange sensations disturbed Bersenev as he returned home that evening. He did not repent of his plan to introduce Yelena to Insarov; he found it entirely natural that his stories about the young Bulgarian should have made such a deep impression on her... after all, he himself had tried to intensify that impression! But a secret and dark emotion had covertly made its nest within his heart; he pined with an unworthy pining. This pining did not, however, prevent him from settling down with *History of the Hohenstaufens* and beginning to read it from the very page at which he had stopped the night before.

XI

Two days later Insarov, true to his word, presented himself at Bersenev's with his things. He had no servant, but without any help set his room in order, arranged the furniture, did the dusting, and swept the floor. He spent a particularly long time fussing over the writing-desk, which would on no account fit into the pier between the windows that had been designated for it; but Insarov, with the taciturn persistence characteristic of him, attained his end. Having settled in, he asked Bersenev to take ten roubles in advance and, equipping himself with a thick walking-stick, set off to survey the environs of his new abode. He returned after about three hours, and to Bersenev's invitation to share his meal replied that he would not refuse to dine within that day, but that he had already talked the matter over with the mistress of the house and would in future obtain his food from her.

'For pity's sake,' Bersenev retorted, 'you will be badly fed: that woman doesn't know how to cook at all. Why don't you want to dine with me? We could split the expense in half.'

'My means do not allow me to dine as you dine,' Insarov replied with a calm smile.

In that smile there was something that did not allow insistence: Bersenev said no more. After dinner he offered to take Insarov to see the Stakhovs; but Insarov replied that he proposed to devote the whole evening to correspondence with his Bulgarians, and therefore asked him to postpone the visit to the Stakhovs to another day. The adamant nature of Insarov's will was already familiar to Bersenev from before; but only now, under the same roof with him, was he finally able to satisfy himself that Insarov never altered any decision he had taken, just as he never put off the fulfilment of a promise he had given. To Bersenev, a thoroughly Russian person, this more than German punctilio at first seemed rather strange, even slightly ridiculous; but he soon grew accustomed to it, and in the end found it, if not estimable, then at any rate most convenient.

On the second day after his move, Insarov rose at four in the morning, quietly toured almost the whole of Kuntsevo, took a bathe in the river, drank a glass of cold milk, and settled down to work; for of work he had not a little: he was studying Russian history, and law, and political economy, translating Bulgarian songs and chronicles, collecting material on the eastern question,* compiling a Russian grammar for Bulgarians, and a Bulgarian one for Russians. Bersenev dropped in to see him and talked to him about Feuerbach.* Insarov listened to him closely, his objections rare, and of a sensible kind; from them it was plain that he was trying to account to himself as to whether he needed to study Feuerbach or whether he could manage without him. Bersenev subsequently led the conversation to his studies, and asked if he would show him something. Insarov read him his translation of two or three Bulgarian songs and expressed a wish to hear his opinion. Bersenev found the translation correct, but not lively enough. Insarov took his comment into consideration. From the songs, Bersenev passed to the contemporary situation in Bulgaria, and now for the first time he noticed the change that came about in Insarov at the mere mention of his motherland: it was not that his face grew flushed or his voice became raised—no! But his whole being seemed to strengthen and aspire forwards, the outline of his lips was more sharply and more implacably marked, while in the depths of his eyes a kind of smouldering and unquenchable fire was lit. Insarov did not like to enlarge on his own journey to his motherland, but would willingly discuss Bulgaria in general with anyone. He would speak, in leisurely tones, of the Turks, of their oppression, of the woe and distress of his fellow-citizens, of their hopes; the concentrated deliberation of a single and inveterate passion was audible in his every word.

'And yet, for all one knows,' Bersenev thought meanwhile, 'the Turkish Aga may have paid the price for the death of Insarov's mother and father.'

Insarov had not yet fallen silent when the door opened and on the threshold Shubin appeared.

He entered the room in a manner that was somehow too familiar and good humoured; Bersenev, who knew him well, realized at once that something was upsetting him.

'Let me introduce myself without ceremony,' he began with a light and open expression on his face. 'My name is Shubin; I am a friend of this young man.' (He pointed to Bersenev.) 'Why, you are Mr Insarov, are you not?'

'I am Insarov.'

'Then give me your hand and let us become acquainted. I don't know if Bersenev has told you about me, but he has told me a great deal about you. Have you moved here? Excellent! Please don't take exception to my looking at you so hard. I am a sculptor by trade, and I can see that very soon I shall be asking your permission to model your head.'

'My head is at your service,' Insarov said quietly.

'Now what shall we do today—eh?' Shubin began, suddenly sitting down on a rather low chair, and leaning with both hands on his widely spread knees. 'Andrei Petrovich, does your honour have a plan for today? The weather is wonderful; such an aroma of hay and dry strawberries... as if one were drinking nursery tea. We ought to think up something clever. Let us show Kuntsevo's new inhabitant all its numerous beauties.' ('Yes, there's something upsetting him,' Bersenev continued to reflect.) 'Well, why art thou silent, Horatio, my friend? Open thy prophetic lips. Shall we think up something clever, or shan't we?'

'I don't know', Bersenev observed, 'what Insarov's plans are. I think he intends to work.'

Shubin turned round on the chair.

'Do you want to work?' he asked, speaking through his nose slightly.

'No,' Insarov replied. 'Today I can devote to a walk.'

'Ah!' Shubin said quietly. 'Well, that's splendid. Come on, Andrei Petrovich, my friend, cover that wise head of yours with a hat, and let us go where our eyes look. Our eyes are young—they look a long way. I know a truly vile little inn where they'll give us a truly loathsome little dinner; but we shall enjoy ourselves enormously. Let us be off.'

Half an hour later all three of them were walking along the bank of the Moscow River. Insarov turned out to be wearing a rather strange, large-eared peaked cap that inspired Shubin with an enthusiasm that was not quite natural. Insarov stepped along without hurry, looking, breathing, talking, and smiling calmly: he had given up this day to relaxation and amusement, and was taking full pleasure in it. 'That's how well-behaved little boys go walking on Sundays,' Shubin whispered in Bersenev's ear. Shubin himself fooled about greatly, running on ahead, stopping in the pose of certain statues, somersaulting on the grass: Insarov's composure did not so much irritate him as make him behave affectedly. 'What are you fidgeting about like that for, Frenchman?' Bersenev observed to him once or twice. 'Yes, I'm a Frenchman, half

French,' Shubin retorted to him, 'and you need to draw a line between jesting and earnest, as a waiter at an inn used to say to me.' The young men turned away from the river and walked along a deep narrow rut between two walls of tall golden rye; a bluish shadow fell on them from one of these walls; the radiant sun seemed to glide along the top of the ears of grain; the skylarks sang, the quails called; everywhere there were green grasses, plants, and herbs; the warm breeze stirred and lifted their leaves, shaking the heads of the flowers. After long travelling, rests, chatter (Shubin even tried to play leapfrog with a toothless muzhik who happened to be passing and who kept on laughing, no matter what the gentlemen did with him), the young men reached the the 'truly vile' little inn. The waiter very nearly knocked each one of them down, and did indeed serve them a very poor dinner, with some kind of Trans-Balkan wine which, as a matter of fact, did not prevent them from enjoying themselves with all their heart and soul, as Shubin had predicted they would; he enjoyed himself more loudly than any of them—and least of any of them. He drank the health of the obscure but great Venelin, the health of the Bulgarian King Krum, Khrum, or Khrom, who had lived very nearly in the age of Adam.*

'In the ninth century,' Insarov corrected him.

'The ninth century?' Shubin exclaimed. 'Oh, what luck!'

Bersenev noticed that in the midst of all his pranks, escapades and jokes Shubin still seemed to be examining Insarov, probing him, and experiencing an inner unease—while Insarov remained calm and serene as before.

At last they went home, got changed, and so as not to depart from the mood they had established since morning, decided to go and visit the Stakhovs that very evening. Shubin ran on ahead to inform them of their arrival.

XII

'The Great Hero Insarov is about to visit!' he solemnly exclaimed as he entered the Stakhovs' drawing-room, where just then only Yelena and Zoya were present.

'*Wer?** Zoya asked in German. Taken unawares, she always expressed herself in her native language. Yelena straightened up. Shubin looked at her with a playful little smile on his lips. She was annoyed, but she said nothing.

'You heard,' he repeated. 'Mr Insarov is coming here.'

'I heard,' she replied, 'and I heard what you called him. I'm surprised at you, truly I am. Mr Insarov has not yet set his foot in the door, yet already you consider it necessary to make trouble.'

Shubin suddenly sank down.

'You are right, you are always right, Yelena Nikolayevna,' he muttered, 'but it was simply a manner of speaking, I swear it was. I've been out walking with him all day, and I can assure you that he is a splendid man.'

'I did not ask you about that,' Yelena said quietly, and got up.

'Is Mr Insarov young?' asked Zoya.

'He is a hundred and forty-four,' Shubin replied with annoyance.

The boy servant announced the arrival of the two friends. They entered. Bersenev presented Insarov. Yelena asked them to be seated and herself sat down, while Zoya set off upstairs: Anna Vasilyevna must be given advance warning. A conversation began, a rather insignificant one, like all first conversations. Shubin observed from the corner without a word, but there was nothing to observe. In Yelena he perceived the traces of a repressed vexation with him, Shubin—and that was all. He looked at Bersenev and at Insarov and, as a sculptor, compared their faces. 'Both', he thought, 'lack beauty; the Bulgarian has a typical, sculptural face; just now it is well lit; the Great Russian asks rather for painting: there are no lines, there is physiognomy. But perhaps it is possible to fall in love with either of them. She is not in love yet, but she will love Bersenev,' he decided to himself. Anna Vasilyevna appeared in the drawing-room and the conversation took a thoroughly 'suburban' turn—emphatically 'suburban', and not 'country'. It was a conversation that varied greatly in the abundance of subjects discussed;

but was broken every three minutes or so by short, rather wearisome pauses. In one of these pauses Anna Vasilyevna turned to Zoya. Shubin understood her silent hint and made a sour face, but Zoya sat down at the piano and played and sang all her pieces. Uvar Ivanovich had been about to emerge from behind the door, but twiddled his fingers and beat a retreat. After that, tea was served, and after that the whole company took a stroll in the garden... Outside it grew dark, and the guests moved off.

Insarov really made less of an impression on Yelena than she had expected, or, to be more precise, the impression he made on her was not the one she had expected. She liked his straightforwardness and ease of manner, and she liked his face; but Insarov's whole being, with its firm composure and everyday simplicity, somehow did not accord with the image that Bersenev's stories had left in her head. Yelena, without herself suspecting it, had anticipated something more 'fatal'. 'But', she thought, 'he spoke very little today, and I am to blame for that; I did not ask him questions; let us wait for another occasion... but he has expressive eyes, and they are honest ones!' She felt that what she wanted to do was not to bow down before him, but to give him a hand in friendship, and she was bewildered: this was not how she had imagined men like Insarov, who were 'heroes'. This last word reminded her of Shubin and, already lying in bed now, she flushed and grew angry.

'How did you like your new friends?' Bersenev asked Insarov as they returned.

'I liked them very much,' Insarov replied, 'especially the daughter. She must be a wonderful girl. She gets excited, but it is a good excitement.'

'One will have to visit them more often,' Bersenev remarked.

'Yes, one will,' Insarov said quietly, and made no more comment until they reached the house. Then he at once shut himself up in his room, but a candle burned there long after midnight.

Bersenev had not yet managed to read a page of Raumer when a handful of fine gravel rapped against the panes of his window. He involuntarily started, opened the window, and caught sight of Shubin, as pale as a piece of white linen.

'What a restless fellow you are! You're a nocturnal moth!' Bersenev began.

'Sh!' Shubin interrupted him. 'I have come to you by stealth, like Max to Agatha.* I really must have a few words with you alone.'

'Then come into the room.'

'No, there's no need,' Shubin retorted, and leaned his elbows on the window ledge—it's more fun like this, more like in Spain. In the first place, I congratulate you: your shares have risen in value. Your much-vaunted "unusual man" has failed. I can vouch for that. And to prove my impartiality to you, listen: here is Mr Insarov's service record. Talents: none, poetry: nix, capacity for work: a great deal, memory: large, mind: not varied or profound, but sensible and lively; dryness and strength, and even the gift of eloquence when the talk is of his —between ourselves—most tedious Bulgaria. Well? Would you say that I am being unfair? One more observation: you will never be on *thou* terms with him, and no one ever has been; I, as an artist, am repugnant to him, which I am proud of. Dryness, dryness, and he is capable of grinding us all into powder. He is bound to his land— not like our empty vessels, which fawn upon the people, saying: pour living water into us! But then, his task is easier, more comprehensible: all he has to do is turf out the Turks, and hey presto! But none of these qualities, thank God, appeal to women. There is no fascination, no *charm*; not like there is in you and me.'

'Why are you dragging me into it?' Bersenev muttered. 'And you're not right about the other things, either: you are not at all repugnant to him, and he is on *thou* terms with his compatriots... I know that.'

'That's a different matter! For them he is a hero; but I must admit, I imagine heroes differently; a hero does not need to be able to talk: a hero bellows like a bull; but then if he moves a horn the walls come tumbling down. And he himself doesn't need to know why he moves it, he simply moves it. Though, as a matter of fact, it's possible that in our times heroes of a different calibre are required.'

'Why does Insarov interest you so much?' Bersenev asked. 'Did you really come here at the double in order to describe his character to me?'

'I came here', Shubin began, 'because at home I was feeling very sad.'

'Well I never! You're not going to start crying again, are you?'

'That's right, laugh! I came here because I am in a fury with myself, because I am being gnawed by despair, vexation, jealousy...'

'Jealousy? Of whom?'

'Of you, of him, of everyone. I am tormented by the thought that if I had understood her earlier, if I had got down to brass tacks with a bit of skill... But what's the use of talking! The end of it will be that I'll just laugh, fool around, "make trouble", as she says, and then go off and hang myself.'

'Somehow I do not think you will,' Bersenev observed.

'On a night like this, of course, no; but let us live until autumn. On a night like this people also die, but from happiness. Ah, happiness! The shadow of each tree, as it extends across the road, seems to be whispering now: "I know where happiness is... Would you like me to tell you?" I was going to ask you if you'd like to take a walk, but you are now under the influence of prose. Sleep, and may you dream of mathematical diagrams! But my soul is being torn apart! You, gentlemen, see a man laughing, and that means, in your view, that he is at ease; you can prove to him that he is contradicting himself— in other words, he is not suffering... Never mind!'

Shubin quickly walked away from the window. 'Annushka!' Bersenev was on the point of calling after him, but restrained himself: Shubin really did look pale and upset. After a minute or two, Bersenev even fancied he heard sobbing: he stood up, opened the window; all was quiet; only somewhere in the distance someone, who must have been a passing muzhik in his cart, was slowly singing *Step' mozdokskaya*.*

XIII

DURING the first two weeks after his move to the vicinity of Kuntsevo, Insarov visited the Stakhovs no more than four or five times; Bersenev went to their house every other day. Yelena was always glad of his company, a lively and interesting conversation invariably sprang up between them, yet he would often return home looking sad. Shubin hardly showed his face; he devoted himself to his art with feverish activity: either stayed in his room in seclusion, rushing out from it now and then in a smock that was stained all over with clay, or spent the days in Moscow, where he had a studio where he received visits from the models and Italian moulders who were his friends and teachers. Yelena never once talked to Insarov as she would have liked to; when he was not there she prepared to ask him about many things, but when he arrived she had a bad conscience about her preparations. Insarov's composure itself embarrassed her: it seemed to her that she had no right to make him speak, and she decided to wait; all this notwithstanding, with each of his visits, no matter how insignificant were the words that passed between them, she felt that he attracted her more and more; but she had no occasion to be alone with him, and in order to become close to someone one must talk to him *tête-à-tête* at least once. She talked about him a great deal to Bersenev. Bersenev realized that Yelena's imagination had been struck by Insarov, and he was pleased that his friend had not failed, as Shubin had claimed; with ardour, right down to the least details, he told her all that he knew about him (often, when we want to make ourselves liked by another person, in conversation with him we extol our friends, almost never suspecting as we do so that we also praise ourselves), and only now and again, when Yelena's pale cheeks slightly blushed, and her eyes shone and widened, that unworthy sadness he had felt before would stab his heart.

One day, Bersenev arrived at the Stakhovs' at an unusual hour: eleven in the morning. Yelena came out into the reception room to meet him.

'Imagine,' he began with a forced smile. 'Our friend Insarov has gone missing.'

'Gone missing?' Yelena said.

'Yes. He walked off somewhere the day before yesterday, in the evening, and hasn't been seen since.'

'Did he not tell you where he was going?'

'No.'

Yelena sank onto a chair.

'He has probably set off for Moscow,' she said quietly, trying to appear indifferent and at the same time marvelling at the fact that she was trying to appear so.

'I don't think so,' Bersenev rejoined. 'He did not go alone.'

'With whom did he go?'

'The day before yesterday, before dinner, two men who must have been his compatriots presented themselves.'

'Bulgarians? How do you know that?'

'Because as far as I could hear, they were talking to him in a language I didn't know, though it was a Slavic one... Now, you always say there is very little that is mysterious about Insarov, Yelena Nikolayevna: but what could be more mysterious than that visit? Picture it: they went in to see him—and then they were shouting and arguing, with such wildness and malice... He was shouting, too.'

'He, too?'

'Yes. Shouting at them. They seemed to be making complaints to one another. And if you had seen those visitors! They had swarthy, broad-cheekboned, stupid faces, with hawk-like noses, each over forty, poorly dressed, covered in dust and sweat, artisans by the look of them—not artisans and not gentlemen... God knows what sort of men they were.'

'And he set off with them?'

'Yes. He gave them something to eat and walked off with them. The landlady told me—the two of them ate the whole of an enormous pot of kasha.* She said they gobbled it down in one go, like wolves.'

Yelena gave a slight, ironic smile.

'You'll see,' she said quietly. 'It will all be resolved in some very prosaic way.'

'God grant it! Only you are wrong to use that word. There is nothing prosaic about Insarov, even though Shubin says there is...'

'Shubin!' Yelena interrupted and shrugged her shoulders. 'But you must admit that those two gentlemen, gobbling their kasha...'

'Themistocles ate on the eve of the Battle of Salamis,'* Bersenev observed with a smile.

'Yes; but the next day there was a battle. Anyway, let me know when he returns,' Yelena added, and tried to vary the conversation, but it remained strained.

Zoya appeared and began to tiptoe about the room, thereby letting them know that Anna Vasilyevna had not yet woken up.

Bersenev left.

In the evening of the same day, a note from him was brought to Yelena. 'He has returned,' he wrote to her, 'sunburned and covered in dust right up to the eyebrows; but why and where he went, I do not know; perhaps you will find out?'

'Perhaps *I* will?' Yelena said in a whisper. 'Do you suppose that Insarov talks to me?'

XIV

ON the following day, just after one o'clock, Yelena stood in the garden facing a small enclosure in which she was raising two mongrel puppies. (The gardener had found them under the fence and had brought them to the young mistress, of whom the laundrywomen had told him that she loved 'all kinds of beasts and creatures'.) She looked into the enclosure, satisfied herself that the puppies were alive and that they had fresh straw spread under them, turned round, and very nearly uttered a scream: straight towards her, along the avenue, Insarov was approaching, alone.

'Hello,' he said quietly as he drew near to her, and took off his peaked cap. She noticed that he really had grown very sunburned in the last three days. 'I was going to come here with Andrei Petrovich, but he seems to have been delayed; so I set off without him. There is no one around in your house: they are all either asleep or out walking, and I came here.'

'You sound as though you are apologizing,' Yelena replied. 'You really do not need to. We are all very glad to see you... Let us sit down on the bench, in the shade.'

She sat down. Insarov took a place beside her.

'You have not been at home of late, I believe?' she began.

'No,' he replied, 'I have been away... Did Andrei Petrovich tell you?'

Insarov glanced at her, smiled and began to toy with his cap. In smiling, he blinked his eyes quickly and pushed his lips forward, which gave him a very good-natured look.

'Andrei Petrovich probably also told you that I went away with some... hooligans,' he said quietly, continuing to smile.

Yelena felt slightly uncomfortable, but sensed at once that with Insarov one must always speak the truth.

'Yes,' she said decisively.

'And what did you think of me?' he asked her suddenly.

Yelena raised her eyes to him.

'I thought,' she said quietly... 'I thought that you always know what you are doing, and that you are not capable of doing anything bad.'

'Well, thank you for that. You see. Yelena Nikolayevna,' he began, sitting closer to her in a way that was somehow trusting, 'there is a little family of us here; among us there are men of scant education; but all are firmly committed to the common cause. Unfortunately quarrels cannot be avoided, but they all know me and trust me; well, and so they asked me to go and settle a quarrel. I went.'

'Far from here?'

'I made a journey of sixty versts from here, to Troitsky Posad. There are also some of our men at the monastery there. At any rate, my efforts were not in vain: I sorted the matter out.'

'And was it hard for you?'

'Yes, it was. One of them was very stubborn. He didn't want to repay some money.'

'What? Was the quarrel about money?'

'Yes; and not very much money. What did you think it was about?'

'And you travelled sixty versts for a trivial matter like that? You lost three days?'

'It is not a trivial matter, Yelena Nikolayevna, when one's fellow countrymen are involved. To refuse to help then is a sin. I see that you don't even refuse puppies help, and I praise you for that. As for my losing time, it does not matter, I shall make it up later. Our time does not belong to us.'

'To whom does it belong, then?'

'Why, to all who have need of us. I have told you all this, off the cuff, as I value your opinion. I imagine that Andrei Petrovich surprised you!'

'You value my opinion,' Yelena said in an undertone... 'Why?'

Insarov smiled again.

'Because you are a good young lady, not a female aristocrat... that is all.'

A short silence ensued.

'Dmitry Nikanorovich,' Yelena said, 'do you know that this is the first time you have been so open with me?'

'How so? It seems to me that I have always told you everything that was in my thoughts.'

'No, this is the first time, and I am very glad about it, and I also want to be open with you. May I be?'

Insarov began to laugh, and said:

'You may.'

'I warn you that I am very inquisitive.'

'It does not matter, speak.'

'Andrei Petrovich has told me a great deal about your life, about your boyhood. I know about one circumstance, one dreadful circumstance... I know that after that, you made a visit to your motherland... For goodness sake, do not answer if my question appears indelicate, but I am tormented by a thought... Tell me, did you meet that man...'

Yelena caught her breath. She felt both ashamed and afraid of her own boldness. Insarov looked at her fixedly, slightly narrowing his eyes, and touching his chin with his fingers.

'Yelena Nikolayevna,' he began at last, and his voice was quieter than usual, which almost frightened Yelena. 'I know which man you referred to just now. No, I did not meet him, and thank God! I did not look for him. I did not look for him, not because I did not consider myself within my rights to kill him—I would have killed him entirely without qualm—but because there is no place for personal vengeance when what matters is a national, public revenge... or no, that word will not do... when what matters is the freeing of a nation. One would prevent the other. In the end he will not escape... He will not escape,' he repeated and shook his head.

Yelena looked at him sideways.

'Do you love your motherland very much?' she articulated, shyly.

'It is still too early to know,' he replied. 'When one of us dies for it, then one may say that he loved it.'

'If you were deprived of the possibility of returning to Bulgaria,' Yelena went on, 'would you find it very hard to be in Russia?'

Insarov lowered his gaze.

'I do not think I could endure that,' he said.

'Tell me,' Yelena began again, 'is it hard to learn Bulgarian?'

'Not in the slightest. A Russian should be ashamed not to know Bulgarian. A Russian should know all the Slavic dialects. Would you like me to bring you some Bulgarian books? You will see how easy it is. What songs we have! They are as good as the Serbian ones. But wait, I will translate one of them for you. It concerns... Do you know a little bit of our history, perhaps?'

'No, I don't know any of it,' Yelena answered.

'Wait, I will bring you a book. From it you will learn the principal facts, at least. Here is the song, then, listen... Though, as a matter of fact, I would do better to bring you a written translation. I am sure you will come to love us: you love all who are oppressed. If you only knew what a land of plenty ours is! And yet it is being trampled, tormented,'

he began again with an involuntary movement of his hand, and his
face grew dark, 'they have taken everything from us, everything: our
churches, our rights, our land; they drive us like a herd of cattle, the
filthy Turks, they slit our throats...'

'Dmity Nikanorovich!' Yelena exclaimed.

He paused.

'Forgive me. I cannot talk about this with composure. But you asked
me just now if I loved my motherland. What else is there on the earth
to love? Which alone is constant, above all doubts, impossible not to
believe in after God? And when that motherland is in need of you...
Take heed of this: the last muzhik, the last beggar in Bulgaria and
I—we want the very same thing. We all of us have one single aim.
Try to understand what certitude and strength that gives us!'

Insarov fell silent for a moment and again began to talk about
Bulgaria. Yelena listened to him with a devouring, profound, and sad
attention. When he had finished, she asked him again:

'So you would not stay in Russia, not on any account?'

And when he left, for a long time she watched him go. That day
he became another person for her. The man she followed with her
eyes was not the man she had met two hours before.

From that day onwards, he began to visit increasingly often, and
Bersenev increasingly seldom. Between the two friends something
strange established itself, something they both felt well aware of, but
to which they could not put a name, and were afraid to interpret. In
this way, a month went past.

XV

ANNA VASILYEVNA liked to stay at home, as the reader already knows;
but sometimes, quite unexpectedly, there was manifested in her an
overwhelming desire for something out of the ordinary, some astonishing *partie de plaisir*; and the more difficult this *partie de plaisir* was,
the more preparations and arrangements it required, the more Anna
Vasilyevna herself was made agitated by it, the more she enjoyed it.
If this mood assailed her in winter, she would have two or three boxes
reserved beside one another, gather all her acquaintances together,
and set off for the theatre, or even a masked ball; in summer she
would go out of town, somewhere as far away as possible. On the following day she would complain of a headache, groan, and lie in bed
all day, but after a month or two the thirst for something 'out of the
ordinary' would start to burn in her again. This was what happened
now. Someone mentioned the beauties of Tsaritsyno* in her presence, and Anna Vasilyevna suddenly announced that she intended
to go to Tsaritsyno the day after next. A state of alarm arose in
the house: an express messenger galloped off to Moscow to fetch
Nikolai Artemyevich; riding with him was the butler, to buy in wine,
pâté, and comestibles of every sort; Shubin was instructed to hire a
barouche (a carriage alone would not be sufficient) and to have relay
horses prepared; the boy servant twice ran over to Bersenev and
Insarov, and brought them two invitations written first in Russian,
and then in French by Zoya; as for Anna Vasilyevna, she fussed
over the young ladies' travelling costume. Meanwhile the *partie de
plaisir* very nearly came unstuck: Nikolai Artemyevich arrived from
Moscow in a sour and ill-disposed, *frondeur*-ish condition of spirit
(he was still in a huff with Avgustina Khristianovna) and, having
learned what was up, determinedly announced that he would not
go; that to gallop from Kuntsevo to Moscow and from Moscow to
Tsaritsyno, and from Tsaritsyno back to Moscow, and from Moscow
back to Kuntsevo was absurd—and, what was more, he added, only
when they could prove to him that it was any more fun to be at
one point on the terrestrial globe rather than at another point on it,
would he go. Of course, no one was able to prove this to him, and
Anna Vasilyevna, faced with the lack of a reliable cavalier, was on the

point of giving up the *partie de plaisir* when she remembered Uvar
Ivanovich and in her distress asked for him to be summoned from
his little room, saying: 'A drowning man clutches at a straw.' He was
woken; he came downstairs, listened in silence to Anna Vasilyevna's
plan, twiddled his fingers, and to general amazement, agreed. Anna
Vasilyevna gave him a kiss on the cheek and called him her darling;
Nikolai Artemyevich smiled contemptuously and said: *'Quelle bourde!'**
(he liked on occasion to use *chic* French expressions)—and next
morning, at seven o'clock, the carriage and barouche, laden to the
rooftops, rolled out of the courtyard of the Stakhovs' dacha. In the
carriage sat the ladies, a maid, and Bersenev; Insarov sat on the box;
while Uvar Ivanovich and Shubin rode in the barouche. Uvar Ivanovich
had himself, with a movement of a finger, beckoned to Shubin to join
him; he knew that Shubin would tease him all the way, but between
the 'power of the black earth' and the young artist there existed some
strange bond and quarrelsome candour. On this occasion, however,
Shubin left his fat friend in peace: he was silent, distracted, and
mild.

The sun already stood high in the cloudless azure when the carriages rolled up to the ruins of Tsaritsyno Palace, gloomy and menacing even at midday. The entire company got out onto the grass and
at once set off into the park. Yelena and Zoya, with Insarov, led the
way; behind them, with an expression of perfect happiness on her face,
Anna Vasilyevna stepped along arm in arm with Uvar Ivanovich. He
was panting and waddling from side to side, a new straw hat was
cutting into his forehead, and his feet were burning in his boots, but
he too was enjoying himself; Shubin and Bersenev brought up the
rear. 'We shall form the reserves, brother, like veterans,' Bersenev
whispered to Shubin. 'Bulgaria is out at the front now,' he added,
indicating Yelena with his eyebrows.

The weather was splendid. Everything around blossomed, hummed,
and sang, in the distance shone the water of the ponds; a festive,
radiant emotion seized the soul. 'Oh, how lovely! Oh, how lovely!'
Anna Vasilyevna kept repeating without cease; Uvar Ivanovich would
wag his head approvingly in reply to her ecstatic exclamations and
once even quietly ventured: 'What can one say?' From time to time
Yelena exchanged words with Insarov; Zoya held the brim of her broad
hat with two dainty fingers, coquettishly bringing her small feet, clad
in light-grey shoes with blunt toecaps, out from under her pink *barège*

dress, and looking now to the side and now to the rear. 'Aha!' Shubin exclaimed in an undertone, suddenly. 'Zoya Nikitishna seems to be looking round. I'm going to go over to her. Yelena Nikolayevna now despises me, but you, Andrei Petrovich, she respects, which comes to the same thing. I'm off now; I've had enough of moping. As for you, my friend, I advise you to engage in some botany; in your position that is the best thing you could devise; it will also do you good from an academic point of view. Farewell!' Shubin ran off to join Zoya, offered her his arm in a crook, and, saying: '*Ihre Hand, Madame*', snatched her along and set off with her. Yelena stopped, summoned Bersenev, and also took his arm, but continued to talk to Insarov. She was asking him the words in his language for lily of the valley, maple, oak, lime... ('Bulgaria!' poor Andrei Petrovich thought.)

Suddenly a cry was heard in front; all raised their heads; Shubin's cigar case flew into a bush, thrown by the hand of Zoya. 'Just you wait, I'll get even with you!' he exclaimed, clambered into the bush, found the cigar case there, and returned to Zoya; but hardly had he done so, when once again his cigar case flew across the path again. Some five times was this caper repeated, he laughing and threatening, Zoya merely smiling on the quiet and huddling up like a little cat. At last he caught her fingers and squeezed them so hard that she squealed and for a long time afterwards blew on her hand, pretending to be angry, while he hummed something into her ear.

'Aren't they naughty, the youngsters,' Anna Vasilyevna observed gaily to Uvar Ivanovich.

Uvar Ivanovich twiddled his fingers.

'What do you think of Zoya Nikitishna?' Bersenev said to Yelena.

'And what about Shubin?' she replied.

Meanwhile the whole company had approached the pavilion that is known by the name of Milovidova, and stopped in order to admire the spectacle of the Tsaritsyno ponds. They stretched one after the other for several versts; dense woods stood dark beyond them. The sward of grass that covered the entire slope of the hill down to the main pond imparted an extraordinarily vivid, emerald colour to the water. Nowhere, not even by the bank, did a wave swell or foam gleam white; not even a ripple traversed the smooth and even surface. It was as though a solidified mass of glass had heavily and radiantly settled in an enormous font, and the sky had sunk to the bottom of it, and the curly trees were motionlessly looking at themselves in its transparent

bosom. Everyone admired the view, long and in silence; even Shubin
piped down, even Zoya fell to reflection. At last they all expressed a
unanimous wish to go out on the water. Shubin, Insarov, and Bersenev
chased one another down the grass. They found a large painted boat;
found two oarsmen and summoned the ladies. The ladies came down
to them; Uvar Ivanovich cautiously descended after the ladies. As he
entered the boat, there was much laughter. 'Take care, *barin*, do not
drown us,' one of the oarsmen observed, a young, snub-nosed lad in
an Alexandrian shirt.* 'Now then, jackanapes!' Uvar Ivanovich said.
The boat cast off. The young men made a move to take to the oars,
but it turned out that of them only Insarov knew how to row. Shubin
proposed that they sing a Russian song in chorus, and struck up: 'Down
Mother Volga...' Bersenev, Zoya, and even Anna Vasilyevna caught
up the refrain (Insarov could not sing), but disunion developed; at
the third line the singers lost their thread, and Bersenev alone tried
to continue in a bass voice: 'Nothing in the waves is seen'—but also
soon became confused. The oarsmen exchanged winks and grinned without saying anything. 'Well?' Shubin addressed them. 'Is it plain that
the ladies and gentlemen don't know how to sing?' The fellow in the
Alexandrian shirt merely shook his head. 'Then, wait, snub-nose,'
Shubin retorted. 'Right, we'll show you. Zoya Nikitishna, sing us
Niedermeyer's "Le lac".* Stop rowing!' The wet oars rose into the air,
like wings, and hung there motionless, resonantly shedding drops of
water; the boat floated a little further and stopped, beginning to spin
round slightly on the water, like a swan. Zoya struck a pose... '*Allons!*'
Anna Vasilyevna said, affectionately... Zoya threw off her hat and began
to sing: '*O lac! l'année à peine a fini sa carrière...*'*

Her small but pure little voice fairly whirled across the mirror of the
pond; far away in the woods each word echoed; it was as though there,
too, someone was singing in a clear and mysterious, but inhuman,
unearthly voice. When Zoya had finished, a loud 'bravo' came from one
of the bank pavilions and out of it popped several red-faced Germans
who had come to Tsaritsyno to do some carousing. Some of them wore
no coats, or neckties, or even waistcoats, and cried '*bis!*' so violently
that Anna Vasilyevna told the oarsmen to row to the other end of the
pond as quickly as possible. Before the boat touched bank, however,
Uvar Ivanovich again succeeded in astonishing his friends: having
noticed that in one part of the woods the echo reproduced each sound
with especial clarity, he suddenly began to call like a quail. At first

they all gave a start, but then at once felt genuine delight, for Uvar Ivanovich's call was very true and lifelike. This encouraged him, and he tried to miaow like a cat; but his miaowing was not of the same quality; he called a quail again, looked at them all, and fell silent. Shubin rushed to kiss him; he pushed Shubin away. At that moment, the boat moored, and the whole company disembarked on the bank.

In the meantime the coachman, with the lackey and the maid-servant, had brought the baskets from the carriage and prepared a dinner on the grass beneath the old lime trees. They all found places around the spread-out tablecloth and began to tuck in to the pâté and other comestibles. All had excellent appetites, but Anna Vasilyevna would now and then play the part of the hostess, trying to persuade her guests to eat just a little more and asserting that in the open air this was very good for the health; she addressed one such homily to Uvar Ivanovich himself. 'Don't worry,' he muttered to her with his mouth stuffed full. 'The Lord has given us such a glorious day!' she kept repeating ceaselessly. One could hardly recognize her: she seemed to have grown twenty years younger. Bersenev noticed this. 'Yes, yes,' she said. 'I too was something in my day: you would not have turned up your nose at me.' Shubin had placed himself next to Zoya, and ceaselessly kept pouring wine for her; she would refuse, he would try to persuade her, in the end drink the glass himself, and then again try to make her accept one; he also assured her that he wanted to lean his head on her knees; she would on no account permit him 'such a great liberty'. Yelena seemed more serious than the rest of them, but in her heart there was a wonderful calm, of a kind she had long not experienced. She felt infinitely well-disposed, and wanted to have beside her not only Insarov, but Bersenev, too... Andrei Petrovich dimly realized what this meant, and furtively sighed.

The hours flew; the evening drew near. Anna Vasilyevna was suddenly all of a flutter. 'Oh, goodness, how late it is,' she said. 'We have lived and drunk our fill, gentlemen; now it is time to wipe our beards.' She began to bustle about, and so did they all, rose and walked in the direction of the palace, where the carriages were. As they passed the ponds, they all stopped in order to admire Tsaritsyno one last time. Everywhere burned bright, pre-evening colours; the sky glowed, the leaves shone with iridescence, stirred by the breeze that had risen; like molten gold streamed the distant waters; sharply distinguished from the dark greenness of the trees were the reddish turrets and pavilions

scattered here and there about the park. 'Farewell, Tsaritsyno, we shall
not forget our visit of today!' Anna Vasilyevna said softly... But at
that moment, and as if in confirmation of her last words, a strange
event took place, one that really was not all that easy to forget.

And namely: no sooner had Anna Vasilyevna sent her farewell greeting to Tsaritsyno, than suddenly, a few paces from her, behind a tall
lilac bush, disorderly exclamations, guffawing, and shouts broke out
—and a whole throng of tousle-haired men, those same devotees of
singing who had so zealously applauded Zoya, came pouring out onto
the path. The gentleman devotees appeared to be thoroughly one over
the eight. At the sight of the ladies, they stopped; but one of them,
enormous in stature, with a bull-like neck and inflamed, bull-like eyes,
detached himself from his companions and, awkwardly bowing and
swaying as he walked, approached Anna Vasilyevna, who was petrified
with fright.

'*Bonjour*, madame,' he said in a hoarse voice. 'How is your health?'
Anna Vasilyevna recoiled.

'But why,' the giant continued in his poor Russian, 'did you not
want to sing *bis*, when our company cried *bis*, and *bravo*, and *foro*?'

'Yes, yes, why?' voices said from the ranks of the company.

Insarov was about to step forward, but Shubin stopped him and
shielded Anna Vasilyevna himself.

'Permit me,' he began, 'respected stranger, to express to you the
unfeigned wonder into which you plunge us by your actions. You,
as far as I can judge, belong to the Saxon branch of the Caucasian
tribe; consequently, we must assume in you a knowledge of the social
proprieties, yet here you address a lady to whom you have not been
introduced... Pleased be assured that at another time I in particular
would be very glad to make your closer acquaintance, for I observe
in you such a phenomenal development of the biceps, triceps, and
deltoid muscles that I, as a sculptor, would consider it a genuine stroke
of good fortune to have you as my model; but on this occasion, please
leave us in peace.'

The 'respected stranger' heard out Shubin's speech, his head contemptuously twisted to one side, his hands on his hips.

'I have nothing understood of what you say,' he said quietly at last.
'You think perhaps I am a cobbler or a watchmaker? Eh! I am *offizier*,
I am official, yes.'

'I do not doubt it,' Shubin began.

'And this is what I say,' the stranger continued, sweeping him aside with his powerful arm like a branch from a road, 'I say: why did you not sing *bis* when we shouted *bis*? And now I shall immediately, this moment, go away, only it's necessary for this *Fräulein*, not this madame, not, that is not necessary, but this one or that one (he pointed to Yelena and Zoya), to give me *einen Kuss*, as we say in German, a little kiss, yes: well? It is nothing.'

'Nothing, *einen Kuss*, it is nothing,' voices said from the ranks of the company again.

'*Ih! der Sakramenter!*' choking with laughter, one by-now completely befuddled German said.

Zoya caught at Insarov's arm, but he tore himself away from her and stood directly in front of the large-bodied jackanapes.

'Be so good as to go away,' he said to him in a voice not loud, but sharp.

The German guffawed heavily.

'Go away? Now I like that! May I not also come out for a walk? Go away? Why away?'

'Because you have had the audacity to importune a lady,' Insarov said, and suddenly turned pale, 'because you are drunk.'

'What? I drunk? Do you hear? *Hören Sie das, Herr Provisor?* I am *offizier*, and he dares... Now I demand *Satisfaction*! *Einen Kuss will ich!*'

'If you take one more step...' Insarov began.

'Well? And what then?'

'I will throw you into the water.'

'Into the water? *Herr Je*... Is that all? Well, let us see, that is very interesting, into the water...'

The *offizier* raised his arms and moved forward, but suddenly something extraordinary occurred: he grunted, the whole of his enormous figure swayed and rose from the ground, his legs kicked in the air and, before the ladies had time to scream, before anyone was able to fathom how it could happen, the *offizier*, with all his bulk, fell into the pond with a heavy splash, and at once disappeared below the watery spray.

'Aie!' the ladies squealed in consort.

'*Mein Gott!*' voices were heard to say from the other direction.

A minute went by... and then a round head, plastered all over with wet hair, appeared above the water; it emitted bubbles, that head; two hands convulsively floundered next to its lips...

'He'll drown, rescue him, rescue him!' Anna Vasilyevna cried to Insarov, who stood on the bank, his legs apart, and breathing deeply.

'He'll swim out,' he said with a contemptuous and unpitying carelessness. 'Come along,' he added, taking Anna Vasilyevna by the arm. 'Come along, Uvar Ivanovich, Yelena Nikolayevna.'

'Ah... ah... oh... oh...' came the howl, just then, of the unfortunate German, who had managed to grasp hold of the reeds by the bank.

They all set off after Insarov, and all had to pass the 'company' itself. But, deprived of their chief, the revellers grew quiet and did not utter a single word; only one, the bravest of them, muttered, shaking his head: 'Well, that is really... that is God only knows what... after that'; and another even removed his hat. Insarov looked very menacing to them, and no wonder: something malevolent, something dangerous had appeared on his face. The Germans rushed to haul their comrade out, and he, as soon as he found himself on dry land, began tearfully to curse and shout after those 'Russian rascals' that he was going to complain, that he would go and see his excellency Count von Kieseritz himself...

But the 'Russian rascals' paid no attention to his exclamations and hurried as fast as possible towards the palace. All were silent as they walked through the grounds, and only Anna Vasilyevna moaned slightly. But once they drew near to the carriages, they stopped, and an irrepressible, unabating laughter, like that of Homer's denizens of heaven,* rose among them. First Shubin broke into a shriek, like a madman's, Bersenev was next, with a rattle like dried peas, then Zoya scattered her delicate pearls, Anna Vasilyevna also suddenly began to shake uncontrollably, even Yelena could not help smiling, and at last not even Insarov could hold his ground. But louder than all, and longer than all, and more violent than all, was the guffawing of Uvar Ivanovich: he laughed until his sides split, until he sneezed and choked. He would calm down a little, and say through his tears: 'I... thought... what's that bang?... and that was him... flat on his face...' And together with the last, convulsively forced-out word, a fresh explosion of laughter would shake his entire constitution. Zoya would egg him on more. 'I saw him with his legs in the air...' she would say. 'Yes, yes,' Uvar Ivanovich would chime in, 'his legs, his legs... and then bang! And he fell in f-l-at on his face!...' 'But how did he ever contrive to do it? After all, the German was three times his size?' Zoya asked. 'I'll tell you how,' Uvar Ivanovich replied, drying his eyes, 'I saw it: he put one arm round his back, tripped him up and then bang! I heard it: what's that?... and he fell in, flat on his face...'

The carriages had long ago set off on their way, the palace of Tsaritsyno was lost from view, but Uvar Ivanovich still could not get over it. Shubin, who once again rode with him in the barouche, put him to shame at last.

Insarov, on the other hand, had a bad conscience. He sat in the carriage opposite Yelena (Bersenev was lodged atop the box) and was silent; she also was silent. He thought that she was blaming him; but she was not. At the initial moment she had been very frightened; after that, she had been struck by the expression of his face; and after that, she had thought about it all. It was not completely clear to her what she had thought about. The feeling she had experienced in the course of the day had vanished: that she was aware of; but it had been replaced by something else, which for the present she did not understand. The *partie de plaisir* had lasted too long: the evening had imperceptibly passed into night. The carriage raced swiftly now next to ripening cornfields, where the air was sultry and fragrant and smelt of grain, now next to broad meadows, and their sudden coolness struck their faces like a gentle billow. The sky seemed to smoke at the edges. At last the moon came out, lustreless and red. Anna Vasilyevna drowsed; Zoya leaned out of the window and looked at the road. At last it occurred to Yelena that she had not spoken to Insarov for more than an hour. She addressed him with an insignificant question; he replied to her at once, with joy. Indistinct sounds began to float on the air; it was as if thousands of voices were talking far away: Moscow raced towards them. Ahead of them tiny lights began to flicker; there were more and more of them; at last, stones began to knock beneath the wheels. Anna Vasilyevna woke up; everyone in the carriage began to talk, although no one could hear what it was about: so violently did the roadway thunder beneath the two carriages and the horses' thirty-two hooves. Long and boring did the ride from Moscow to Kuntsevo seem; all slept or were silent, nestling their heads into various corners; Yelena alone did not close her eyes: she had them fixed on the dark figure of Insarov. Shubin was assailed by sadness: the breeze blew in his face and irritated him; he muffled himself in the collar of his greatcoat and very nearly began to cry. Uvar Ivanovich kept up a contented snoring, swaying to right and to left. At last the carriages stopped.

Two lackeys helped Anna Vasilyevna out; she went quite to pieces and, in parting from her travelling companions, declared to them that she was scarcely still alive; they began to thank her, but she could only keep saying: 'Scarcely alive.' Yelena shook hands with Insarov for the first time and for a long time sat at the window without undressing; while Shubin seized the moment to whisper to Bersenev, as he left:

'One can't say he's not a hero: he throws drunken Germans in the water!'

'That's more than you did, anyway,' Bersenev retorted, and set off home with Insarov.

Dawn was already breaking in the sky as the two friends returned to their quarters. The sun was not yet rising, but a chill had begun to stir, a grey dew covered the grass, and the first larks chimed high upon high in the half-dusky vault of the air, from where, like a solitary eye, the large last star looked down.

XVI

SOON after making Insarov's acquaintance, Yelena began (for the fifth or sixth time) to keep a diary. Here are some fragments from it:

June... Andrei Petrovich brings me books, but I cannot read them. To admit this to him makes me feel ashamed; to return the books to him, to lie, to say that I have read them—I don't want to do that. I think it would upset him. He takes note of everything about me. I think he is very attached to me. He is a very good man, Andrei Petrovich.

. . . What do I want? Why is my heart so heavy, so languid? Why do I look with envy at the passing birds? I think I would like to fly with them, fly—where, I do not know, only far, far away from here. And is it not sinful, this desire? Here I have a mother, a father, a family. Do I not love them? No, I do not love them as I would like to love them. I am afraid to say it aloud, but it is true. Perhaps I am a great sinner; perhaps I feel so sad because I have no peace. A hand lies on me, and is choking me. As though I were in a prison, and the walls were about to topple down on me at any moment. But why do other people not feel this? Whom shall I love, if I am cold to my own? It seems that dear Papa is right: he reproaches me for loving only dogs and cats. I must give some thought to that. I do not pray enough; one must pray... Yet I think I would be capable of love!

. . . I still feel afraid in Mr Insarov's presence. I do not know why; after all, I am not very young, and he is so straightforward and kind. Sometimes his face looks very serious. He is probably not much interested in us. I can feel that, and am almost ashamed to take up his time. Andrei Petrovich is another matter. I could chatter to him all day. But he always talks about Insarov. And what terrible details! I dreamed of him last night with a dagger in his hand. And he seemed to be saying to me: 'I shall kill you and kill myself.' What nonsense!

. . . Oh, if only someone would say to me: this is what you must do! To be good—that is not enough; to do good... yes; that is the main thing in life. But how to do good? Oh, if only I could master myself! I don't understand why I so often think about Mr Insarov. When he comes and sits and listens attentively, but makes no effort himself, and does not make a fuss, I look at him, and I like it—but that is all;

but when he leaves, I keep remembering his words and feel annoyed with myself and even become upset... I myself do not know why. (He speaks French badly, and is not ashamed—that appeals to me.) As a matter of fact, though, I always think a great deal about new people. While talking with him, I suddenly remembered our butler, Vasily, who hauled a one-legged old man out of a burning cottage and himself almost perished. Papa called him a plucky fellow, Mama gave him five roubles, and I felt I wanted to bow down at his feet. He, too, had a straightforward, even stupid face, and later he became a drunkard.

   . . . Today I gave a half-copeck to a beggar-woman, and she said to me: why are you so sad? And I had no idea that I looked so sad. I think it is because I am alone, always alone, with all my goodness, with all my badness. There is no one to whom I can reach out a hand. Whoever approaches me, I do not want; whoever I would like... he goes past.

   . . . I do not know what is wrong with me today; my head is confused, I am ready to fall on my knees and ask and beg for mercy. I do not know who is doing it, or how, but it is as though I were being killed, and inwardly I cry out and rebel; I weep and cannot be silent... My God, my God! curb in me these outbursts! You alone can do it, all else is powerless: neither my paltry alms-giving, nor my studies—nothing, nothing can help me. I wish I could go away somewhere and work as a serving-maid, truly I do: I would find it easier.

   What is the purpose of youth, what is the purpose of my life, why do I have a soul, what is all this for?

   . . . Insarov, Mr Insarov—truly, I do not know what to write—continues to occupy me. I want to know what he has there, in his soul. He seems so open, so accessible, but I cannot see anything. Sometimes he looks at me with eyes that are somehow searching... or is that merely my imagination? Paul keeps teasing me—I am angry with Paul. What does he want? He is in love with me... and I do not want his love. He is in love with Zoya, too. I am unfair to him; yesterday he told me I did not know how to be unfair by half measures... that is true. It is very bad.

   Oh, I feel that one needs unhappiness, or poverty, or illness, otherwise one gives oneself airs.

   . . . Why did Andrei Petrovich tell me about those two Bulgarians today. He told me about them as if with some intention. What business is Mr Insarov of mine? I am angry with Andrei Petrovich.

. . . I take my pen and do not know how to start. How unexpected it was when he began to talk to me in the garden today! How affectionate and trusting he was! How quickly it happened! As if we were old, old friends, and had only just recognized each other. How is it possible that until now I did not understand him? How close he is to me now! And what is surprising is that: I have become much calmer now. I find it comical: yesterday I was angry with Andrei Petrovich, and with him, even called him *Mr Insarov*, yet today... Here at last is an upright man, a man one can rely on. This one does not lie; he is the first man I have met who does not lie; all the rest of them lie, everyone lies. Andrei Petrovich, dear, good man, what am I doing insulting you? No! Andrei Petrovich is, perhaps, more learned than him, even, perhaps, more intelligent... But, I don't know what it is, in front of him he seems such a little boy. When *he* talks about his motherland, he grows and grows, and his face becomes handsome, and his voice like steel, and no, I think that then there is no one in the world before whom he would lower his eyes. And he does not only talk—he has acted and will act. I shall ask him about it... How suddenly he turned to me and smiled at me!... Only brothers smile like that. Oh, how pleased I am! When he came to see us the first time, I never thought we would so soon be friends. And now I am even glad that I was indifferent the first time... Indifferent! Am I really not indifferent now?

. . . It is a long time since I have felt such inner calm. It is so quiet inside me, so quiet. And there is no point in writing things down. I see him frequently, and that is all. What more can one write?

. . . Paul has shut himself away; Andrei Petrovich has begun to visit less frequently... poor fellow! I think he... But that can never be. I like talking to Andrei Petrovich: never a word about himself, always about something practical and useful. Not like Shubin. Shubin is decorative, like a butterfly, and he admires his own decorativeness; butterflies do not do that. As a matter of fact, both Shubin and Andrei Petrovich... I know what I want to say.

. . . *He* enjoys visiting us, I can see that. But why? What has he found in me? It is true that we have similar tastes: he and I, we are neither of us fond of verses, and neither of us is a good judge of art. But how much better he is than me. He is calm, while I am in perpetual unease; he has a road, he has a goal—but I, where am I bound? Where is my nest? He is calm, but all his thoughts are far away. The time will come when he will leave us all for ever, return to his home, down there, across the sea. What of it? God speed him on his way! But I shall always be glad that I got to know him while he was here.

Why is he not Russian? No, he could never be Russian.

Mama likes him, too; she says: a modest man. Kind Mama! She does not understand him. Paul says nothing: he has realized that I find his hints unpleasant, but he is jealous of him. The spiteful boy! And what right has he? Have I ever...

This is all nonsense! Why does all this come into my head?

. . . Yet it is strange, is it not, that so far, now at the age of twenty, I have never loved anyone? I think that D. (I shall call him D., I like that name: Dmitry) has such serenity of soul because he has completely devoted himself to his cause, his dream. Why should he ever be uneasy? Someone who has completely devoted himself... completely... completely... nothing touches him, he is no longer answerable for anything. It is not *I* who wills: *it* wills. I note by the way, that we like the same flowers, he and I. I picked a rose today. One petal fell off, and he picked it up... I gave him the whole rose.

For some time now I have been having strange dreams. What can that mean, I wonder?

. . . D. comes to see us often. Yesterday he stayed all evening. He wants to teach me Bulgarian. I like being with him, it's like being at home. Better than being at home.

. . . The days are flying... And I like it, and feel terrified for some reason, and want to thank God, and am not far from tears. Oh, warm, radiant days!

. . . I still feel light and easy, as before and only sometimes, sometimes slightly sad. I am happy. Am I happy?

. . . I shall not forget yesterday's outing for a long time. What strange, new, terrible impressions! When he suddenly took hold of that giant and hurled him into the water, like a ball, I was not frightened... but he frightened me. And afterwards—how ominous a face, almost savage! When he said: 'He'll swim out'! That made my heart turn over. So it must be that I have not understood him. And later, when everyone was laughing, when I was laughing, how sorry I was for him! He was ashamed, I could feel that, and he was ashamed in my presence. He told me that later in the carriage, in the dark, when I was trying to see him and was afraid of him. Yes, he is not to be trifled with, and he knows how to intervene in a situation. But why that anger, those trembling lips, that venom in his eyes? Or can it not be otherwise, perhaps? One cannot be a man, a fighter, and remain meek and mild? 'Life is a crude business,' he said to me recently. I repeated that remark to Andrei Petrovich; he did not agree with D. Which of them is right? Yet how that day began! How I enjoyed walking beside him, even though in silence... But I am glad it happened. Apparently it was meant to.

. . . Again unease... I am not quite well.

. . . All these recent days I have not written in this notebook, because I have not felt like writing. I felt that whatever I wrote, it would not be what was in my soul... And what is in my soul? I had a long conversation with him, which revealed many things to me. He told me about his plans (incidentally, now I know where he got that scar on his cheek... My God! When I think that was condemned to death, that he only just escaped, that he was wounded...). He has presentiments of war, and is glad about it. And yet, in spite of all this, I have never seen D. so sad. What can he... he!... be so sad about? Papa came back from town, found us both together, and looked at us rather strangely. Andrei Petrovich arrived; I noticed that he has become very thin and pale. He reproached me, saying I was dealing with Shubin in too cold and offhand a manner. Yet I had completely forgotten about Paul. When I see him, I shall try to expiate my guilt. I have no time for him now... nor for anyone in the world. Andrei Petrovich spoke to me with a kind of compassion. What is the meaning of all this? Why is it so dark around me and in me? It seems to me that around me and in me something mysterious is taking place, that I must find the word...

. . . I did not sleep last night, I have a headache. What is the point of writing? Today he left so soon, and I wanted to talk to him... It is as if he were avoiding me. Yes, he is avoiding me.

. . . The word is found, light has illumined me! O Lord! Take pity on me... I am in love!

XVII

THAT same day, as Yelena wrote this last, fateful entry in her diary, Insarov sat in Bersenev's room, and Bersenev stood before him with an expression of bewilderment on his face. Insarov had just told him of his intention to move back to Moscow the very next day.

'For pity's sake!' Bersenev exclaimed. 'The most beautiful time of the year is beginning now. What are you going to do in Moscow? Why this sudden decision? Or have you received some news?'

'I have received no news,' Insarov rejoined, 'but, for reasons of my own, I cannot stay here.'

'But how is it possible...'

'Andrei Petrovich,' Insarov said, 'kindly do not insist, I beg you. It is hard for me to part from you, but there is nothing for it.'

Bersenev looked at him fixedly.

'I know', he said, 'that you will not be persuaded. So the matter is decided?'

'Completely decided,' Insarov replied, stood up, and walked away.

Bersenev paced about the room, took his hat, and set off for the Stakhovs'.

'You have something to tell me,' Yelena said to him as soon as they were alone together.

'Yes; how did you guess?'

'It doesn't matter. Tell me, what is it?'

Bersenev informed her of Insarov's decision.

Yelena turned pale.

'What is the meaning of it?' she articulated at last, with difficulty.

'You know', Bersenev said quietly, 'that Dmitry Nikanorovich does not like to give explanations for his actions. But I think... Let us sit down, Yelena Nikolayevna, you do not seem quite well... I believe that I can guess what the real reason for this sudden departure is.'

'What, what is the reason?' Yelena repeated, tightly, without being aware of it, clutching Bersenev's hand in hers, which now was cold.

'Look, you see,' Bersenev began with a sad smile, 'how should I explain this to you?' In order to do so, I shall have to return to the spring of this year, to the time when I got to know Insarov more closely. I met him then, at the house of one of my relatives; this relative had a daughter, a very pretty one. It seemed to me that Insarov was not indifferent to her, and I told him that. He began to laugh and replied to me that I was wrong, that his heart had not suffered, but that he would go away immediately if anything like that ever happened to him, as he did not want—these were his own words—to betray his cause and his duty for the satisfaction of a personal emotion. 'I am a Bulgarian,' he said, 'and I do not need the love of a Russian...'

'Well... and so now what... do you...' Yelena said in a whisper, involuntarily turning her head like a person expecting a blow, but still not releasing Bersenev's hand from her grasp.

'I think,' he said quietly, also lowering his voice, 'I think that now what then I wrongly presupposed has taken place.'

'In other words... you think... do not torment me!' the words broke suddenly from Yelena.

'I think,' Bersenev continued hurriedly, 'that Insarov has fallen in love with a Russian girl, and, in accordance with his promise, has decided to flee.'

Yelena clutched his hand even tighter, and inclined her head even lower, as though in an endeavour to hide from a stranger's gaze the blush of shame that suddenly spilled like flame across the whole of her face and neck.

'Andrei Petrovich, you are as kind as an angel,' she said, 'but will he come to say farewell, do you suppose?'

'Yes, I should think so, certainly he'll come, because he will not want to leave...'

'Tell him, tell him that...'

But at this point the unhappy girl could not hold out any longer: tears gushed from her eyes, and she ran out of the room.

'So she loves him that much,' Bersenev thought, as he slowly returned home. 'I did not expect that; I did not expect it already to be so strong. I am kind, she says,' he continued his reflections... 'Who can say what feelings and what promptings led me to tell Yelena all this? But it was not from kindness, not from kindness. All merely the accursed desire to find out whether the dagger was really in the wound. I ought to be pleased—they love each other, and I helped them... "A future mediator between science and the Russian public," Shubin calls me; apparently it was written into my birthright to be a mediator. But what if I am wrong? No, I am not wrong...'

Andrei Petrovich felt bitter, and could not concentrate on Raumer.

The next day, at about two, Insarov presented himself at the Stakhovs'. As if on purpose, at that time a female guest sat in Anna Vasilyevna's drawing-room, the wife of the local priest who lived nearby, a very good and honourable woman, who had had a slightly unpleasant encounter with the police because she had conceived the idea of bathing, in the full heat of the day, in a pond near a road along which some important general's family used to drive. The presence of a stranger was at first rather agreeable to Yelena, whose face lost its last drop of colour as soon as she heard Insarov's footsteps; but her heart froze at the thought that he might say farewell without having spoken to her alone. As for him, he seemed embarrassed, and avoided her gaze. 'Is he really going to say farewell now?' thought Yelena. Indeed, Insarov was about to address Anna Vasilyevna; Yelena hastily stood up and beckoned him to one side, to the window. The priest's wife was astonished, and tried to turn away; but so tight were her corsets, that they made a creaking sound with every movement she made. She remained where she was.

'Listen,' Yelena said quickly, 'I know why you have come; Andrei Petrovich told me of your intention, but I beg you, I implore you not to take your farewell of us today, but to come here tomorrow rather early, at about eleven. There are a couple things I want to tell you.'

Insarov silently inclined his head.

'I shall not detain you... Do you promise me?'

Insarov bowed again, but said nothing.

'Lenochka, come here,' Anna Vasilyevna said quietly. 'Look what a splendid handbag your mother has.'

'I made it myself,' the priest's wife remarked.

Yelena came away from the window.

Insarov stayed at the Stakhovs' no more than a quarter of an hour. Yelena watched him on the sly. He shifted from one foot to the other, was unsure where to look, as before, and left in a rather strange and sudden manner; he seemed to vanish.

That day passed slowly for Yelena; even more slowly did the long, long night extend. Now Yelena sat on the bed, hugging her knees and putting her head on them, now went to the window, putting her hot forehead to the cold glass, thinking and thinking, thinking the same thoughts to the point of exhaustion. Her heart had either turned to stone or vanished from her breast; she could not feel it, but the veins throbbed painfully in her head, her hair burned, and her lips were dry. 'He will come... he has not said farewell to Mamma... he will not deceive me... Is what Andrei Petrovich said really true?... He did not promise to come in so many words... Have I really parted from him for ever?' Such were the thoughts that would not leave her... truly, would not leave her: they did not arrive, did not return —they constantly swirled within her, like a mist. 'He loves me!'— suddenly flared within her whole being, and she stared fixedly into the darkness; a secret smile seen by no one parted her lips... but she at once shook her head, put her folded hands to the back of her neck again, and again, like a mist, the earlier thoughts swirled within her. Before morning she undressed and went to bed, but could not fall asleep. The sun's first fiery rays struck her room... 'Oh, if he loves me!' she exclaimed suddenly and, unabashed by the light that illumined her, opened her arms...

She got up, dressed, went downstairs. No one was yet awake in the house. She went into the garden; but in the garden it was so quiet, and green, and fresh, so trustingly did the birds chirrup, so joyfully did the flowers peep out, that she felt frightened. 'Oh!' she thought, 'if that is true, there is not a single blade of grass more happy than I, but is it true?' She returned to her room and, so as to kill the time somehow, began to change her dress. But everything fell or slipped out of her hands, and she was still sitting half-dressed before her dressing-table mirror when she heard the call to morning tea. She went downstairs; her mother noticed her pallor, but merely said: 'How interesting you look today,'—and, glancing at her, added: 'That dress suits you very well; you must always put it on when you want to appeal to someone.' Yelena made no reply and sat down in a corner. Meanwhile it struck nine; there were only two hours left until eleven. Yelena sat down with a book; then she took up her sewing, then the book again; then she vowed to herself to walk along a certain avenue a hundred times, and did so, a hundred times; then for a long time she watched Anna Vasilyevna play patience... and glanced at her watch: it was not yet ten. Shubin arrived in the drawing-room. She tried to talk to him and apologized to him, without knowing what for... Her every word caused her not so much effort as an extreme sense of bewilderment. Shubin leaned over her. She expected mockery, raised her eyes, and saw before her his sad and friendly face... She smiled at that face. Shubin smiled back at her, and quietly went out. She wanted to call him back, but could not immediately remember his name. At last it struck eleven. She began to wait, wait, wait and listen. Now she could no longer do anything; she had even ceased to think. Her heart came to life again and began to beat louder, louder, and it was a strange thing: the time seemed to race more quickly. Quarter of an hour passed, then half an hour, then it seemed to her that several more minutes passed, and suddenly she gave a start: the clock struck not twelve, but one. 'He will not come, he is leaving without saying farewell...' This thought, together with her blood, truly rushed into her head. She felt her breath catch, felt she was about to break into sobs... She ran up to her room and fell on her bed, face-down on folded arms.

For half an hour she lay there motionless; through her fingers, tears trickled on to the pillow. She suddenly raised herself, and sat up; something strange was taking place within her: her face changed, of their own accord her moist eyes dried and began to shine, her eyebrows moved together, her lips tightened. Another half-hour passed. For the last time, Yelena strained an ear in case the familiar voice might come to greet her, stood up, put on her hat and gloves, threw her cape on her shoulders, and slipping out of the house unnoticed, walked with agile steps along the road that led to Bersenev's lodgings.

XVIII

YELENA walked with her head lowered and her eyes directed motionlessly forward. She did not fear anything, she did not weigh the pros and cons of anything; she wanted to see Insarov one more time. She walked, not noticing that the sun had long ago gone in, obscured by heavy black clouds, that the wind was soughing fitfully in the trees and making her dress swirl, that dust rose suddenly and rushed in columns along the road... Large drops of rain began to fall, and she did not notice it, either; but it grew ever heavier and more intense, lightning flashed, thunder rolled. Yelena stopped and looked around... To her good fortune, not far from the place where the storm had overtaken her, there was a dilapidated and derelict roadside chapel above a ruined well. She ran to it and went in under the low roof. The rain was lashing down in torrents; the sky was completely overcast. With a silent sense of despair, Yelena gazed at the close mesh of swiftly falling drops. Her last hope of seeing Insarov disappeared. An old beggar-woman came into the chapel, shook herself, and said with a bow: 'Because of the rain, kind mother,'—and, sighing and groaning, sat down on the ledge beside the well. Yelena lowered her hand into her pocket: the old woman noticed this movement, and her face, wrinkled and yellow, though once it had been attractive, came to life. 'Thank you, dear lady who tends and feeds us,' she began. Yelena had no purse in her pocket, but the old woman was already stretching out her hand...

'I have no money with me, grandmother,' said Yelena, 'but here, take this, it may be of some use for something.'

She gave the old woman her handkerchief.

'O-oh, my pretty one,' the beggar-woman said, 'but what would I be doing with your hanky? Perhaps I could give it to my granddaughter when she goes to be wed. May the Lord send you blessings for your kindness!'

A peal of thunder rolled.

'Lord Jesus Christ,' the old woman muttered, and crossed herself three times. 'Yes, I thought so, I've seen you before,' she added after a short while. 'Yes, you were the one who gave me Christian alms, weren't you?'

Yelena looked closely at the old woman, and recognized her.

'Yes, grandmother,' she replied. 'And you asked me why I was so sad.'

'That's right, my little pigeon, that's right. I was sure I knew who you were. And even now you are living in sorrow. And your hanky here is wet, I think, with tears. Oh, you young things, you all have the same sadness, a lot of unhappiness!'

'What sadness is that, grandmother?'

'What is it? Eh, pretty young lady, you can't use your cunning on me, an old woman. I know what you're grieving about: your unhappiness is not all on its own. After all, I too was young once, my bright light, I also went through those torments. Yes. But for your kindness, here, I'll tell you this: if a good man crosses your path, and he's not an empty-headed fellow, hold on to him; hold on to him tighter than death. If it's to be, then it's to be, and if it's not to be, then that is probably how God wants it. Yes. Why do you marvel at me? I'm a fortune-teller. Do you want me to take all your unhappiness away with your hanky? I'll do that, and that will be the end of it. Look, the rain is lighter now; you wait a bit more, but I'll be on my way. I won't be the first he's wetted. Now remember, little pigeon: sadness comes, and sadness goes, and then there's not a trace of it. May the Lord have mercy!'

The beggar-woman raised herself from the ledge, left the chapel, and trudged off on her way. In astonishment, Yelena watched her go. 'What can this mean?' she whispered involuntarily.

The rain became a lighter and lighter drizzle, and the sun showed itself for a moment. Yelena was already preparing to leave her refuge... Suddenly, at ten paces from the chapel, she saw Insarov. Wrapped in a cloak, he was walking along the same path by which Yelena had come; he seemed to be hurrying home.

She rested her arm on the decrepit railing of the steps, wanted to call him, but her voice failed her... Insarov had already gone past, without raising his head...

'Dmitry Nikanorovich!' she got out at last.

Insarov suddenly stopped, looked round... For an initial moment he did not recognize Yelena, but at once approached her.

'You! You're here!' he exclaimed.

Without saying anything, she retreated into the chapel. Insarov followed her.

She continued to say nothing, and merely stared at him with a kind of long, gentle gaze. He lowered his eyes.

'Have you come from our house?' she asked him.

'No... not from yours.'

'Oh?' Yelena repeated, trying to smile. 'So this is how you keep your promises! I waited for you all morning.'

'If you remember, Yelena Nikolayevna, I did not promise anything yesterday.'

Again Yelena almost smiled, and passed her hand across her face. Both face and hand were very pale.

'I suppose you were going to leave without saying farewell to us?'

'Yes,' Insarov said, sternly and voicelessly.

'What? After our friendship, after those conversations, after everything... I suppose that if I had not met you by chance...' (Yelena's voice began to resonate, and she fell silent for a moment) 'you would have left, and would not have shaken my hand for the last time, and would have felt no regret?'

Insarov turned away.

'Please, Yelena Nikolayevna, do not talk that way. I feel unhappy enough as it is. Believe me, my decision cost me a great effort. If you only knew...'

'I don't want to know why you are going,' Yelena interrupted him, with alarm. 'Evidently it is necessary. Evidently we must part. You would not want to upset your friends without reason. But do friends part like this? After all, you and I are friends, are we not?'

'No,' said Insarov.

'What?' Yelena said softly. Her cheeks were covered by a light blush.

'It is precisely because we are not friends that I am leaving. Do not compel me to say what I do not want to say, what I shall not say.'

'You were open with me before,' Yelena articulated with slight reproach. 'Do you remember?'

'Then I was able to be open, then I had nothing to hide. But now...'

'Yes?' Yelena asked.

'But now... But now I must go. Farewell.'

Had Insarov raised his eyes to Yelena at that moment, he would have observed that the more morose and gloomy he became, the brighter grew her face; but he stared doggedly at the floor.

'Well, farewell, Dmitry Nikanorovich,' she began. 'But at least, since we have already met, now give me your hand.'

Insarov began to extend his hand.

'No, I cannot do that, either,' he said quietly, and turned away again.

'You can't?'

'No. Farewell.'

And he moved towards the exit of the chapel.

'Wait a little longer,' said Yelena. 'It is as if you were afraid of me. But I am braver than you,' she added with a sudden light tremor that passed through her whole body. 'I can tell you... would you like me to?... why you found me here. Do you know where I was going?'

Insarov looked at Yelena in astonishment.

'I was going to see you.'

'To see me?'

Yelena covered her face.

'You wanted to make me say that I love you,' she whispered. 'There... I have said it.'

'Yelena!' Insarov cried out.

She took his hands, looked at him, and fell onto his breast.

He embraced her tightly and said nothing. He did not need to tell her that he loved her. From his exclamation alone, from that instant transformation of his whole person, from the way that this breast, to which she clung so trustfully, rose and fell, from the way that the tips of his fingers touched her hair, Yelena was able to tell that she was loved. He said nothing, and she did not need any words. 'He is here, he loves me... what more can there be?' The silence of bliss, the silence of the untroubled refuge, the goal attained, that heavenly bliss that gives death itself both meaning and beauty, filled her entirely with its divine wave. She desired nothing, because she possessed everything. 'O my brother, my friend, my darling!' her lips whispered, and she herself did not know whose heart this was, his or hers, that so sweetly throbbed and melted within her breast.

But he stood motionless, with his tight embrace he surrounded this young life that had given itself to him, on his breast he felt this new, infinitely precious burden; a feeling of tender emotion, a feeling of indescribable gratitude utterly routed his firm soul, and tears he had never before experienced welled from his eyes...

She, however, did not weep; she merely kept repeating: 'O my friend, O my brother!'

'So you will come with me everywhere?' he said to her a quarter of an hour later, surrounding and supporting her in his embrace as before.

'Everywhere, to the ends of the earth. Where you will be, I will be.'

'And you do not deceive yourself, you know that your parents will never consent to our marriage?'

'I do not deceive myself; I know that.'

'You know that I am poor, almost destitute?'

'I do.'

'That I am not a Russian, that I am not destined to live in Russia, that you will have to tear up all your links with your fatherland, with your kinsfolk?'

'I do, I do.'

'Do you also know that I have dedicated myself to a cause that is difficult and thankless, that I... that we shall have to submit not only to danger, but also to deprivation and degradation, perhaps?'

'I know, I know it all... I shall love you.'

'That you will have to put behind you all that you are accustomed to, that there, alone, among strangers, you will perhaps be compelled to work...'

She put her hand on his lips.

'I love you, my darling!'

Hotly he began to kiss her pink, narrow hand. Yelena did not take it from his lips and with a kind of childish joy, with laughing curiosity watched as he covered it, that hand of hers, with kisses, now the hand itself, now its fingers...

Suddenly she blushed and hid her face against his breast.

Tenderly he raised her head and looked fixedly into her eyes.

'Hail, then,' he said to her, 'my wife before men and before God!'

XIX

An hour later Yelena, with her hat in one hand and her cape in the other, walked quietly into the drawing-room of the dacha. Her hair had come slightly uncurled, there was a small pink spot on each of her cheeks, the smile would not leave her lips, her eyes were narrowed and, though half-closed, also smiling. She could hardly move her feet for tiredness, and she found this tiredness pleasant: indeed, she found everything pleasant. It all seemed to her charming and tender. Uvar Ivanovich sat by the window; she went over to him, put her hand on his shoulder, stretched, and almost involuntarily began to laugh.

'What is it?' he asked, surprised.

She did not know what to say. She felt like kissing Uvar Ivanovich. '*Flat* on his face!...' she said quietly, at last.

But Uvar Ivanovich did not even raise an eyebrow, and continued to stare at Yelena in surprise. She dropped both her hat and her cape on top of him.

'Dear Uvar Ivanovich,' she said, 'I want to sleep, I am tired'—and once more she began to laugh, and fell into an armchair beside him.

'Hm,' Uvar Ivanovich grunted, and began to twiddle his fingers. 'One ought to, yes...'

But Yelena looked around her and thought: 'I shall soon have to part with all this... and it is strange: there is in me neither fear, nor doubt, nor regret... No, I feel sorry for Mama!' Then again before her the chapel appeared, his voice sounded in her ears again, she felt his arms around her. Her heart stirred joyfully but faintly: the languor of happiness lay upon it, too. She remembered the old beggar-woman. 'Indeed, she took away my unhappiness,' she thought. 'Oh, how happy I am! How undeservedly! How soon!' Had she let go of herself just a fraction, she would have wept sweet, never-ending tears. She only held them back by laughing. Whatever posture she took, it seemed to her that it could not be better or more comfortable: as if she were being lulled in a cradle. All her movements were slow and soft; what had become of her haste, her angular awkwardness? Zoya came in: Yelena decided that she had never seen a more delightful little face; Anna Vasilyevna came in: Yelena felt a prick of conscience, but with what tenderness did she embrace her good, kind mother and kiss her forehead, near the hair that had already grown slightly grey! Then she went up to her room: how everything smiled to her there! With what a sense of bashful triumph and submission she sat down on her bed, that same little bed where three hours earlier she had passed such bitter moments! 'And yet even then I knew that he loved me,' she thought, 'and even before that... Oh, no, no, that is a sin.' '"You are my wife..."' she whispered, covering her face with her hands, and then threw herself to her knees.

Towards evening she became more reflective. Sadness assailed her at the thought that it would be some time before she saw Insarov again. He could not remain at Bersenev's lodgings without arousing suspicion, and so Yelena and he had determined on a plan: Insarov was to return to Moscow and come to visit them a couple of times before the autumn; she, on her part, promised to write him letters and, if possible, arrange a meeting with him somewhere near Kuntsevo. When it was time for evening tea, she came down to the drawing-room and there found all her family, and Shubin, too, who gave her a keen glance as soon as she appeared; she wanted to talk to him in friendly fashion, in their old way, but was afraid of his perspicacity, afraid of herself. It seemed to her that it was not without reason that he had left her alone for more than two weeks. Soon Bersenev arrived, bringing Anna Vasilyevna a greeting from Insarov, together with an apology for returning to Moscow without having presented his respects to her. Insarov's name was spoken for the first time that day in Yelena's presence; she felt herself blush; at the same time, she knew that she ought to express regret at the sudden departure of such a good friend, but could not constrain herself to such dissembling and continued to sit in motionless silence, while Anna Vasilyevna sighed and grieved. Yelena tried to stay near Bersenev; she did not fear him, even though he knew part of her secret; under his wing she sought to escape from Shubin, who continued to look at her now and again—not mockingly, but attentively. Bersenev, too, was puzzled during the course of the evening: he had expected Yelena to look more melancholy. Fortunately for her, between him and Shubin an argument about art sprang up; she moved away, listening to their voices as in a dream. Little by little, not only they but the whole room, all that surrounded her, seemed to her like a dream—everything: the samovar on the table, Uvar Ivanovich's short waistcoat, Zoya's sleek fingernails, and the oil portrait of Grand Prince Konstantin Pavlovich on the wall: it all receded, it was all immersed in a fog, ceased to exist. She merely felt sorry for them all. 'What are their lives for?' she thought.

'Are you sleepy, Lenochka?' her mother asked.

She did not hear her mother's question.

'A semi-true statement, you say?' These words, spoken sharply by Shubin, suddenly aroused Yelena's attention. 'For pity's sake,' he went on, 'that is where the savour lies. True statements are depressing—they aren't Christian. Untrue statements make people feel indifferent—such statements are simply stupid. While half-true statements make them show annoyance and impatience. For example, if I were to say that Yelena Nikolayevna is in love with one of us, what sort of statement would that be, eh, my good sir?'

'Oh, Monsieur Paul,' said Yelena, 'I should like to show you my annoyance, but really, I cannot. I am very tired.'

'Then why don't you go to bed?' said Anna Vasilyevna, who herself often dozed in the evening and therefore liked to send others off to their rooms to sleep. 'Say goodnight to me, and off you go. Andrei Petrovich will excuse you.'

Yelena gave her mother a kiss, bowed to them all, and went. Shubin saw her to the door.

'Yelena Nikolayevna,' he whispered to her on the threshold, 'you may trample on Monsieur Paul, you may walk all over him without pity, but Monsieur Paul blesses you, and your feet, and the shoes on your feet, and the soles of your shoes.'

Yelena gave a shrug of her shoulder, reluctantly offered him her hand—not the one Insarov had kissed—and, having returned to her room, at once undressed, got into bed, and fell asleep. She slept a deep, untroubled sleep... Not even children sleep this way: only a convalescent baby sleeps this way, as its mother sits beside its cradle and looks at it and listens to its breathing.

XX

'COME to my room for a moment,' Shubin said to Bersenev as soon as the latter had said goodnight to Anna Vasilyevna. 'I have something to show you.'

Bersenev set off with him to the outbuilding. He was struck by the large number of studies, statuettes, and busts, wrapped in wet rags and placed in every corner of the room.

'I say, you seem to be working in earnest,' he observed to Shubin.

'Well, one has to do something,' the other replied. 'If one doesn't succeed at one thing, one must try something else. Though, as a matter of fact, I, like a Corsican, am engaged more in vendetta than in pure art. *Trema, Bisanzia!*'*

'I don't understand,' Bersenev said.

'Wait and see. Now, dear friend and benefactor, be so good as to take a look at my vendetta number one.'

Shubin unwrapped one of the figures, and Bersenev saw a bust that was an excellent likeness of Insarov. The features of the face had been precisely captured by Shubin, right down to the last detail, and he had given it a wonderful expression: honest, noble, and bold.

Bersenev was ecstatic.

'Why, that is simply splendid!' he exclaimed. 'I congratulate you. It ought to be in an exhibition! Why do you call this magnificent work a vendetta?'

'Because, sir, I intend to present this, as you are good enough to call it, magnificent work to Yelena Nikolayevna as a gift on her name-day. Do you understand the allegory? We are not blind, we see what is happening around us, but we are gentlemen, dear sir, and we take our revenge in gentlemanly fashion.'

'And here,' Shubin added, unwrapping another small figure, 'since, according to the latest aesthetics, the artist enjoys the enviable right to embody within himself all kinds of loathsomeness, exalting it into the pearl of creation, we, in the exaltation of this pearl, number two, have taken our revenge not as gentlemen at all, but simply *en canaille*.'*

He deftly tugged off the covering cloth, and before Bersenev's gaze appeared a statuette, in the style of Dantan,* also representing Insarov.

Anything more wicked or witty it would have been impossible to
devise. The young Bulgarian was portrayed as a ram, rising up on its
hind-legs and lowering its horns to strike. Stupid pomposity, fervour,
stubbornness, gaucherie, and narrow-mindedness were imprinted in
no uncertain terms on the physiognomy of 'the spouse of fine-fleeced
ewes', and yet the resemblance was so striking, so unmistakable, that
Bersenev could not but burst out laughing.

'Well? Amusing, eh?' Shubin said. 'Do you recognize the hero?
Do you think I should also send this one to an exhibition? This one,
my dear chap, I am going to give myself on my own name-day... Your
excellency, allow me to perform a trick!'

And Shubin jumped up and down two or three times, kicking himself behind with the soles of his shoes.

Bersenev picked up the covering cloth from the floor and threw it
back on to the statuette.

'Oh, you magnanimous fellow!' Shubin began. 'Now who was it in
history who was considered especially magnanimous? Oh, never mind!
And now,' he went on sadly and solemnly unwrapping a third, rather
large mass of clay, 'you will see something that will prove to you your
friend's humility and sagacious wisdom. You will be satisfied that
he, again as a true artist, feels the need and usefulness of his own
forthright criticism. Behold!'

The covering cloth was raised, and Bersenev saw two heads, placed
side by side and close to each other, as though they had grown together
... At first he did not grasp the point of it, but, looking closer, recognized one of them as Annushka, and the other as Shubin himself. They
were, however, more like caricatures than portraits. Annushka was
represented as an attractive, buxom wench with a low forehead, dis-
tended eyelids, and a pertly upturned nose. Her thick lips smirked
brazenly; her entire face expressed sensuality, unconcern, and boldness,
not without good nature. Shubin had depicted himself as a haggard,
emaciated playboy with hollow cheeks, helplessly trailing wisps of
insubstantial hair, a vacuous expression in dimmed eyes, and a nose
as pointed as that of a corpse.

Bersenev turned away in disgust.

'Quite a pair, eh, brother?' Shubin said quietly. 'You wouldn't like to
think up a decent title for it, would you? I've already thought up titles
for the other two. Under the bust it will say: "The hero intending to
save his motherland". Under the statuette: "Beware, sausage-makers!"

And under this one—what do you think?—"The future of the artist Pavel Yakovlevich Shubin..." Would that do?'

'Stop it,' Bersenev rejoined. 'Was it really worth wasting your time on such...' He could not immediately think of a suitable word.

'Filth, you mean? No, brother, I'm sorry, but if anything is to be exhibited, it's this group.'

'Filth is what it is,' Bersenev repeated. 'And what sort of nonsense is this, anyway? You as a person are entirely lacking in traces of the kind of development with which, alas, our artists have been so plentifully endowed to date. All you have done here is to slander yourself.'

'Do you think so?' Shubin said gloomily. 'If I am lacking in them, and if they become established in me, the guilt will be borne by only... one person. Do you know,' he added, tragically knitting his brows, 'that I have already tried drink?'

'Do not tell lies!'

'I have tried it, I swear to God,' Shubin retorted, suddenly grinning and cheering up, 'and it's horrible, brother, it won't go down, and afterwards one's head feels like a drum. The great Lushchikhin himself—Kharlampy Lushchikhin, the greatest soak in Moscow, and, some say, in all Great Russia—declared that I will never be any good at it. In his words, the bottle says nothing to me.'

Bersenev began to raise his hand against the group, but Shubin stopped him.

'No, brother, do not strike them down; they will serve as a lesson, as a scarecrow.'

Bersenev began to laugh.

'In that case, very well, I will spare your scarecrow,' he said quietly, 'and long live pure, eternal art!'

'Hear, hear!' Shubin chimed in. 'With it, the good is better and the bad of less account.'

The friends shook hands firmly, and went their separate ways.

XXI

YELENA's initial feeling on awakening was a joyful trepidation. 'Can it be? Can it really be?' she kept wondering, and her heart thrilled with happiness. Memories surged over her... she was engulfed by them. Then, once again, she was visited by that blissful, ecstatic silence. During the morning, however, Yelena was gradually assailed by unease, and in the days that followed she felt both languor and boredom. While it was true that now she knew what she wanted, this made her mind no easier. That unforgettable meeting had thrown her for ever out of her earlier routine: she was no longer caught in it, she was far away, yet meanwhile around her everything happened in its usual order, everything took its normal course, as though nothing had altered; the old life went on as before, counting, as it had done earlier, on her participation and co-operation. She tried to begin a letter to Insarov, but did not succeed with that, either: when the words came out on to the paper they seemed either dead or false. She finished her diary, drawing a thick line under the last entry. That was the past, and now with all her thoughts, with the whole of her being, she passed into the future. It was hard for her. To sit with her mother, who suspected nothing, to listen to everything she said, to reply to her, to talk to her—seemed almost criminal to Yelena; she sensed within herself the presence of a kind of falsehood; she felt angry, though she had nothing to blush for; several times there rose within her soul an almost overwhelming desire to tell all without concealment, no matter what happened afterwards. 'Why,' she wondered, 'did not Dmitry take me away from that chapel to where he wanted to go? Did he not tell me that I was his wife before God? What am I doing here?' Suddenly she began to avoid everyone, even Uvar Ivanovich, who was more bewildered—and twiddled his fingers more—than ever. Now all that surrounded her no longer seemed tender, or charming or even a dream: it weighed on her bosom like a nightmare, with a dead, immobile burden; it seemed to reproach her, to be indignant with her, and not want to know about her... As if it were saying: 'Whatever you do, you are still ours.' Even her poor foster-children, the oppressed birds and creatures, looked at her—at least, so it seemed to her—with mistrust and hostility. She became ashamed and embarrassed about her own feelings. 'After all, this is still my home,' she thought, 'my family, my motherland...' 'No, it is no longer your motherland, no longer your family,' another voice kept telling her. Terror seized her, and she was vexed at her own cowardice. The hard times were only just beginning, and already she was losing patience... Was that what she had promised?

It took her some time to regain her self-control. But a week went by, another... Yelena calmed down a little and became accustomed to her new situation. She wrote two short notes to Insarov, and took them to the post office herself—because of both shame and pride, not on any account could she have brought herself to entrust them to the maid. She was already beginning to wait for him... But in his stead, one fine morning Nikolai Artemyevich arrived.

XXII

No one in the home of retired guards lieutenant Stakhov had ever seen him look as sour, and at the same time as self-assured and important, as he did that day. He entered the drawing-room in his coat and hat—entered slowly, his legs wide apart, and clacking his heels; he drew near to the mirror and spent a long time looking at himself, shaking his head with calm severity and biting his lips. Anna Vasilyevna greeted him with outward excitement and secret joy (she never greeted him in any other way); he did not even take off his hat, did not greet her, and silently let her kiss his chamois leather glove. Anna Vasilyevna began to ask him about his course of treatment—he made no reply to her; Uvar Ivanovich appeared—he glanced at him and said: 'Bah!' With Uvar Ivanovich he was in general cold and condescending, though he recognized in him 'traces of the real Stakhov blood'. It is well known that nearly all Russian noble families are convinced of the existence of exclusive, hereditary traits that are peculiar to them alone: we have more than once heard talk 'between ourselves' of 'Podsalaskin noses' and 'Perepreyev necks'. Zoya came in, and curtseyed to Nikolai Artemyevich. He grunted, sat down in an armchair, demanded coffee, and only then removed his hat. His coffee was brought; he drank a cup and, looking at them all in turn, muttered through his teeth: '*Sortez, s'il vous plaît*', and then, turning to his wife, added: '*Et vous, madame, restez, je vous prie.*'*

Everyone went out except Anna Vasilyevna. Her head began to quiver with excitement. The solemn quality of Nikolai Artemyevich's manner had given her a shock. She was expecting something extraordinary.

'What on earth?...' she exclaimed, as soon as the door had closed.

Nikolai Artemyevich cast an indifferent glance at Anna Vasilyevna. 'Nothing much, and where did you acquire this manner of at once adopting the look of some kind of victim?' he began, quite needlessly turning down the corners of his mouth at every word. 'I simply wanted to give you advance notice that we shall be having a new guest to dinner today.'

'Who is it?'

'Kurnatovsky, Yegor Andreyevich. You don't know him. He's a chief secretary at the Senate.'

'He is coming to dine with us today?'

'Yes.'

'And you asked everyone to leave the room merely in order to tell me this?'

Nikolai Artemyevich again cast a glance at Anna Vasilyevna, this time an ironic one.

'Does it surprise you? Don't be so quick to be surprised.'

He fell silent. Anna Vasilyevna also said nothing for a while.

'I should like...' she began.

'I know you have always considered me an "immoral" man,' Nikolai Artemyevich suddenly began.

'I?' Anna Vasilyevna muttered in amazement.

'And perhaps you are right. I will not deny that I have indeed on occasion given you reasonable cause for dissatisfaction' ('the grey horses!' flickered through Anna Vasilyevna's head), 'although you your-self must admit that in the state of your constitution...'

'But I make not the slightest accusation against you, Nikolai Artemyevich.'

'*C'est possible*. At any rate, I do not intend to vindicate myself. Time will vindicate me. I consider it my duty to assure you, how-ever, that I know my obligations and am able to take care of... the interests of the... the interests of the family that has been entrusted to me.'

'What can this mean?' thought Anna Vasilyevna. (She could not have known that the evening before, at the English Club, in the sofa corner, there had arisen a discussion about the inability of Russians to make 'speeches'. 'Which of our countrymen knows how to speak in public? Name someone!' exclaimed one of the disputants. 'What about Stakhov, for instance?' another replied, and pointed to Nikolai Artemyevich, who had been standing right there and had very nearly squeaked with satisfaction.)

'For example,' Nikolai Artemyevich went on, 'my daughter, Yelena. Do you not consider that it is time for her at last to take a firm step upon the path of... to get married, I mean. These sophistries and philosophizings are all very well, but only to a certain degree, to a certain age. It is time for her to leave her mists behind, abandon the company of all these artists, scholars, and Montenegrins, and become like everyone else.'

'How am I to understand your words?' asked Anna Vasilyevna.

'Be so good as to listen to what I have to say,' Nikolai Artemyevich replied, still with the same downward turn of his lips. 'I will tell you directly, without beating about the bush: I have become acquainted, I have made friends with this young man—Mr Kurnatovsky—in the hope of having him as my son-in-law. I dare to think that, once having seen him, you will not accuse me of partiality or hastiness of judgement.' (As Nikolai Artemyevich spoke, he admired his own eloquence.) 'Of excellent education, he is a lawyer, has fine manners, is thirty-three years of age, a chief secretary, a collegiate councillor, and has the ribbon of the Order of St Stanislas.* You will, I hope, do me the fairness of not supposing that I am one of those *pères de comédie** who never stop raving about honours and ranks; but you yourself told me that Yelena Nikolayevna likes businesslike, positive men: Yegor Andreyevich is a first-class business operator in his field; now, on the other hand, my daughter has a weakness for generous actions: so let me tell you that as soon as he attained the possibility, the possibility, you understand, of living comfortably on his salary, Yegor Andreyevich instantly renounced the annual sum his father had granted him in favour of his brothers.'

'And who is his father?' asked Anna Vasilyevna.

'His father? His father is also a famous man in his own way, of the very highest morality, *un vrai stoïcien*,* a retired major, it appears, who manages all the estates of the counts B——'

'Ah!' Anna Vasilyevna said quietly.

' "Ah"? What do you mean, "Ah"?' Nikolai Artemyevich put in. 'Is it possible that you, too, are infected by prejudice?'

'But I did not say anything,' Anna Vasilyevna began...

'Yes, you did, you said "Ah"... However that may be, I considered it necessary to warn you about my mode of thinking and dare to suppose... dare to hope that Mr Kurnatovsky will be received *à bras ouverts*.* This is not some Montegrin.'

'Of course; only I shall have to send for our cook, Vanka, and tell him to add another course to our dinner.'

'You will understand that I shall play no role in that...' Nikolai Artemyevich said, stood up, put on his hat, and whistling as he went (he had heard from someone that one should only whistle at one's dacha and in the riding-hall), set off to take a walk in the garden. Shubin looked at him from the window of his outbuilding, and silently stuck out his tongue.

At ten to four a carriage drove up to the front steps of the Stakhov dacha, and a man, still young, of fine appearance, simply and elegantly dressed, got out of it and asked to be announced. This was Yegor Andreyevich Kurnatovsky.

This, among other things, was what Yelena wrote to Insarov the following day:

'Congratulate me, dear Dmitry, I have a fiancé. He dined with us yesterday; it seems that papa got to know him at the English Club and invited him. Of course, when he arrived yesterday he was not my fiancé. But good, kind Mama, to whom Papa conveyed his hopes, whispered in my ear what kind of guest this was. His name is Yegor Andreyevich Kurnatovsky; he works as a chief secretary at the Senate. I shall first describe his appearance to you. He is small of stature, shorter than you, well built; his features are regular, he has short hair, and large side-whiskers. His eyes are small (like yours), dark-brown and quick, his lips are flat and broad; his eyes and lips have a constant smile, which is somehow official; as though it were on watch. He conducts himself in a very straightforward way, speaks distinctly, and everything about him is distinct: he walks, laughs, and eats as though he were doing business. "How she has studied him!" you are thinking, perhaps, at this moment. Yes, I have; so that I may describe him to you. And in any case, how can one help studying one's fiancé? There is something iron-hard about him... at once obtuse and superficial—and honest; indeed, he is said to be very honest. You are also iron-hard, my darling, but not like this man. At table he sat beside me, Shubin sat opposite us. At first the conversation was about commercial enterprises of some kind: he is said to know a great deal about them and very nearly gave up his civil service post in order to take charge of a large factory. He missed his vocation there! Then Shubin began to talk about the theatre; Mr Kurnatovsky declared, and —I must admit—without false modesty, that he understands nothing of art. That reminded me of you... but I thought: no, Dmitry and I don't understand art, but in a different way. This man seemed to be saying: I don't understand it, and in any case it isn't necessary, though in a well-ordered state it is tolerated. To St Petersburg and *comme il faut** he was, however, rather indifferent: he once even called himself a proletarian. "We are unskilled labourers," he said. I thought: if Dmitry had said that, I would not have liked it, but let this man say it! Let him boast! With me he was very polite; but I kept feeling as though I were being spoken to by a very, very condescending superior. When he wanted to praise someone, he would say that the person had *principles*—that was his favourite word. I have no doubt that he is self-assured, hard-working, capable of self-sacrifice (you see: I am impartial), or rather, of sacrificing his own advantage, but he is a great despot. Woe to anyone who ends up in his hands! At table they began to talk about bribes...

‘ "I realize," he said, "that in many cases the person who takes the bribe is not to blame; he cannot act any other way. And yet, if he is caught, he must be crushed."

‘I uttered a cry.

‘ "Crush someone who is not guilty?"

‘ "Yes, for the sake of principle."

‘ "Which one?" Shubin asked.

‘Kurnatovsky, half in confusion, half in surprise, said:

‘ "There is no need to explain that."

‘Papa, who, I think, regards him with reverence, inserted a remark to the effect that no, of course there was no need to explain it, and, to my annoyance, this conversation came to an end. In the evening Bersenev arrived and got into a dreadful argument with him. Never have I seen our good, kind Andrei Petrovich in such a lather. Mr Kurnatovsky did not at all refute the value of learning, the universities, and so on... and yet I understood Andrei Petrovich's outrage. Mr Kurnatovsky views it all as a kind of gymnastics. Shubin came to me after table and said: "This fellow and a certain other person" (he cannot bring himself to say your name) "are both practical men, but see what a difference exists between them: in the one, there is an authentic, living, life-given ideal; but in the other there is not even a sense of duty, but simply an official honesty and efficiency with no substance." Shubin is clever, and I have remembered his words for you; but in my opinion, what is there in common between you? You *believe*, but he does not, because to believe only in oneself is *impossible*.

‘He left late, but Mama managed to tell me that he had liked me, that Papa was delighted... Perhaps he said of me that I have principles? I nearly told Mama that I was very sorry, but I already had a husband... Why does Papa dislike you so? I am sure we can persuade Mama round somehow...

'Oh, my darling! I have described this gentleman to you in such detail in order to dull my longing. Without you, I am not alive, I see you constantly, hear you... I await you, only not here at our home, as you wanted—think how painful and awkward it would be for us!— but where I wrote to you about, you know—in that copse... Oh, my darling! How I love you!'

XXIII

SOME three weeks after Kurnatovsky's first visit, Anna Vasilyevna, much to Yelena's delight, moved to Moscow and her large wooden house by the Prechistenka,* a house with columns, white lyres and garlands above each window, with a mezzanine floor, outbuildings, a front garden, an enormous turfed courtyard, a well in the courtyard, and a dog's kennel beside the well. Anna Vasilyevna had never left her dacha so early before, but this year the first autumn frosts made her gumboils 'act up'; Nikolai Artemyevich, for his part, having completed his course of treatment, had begun to miss his wife; in addition, Avgustina Khristianovna had gone to stay with her cousin in Reval; a foreign family arrived in Moscow demonstrating 'plastic poses', *des poses plastiques*, the *Moscow Gazette*'s description of which had powerfully awoken Anna Vasilyevna's curiosity. In short, to stay at the dacha any longer turned out to be inconvenient and even, in the words of Nikolai Artemyevich, incompatible with the fulfilment of his 'predeterminations'. The last two weeks seemed very long to Yelena. Kurnatovsky called twice, each time on a Sunday; on other days he was busy. While the purported reason for his visit was Yelena, he spent more time talking to Zoya, who liked him very much. '*Das ist ein Mann!*' she thought to herself as she looked at his swarthy, manly face, and listened to his self-assured, condescending talk. In her opinion, no one had such a wonderful voice, no one else was able to say so beautifully things such as: 'I had the *hon*our', 'I am most gratified'. Insarov did not come to the Stakhovs', but Yelena did see him once in a small copse above the Moscow River, where she had appointed a rendezvous with him. They scarcely had time to say more than a few words to each other. Shubin returned to Moscow with Anna Vasilyevna; Bersenev a few days later.

Insarov was sitting in his room, for a third time reading the letters that had been brought to him from Bulgaria by 'courier'; it was considered too risky to send them by post. They alarmed him greatly. Events in the East were developing quickly; the occupation of the Principalities by Russian forces* was worrying everyone; a storm was brewing, and a breath of imminent and ineluctable war could already be sensed. All around, the conflagration was taking hold, and no one could predict where it would go next, or where it would end; old injuries, ancient hopes—all had begun to stir. Insarov's heart beat violently: *his* hopes, too, were being realized. 'But is it not too soon? Will it not all be in vain?' he thought, as he clenched his fists. 'We are not ready yet. But so be it! I will have to go.'

There was a slight rustling sound outside the door, the door quickly opened wide, and into the room walked Yelena.

Insarov trembled all over, rushed towards her, fell on his knees before her, embraced her waist, and pressed his head hard against it.

'Did you not expect me?' she began, barely able to draw breath. (She had quickly run all the way up the staircase.) 'Darling! Darling!' She put both her hands on his head and looked round. 'So this is where you live! It did not take me long to find you. Your landlady's daughter showed me the way. We moved back here to town the day before yesterday. I was going to write to you, but then thought I had better come in person. I've only come to see you for a quarter of an hour. Get up and bolt the door.'

He rose to his feet, nimbly bolted the door, returned to her, and took her by the hands. He was unable to speak; joy was choking him. With a smile, she looked him in the eyes... there was so much happiness in them... She felt embarrassed.

'Wait,' she said, tenderly withdrawing her hands from him, 'let me take off my hat.'

She untied the bands of her hat, threw it off, released her cape from her shoulders, straightened her hair, and sat down on the small old sofa. Insarov did not move, and stared at her like one enchanted.

'But sit down,' she said, not taking her eyes off him, and indicating the place next to herself.

Insarov sat down, though not on the sofa but on the floor, at her feet.

'Here now, take my gloves off for me,' she said quietly in an uneven voice. She was starting to feel afraid.

He proceeded first to unfasten, then to pull off one of the gloves, half removed it and eagerly put his lips to the soft, delicate hand that gleamed white beneath it.

Yelena gave a start, and tried to ward him off with her other hand, but he began to kiss her other hand, too. Yelena drew it towards her, he threw back his head, she looked him in the face, leaned forward— and their lips fused...

A moment passed... She tore herself away, stood up, whispered: 'No, no,' and quickly walked over to the writing-desk.

'After all, I am the lady of the house here, and you must have no secrets from me,' she said, trying to appear untroubled and turning her back to him. 'What a lot of papers! What letters are these?'

Insarov furrowed his brow.

'These letters?' he said quietly, getting up off the floor. 'You may read them.'

Yelena twirled them in her hand.

'There are so many of them, and they are written in such a small hand, and I must go soon... Let them be! They're not from a rival, are they?... And they're not in Russian, either,' she added, leafing through the thin sheets.

Insarov drew near to her and touched her waist. She suddenly turned round to face him, smiled brightly at him, and leaned against his shoulder.

'These letters are from Bulgaria, Yelena; my friends are writing to me, they are summoning me.'

'Now? There?'

'Yes... now. While there is still time, while it is still possible to get there.'

She suddenly threw both arms around his neck.

'Well, you'll take me with you, won't you?'

He pressed her to his heart.

'Oh, my dear girl, oh, my heroine, how you uttered those words! But is it not sinful, is it not reckless for me, me, a homeless, solitary man, to entice you away with me?... And to where!'

She put her hand over his mouth.

'Shh... or I shall get angry and never come to see you again. Is not everything decided, is not everything settled between us? Am I not your wife? Does a wife part from her husband?'

'Wives do not go to war,' he said quietly, with a half-sad smile.

'Yes, that is true, when they can stay at home. But do you think I would be able to stay here?'

'Yelena, you are an angel!... But think: I may have to leave Moscow... in two weeks' time. I can no longer think of university lectures, or of finishing my work.'

'What is this?' Yelena interrupted. 'You will soon have to leave? Well, if you want, I will remain with you now, this moment, this very instant, will remain with you for ever, and will not return to my own home, do you want that? Let us go now, do you want to?'

Insarov enclosed her in his arms with redoubled strength.

'Then let God punish me', he exclaimed, 'if I am doing wrong! From this day we are united for ever!'

'Shall I stay?'

'No, my pure girl; no, my treasure. Today you shall go home, but be ready. This deed cannot be done at once; we must consider it all properly. You will need money, a passport...'

'I have money,' Yelena interrupted. 'Eighty roubles.'

'Well, that is not much,' observed Insarov, 'though anything will come in handy.'

'But I can get more, I shall borrow, I shall ask Mama... No, I shan't... But I can sell my watch... I have earrings, two bracelets... lace.'

'Money is not the important thing, Yelena; the passport, your passport, how are we to get that?'

'Yes, how are we to get that? Must I absolutely have a passport?'

'Yes, you must.'

Yelena smiled thinly.

'The things that come into my head! I remember, when I was only a little girl... Our housemaid ran away. She was caught, and pardoned, and she lived with us for a long time... And yet she was always called "Tatyana the Runaway". I never thought then that one day I might be a runaway like her.'

'Yelena, have you no shame?'

'Why? Of course, it's better to go with a passport. But if one can't...'

'We shall arrange all that afterwards, afterwards, you must wait,' Insarov said quietly. 'Just let me take a look round, let me give it some thought. You and I shall discuss everything properly. And I have money, too.'

Yelena drew aside with her hand the hair that had fallen onto his forehead.

'Oh, Dmitry! What fun it will be for us to go together!'

'Yes,' said Insarov. 'But when we get there, to the place we are going...'

'What of it?' Yelena interrupted. 'Won't it be fun to die together, too? But no, why should we die? We shall live, we are young. How old are you? Twenty-six?'

'Yes.'

'And I am twenty. We still have much time ahead of us. Ah! You wanted to run away from me, did you? You did not want a Russian love, Bulgarian? Let us see now how you get away from me! But what would have happened to us had I not gone to see you that day?'

'Yelena, you know what compelled me to go away.'

'Yes, I do: you fell in love, and were frightened. But did you really not suspect that you, too, were loved?'

'On my honour I swear it, Yelena, I did not.'

Swiftly and unexpectedly, she gave him a kiss.

'And it's for that that I love you. But now farewell.'

'Can you not stay longer?' Insarov asked.

'No, my darling. Do you think it was easy for me to get away alone? The quarter of an hour was up long ago.' She put on her cape and hat. 'But come and see us tomorrow evening. No, the evening after tomorrow. It will be strained and tedious, but there's nothing to be done: at least we shall see each other. Farewell. Let me out.' He embraced her for the last time. 'Aie! Look, you have broken my chain. Oh, my clumsy one! Well, it doesn't matter. So much the better. I shall go over to Kuznetsky Bridge,* and hand it in to be repaired. If they ask me, I shall say I was at Kuznetsky Bridge.' She gripped the door handle. 'By the way, I forgot to tell you: Monsieur Kurnatovsky will probably make me a proposal in a few days' time. But I shall make him... one of these.' She put the thumb of her left hand to the tip of her nose and waggled her other fingers in the air. 'Goodbye. Until our meeting. Now I know the way... And don't waste any time...'

Yelena opened the door a little, listened closely, turned round to face Insarov, nodded her head, and slipped out of the room.

For about a minute Insarov stood in front of the closed door, also listening closely. The door into the courtyard downstairs slammed shut. He went over to the sofa, sat down, and covered his eyes with his hand. Nothing like this had ever happened to him before. 'How have I deserved such love?' he thought. 'Is this not a dream?'

But the faint scent of mignonette that Yelena had left in his poor, dark room reminded him of her visit. Together with it, in the air there still seemed to remain the sounds of her young voice, the rustle of her light, young steps, and the warmth and freshness of her young, virginal body.

XXIV

INSAROV decided to wait for the news to be even more positive, but began to prepare for his departure. It was a very difficult matter. For him no real obstacles lay ahead: all he had to do was obtain a passport on demand—but what was to happen to Yelena? To secure a passport for her by legal means was impossible. To marry in secret, and then present themselves to her parents... 'They would let us go then,' he thought. 'But what if they did not? We would go all the same... But what if they filed a complaint... what if... No, it's better to try to obtain a passport by some means or other.'

He decided to consult (without, of course, mentioning any names) an acquaintance of his, a retired, or discharged, public procurator, an old and experienced expert in all kinds of secret matters. This respected man did not live close at hand: Insarov spent a whole hour trundling in a vile little cab to see him, and to cap it all did not find him at home; and on the homeward journey got soaked to the skin, thanks to a sudden deluge of rain. The following morning Insarov, in spite of a rather severe headache, set off for the retired public procurator a second time. The retired public procurator listened to him attentively, taking snuff from a snuffbox adorned with a picture of a full-breasted nymph, and watching his guest sideways out of sly little eyes that were also the colour of snuff, heard him out and demanded 'more determinacy in the factual data'; but, having noticed that Insarov was reluctant to go into detail (Insarov had, after all, come to see him only against the promptings of his heart), confined himself to advising him above all to furnish himself with *pieniadze** and requested him to come back for another visit—'when', he added in a Polish accent, inhaling the snuff over the open box, 'trust will arrive and mistrust will depart'. 'But a passport', he continued, as if to himself, 'is the work of human hands; you are travelling, let us say: who is to know whether you are Marya Bredikhina, or Karolina Fogelmeyer?' A sense of revulsion stirred in Insarov, but he thanked the public procurator and promised to return in a few days' time.

That same evening he went to the Stakhovs'. Anna Vasilyevna greeted him with affection, chided him for having quite forgotten them, and finding that he looked pale, enquired about his health. Nikolai

Artemyevich said not a word to him, and merely surveyed him with a reflectively casual curiosity; Shubin treated him coldly; but Yelena amazed him. She was waiting for him; she had put on for him the same dress she had worn on the day of their first meeting in the wayside chapel; but so calmly did she greet him, so amiable was she, so untroubled and cheerful that, looking at her, no one would have thought that the fate of this girl was already decided and that it was the secret consciousness of a happy love alone that endowed her features with animation, lent lightness and charm to all her movements. She, not Zoya, poured the tea, joked, and chatted; she knew that Shubin would observe her, that Insarov would be incapable of donning a mask, of feigning indifference, and had armed herself beforehand. She was not wrong: Shubin did not take his eyes off her, and Insarov was very silent and gloomy throughout the whole evening. Yelena was so happy that she felt like teasing him.

'Well?' she asked him suddenly. 'How is your plan progressing?' Insarov was disconcerted.

'What plan?' he said.

'Have you forgotten?' she replied, laughing into his face: he alone was able to understand the meaning of that happy laughter. 'Your Bulgarian anthology for Russians?'

'*Quelle bourde!*' Nikolai Artemyevich muttered through his teeth.

Zoya sat down at the piano. Yelena gave a barely perceptible shrug of her shoulder and with her eyes showed Insarov to the door, as though letting him off. Then, in a measured way, she touched the table twice with her finger, and looked at him. He realized that she was appointing a rendezvous with him for two days hence, and she quickly smiled when she saw he had understood. Insarov stood up and began to take his leave: he felt unwell. Kurnatovsky appeared. Nikolai Artemyevich leapt to his feet, raised his right hand above his head, and gently lowered it on to the chief secretary's palm. Insarov remained for a few more minutes, in order to take a look at his rival. Yelena shook her head at him slyly, in stealth, the master of the house did not consider it necessary to introduce the two men to each other, and Insarov left, for the last time exchanging a look with Yelena. Shubin thought and thought—and then began furiously to argue with Kurnatovsky on a question of law about which he had not the faintest idea.

Insarov lay awake all night, and in the morning felt ill; however, he set about putting his papers in order and writing letters, but his head was heavy and somehow confused. By dinner, he had a fever: he was unable to eat anything. The fever swiftly grew worse towards evening; now rheumatic pain appeared in all his limbs, and a tormenting headache. Insarov lay down on that same small sofa where Yelena had so recently sat; he thought: 'I am justly punished, why did I go trailing off to see that old rogue?'—and tried to fall asleep... But illness had already taken possession of him. With terrible force, his veins began to throb within him, his blood burned intensely, his thoughts began to wheel like birds. He fell into oblivion. Like one physically overwhelmed, he lay supine, and suddenly it seemed to him that someone was quietly guffawing and whispering over him; with an effort he opened his eyes, the light from the guttering candle flashed above him like a knife... What was this? Before him the old public procurator, in a *tarmalama** dressing-gown, belted with a foulard, as he had seen him the day before... 'Karolina Fogelmeyer,' the toothless mouth muttered. Insarov stared, and the old man expanded, swelled up, grew, now he was no longer a human being—he was a tree... Insarov had to climb along the steep branches. He clung on, then fell chest-first on to a sharp stone, and Karolina Fogelmeyer was squatting there, looking like a market woman, and babbling: '*Pirozhki, pirozhki, pirozhki**— and there was blood, and swords gleaming unendurably... Yelena!... And everything vanished in a crimson chaos.

XXV

'SOME fellow or other has come to see you, goodness knows what he is, a locksmith, or something,' Bersenev's servant, who was distinguished for his stern treatment of his master and his sceptical turn of mind, said the following evening. 'He wants to see you.'

'Tell him to come in,' Bersenev said quietly.

The 'locksmith' entered. Bersenev recognized him as the tailor, the landlord of the apartment where Insarov lived.

'What is it?' he asked him.

'I have come to see your honour,' the tailor began, slowly shifting from foot to foot, and from time to time gesturing in the air with his right hand as he gripped his cuff with its last three fingers. 'Our tenant, goodness knows, is very ill.'

'Insarov?'

'Indeed, sir, our tenant. Goodness knows, yesterday morning he was on his feet, but in the evening he asked for a drink, our missus took him some water, but at night he began a-babbling, we could hear him, because there's a partition, not a wall; and this morning he'd lost his tongue and was lying there on his back, and the fever on him, Lord of mine! I thought, goodness knows, he looks as though he may die; I thought, we'll have to let the police station know. Because he's on his own; but the missus said: "You go and see the other tenant. The one who went to rent a room at the dacha: maybe he'll have some advice or come here himself." So here I have come to see your honour, because we can't, that's to say...'

Bersenev seized his peaked cap, stuffed a rouble into the tailor's hand, and at once set off with him at a gallop to Insarov's apartment.

He found Insarov lying on the sofa unconscious, with his clothes still on. His face was terribly altered. Bersenev at once told the landlord and his wife to undress him and carry him to the bed, while he himself rushed for a doctor and brought him back with him. The doctor prescribed leeches, Spanish fly, and calomel, all to be applied together, and ordered blood-letting.

'Is he in danger?' Bersenev asked.

'Yes, indeed he is,' the doctor replied. 'He has a very bad inflammation of the lungs; full-blown pneumonia, and his brain may be affected, too—but he is young. On the other hand, at the moment his own strength is working against him. You have sent for me too late, but we shall do all that science demands.'

The doctor was still a young man, and believed in science.

Bersenev stayed the night. The landlord and his wife proved to be kindly and even practical people, as soon as someone appeared in order to tell them what to do. The doctor's assistant arrived—and the ordeals by medicine began.

Towards morning Insarov recovered consciousness for a few minutes, recognized Bersenev, asked: 'Am I not well, then?', looked around him with the dull and languid bewilderment of the seriously ill, and fell back into oblivion again. Bersenev went home, changed his clothes, took some books with him, and returned to Insarov's apartment. He had decided to stay there, for the near future at least. He closed off Insarov's bed with the screen, and made a little place for himself around the sofa. Slowly and gloomily the day passed. Bersenev absented himself only in order to have his dinner. Evening set in. He lit a candle with a shade round it, and settled down to read. All was quiet. From the room behind the partition where the landlord and his wife lived there came now a suppressed whisper, now a yawn, now a sigh... Someone with them sneezed, and was cursed in a whisper; from behind the screen came the sound of heavy and unsteady breathing, broken from time to time by a short groan and the anguished tossing of a head on a pillow... Strange thoughts came to Bersenev. He was in the room of a man whose life was hanging by a thread—a man whom, he knew, Yelena loved... He remembered the night when Shubin had caught up with him and told him that she loved him, him Bersenev! But now... 'What am I to do now?' he wondered. 'Tell Yelena of his illness? Wait? This news is sadder than the news I once brought her: strange how fate always makes me their intermediary!' He decided that it was better to wait. His gaze fell to the table, which was covered in heaps of papers... 'Will he fulfil his plans?' Bersenev wondered. 'Will it all really come to nothing?' And he began to feel sorry for this young, expiring life, and he vowed to himself that he would save it...

It was not a good night. The sick man raved a great deal in his delirium. Several times Bersenev got up from his small sofa, approached the bed on tiptoe, and sadly listened to Insarov's incoherent babbling. Only once did Insarov say with sudden clarity: 'I don't want you to, I don't want you to, you mustn't...' Bersenev started, and looked at Insarov: his face, at once full of suffering and deathly pale, was immobile, and his arms lay helpless... 'I don't want you to,' he repeated, barely audibly.

In the morning the doctor came, shook his head, and prescribed more medicine.

'The crisis is still a long way off,' he said, putting on his hat.

'And after the crisis?' Bersenev asked.

'After the crisis? The result can be of only two kinds: *aut Caesar, aut nihil*.'*

The doctor left. Bersenev walked up and down the street a few times: he needed fresh air. He returned and settled down with a book. Raumer he had finished long ago: now he was studying Grote.*

The door suddenly creaked softly, and the head of the landlady's daughter, covered as usual by a heavy shawl, looked into the room.

'The young lady is here,' she began in a low voice, 'the one who gave me ten-copeck piece that time...'

The landlady's daughter's head abruptly vanished, and in its place Yelena appeared.

Bersenev leapt up like a man who had been stung; but Yelena did not move, did not cry out... It seemed that in a trice she had understood it all. A terrible pallor covered her face, she walked over to the screen, glanced behind it, threw up her hands, and stood stock-still. In a moment she would have rushed to Insarov, but Bersenev stopped her.

'What are you doing?' he said in a trembling voice. 'You could kill him!'

She reeled back. He led her over to the sofa and made her sit down.

She looked him in the face, then up and down, and then fixed her eyes on the floor.

'Is he dying?' she asked, so coldly and calmly that Bersenev was frightened.

'For God's sake, Yelena Nikolayevna,' he began, 'why do you say that? He is ill, it is true—and rather dangerously so... But we shall save him, that I guarantee you.'

'Is he unconscious?' she asked him, as before.

'Yes, he is oblivious now... That always happens at the beginning of these illnesses, but it does not mean anything, nothing at all, I assure you. Here, drink some water.'

She raised her eyes to him, and he realized that she had not heard his replies.

'If he dies,' she said quietly, still in the same voice, 'I too shall die.'

At that moment Insarov uttered a slight groan; she began to tremble, clutched her head, then began to unfasten the bands of her hat.

'What is this you are doing?' Bersenev asked her.

She made no reply.

'What are you doing?' he repeated.

'I shall stay here.'

'What... for a long time?'

'I don't know, perhaps all day, a night, for ever... I don't know.'

'For God's sake, Yelena Nikolayevna, come to your senses. I, of course, could never have expected to see you here; but all the same, I... assume that you have only come here for a short time. Remember, your absence may be noticed at home...'

'And what of it?'

'They will come looking for you... They will find you...'

'And what of it?'

'Yelena Nikolayevna! You see... He cannot protect you now.'

She lowered her head, as though reflecting, brought her handkerchief to her lips, and with shocking violence, convulsive sobs suddenly broke from her... She threw herself face down on the sofa, trying to stifle them, but her whole body kept rising and struggling like a bird that had just been caught.

'Yelena Nikolayevna... for God's sake...' Bersenev kept saying above her.

'Ah? What is it?' Insarov's voice suddenly uttered out loud.

Yelena straightened up, and Bersenev almost froze on the spot... After a moment or two, he went over to the bed... Insarov's head lay helpless as before on the pillow; his eyes were closed.

'Is he delirious?' Yelena whispered softly.

'I think so,' Bersenev replied, 'but it is nothing; it is also one of the things that always happens, especially if...'

'When did he fall ill?' Yelena interrupted.

'The day before yesterday; I have been here since yesterday. Rely on me, Yelena Nikolayevna. I shall not leave him; every means will be expended. If necessary, we will call a doctors' council.'

'He will die without me,' she exclaimed, wringing her hands.

'I give you my word that I will inform you daily of the course of his illness, and if any real danger should approach...'

'Swear to me that you will send for me at once, no matter at what time, day or night; write a note directly to me... Such questions are of no account to me now. Do you hear? Do you promise to do that?'

'I promise, before God.'

'Swear it on oath.'

'I swear it.'

She suddenly seized his hand and, before he could pull it away, pressed it to her lips.

'Yelena Nikolayevna... what are you doing?' he mouthed.

'No... no... don't...' Insarov articulated incoherently, and gave a heavy sigh.

Yelena walked over to the screen, bit her handkerchief between her teeth, and looked for a long, long time at the sick man. Silent tears trickled down her cheeks.

'Yelena Nikolayevna,' Bersenev said to her, 'he may recover consciousness, and recognize you; I don't know if that would be a good thing. Moreover, I expect the doctor to arrive at any moment now...'

Yelena took her hat from the sofa, put it on and stood still. Her gaze wandered sadly about the room. She seemed to be remembering...

'I cannot leave,' she whispered quietly at last.

Bersenev pressed her hand.

'Gather your strength,' he said, 'calm yourself; you are leaving him in my care. I shall come and see you this very evening.'

Yelena glanced at him, said: 'Oh, my kind friend!'—burst out sobbing, and rushed from the room.

Bersenev leaned against the door. A sorrowful and bitter feeling, that was not without a strange consolation, pinched his heart. 'My kind friend!' he thought, and gave a shrug of his shoulder.

'Who is here?' Insarov's voice said.

Bersenev walked over to him.

'I am here, Dmitry Nikanorovich. What can I get you? How do you feel?'

'Are you on your own?' the sick man asked.

'Yes, I am.'

'And she?'

'Whom do you mean?' Bersenev said, almost in fear.

Insarov was silent.

'The mignonette,' he whispered, and again his eyes closed.

XXVI

FOR a whole eight days Insarov hovered between life and death. The doctor called constantly, taking an interest, again as a young man, in a patient who was seriously ill. Shubin heard about Insarov's dangerous condition and paid him a visit; his compatriots—Bulgarians—appeared; among them Bersenev recognized the two strange figures who had aroused his bewilderment by their unexpected visit to the dacha; all expressed sincere concern, and some offered to take over from Bersenev at the sick man's bedside; but he would not consent to this, remembering the promise he had given to Yelena. He saw her every day and privately conveyed to her—sometimes in words, sometimes in a short little note—every detail of the course of the illness. With what sinking of the heart did she await him, how she listened to him and plied him with questions! She constantly yearned to go and see Insarov, but Bersenev implored her not to: Insarov was rarely alone. On the first day, when she had learned of his illness, she herself had very nearly been taken ill; as soon as she got home she locked herself in her room; but she had been called down to dinner, and had appeared in the dining-room looking so dreadful that Anna Vasilyevna had been frightened and wanted to put her to bed without delay. Yelena, however, had managed to master herself. 'If he dies,' she kept saying, 'I too will not be here.' This thought calmed her and gave her the strength to appear indifferent. As a matter of fact, no one was much troubled by it: Anna Vasilyevna was fussing with her gumboils; Shubin was working like a maniac; Zoya had lapsed into melancholy and was preparing to read *Werther*;* Nikolai Artemyevich was very unhappy about the frequent visits of the 'scholar', all the more so as his 'predeterminations' regarding Kurnatovsky were making slow progress: the practical-minded chief secretary was puzzled, and biding his time. Yelena did not even thank Bersenev: there are good turns for which it is unnatural and embarrassing to give thanks. Only once, on her fourth meeting with him (Insarov had had a very bad night and the doctor had hinted that a council of specialists might be needed), only at this meeting had she reminded him of the oath he had sworn. 'Well, in that case let us go,' he told her. She stood up and was about to go and dress. 'No,' he said quietly, 'let us wait until tomorrow.' By the evening, Insarov's condition had eased a little.

For a week this torment continued. Yelena seemed calm, but was unable to eat anything, and could not sleep at nights. There was a dull aching in all her limbs; a dry, hot smoke seemed to fill her head. 'Our young mistress is melting like a candle,' her maid said of her.

At last, on the ninth day, the crisis was attained. Yelena was sitting in the drawing-room beside Anna Vasilyevna and, scarcely conscious of her actions, was reading to her from the *Moscow Gazette*; Bersenev came in. Yelena glanced at him (how quick, and shy, and penetrating, and troubled was the first glance she cast at him each time he arrived!) and realized at once that he had brought good news. He was smiling; he nodded to her slightly: she rose to greet him.

'He has regained consciousness, he is saved, in a week's time he will be quite well again,' he whispered to her.

Yelena stretched out her arms, as if warding off a blow, and said nothing—but her lips began to tremble, and a scarlet colour suffused her whole face. Bersenev began to talk to Anna Vasilyevna, and Yelena went to her room, fell on her knees, and began to pray, to give thanks to God... Light, radiant tears flowed from her eyes. She suddenly felt an extreme weariness, put her head on the pillow, whispered 'Poor Andrei Petrovich!'—and instantly fell asleep, with wet eyelashes and cheeks. It was a long time since she had either slept or wept.

XXVII

BERSENEV'S words were only partially realized: the danger passed, but Insarov's strength recovered slowly, and the doctor spoke of a deep and general shock to the whole system. Even so, the sick man left his bed and began to walk about the room; Bersenev had moved back to his lodgings; but each day he would look in to see his still-enfeebled companion, and each day, as previously, inform Yelena of the condition of his health. Insarov did not dare to write to her and only obliquely, in conversations with Bersenev, alluded to her; while Bersenev, with feigned indifference, told him of his visits to the Stakhovs', trying all the same to let him know that Yelena had been very upset, and that now she was calmer. Yelena also did not write to Insarov; she had something else on her mind.

One day—Bersenev had just told her with a cheerful look that the doctor had allowed Insarov to eat a cutlet and that he would probably soon be out and about—she reflected, lowered her eyes...

'Guess what I want to tell you,' she said quietly.

Bersenev was disconcerted. He understood her.

'Probably', he said, glancing to one side, 'you want to tell me that you would like to see him.'

Yelena reddened a little and, barely audibly, articulated:

'Yes.'

'Well? I should think that would be very easy for you.' 'Ugh!' he thought. 'What a vile feeling I have in my heart!'

'You mean that I already saw him earlier...' Yelena said quietly. 'But I'm afraid... now, you say, he is seldom alone.'

'It would not be difficult for me to help you in this,' Bersenev retorted, still without looking at her. 'I could not warn him in advance, of course; but give me a note. Who can forbid you to write to him as a good friend about whom you are concerned? There is nothing blame-worthy in that. Make a... or rather, write to him, and tell him when you will...'

'I'm too ashamed,' Yelena whispered.

'Give me a note, I will take it to him.'

'That isn't necessary, but I was going to ask you... Please don't be angry with me, Andrei Petrovich... don't come and see him tomorrow.'

Bersenev bit his lip.

'Ah! Now I understand, it's very clear, very clear.' And, after adding a few more words, he quickly went on his way.

'So much the better, so much the better,' he thought as he hurried home. 'I have learned nothing new, but so much the better. Why should I cling to the edge of another's nest? I repent of nothing, I have done what my conscience commanded, but now I have had enough. Let them go! Not without reason did my father say to me: "You and I, brother, are not sybarites, we're not aristocrats, not darlings of fortune or nature, we are not even martyrs—we are toilers, toilers and toilers. So put on your leather apron, toiler, and stand at your workman's lathe, in your dark workshop! As for the sun, let it shine for others! In our godforsaken lives we too have our pride and our happiness!"'

The following morning Insarov received a short little note in the post. 'Expect me,' Yelena wrote to him, 'and give instructions that everyone be refused entrance. A.P. is not coming.'

XXVIII

INSAROV read Yelena's note—and at once began to set his little room in order, asked the landlady to remove the bottles of medicine, took off his dressing-gown, and put on his frock-coat. With weakness and joy his head whirled and his heart pounded. His legs gave way beneath him: he lowered himself on to the sofa and began to look at his watch. 'It's now a quarter to twelve,' he said to himself. 'She cannot possibly be here before twelve, so I shall think about something else for quarter of an hour, otherwise I shall not be able to endure. She cannot possibly be here before twelve...'

The door opened wide and in a light silk dress, her face pale and fresh, young and happy, Yelena came in and, with a faint cry of joy, fell on his breast.

'You're alive, you are mine,' she kept saying, embracing his head, and caressing it. He stood stock-still, he gasped for breath at this closeness, this physical contact, this happiness.

She sat down beside him, nestled close against him, began to look at him with that laughing, caressing, and tender gaze that shines only in a woman's loving eyes.

Her face was suddenly sad.

'How thin you are, my poor Dmitry,' she said, moving her hand across his cheek. 'What a beard you have!'

'You too are thin, my poor Yelena,' he replied, trying to catch her fingers with his lips.

Cheerfully she shook her curls.

'It doesn't matter, Dmitry! Now we shall get well again! The storm broke as it did that day when we met in the wayside chapel, broke and passed. Now we shall live!'

He answered her only with a smile.

'Oh, what days, Dmitry, what cruel days! How is it possible for people to outlive those whom they love? Each time I knew beforehand what Andrei Petrovich would say, truly I did: my life fell and rose together with yours. Get well and prosper, my Dmitry!'

He did not know what to say to her. He felt like throwing himself at her feet.

246 *On the Eve*

'There is another thing that I observed,' she continued, turning back his hair, '(I made many observations all that time, at my leisure)—when one is very, very unhappy—with what stupid attention one follows all that is happening around one! Truly, sometimes I used to lose myself in contemplation of a fly, yet in my soul there was such cold and terror! But all that has passed, passed, has it not? All is light ahead of us, is it not?'

'For me you are ahead,' Insarov replied. 'For me it's light.'

'And for me! But do you remember that day when I was with you, not the last time... no, not the last time,' she repeated with an involuntary shudder, 'but when you and I were talking, I don't know why, I mentioned death; I had no idea then that death was lying in wait for us. But you are well now, aren't you?'

'I am much better, I am almost well.'

'You are well, you did not die. Oh, how happy I am!'

A brief silence ensued.

'Yelena?' Insarov inquired of her.

'What, my darling?'

'Tell me, did it ever occur to you that this illness was sent to us as a punishment?'

Yelena gave him a serious look.

'That thought did occur to me, Dmitry. But I reflected: for what would I be punished? What duty have I violated, against what have I sinned? Perhaps my conscience is not like that of others, but it was silent; or is it perhaps in your regard that I am guilty? I am standing in your way, I am stopping you...'

'You will not stop me, Yelena, we shall go together!'

'Yes, Dmitry, we shall go together, I shall follow you... That is my duty. I love you... I know no other duty.'

'Oh, Yelena!' Insarov said quietly. 'What indestructible chains your every word places upon me!'

'Why talk of chains?' she caught up. 'You and I are free human beings. Yes,' she continued, looking reflectively at the floor, with one hand smoothing his hair as before, 'I have experienced many things of late, things I had never had any idea of! If anyone had predicted that I, a young lady, well-bred, would leave my home on my own under various false pretexts, and go where? To a young man's lodgings—what indignation I should have felt! And it has all come true, and I feel no indignation at all. I swear to God I don't,' she added, and turned round to face Insarov.

He gazed at her with such an expression of worship that she quietly lowered her hand from his hair to his eyes.

'Dmitry!' she began again. 'You don't know, do you, but I saw you there, on that dreadful bed, I saw you in the clutches of death, unconscious...'

'You saw me?'

'Yes.'

He was silent.

'Bersenev was here, too?'

She nodded.

Insarov leaned towards her.

'Oh, Yelena!' he whispered softly. 'I do not dare to look at you.'

'Why? Andrei Petrovich is so good and kind! I was not ashamed with him. And why should I be ashamed? I am ready to tell the whole world that I am yours... And I trust Andrei Petrovich like a brother.'

'He saved me!' Insarov exclaimed. 'He is the most noble, the kindest of men.'

'Yes... And do you know that I owe him everything? Do you know that he was the first person to tell me that you loved me? And if I could reveal everything... Yes, he is the most noble of men.'

Insarov looked fixedly at Yelena.

'He is in love with you, isn't he?'

Yelena lowered her eyes.

'He loved me,' she said in an undertone.

Insarov tightly squeezed her hand.

'Oh you Russians,' he said, 'you have hearts of gold!' He too, he looked after me, he did not sleep at nights... And you, you, my angel... Never a reproach, never a hesitation... And all of it for me, for me...'

'Yes, all of it for you, because you are loved. Oh, Dmitry! How strange this is! I think I have already told you about this—but it doesn't matter, I like repeating it, and you will like hearing it—when I saw you the first time...'

'Why are there tears in your eyes?' Insarov interrupted her.

'In my eyes? Tears?' She wiped her eyes with her handkerchief. 'Oh, stupid man! He still does not know that one may also cry from happiness. This is what I wanted to say: the first time I saw you I did not see anything special in you, truly. I remember that at first Shubin appealed to me much more, though I never loved him, and as for Andrei Petrovich—oh! there was a moment when I thought: is not *he* the one? But you were nothing to me; yet later... later... you took my heart in both your hands!'

'Have mercy on me,' Insarov said quietly. He wanted to stand up, but at once sank back on to the sofa.

'What's wrong?' Yelena asked in concern.

'Nothing... I am still a little weak... This happiness is still too much for me.'

'Then sit quietly. You mustn't move about, mustn't excite yourself,' she added, admonishing him with her finger. 'And why have you taken off your dressing-gown? It's too soon for you to be striding about! Sit down, and I will tell you stories. Listen and keep quiet. After your illness it's not good for you to talk so much.'

She began to tell him about Shubin, about Kurnatovsky, about what she had been doing for the past two weeks, about how, judging from the newspapers, war was inevitable and that, consequently, as soon as he was completely recovered, they would have to find the means for their departure, with not a moment to lose... All this she told him, sitting beside him and leaning on his shoulder...

He listened to her, listened, now turning pale, now flushing... several times he wanted to stop her—and suddenly sat straight up.

'Yelena,' he said in a voice that was somehow strange and sharp. 'Leave me, go away.'

'What?' she said softly, in amazement. 'Are you feeling ill?' she added quickly.

'No... I feel all right... but, please, leave me.'

'I don't understand. You are driving me away?... What are you doing?...' she said suddenly: he leaned forward on the sofa so that he almost touched the floor, and pressed his lips to her feet. 'Don't do that, Dmitry... Dmitry...'

He raised himself.

'Then leave me! You see, Yelena, when I fell ill, I did not lose consciousness right away; I knew that I was on the brink of doom; even in my fever, in my delirium, I realized, I dimly sensed, that death was coming to me, I said farewell to life, to you, to everyone, I parted with hope... And then suddenly this rebirth, this light after darkness, you... you... beside me, with me... your voice, your breathing... It is beyond my strength! I feel that I love you passionately, I hear you call yourself mine, and I cannot be answerable for anything... Please go away!'

'Dmitry,' Yelena whispered softly, hiding her head on his shoulder. Only now did she understand.

'Yelena,' he continued, 'I love you, you know that, I am ready to give up my life for you... Then why have you come to me now, when I am weak, when I am not my own master, when all my blood is on fire?... You are mine, you say... you love me...'

'Dmitry,' she repeated, flushed all over, and pressed herself even closer to him.

'Yelena, have pity on me—go away, I feel I may die—I will not survive these outbursts... the whole of my soul is striving towards you... Think, death almost separated us... and now you are here, you are in my arms... Yelena...'

She began to tremble.

'So take me, then,' she whispered, barely audibly...

XXIX

Nikolai Artemyevich was pacing to and fro about his study, beetle-browed. Shubin sat by the window, legs crossed, calmly smoking a cigar.

'Do stop pacing from one corner of the room to another like that,' he said, knocking the ash from his cigar. 'I keep thinking you're going to say something, and I follow you with my eyes until my neck is sore. Your walk, moreover, has something strained and melodramatic about it.'

'All you want to do is make jokes,' Nikolai Artemyevich replied. 'You don't want to enter into my situation; you don't want to see that I've grown accustomed to this woman, that I am attached to her, that her absence cannot but torment me. October is here, winter is just around the corner... What can she be doing in Reval?'

'She must be knitting stockings... for herself; herself... not you.'

'Laugh away, laugh away; but I will tell you that I know no other woman like her. Such honesty, such selflessness...'

'Did she try to cash the promissory note?' Shubin asked.

'Such selflessness,' Nikolai Artemyevich repeated, raising his voice, 'that it is astonishing. They tell me that there are a million other women in the world; but I say: show me that million; show me that million, say I; *ces femmes—qu'on me les montre!** She does not write to me, either, that is what is so devastating.'

'You are as eloquent as Pythagoras,' Shubin observed, 'but do you know what I would advise you?'

'What?'

'When Avgustina Khristianovna returns... you understand me?'

'Well, yes, but so what?'

'When you see her... You follow the development of my thought?'

'Well, yes, yes.'

'Try beating her a bit: something might come of it?'

Nikolai Artemyevich turned away in indignation.

'I thought he was really going to give me some sensible advice. But what can one expect from him? An artist, a man without principles...'

'Without principles! And yet I am told that your favourite, Mr Kurnatovsky, a man of principles, won a hundred roubles in silver from you yesterday at cards. That was not very tactful, you must admit.'

'What of it? We were playing the commercial game. Of course, I might have expected... But he is so little appreciated in this house...'

'I know what was in his mind,' Shubin chipped in: ' "No matter! Father-in-law or no father-in-law, that is still hidden in the urn of Fate, but a hundred roubles will come in handy for a man who does not take bribes." '

'Father-in-law? What kind of father-in-law am I, damn it? *Vous revez, mon cher*.* Of course, any other girl would be overjoyed to have such a fiancé. Judge for yourself: the man is sharp and clever, worked his way up in the world unaided, drudged in two guberniyas . . .'*

'In —— guberniya he led the governor by the nose,' Shubin observed.

'That may very well be so. I expect it was the right thing to do. He's a practical man, a businesslike man...'

'And good at cards, too,' Shubin observed again.

'Well, yes, and good at cards, too. But Yelena Nikolayevna... Is it really possible to understand her? I should like to know where the man is who could undertake to ascertain what it is she wants. Now she is cheerful, now she frets; she suddenly becomes so thin that one can't bear to look at her, and then suddenly puts on weight again, and all this without any obvious cause...'

An uncomely lackey entered, bearing a cup of coffee, a jug of cream, and some rusks on a tray.

'The father likes the intended bridegroom,' Nikolai Artemyevich continued, waving a rusk in the air, 'but what does the daughter care? It all worked well in the old, patriarchal days, but now we have changed all that. *Nous avons changé tout ça*. Now a young lady talks with whom she pleases and reads what she pleases; sets off through Moscow alone, with no lackey, with no maid, as if she were in Paris; and it is all accepted. A day or two ago I ask: where is Yelena Nikolayevna? It pleased her ladyship to go out, they say. Where to? We do not know. Do you call that—order?'

'Oh, take your cup and let the servant go,' Shubin said quietly. 'You yourself say that one should not talk *devant les domestiques*,' he added in a low voice.

The lackey glowered at Shubin, and Nikolai Artemyevich took the cup, poured some cream for himself, and raked up a dozen or so rusks.

'What I mean,' he began, as soon as the lackey went out, 'is that I count for nothing in this house. 'That is all. Because in our time everyone judges by external appearances; a man may be empty and stupid, but if he comports himself grandly—he is respected; while another may, perhaps, possess talents that might... might be of great use, but out of modesty...'

'Are you a statesman, Nikolenka?' Shubin asked in a thin little voice.

'Enough of your clowning!' Nikolai Artemyevich exclaimed with anger. 'You forget yourself! There is another proof for you that I count for nothing in this house, nothing!'

'Anna Vasilyevna is keeping you down... poor dear chap!' Shubin said, stretching. 'Eh, Nikolai Artemyevich, we're a couple of sinners, you and I. You'd better get Anna Vasilyevna a little present of some kind. It's her birthday soon, and you know how she prizes the slightest sign of attention on your part.'

'Yes, yes,' Nikolai Artemyevich answered hurriedly, 'I'm most grateful to you for reminding me. Indeed, indeed... absolutely. And actually, I do have a little item: a brooch thing, I bought it at Rosenstrauch's the other day; only I don't know if it will do for her?'

'You bought it for the other one, the lady resident of Reval, did you not?'

'Well, I... yes... I thought...'

'Oh, in that case it will surely do.'

Shubin rose from the chair.

'Where shall we go this evening, Pavel Yakovlevich, ah?' Nikolai Artemyevich asked him, peering affectionately into Shubin's eyes.

'But you're going to the club.'

'After the club... after the club.'

Again, Shubin stretched.

'No, Nikolai Artemyevich, I must work tomorrow. Some other time.' And he went out.

Nikolai Artemyevich scowled, paced once or twice about the room, took from the writing-desk a small velvet box that contained the 'brooch thing', and examined it for a long time, wiping it with his foulard. Then he sat down in front of the mirror and began painstakingly to comb his thick black hair, with a solemn expression on his face inclining his head now to the right, now to the left, his tongue stuck in his cheek and his eyes fixed constantly on his parting. Someone coughed behind his back: he glanced round and saw the lackey who had brought him his coffee.

'What do you want?' he asked him.

'Nikolai Artemyevich!' the lackey said, not without a certain solemnity. 'You are our *barin*!'

'I am aware of that: what else?'

'Nikolai Artemyevich, please don't be angry with me, sir; only, I've been in your service since I was little, and so my servile diligence makes me an-obligated to inform your grace...'

'What on earth are you talking about?'

The lackey stood humming and hawing.

'You see, sir,' he began, 'your grace told me that you don't know where her ladyship Yelena Nikolayevna goes when she's not here. I have become informed of that.'

'What rubbish are you talking, fool?'

'That is all as you wish, sire, but only three days ago I saw her ladyship enter a certain house, sir.'

'Where? What? What house?'

'In —— Lane, near Povarskaya. Not far from here. I asked the yardkeeper: yardkeeper, I said, what sort of tenants do you have here?'

Nikolai Artemyevich began to stamp his feet.

'Be silent, good-for-nothing! How dare you?... Yelena Nikolayevna, out of the kindness of her heart, goes visiting the poor, and you... Out, fool!'

The frightened lackey began to rush towards the door.

'Wait!' exclaimed Nikolai Artemyevich. 'What did the yardkeeper tell you?'

'Why n-nothing, sir. A s-student, he said.'

'Be silent, good-for-nothing! Listen here, villain: if you ever tell anyone about this, even in your sleep...'

'For mercy's sake, sir...'

'Be silent! If you so much as let out a squeak... if anyone... if I find out... You will not even find a place with me beneath the ground! Do you hear? Make yourself scarce!'

The lackey disappeared.

'Oh my God! What does this mean?' Nikolai Artemyevich thought, when he was left alone. 'What did that blockhead say to me? Eh? However, I must find out what sort of house that is, and who lives there. I must go myself. That is what it has come to, at last!... *Un laquais! Quelle humiliation!*'

And, loudly repeating: '*Un laquais*', Nikolai Artemyevich locked the brooch in the writing-desk and set off to see Anna Vasilyevna. He found her in bed, with a bound-up cheek. But the sight of her sufferings merely irritated him, and he very soon reduced her to tears.

XXX

MEANWHILE the storm that had been gathering in the East broke. Turkey declared war on Russia; the term appointed for the evacuation of the principalities was up; it would not now be long until the day of the Sinope Massacre.* The last letters Insarov received insistently summoned him to the motherland. His health was still not recovered: he coughed, experienced asthenia, had mild attacks of fever, but was almost never at home. His soul was on fire; he no longer thought about illness. He travelled about Moscow ceaselessly, had surreptitious meetings with various persons, sat up writing for nights on end, went missing for days on end; to his landlord he said that he would soon be vacating the room, and made him a gift of his modest furniture in advance. Yelena, for her part, also got ready for the departure. One inclement evening she sat in her room and, as she hemmed some shawls, with involuntary melancholy listened to the howling of the wind. Her maidservant came in and told her that her father was in her mother's bedroom and was asking her to go there... 'Your mother is crying,' she whispered as Yelena went, 'and your father is angry.'

Yelena shrugged slightly, and went into Anna Vasilyevna's bedroom. Nikolai Artemyevich's good-natured spouse lay half-reclining in a tip-up armchair, sniffing a handkerchief soaked in eau-de-cologne; he himself stood by the fireplace, with all his buttons done up, in a high, stiff cravat and a tightly starched collar, his bearing vaguely reminiscent of some parliamentary orator. With an oratorical movement of his hand, he showed his daughter to a chair, and when, failing to understand his movement, she looked at him questioningly, he said with quiet dignity, though without turning his head: 'Pray be seated.' (Nikolai Artemyevich always used this type of address* to his wife— to his daughter, only in extraordinary circumstances.)

Yelena sat down.

Anna Vasilyevna tearfully blew her nose. Nikolai Artemyevich put his right hand under the breast of his frock-coat.

'I have called you here, Yelena Nikolayevna,' he began after a lengthy silence, 'in order to have an explanation with you, or, rather, to request an explanation from you. I am displeased with you, or rather, no: that is putting it too mildly; your behaviour distresses me, offends me—me, and your mother, too... your mother, whom you see here.'

Nikolai Artemyevich employed only the bass notes of his voice. In silence, Yelena looked at him, and then at Anna Vasilyevna—and turned pale.

'There was a time,' Nikolai Artemyevich began again, 'when daughters did not permit themselves to look down upon their parents, when parental authority made the disobedient tremble. That time has passed, regrettably; or thus, at least, do many people suppose; but believe me, there are still laws, which do not permit... do not permit... in short, there are still laws. Pray take notice of that fact: there are laws...'

'But Papa!' Yelena began...

'I pray you not to interrupt me. Let us convey ourselves mentally into the past. Anna Vasilyevna and I have fulfilled our duty. Anna Vasilyevna and I have spared nothing for your upbringing: neither expense, nor care. As to the benefit you have derived from all this care, this expense—that is another matter; but I had the right to suppose that you would at least hold sacred those principles of morality which... which to you, as our only daughter, we have... *que nous avons inculqués*, which we have inculcated in you. We had the right to suppose that no new "ideas" would affect this, as it were, sacred realm. And yet, what do we find? I pass over the frivolity, characteristic of your sex and age... but who could have expected that you would forget yourself so far that...'

'Papa,' Yelena said quietly. 'I know what you want to say...'

'No, you do not know what I want to say!' Nikolai Artemyevich cried in a falsetto, having suddenly, and in equal measure, broken faith with the majesty of his parliamentary bearing, the smooth solemnity of his speech, and the bass notes of his voice. 'You do not know, insolent girl!'

'For the love of God, Nikolai Artemyevich,' Anna Vasilyevna murmured softly, '*vous me faites mourir*.'*

'Do not say that to me, *que je vous fais mourir*, Anna Vasilyevna! You cannot imagine what you are about to hear—prepare yourself for the worst, I warn you!'

Anna Vasilyevna was utterly stupefied.

'No,' Nikolai Artemyevich continued, turning to Yelena, 'you do not know what I want to say!'

'I am guilty before you both,' she began...

'Ah, at last!'

'I am guilty before you,' Yelena continued, 'for not having confessed long ago...'

'And do you realize', Nikolai Artemyevich interrupted her, 'that I can annihilate you with a single word?'

Yelena raised her eyes to him.

'Yes, madam, with a single word! There is no need to stare!' (He folded his arms on his chest.) 'Permit me to enquire: are you acquainted with a certain house in —— Lane, near Povarskaya? Have you visited that house?' (He stamped his foot.) 'Answer, good-for-nothing girl, and do not think of using cunning! The servants, the servants, lackeys, madam, *des vils laquais* saw you go there, to your...'

Yelena flushed all over, and her eyes began to gleam.

'I have no reason to use cunning,' she said. 'Yes, I have visited that house.'

'Splendid! Do you hear, do you hear, Anna Vasilyevna? And I expect you probably know who lives in it?'

'Yes, I do: my husband...'

Nikolai Artemyevich goggled in disbelief.

'Your...'

'My husband,' Yelena repeated. 'I am married to Dmitry Nikanorovich Insarov.'

'You?... married?...' Anna Vasilyevna said barely audibly.

'Yes, mama... Forgive me... Two weeks ago we were married in secret.'

Anna Vasilyevna fell into her chair; Nikolai Artemyevich took two steps back.

'Married? To that ragamuffin, that Montenegrin? The daughter of the nobleman of ancient stock, Nikolai Stakhov, has married a vagrant, a *raznochinets*!* Without the blessing of her parents! And you suppose that I will leave the matter there? That I will not make official complaints? That I will allow you... that you... that... You shall go to a nunnery, and he to the convict regiments! Anna Vasilyevna, kindly tell her this instant that you are disinheriting her.'

'Nikolai Artemyevich, for the love of God!' Anna Vasilyevna moaned quietly.

'And when, in what manner did this happen? Who wed you? Where? How? My God! What will my friends say now, the whole world? And you, shameless dissembler, thought that you could go on living under your parents' roof after such an action? Were you not afraid... of a celestial thunderbolt?'

'Papa,' Yelena said (she was trembling from top to toe, but her voice was firm), 'you are free to do with me as you will, but you have no right to accuse me of shamelessness and dissembling. I did not want... to cause you distress in advance, but I would have no choice but to tell you everything in a few days' time, because my husband and I are going away from here next week.'

'Going away? Where to?'

'To his motherland, Bulgaria.'

'To the Turks!' Anna Vasilyevna exclaimed, and swooned unconscious.

Yelena rushed to her mother.

'Get thee hence!' roared Nikolai Artemyevich, and seized his daughter by the arm. 'Get thee hence, unworthy one!'

But at this moment the door of the bedroom opened, and a pale head with glittering eyes appeared; it was Shubin's head.

'Nikolai Artemyevich!' he shouted at the top of his voice. 'Avgustina Khristianovna has arrived and calls you to her!'

Nikolai Artemyevich turned round in fury, shook his fist at Shubin, paused for a moment, and quickly left the room.

Yelena fell at her mother's feet and hugged her knees.

Uvar Ivanovich lay on his bed. A shirt without a collar, but with a large stud, enveloped his fat neck, falling open in broad, untrammelled folds over his almost feminine breast and exposing to view a large, cypresswood cross, and an amulet. A light coverlet draped his extensive limbs. A candle burned dimly on the night table, beside a tankard of kvass, and at Uvar Ivanovich's feet, on the bed, sat a mournful Shubin.

'Yes,' he said reflectively, 'she is married and is getting ready to leave. Your little nephew has caused a rumpus, bawling all over the house; locked himself away in the bedroom for secrecy, yet not only the lackeys and the maids, but even the coachmen could hear it all! Even now he's still ranting and raving, he almost knocked me down, keeps roaring about his paternal curse like a bear with a sore head; but he's quite ineffective. Anna Vasilyevna is broken-hearted, but she is far more distressed about her daughter's departure than about her married state.'

Uvar Ivanovich twiddled his fingers.

'A mother,' he said. 'Well... after all.'

'Your nephew', Shubin continued, 'is threatening to file complaints with the Metropolitan,* with the Governor-General, with the Minister, but she'll leave all the same in the end. Who can get any fun out of ruining his own daughter? He'll strut like a cockerel and then put his tail back down where it belongs.'

'They don't have... the right,' Uvar Ivanovich observed, and took a sip from the tankard.

'Indeed, indeed. But what a swarm of condemnation, gossip, and rumour will be stirred in Moscow! She was not afraid of that... As a matter of fact, she is above it. She is going away—and where to? It's dreadful even to think of it! Such a long way away, to such a godforsaken spot! What will await her there? I see her leaving some wayside inn at night, in a snowstorm, in thirty degrees of frost. Parting from her motherland, her family; but I understand her. Whom does she leave behind? With whom has she associated? Folk like Kurnatovsky, Bersenev, you and I; and those are the best of them. What is there to feel sorry about there? The only bad part of it is that they say her husband—damn it, my tongue somehow refuses to get itself round that word—Insarov, they say, is coughing blood; that is the bad part. I saw him the other day, with a face you could have modelled a Brutus* from right there and then... Do you know who Brutus was, Uvar Ivanovich?'

'How would I know? A man.'

'Precisely: "this was a man". Yes, a marvellous face, but unhealthy, very unhealthy.'

'For fighting... it doesn't matter,' Uvar Ivanovich said.

'For fighting it doesn't matter, exactly: you're expressing yourself most lucidly today, if I may say so. But for living it does matter. And after all, that is what she wants to do with him—live with him.'

'A young affair.'

'Yes, a young affair, a glorious, bold affair. Death, life, struggle, downfall, triumph, love, freedom, motherland... Wonderful, wonderful. God grant it to everyone! It's rather different from sitting up to one's neck in the mire and trying to make it look as if one doesn't care, when indeed, in essence, one really does care. But there, on the other hand, are tautened strings: play to the whole world, or break!'

Shubin lowered his head to his chest.

'Yes,' he continued, after a long silence. 'Insarov is worthy of her. Though, as a matter of fact, what nonsense that is ! No one is worthy of her. Insarov... Insarov... Why the false humility? Very well, let us admit that he's a brave fellow, he can stand up for himself, though so far he has acted just the same as the rest of us sinners, and in that case are we really such complete nonentities? Well, take me, for example, Uvar Ivanovich, am I a nonentity? Has God not endowed me with anything? Given me no abilities, no talents? Who knows, in time the name of Pavel Shubin may be famous! There's a copper half-copeck coin on your table over there. Who knows, perhaps one day, a century from now, that copper will go towards a statue of Pavel Shubin, erected in his honour by a grateful posterity.'

Uvar Ivanovich propped himself up on his elbow and stared fixedly at the excited artist.

'A distant story,' he said at last, with the customary twiddle of his fingers. 'We are talking of others, but you talk... of yourself.'

'O great philosopher of the Russian land!' exclaimed Shubin. 'Each word you utter is pure gold, and it is not to me but to you that a statue should be erected: I shall make it myself. Just as you lie now there, in that pose, in which it's hard to say if there is more laziness or strength—that is how I shall mould you. Just was the rebuke with which you smote my egotism and my vanity! Yes! Yes! There is no use talking of oneself; there is no use boasting. We have no one yet, there are no human beings, no matter where one looks. It's all small fry, rodents, little Hamlets, samoyeds, or obscurity and the subterranean backwoods, or arrivistes, pourers of emptiness into vacuity, and sticks to beat drums with! Or else it's the other kind: studying themselves with shameful subtlety, constantly feeling the pulse of their every sensation and reporting to themselves: that, they say, is what I feel, that is what I think. A useful, practical occupation! No, if there were any worthwhile human beings among them, this girl, this sensitive soul, would not be leaving us, would not be slipping away like a fish into water! What is this, Uvar Ivanovich? When will our time come? When will some human beings be born among us?'

'Wait a while,' Uvar Ivanovich replied. 'They will come.'

'Will they? Soil! Power of the black earth! "They will come," you say? Look then, I'll write down your words. But why are you dousing the candle?'

'I want to sleep, goodnight.'

XXXI

WHAT Shubin had said was true. The unexpected news of Yelena's marriage very nearly killed Anna Vasilyevna. She took to her bed. Nikolai Artemyevich demanded that she should not admit her daughter to her presence; he seemed to take delight in the chance to show that he was, in the full sense of the word, master of the house, with all the powers of the head of the family: he constantly bellowed and thundered at the servants, every so often repeating: 'I'll show you who I am, I'll make you understand—just wait?' For as long as he was at home, Anna Vasilyevna did not see Yelena, and made do with the presence of Zoya, who obliged her very diligently, all the time thinking to herself: '*Diesen Insaroff vorziehen—und wem?*'* But as soon as Nikolai Artemyevich went away (and this happened rather often: Avgustina Khrisianovna had indeed returned), Yelena would appear in her mother's room— and her mother would look at her in silence, for a long time, with tears in her eyes. This mute reproach penetrated Yelena's heart more deeply than any of the rest; it was not remorse that she felt then, but a deep, infinite pity that was similar to remorse.

'Mama, dear Mama!' she kept saying, kissing her mother's hands. 'But what could I do? I am not guilty, I fell in love with him, I could not do anything else. Blame fate: it was fate that brought me together with a man whom Papa does not like, who is taking me away from you.'

'Oh!' Anna Vasilyevna interrupted her. 'Don't remind me of it. When I remember where you are planning to go to, my heart writhes in agony!'

'Dear Mama,' Yelena replied, 'console yourself with the thought that it could have been worse: I could have died.'

'It doesn't matter, I still don't believe I shall ever see you again. Either you will end your days there in some *shalash*, some shelter made of branches (Anna Vasilyevna imagined Bulgaria as something like the Siberian tundra), or I will not be able to endure the separation...'

'Do not say that, my kind mother, we shall see each other again, God will grant it. And in Bulgaria there are cities just as there are here.'

'What do you mean, cities? There's a war there now; wherever you turn there will be cannons going off, I expect... Are you leaving soon?'

'Yes... if Papa will... He wants to file an official complaint, he's threatening to have us divorced.'

Anna Vasilyevna raised her eyes heavenwards.

'No, Lenochka, he will file no official complaint. I would never have agreed to this marriage, would rather have died; but it's no good trying to undo what's been done, and I will not let my daughter be disgraced.'

Several days passed like this. At last, Anna Vasilyevna summoned her courage, and one evening shut herself up alone with her husband in the bedroom. Everyone in the house fell quiet, and listened. At first, nothing could be heard; then Nikolai Artemyevich's voice began to boom, and after that an argument began, there were cries, some even fancied they heard groans... Shubin, with Zoya and the maids, was on the point of going to the rescue again; but the uproar in the bedroom gradually began to die down, passed into conversation—and was silent. Only now and then were there faint sobbings—and then those, too, came to an end. There was a jangle of keys, the squeaking of the writing-desk being opened was heard... The door opened, and Nikolai Artemyevich appeared. Glancing sternly at all whom he encountered, he set off for the club; but Anna Vasilyevna told Yelena to come and see her, hugged her tightly, and dissolving in bitter tears, said:

'It's all arranged, he won't make any difficulties, and there is nothing to stop you from going away... and deserting us.'

'Will you allow Dmitry to come and thank you both?' Yelena asked her mother as soon as the latter had calmed down a little.

'Wait, my darling, I cannot see our rival now... We shall have time before your departure.'

'Before our departure,' Yelena repeated sadly.

Nikolai Artemyevich had consented 'not to make any difficulties'; but Anna Vasilyevna did not tell her daughter the price he had set on this consent. She did not tell her that she had undertaken to pay all his debts and had given him a thousand silver roubles in cash. Moreover, he had announced to Anna Vasilyevna in no uncertain terms that he did not wish to meet Insarov, whom he continued to call a 'Montenegrin', and on arriving at the club began, quite needlessly, to talk about his daughter's marriage with his card partner, a retired general of the Engineers. 'Have you heard?' he said quietly, with a feigned air of casualness. 'Because of all that learning of hers, my daughter has gone and married some student or other.' The general looked at him through his spectacles, grunted 'Ahem!' and asked him what trumps he was playing.

XXXII

MEANWHILE the day of departure drew near. November was already running to a close, the final dates were expiring. Insarov had long ago finished all his preparations and burned with the desire to escape from Moscow. The doctor, too, hurried him along: 'You need a warm climate,' he told him. 'Here you will not get well.' Impatience also tormented Yelena; she was worried by Insarov's paleness, and by how thin he was. She would often stare at his altered features with involuntary fear. Her position in her parents' home was becoming intolerable. Her mother keened over her as if she were already dead, while her father treated her with cold contempt: the closeness of the separation was secretly torturing him, too, but he considered it his duty, the duty of an injured parent, to conceal his feelings, his weakness. Anna Vasilyevna finally expressed a wish to see Insarov. He was brought to her on the quiet, by the back entrance. When he entered her room, it was a long time before she could begin to talk to him, and she could not even bring herself to look at him: he sat beside her chair, with calm respect awaiting her first word. Yelena sat there also, holding her mother's hand. Anna Vasilyevna raised her eyes at last, said softly: 'God is your judge, Dmitry Nikanorovich,'—and stopped: the reproaches froze on her lips.

'Oh, you are ill,' she exclaimed. 'Yelena, he is ill, this man of yours!'

'I have been unwell, Anna Vasilyevna,' Insarov replied, 'and even now I have not quite regained my health; but I hope that the air of my native land will finally restore me.'

'Yes... Bulgaria!' Anna Vasilyevna murmured, as she thought: 'My God, a Bulgarian, a dying one, with a voice as though out of a barrel, eyes as big as baskets, skin as yellow as dog fennel—and she is his wife, she loves him... why, this is some kind of dream...' But she at once collected herself. 'Dmitry Nikanorovich,' she said, 'do you absolutely... absolutely have to go?'

'Yes, Anna Vasilyevna, I do.'

Anna Vasilyevna looked at him.

'Ah, Dmitry Nikanorovich, may God never make you endure what I am now enduring... But you will promise me to look after her, and love her... You will never have to suffer poverty for as long as I am alive!'

Tears choked her voice. She opened her arms, and both Yelena and Insarov hugged her.

The fateful day arrived at last. It was decided that Yelena should say farewell to her parents at home, but that the journey should begin from Insarov's lodgings. The departure was fixed for twelve. A quarter of an hour before that, Bersenev arrived. He had supposed he would find Insarov's fellow countrymen there to see him off; but they had all gone on ahead, as had the two mysterious persons who are already familiar to the reader (they had served as witnesses at Insarov's wedding). The tailor greeted the 'kind *barin*' with a bow: he had had much to drink, possibly in order to drown his sorrows, but also possibly because he was pleased to be getting the furniture; his wife soon led him away. Everything in the room had been tidied up; a trunk, bound with rope, stood on the floor. Bersenev began to ponder: many memories passed through his soul.

It had long ago struck twelve, and the yamshchik* had already brought the horses, but of the 'young ones' there was still no sign. At last hurried steps were heard on the stairs, and Yelena came in, accompanied by Insarov and Shubin. Yelena's eyes were red: she had left her mother lying in a fainting-fit; the farewell had been very difficult. Yelena had not seen Bersenev for more than a week: of late he had seldom visited the Stakhovs. She had not expected to find him there, cried: 'You! Thank you!'—and hurled herself upon his neck; Insarov also embraced him. A tense silence ensued. What could they say, these three people, what did they feel, these three hearts? Shubin realized the necessity of relieving the tension by a living sound, a word or two.

'Our trio is gathered again,' he began, 'for the last time! Let us submit to the commands of fate, reflect kindly on the past, and with God move on to a new life! "With God upon the distant road...",'* he began to sing, and then stopped. He suddenly felt ashamed and awkward. It is sinful to sing in the place where the deceased lies: and at that moment, in that room, the past he had mentioned was dying, the past of the people who had gathered there. It was dying in order to be reborn in a new life, perhaps . . . But it was dying nonetheless.

'Well, Yelena,' Insarov began, turning to his wife, 'I think that is everything? Everything is paid for, and packed. Now there is only this trunk to be hauled downstairs! Landlord!'

The landlord came into the room together with his wife and daughter. Swaying slightly, he attended to Insarov's command, loaded the trunk onto his shoulders, and quickly ran down the staircase, his heels clattering.

'Now, according to Russian custom, we must sit down,' Insarov observed.

They all sat down: Bersenev lodged himself on the old sofa; Yelena sat beside him; the landlady and her daughter nestled down in the doorway. All were silent; all were smiling forced smiles, and none of them knew why they were smiling; each wanted to say some word of farewell, and each (with the exception, of course, of the landlady and her daughter: they merely watched with eyes a-goggle), each felt that at such moments it is permissible to say only trivial things, that any significant, or intelligent, or simply sincere remark would be somehow out of place, almost false. Insarov was the first to get to his feet, and he began to cross himself... 'Farewell, our little room!' he exclaimed.

There was the sound of kisses, the resonant but cold kisses of parting, half-finished wishes for the journey, promises to write, the last, half-stifled words of farewell...

Yelena, her face in tears, had already got into the sledge-cart; Insarov was solicitously covering her legs with the rug; Shubin, Bersenev, the landlord, his wife, his daughter with the inevitable shawl on her head, the yardkeeper, a passing artisan in a striped overall—all stood by the front steps, when suddenly into the courtyard sailed an opulent sleigh, drawn by a spirited trotter, and out of the sleigh, shaking the snow from the collar of his overcoat, jumped Nikolai Artemyevich.

'Caught you while there is still time,' he exclaimed, and ran towards the sledge-cart. 'Here, Yelena, is our last parental blessing,' he said, bending down to look in under the hood, and, taking from the pocket of his frock-coat a small icon, sewn up in a little velvet bag, hung it around her neck. She burst out sobbing and began to kiss his hands, while the coachman took a half-bottle of champagne and three glasses from the front of the sleigh.

'Well!' said Nikolai Artemyevich, as the tears fairly dripped down on the beaver collar of his overcoat. 'We must see you off... and wish you...' He began to pour the champagne; his hands trembled, the foam rose over the edge and fell on the snow. He took one glass himself, and gave the other two to Yelena and Insarov, who had already managed to get in beside her. 'May God grant you...' Nikolai Artemyevich began, but could not finish the sentence—and drank the wine; the others also drank theirs. 'Now you should drink too, gentlemen,' he added, turning to Shubin and Bersenev, but at that moment the yamshchik started the horses. Nikolai Artemyevich ran beside the sledge-cart. 'See and write to us,' he said in a broken voice. Yelena thrust her head out, said: 'Farewell, Papa, Andrei Petrovich, Pavel Yakovlevich, farewell everyone, farewell, Russia!'—and settled back again. The yamshchik brandished his whip, and began to whistle; the sledge-cart, its runners creaking, turned out of the gate to the right—and disappeared.

XXXIII

IT was a bright day in April. On the wide lagoon separating Venice from the narrow strip of alluvial sea-sand that is called the Lido, a sharp-prowed gondola was gliding, slowly and regularly swaying with each jolt that fell on to the gondolier's long oar. Beneath its low roof, on soft leather cushions, sat Yelena and Insarov.

The features of Yelena's face had not changed much since the day of her departure from Moscow, but their expression was now different: it was more deliberate and stern, and her eyes looked more boldly. Her whole body had blossomed out, and her hair seemed to lie more luxuriantly and thickly along her pale forehead and fresh cheeks. Only on her lips, when she was not smiling, did a barely perceptible crease betray the presence of a secret, constant anxiety. The expression of Insarov's face had, on the other hand, remained the same, but his features had cruelly altered. He had become thinner, had aged, grown pale, and stooped; he coughed almost without cease, a short, dry cough, and his sunken eyes shone with a strange brilliancy. On the way from Russia Insarov had lain ill in bed for nearly two months in Vienna, and had not reached Venice with his wife until the end of March: from there he hoped to cross by way of Zara into Serbia and Bulgaria; the other routes were closed to him. War was already fully under way on the Danube; France and England had declared war on Russia, and all the Slavic lands were in a state of ferment, and preparing for insurrection.

The gondola pulled in at the inner end of the Lido. Yelena and Insarov set off along a narrow sandy path planted with consumptive saplings (they are planted every year, and they die every year), to the outer end of the Lido, towards the sea.

They walked some way along the shore. Before them, the Adriatic rolled its turbid blue breakers; they foamed, hissed, broke, and sliding back, left small shells and pieces of seaweed on the sand.

'What a melancholy place!' Yelena observed. 'I am afraid it may be too cold for you here; but I can guess why you wanted to come.'

'Too cold!' Insarov rejoined with a quick but bitter smile. 'A fine soldier I will make if I'm to fear the cold. No, I came here... I shall tell you why. When I look at this sea, I feel that I am closer to my motherland. After all, it's over there,' he added, extending a hand to the east. 'Now the wind is blowing from that direction.'

'I suppose this wind will bring the boat you are waiting for, won't it?' said Yelena. 'Look, there's a white sail, perhaps that's it?'

Insarov looked into the marine distance, in the direction Yelena had pointed.

'Rendich promised to arrange everything for us within the space of a week,' he observed. 'I think one may rely on him... I say, Yelena, did you hear,' he added with sudden animation, 'it's said that poor Dalmatian fishermen have given up their plumbs—you know, those weights they use to lower their sweep-nets to the bottom—to make bullets! They didn't have any money, and catching fish is their only means of livelihood; but they gave up their last possessions with joy, and are now going hungry. What people they are!'

'*Aufgepasst!*'* a haughty voice cried from behind them. There was a muffled thud of horses' hooves, and an Austrian officer, in a short grey tunic and a green peaked cap, galloped past them . . . They barely had time to move aside.

With a dark look, Insarov watched him go.

'It's not his fault,' Yelena said quietly. 'You know, there is nowhere else for them here to break in their horses.'

'No, it's not his fault,' Insarov rejoined, 'but he set my blood going with his shouting, his moustache, his cap, and the whole of the way he looked. Let's go back.'

'Yes, let's, Dmitry. In any case, it really is windy here. You did not look after yourself following your illness in Moscow, and paid the price for it in Vienna. Now you must show more caution.'

Insarov said nothing, but his earlier bitter smile fleeted across his lips.

'I know what,' Yelena continued, 'let's sail back along the Canale Grande. After all, we have not really seen Venice properly since we arrived. And in the evening, let us go to the theatre: I have two tickets for a box. They say there is a new opera. If you would like to, let us devote today to each other, let us forget about politics, war, everything, let us know only one thing: that we live, breathe, and think together, that we are united for ever... Would you like that?'

'You would like it, Yelena,' Insarov replied, 'and therefore I would like it, too.'

'I knew you would,' Yelena remarked with a smile. 'Let us go, let us go.'

They returned to the gondola, climbed into it, and asked to be taken, in leisurely fashion, along the Grand Canal.

He who has never seen Venice in April will scarcely be familiar with the whole ineffable charm of that enchanting city. The mildness and softness of spring suit Venice, as the blazing summer sun suits magnificent Genoa, and as the gold and purple of autumn suit the great elder, Rome. Like the spring, the beauty of Venice also affects and arouses the desires; it torments and teases the inexperienced heart, like the promise of an imminent, not hard to explain, but mysterious happiness. Everything in it is light and comprehensible, and it is all imbued, as by a drowsy haze, in a kind of enamoured silence; everything in it is silent, and everything is welcoming; everything in it is feminine, starting with its name; not in vain is it alone given the title 'Beautiful'. The massive forms of the palaces and churches stand light and miraculous as the well-proportioned dream of a young god; there is something fairy-tale like, something captivatingly strange in the greenish-grey lustre and silky tints of the canals' mute undulation, in the gondolas' soundless passage, in the absence of raucous urban noise, of raucous clatter, crash, and din. 'Venice is dying. Venice has become deserted,' its inhabitants tell you; but it is possible that it was precisely this final charm, the charm of fading in the very flowering and triumph of beauty, that it earlier lacked. He who has not seen it, does not know it: neither Canaletto nor Guardi (not to mention more recent painters) are able to convey this silvery softness of air, this receding and intimate distance, this marvellous consonance of the most exquisite contours and melting colours. He who has lived out his days and been jaded by life has no cause to visit Venice: to him it will be bitter, like the memory of the dreams of his early days; but it will be sweet to the one who still has all his strength about him, who feels happy and successful; let him bring his happiness under its enchanted skies, and no matter how bright that happiness is, it will gild it even further with an unfading radiance.

The gondola in which Insarov and Yelena sat slowly passed the Riva degli Schiavoni, the Doge's Palace, and the Piazzetta, and then entered the Grand Canal. On both sides marble palaces moved; they seemed to float quietly by, scarcely allowing one's gaze to embrace and comprehend all their beauties. Yelena felt deeply happy; in the azure of her sky there was only one small dark cloud—and it was moving away: Insarov was much better that day. They sailed as far

as the steep arch of the Rialto and turned back. Yelena feared the cold
of the churches for Insarov's sake; but she remembered about the
Accademia di Belle Arti and told the gondolier to go there. They soon
went round all the rooms of that small museum. Being neither con-
noisseurs nor dilettantes, they did not stop before each picture, did
not constrain themselves: a kind of light gaiety unexpectedly took hold
of them. They suddenly found everything very amusing. (Children
know this feeling well.) Much to the scandalized attention of three
—English—visitors, Yelena laughed until she cried at Tintoretto's
St Mark leaping from the sky like a frog into water, in order to rescue
a tortured slave; for his part, Insarov went into transports over the
back and calves of that energetic fellow in the green chlamys who stands
in the foreground of Titian's *Assumption*, raising his arms after the
departing Madonna; the Madonna herself, however—a beautiful,
strong woman, calmly and majestically aspiring to the bosom of God
the Father—struck both Insarov and Yelena; they also liked a stern
and holy painting by old Cima da Conegliano. As they emerged from
the Academy, they again looked round at the three Englishmen, with
long, rabbit-like teeth and dangling side-whiskers, who were walking
behind them—and began to laugh; caught sight of their gondolier with
his short jacket and trousers that were also too short—and began to
laugh; caught sight of a market-woman with a little knot of grey hair
right on the top of her head—and began to laugh more than ever;
looked, at last, each other in the face—and dissolved in laughter, and
as soon as they were back in the gondola—tightly, tightly pressed each
other's hands. They arrived at the hotel, ran to their room, and ordered
dinner to be brought there. Their gaiety did not abandon them at table,
either. They poured wine for each other, drank the health of their
Moscow friends, clapped their hands at the *cameriere** in appreciation
of the savoury fish dish he had served them, and requested insistently
that he bring them *frutti di mare*;* the *cameriere* shrugged his shoulders
and shuffled his feet, and when he came out of their room shook his
head and even whispered once, with a sigh: *poveretti* (poor things!).
After dinner they went to the theatre.

  At the theatre there was a performance of an opera by Verdi, a rather
vulgar opera, if truth be told, but one that had already flown round all
the stages of Europe, and is well known to us Russians: *La Traviata*.*
The season in Venice was over, and none of the singers rose above
the level of mediocrity; they all shouted fit to burst. The role of Violetta

was performed by a singer without reputation and, to judge from the audience's coldness towards her, not much in favour, though she did not lack talent. She was a young, not particularly attractive, grey-eyed girl with a voice that was not quite steady and was already spent and overused. She was dressed in an odd array of shabby finery, to the point of naivety: her hair was covered by a red hairnet, a rather faded blue satin dress constricted her bosom, and she wore thick suede gloves that reached all the way to her angular elbows; and indeed, how was she, the daughter of some Bergamo shepherd, to know how the Parisian *dames aux camélias* dress? She did not know how to comport herself upon stage, either; but in her performance there was much lifelike and unfeigned simplicity, and she sang with that special passionate quality of expression and rhythm that is given to the Italians alone. Yelena and Insarov sat together in a dark box, right beside the stage; the playful mood that had seized them in the Academia di Belle Arti had not yet passed. When the father of the unhappy youth who falls into the temptress's snares appeared on the stage in a pea-green frock-coat and rumpled white wig, crookedly opened his mouth, and, himself embarrassed in advance, emitted a mournful bass tremolo, they both very nearly burst a seam... But Violetta's performance made an impression on them.

'That poor girl is receiving hardly any applause,' said Yelena, 'but I prefer her a thousand times to some self-confident, second-rate celebrity who would pose and put on airs and keep striving for effect. She is in no laughing mood, it seems; look, she does not notice the audience.'

Insarov leaned towards the edge of the box and looked at Violetta closely.

'Yes,' he said, 'she is not joking: there's a whiff of death.'

Yelena fell silent.

The third act began. The curtain rose... Yelena shivered at the sight of the bed, the drawn curtains, the bottles of medicine, the covered lamp... She remembered the recent past... 'And the future? And the present?' flickered through her mind. As if on purpose, in response to the actress's simulated cough, in the box resounded the hollow, genuine cough of Inasarov... Yelena stole a glance at him, and at once gave her features an untroubled, calm expression; Insarov understood her, and also began to smile and, very quietly, join in the singing.

He soon grew quiet again, however. Violetta's performance was becoming better and better, freer and freer. She had thrown off all that was extraneous, all that was superfluous and *had found herself*: a rare and supreme happiness for an artist! She had suddenly crossed that limit that is impossible to define, but beyond which beauty lives. The audience sat up, was astonished. The unattractive girl with her spent voice was beginning to take it into her hands, to take possession of it. But now the singer's voice did not sound spent: it had acquired warmth and strength. 'Alfredo' appeared; Violetta's joyful cry very nearly aroused that storm the name of which is *fanatismo* and before which all out northern howlings are as nothing... A moment—and again the audience thrilled. The duet had begun, the opera's best number, in which the composer has succeeded in expressing all the regrets of a senselessly wasted youth, the final struggle of hopeless and helpless love. Carried along, caught up in a slipstream of common fellow-feeling, with tears of artist's joy and real suffering in her eyes, the singer abandoned herself to the wave that was bearing her aloft, her face became transformed, and before the grim spectre of suddenly approaching death, in such a rush of prayer that rose to the sky did the words break from her: 'Lascia mi vivere... morir si giovane!' ('Let me live... to die so young!'), that the whole theatre began to resound with furious applause and ecstatic cries.

Yelena turned cold all over. She quietly began to seek Insarov's hand with her own, found it, and squeezed it tightly. He responded to her grip; but she did not look at him, nor he at her. This grip was not like the one with which, a few hours earlier, they had greeted each other in the gondola.

They sailed back to their hotel along the Canale Grande. Night had already fallen, a light, soft night. The same palaces moved towards them, but they seemed different now. The ones that the moon illumined gleamed a golden white, and in this very whiteness the details of the ornaments and contours of windows and balconies seemed to disappear; they were more clearly evident on the buildings that were suffused with the gentle gloom of regular shadow. The gondolas with their small red lights seemed to pass even more swiftly and inaudibly; mysteriously their steel crests gleamed, mysteriously the oars rose and fell above the silver fishes of the disturbed current; from here and there came the short, soft cries of the gondoliers (they almost never sing nowadays): of other sounds there were almost none. The hotel where Yelena and Insarov were staying was on the Riva degli Schiavoni; before reaching it, they disembarked from the gondola and strolled several

times around St Mark's Square, beneath the arcades, where in front
of tiny cafés large numbers of idle people thronged. To walk together
with a beloved being in a foreign city, among foreigners, is somehow
peculiarly pleasant: everything seems beautiful and significant, one
wishes everyone good fortune, peace, and the same happiness with
which one is filled oneself. But Yelena could no longer light-heartedly
indulge her sense of happiness: her heart, shaken by her recent impressions, was unable to calm itself; and Insarov, as they passed the
Doge's Palace, pointed silently to the muzzles of the Austrian cannons
that stared out from the lower arches, and pulled his hat down over
his eyes. Besides, he felt tired—and, with a final glance at St Mark's
Cathedral and its domes, where in the rays of the moonlight patches
of phosphorescent light had begun to burn on the bluish lead, they
slowly returned home.

Their little room looked on to the wide lagoon that stretches from
the Riva degli Schiavoni to the Giudecca. Almost facing their hotel
rose the pointed tower of San Giorgio; to the right, high in the air,
glittered the golden sphere of the Dogana—and, decked out like a
bride, the most beautiful of the churches, the Redentore di Palladio,
stood. To the left were the black outlines of the masts and yards of
sailing-boats, the smokestacks of steamers; here and there, like a
broken wing, hung a half-folded sail, and the pennants barely stirred.
Insarov squatted down by the window, but Yelena would not let him
admire the view for long; he had suddenly run a fever, and a kind of
devouring asthenia had taken hold of him. She put him to bed and,
waiting until he had fallen asleep, quietly returned to the window.
Oh, how quiet and tender the night was, with what dove-like mildness the azure air breathed, how it must be that every suffering, every
grief must fall silent and sleep beneath this clear sky, beneath these
holy, innocent rays! 'O God,' thought Yelena, 'why is there death,
why parting, illness and tears? And why is there this beauty, this
sweet sense of hope, why this reassuring sense of an enduring refuge,
of an unfailing safeguard, of an immortal protection? What do they
mean, this smiling, blessing sky, this happy, resting earth? Is it all
really only within ourselves, while beyond us lie eternal cold and
silence? Are we really alone... alone... while there, everywhere, in all
those inaccessible abysses and depths—all, all is alien to us? To what
purpose, then, is this thirst for prayer, this joy in it?' ('Morir si
giovane' began to sound within her soul...) 'Is it really forbidden

to supplicate, to avert, to save... O God! Is it really forbidden to believe in a miracle?' She put her head on her clenched hands. 'Is it over?' she whispered. 'Is it really already over? I was happy not merely for minutes, or hours, or whole days—no, for whole weeks on end. And with what right?' She began to feel afraid of her happiness. 'And what if it is forbidden?' she thought. 'What if it is not given gratis? For that was heaven... but we are human beings, poor, sinful human beings... *Morir si giovane*... O dark spectre, hence! Not for me alone is his life needed!'

'But what if this is a punishment,' she thought again, 'what if we must now render full payment for our guilt? My conscience was silent, it is silent now, but is that any proof of innocence? O God, are we really so criminal? Can it really be that you, who created this night, this sky, want to punish us for having loved? But if that is so, if he is guilty, if I am guilty,' she added on an involuntary impulse, 'then let him, O God, let us both at least die an honourable, glorious death—there, on his native fields, and not here, not in this distant room.'

'And the grief of my poor, lonely mother?' she asked herself, was herself perplexed, and could find no answers to her question. Yelena did not know that the happiness of each person is founded on the unhappiness of another, that even his advantage and comfort require, like a statue a pedestal, the disadvantage and discomfort of others.

'Rendich!' Insarov muttered in his sleep.

Yelena went over to him on tiptoe, leaned over him and wiped the sweat from his face. He tossed on the pillow a little, and fell quiet.

She again approached the window, and again her thoughts took hold of her. She began to persuade and assure herself that there was no cause for fear. She even felt ashamed of her weakness. 'Is there really any danger? He is better, isn't he?' she whispered. 'Why, had we not been at the theatre today, none of this would have occurred to me.' At that moment, high above the water, she saw a white seagull; it had probably been disturbed by a fisherman, and it flew silently, with an uneven trajectory, as if it were spying out a place to land. 'If it flies this way,' Yelena thought, 'that will be a good omen...' The gull began to wheel round, folded its wings and—as though it had been winged by a shot, fell with a doleful cry somewhere far away behind a dark sailboat. Yelena shuddered, had a guilty conscience about shuddering, and then, without undressing, lay down on the bed beside Insarov, who was breathing heavily and quickly.

XXXIV

INSAROV woke up late, with a dull aching in his head and a sense, as he put it, of 'outrageous' weakness in all his body.

'Has Rendich arrived?' was his first question.

'Not yet,' Yelena replied, handing him the latest issue of the *Osservatore Triestino*, in which there was a great deal about the war, the Slavic lands, and the Principalities. Insarov began to read; she set about making coffee for him... Someone gave a knock at the door.

'Rendich,' they both thought, but the person who had knocked said in Russian: 'May I come in?' Yelena and Insarov looked at each other in bewilderment, and then, without waiting for them to reply, a foppishly dressed man with a small, sharp face and small, mobile eyes entered the room. He was beaming all over, as though he had just won an enormous amount of money or heard a most pleasant piece of news.

Insarov rose from his chair.

'You won't recognize me,' the stranger began, going up to him in familiar fashion and amiably bowing to Yelena. 'Lupoyarov, we met in Moscow at the Ye——s', if you remember?'

'Yes, so we did,' said Insarov.

'Indeed we did, indeed we did! Please introduce me to your wife. Madam, I have always had the deepest respect for Dmitry Vasilyevich...' (he corrected himself) 'Nikanor Vasilyevich, and am very happy to at last have the honour of making your acquaintance. Imagine,' he went on, turning to Insarov, 'I only discovered that you were here yesterday evening. I am also staying at this hotel. What a city this Venice is—sheer poetry! The only bad thing about it is the damned Austrians one meets at every step! Oh, I cannot endure these Austrians! Incidentally, did you hear: there has been a decisive battle on the Danube: three hundred Turkish officers killed, Silistria is taken, Serbia has already declared its independence. You, as a patriot, must be delighted, are you not? Even my own Slavic blood is positively on fire! However, I'd advise you to be more cautious; I am sure you are being watched. There's a dreadful amount of spying here! Yesterday a suspicious-looking fellow came up to me and asked me if I was a Russian. I told him I was a Dane... But my dearest Nikanor Vasilyevich, you look unwell. You must look after yourself a little;

madam, you must look after your husband. Yesterday I was running about the palaces and churches like a madman—I say, have you been to the Doge's Palace? What splendour everywhere! Especially that great hall, and the place for Marino Faliero;* there's an inscription there: "Decapitati pro criminibus." I was at the famous prisons, too: and there, how my soul rose up in indignation—I, you will perhaps remember, have always liked to concern myself with social questions and have always strongly opposed the aristocracy—it is there I would like to take the aristocracy's defenders: to those prisons; Byron was right when he said: "I stood in Venice on the bridge of sighs"; though, as a matter of fact, he was an aristocrat, too. I have always been on the side of progress. The younger generation is always on the side of progress. And how do you like the Anglo-French? We shall see how much they'll get done: Boustrapa* and Palmerston. Palmerston has been made prime minister, you know. No, say what you like, the Russian fist is not to be treated lightly. He is a dreadful rogue, that Boustrapa! If you wish, I can lend you *Les Châtiments** by Victor Hugo—it's wonderful! "L'avenir—le gendarme de Dieu"—a little boldly put, but there is strength, strength there. Prince Vyazemsky* also puts it well: "Europe repeats: 'Basgedikler', her eyes on Sinope fixed."* I love poetry. I also have Proudhon's latest book,* in fact I have everything. I don't know about you, but I am glad about the war; as long as they don't summon me back home, but in case they do, I'm going to go from here to Florence, or Rome: one can't go to France, so I plan to go to Spain—the women there are wonderful, they say, only there's poverty and too many insects. I'd go off to California, too, we Russians think nothing of it, except that I promised an editor to do a detailed study of Mediterranean trade. A dull, specialized subject, you may say, but we need, need specialists, we've spent enough time philosophizing, now what's needed is the practical, the practical... You are very unwell, Nikanor Vasilyevich, it's possible that I am tiring you, but never mind, I shall stay a little longer...'

And Lupoyarov continued to chatter like this for a long time, promising, as he left, to return.

Exhausted by the unexpected visit, Insarov lay down on the sofa.

'There,' he said with quiet bitterness, casting a glance at Yelena, 'there is your younger generation! Some of them may put on airs and cut a grand figure, but at heart they are the same idle whistlers as that gentleman.'

Yelena made no rejoinder to her husband; at that moment, she was far more troubled by Insarov's asthenia than by the condition of Russia's entire younger generation... She sat down beside him, took up her work. He closed his eyes and lay motionless, his face pale and thin. Yelena glanced at his sharp-cut profile and his outstretched arms, and a sudden pang of fear shot through her heart.

'Dmitry...' she began.

He roused himself.

'What is it? Has Rendich arrived?'

'Not yet... but what do you think—you've a fever, you really are not well, shouldn't we send for a doctor?'

'That chatterbox has frightened you. It's not necessary. I shall rest for a while, and it will all pass. After dinner we shall go out again... somewhere.'

Two hours passed... Insarov stayed lying on the sofa, but could not sleep, though his eyes were closed. Yelena stayed beside him; she had dropped her work to her knees, and did not move.

'Why are you not sleeping?' she asked him at last.

'Oh, just wait.' He took her hand, and put it under his head. 'There... that's nice. You must wake me as soon as Rendich arrives. If he says that the boat is ready, we shall go at once... We'll have to pack everything.'

'That will not take long,' Yelena replied.

'What was that fellow saying about a battle, about Serbia?' Insarov said after a while. 'He must have made it all up. But we must, must go. There is no time to waste... Be ready.'

He fell asleep, and everything in the room was quiet.

Yelena leaned her head against the back of her chair and stared out of the window for a long time. The weather had changed for the worse; a wind had got up. Large, white clouds were swiftly racing across the sky, a slender mast was swaying in the distance, a long pennant with a red cross ceaselessly rose aloft, fell back, and rose aloft again. The pendulum of the old clock ticked heavily, with a kind of melancholy hiss. Yelena closed her eyes. She had slept badly all the night before; gradually she too fell asleep.

She had a strange dream. She was out on Tsaritsyno Pond in a rowing-boat with some people she did not know. They were sitting still, in silence, and no one was rowing; the boat moved along by itself. Yelena felt no fear, only boredom: she would have liked to know

who these people were and why she was with them. She looked, and
the pond widened, the banks disappeared—it was no longer a pond,
but a troubled sea: enormous, azure, silent waves rocked the boat
majestically; something thunderous and menacing was rising from
the bottom; her unknown fellow passengers suddenly leapt to their
feet, shouting and waving their arms... Yelena recognized their faces:
her father was among them. But a kind of white whirlwind swooped
down on the waves... everything spun round and was mingled
together...

Yelena looked around her: everything around was white, as before;
but this was snow, snow, endless snow. And now she was no longer in
the boat, she was travelling, as she had from Moscow, in a sledge-cart;
she was not alone: beside her sat a small creature, wrapped in an old
coat. Yelena looked more closely: it was Katya, her poor little friend.
Yelena felt afraid: 'Isn't she dead?' she thought.

'Katya, where are we bound for, you and I?'

Katya made no reply, and muffled herself in her coat; she was
shivering. Yelena was cold, too; she looked along the road: a city could
be seen in the distance, through the snowy dust. Tall white towers
with silver cupolas... Katya, Katya, is that Moscow? No, Yelena
thought, that's the Solovets Monastery:* there are many, many tiny
cramped cells, like in a beehive; it's stuffy and cramped in there—
Dmitry is shut up in there. I must set him free... Suddenly a grey,
yawning chasm opened before her. The sledge-cart was falling, Katya
was laughing. 'Yelena. Yelena!' a voice said out of the abyss.

'Yelena!' someone said clearly in her ears. She quickly raised her
head, turned round and froze: Insarov, white as snow, the snow of
her dream, was half sitting up on the sofa and staring at her with large,
bright, terrible eyes. His hair was scattered over his forehead, his lips
had opened strangely. Horror, mixed with a kind of wistful tender
piety, expressed itself in his suddenly altered face.

'Yelena!' he articulated. 'I am dying.'

She fell to her knees with a cry, and pressed herself to his chest.

'It is all over,' Insarov said again, 'I am dying... Farewell, my poor
one! Farewell, my motherland!...'

And he capsized on to his back, on the sofa.

Yelena went running out of the room, began to call for help, and
the *cameriere* rushed off to fetch a doctor. Yelena fell and hugged
Insarov.

At that moment in the doorway a man appeared, broad-shouldered, sunburned, in a thick flannelette coat and a low oilskin hat. He stood there in bewilderment.

'Rendich!' Yelena exclaimed. 'It's you! Look, for the love of God, he's unconscious! What is wrong with him? O God, O God! He went out yesterday, he was talking to me just now...'

Rendich did not say anything and merely stood to one side. Past him nimbly darted a small figure in a wig and spectacles: this was a doctor who was staying at the same hotel. He went close to Insarov.

'Signora,' he said a few moments later, 'the foreign gentleman has passed away—*il signore forestiero è morto*—the cause is an aneurism combined with a disorder of the lungs.'

XXXV

The following day, in the same room, Rendich stood by the window; in front of him, wrapped in a shawl, sat Yelena. Insarov lay in a coffin in the adjacent room. Yelena's face was both frightened and lifeless; on her forehead, between her eyebrows, two small wrinkles had appeared: they gave a tense expression to her immobile eyes. On the window lay an unsealed letter from Anna Vasilyevna. She was inviting her daughter to Moscow, even if only for a month, complaining about her loneliness, about Nikolai Artemyevich, sending greetings to Insarov, asking after his health, and requesting him to give his wife leave of absence.

Rendich was a Dalmatian, a seaman with whom Insarov had become acquainted during his journey to the motherland, and whom he had looked up in Venice. He was a stern, coarse, bold, man, and devoted to the Slavic cause. He despised the Turks and hated the Austrians.

'How long are you due to stay in Venice?' Yelena asked him in Italian. Her voice, too, was void of life, like her face.

'A day, in order to load the boat and not arouse suspicion, and then straight to Zara. My countrymen will not be overjoyed when I tell them. They have been waiting for him for a long time; they were relying on him.'

'They were relying on him,' Yelena repeated automatically.

'When will you bury him?' asked Rendich.

Yelena did not reply at once.

'Tomorrow.'

'Tomorrow? I will stay: I want to throw a handful of earth into his grave. And then I must help you, too. Though it would be better for him to lie in Slavic soil.'

Yelena looked at Rendich.

'Captain,' she said, 'take me with him and sail us to the other side of the sea, away from here. Can that be done?'

Rendich thought.

'Yes, it can, though it will be tricky. We'll have to deal with the damned authorities here. But even supposing we manage to arrange it all and bury him over there; how am I to bring you back again?'

'You will not have to bring me back again.'

'What? But where will you stay?'

'I shall find a place for myself; just take us, take me.'

Rendich scratched the back of his head.

'As you think best, but it will all be very tricky. I'll go and see what I can do; expect me back here in about two hours' time.'

He left. Yelena went into the adjacent room, leaned against the wall and stood there for a long time as if fixed in stone. Then she lowered herself to her knees, but could not pray. In her soul there was no rebuke; she did not dare to enquire of God why he had not spared, had pity, protected, why he had punished beyond the measure of guilt, if indeed guilt there had been? Each of us is already guilty by the fact of being alive, and there is no great thinker, no benefactor of mankind, who because of the good he has wrought may rely on having the right to live... But Yelena could not pray: she was fixed in stone.

That same night a wide rowing-boat cast off from the hotel where the Insarovs had stayed. In the boat were Yelena and Rendich, and a long box covered with black cloth. They rowed for about an hour and at last reached a small, two-masted craft that lay at anchor right at the mouth of the harbour. Yelena and Rendich boarded the craft; the sailors carried the box on board. At around midnight a storm got up, but by early morning the craft had already passed the Lido. During the day the storm broke with terrible force, and experienced seamen in the offices of Lloyd's shook their heads and expected no good. The Adriatic Sea between Venice, Trieste, and the Dalmatian coast is exceedingly dangerous.

Some three weeks after Yelena's departure from Venice, Anna Vasilyevna received the following letter in Moscow:

My dear parents,

I am saying farewell to you for ever. You will not see me again. Yesterday Dmitry passed away. Today I am leaving for Zara with his body. I shall bury him, and as for what will happen to me, I do not know! But I no longer have any motherland but Dmitry's. An insurrection is in the making there, and there are preparations for war; I shall join the Sisters of Mercy; I shall tend the sick and wounded. I do not know what will happen to me, but after Dmitry's death, too, I shall remain faithful to his memory, to the cause to which he devoted all his life. I have learned Bulgarian and Serbian... I shall probably not come through this—so much the better. I am brought to the edge of the abyss, and must fall. Fate did not unite us in vain: who knows, it may be that I killed him; now it is his turn to entice me after him. I was in search of happiness—and it may be that I shall find death. Evidently that is how it was supposed to be; evidently there was guilt... But death covers up and reconciles everything—is it not true? Forgive me all the distress I have caused you; it was not in my power to act otherwise. But return to Russia—why? What can one do in Russia?

Accept my final kisses and blessings, and do not censure me.

Ye.

Since that day about five years have gone by, and no further news of Yelena has arrived. All letters and enquiries have remained fruitless; in vain did Nikolai Artemyevich, after the conclusion of peace, make a visit to Venice and Zadar; in Venice he discovered what the reader already knows, and in Zadar no one could give him any positive information about Rendich and the craft he had hired. There were dark rumours that several years earlier, after a violent storm, the sea had thrown a coffin ashore in which the corpse of a man had been found... According to other, more trustworthy, information, this coffin had not been thrown up by the sea at all, but had been brought beside the shore and buried there by a foreign lady who had travelled from Venice; some added that this lady had later been seen in Herzegovina among the troops that were mustering there at the time; there were even descriptions of her dress—black from head to foot. Whatever the truth of the matter, Yelena's trace had disappeared irrevocably, for ever, and no one knows whether she is still alive, is hiding somewhere, or whether her small role in life is over, along with her light ferment, and death's turn has arrived. It sometimes happens that a person, waking up, wonders with involuntary alarm: 'Am I really thirty... forty... fifty years old? How can life have passed so quickly? How can death have moved so close?' Death, like a fisherman who has caught a fish in his net and leaves it in the water for a time: the fish still swims about, but the net is over it, and the fisherman will snatch it out—when he wants to.

What has happened to the other persons in our story?

Anna Vasilyevna is still alive; she has aged a great deal after the blow that struck her, complains less, but is far more prone to melancholy. Nikolai Artemyevich has also aged, and gone grey, and has parted from Avgustina Khristianovna... Nowadays he curses anything that is foreign. His housekeeper, an attractive woman of about thirty, a Russian, goes about in silk dresses and wears gold rings and earrings. Kurnatovsky, as a man of temperament and, in his quality of vigorous *brun*, an admirer of pretty blondes, has married Zoya; she shows him great obedience, and has even ceased to think in German. Bersenev is living in Heidelberg; he was sent abroad at public expense; he has visited Berlin and Paris, and does not waste his time; he will make an able professor. The learned public has taken note of two articles by him: 'On Some Special Characteristics of Ancient German Law in the Matter of Judicial Punishment' and 'On the Significance of the Urban Principle in the Question of Civilization', and it is merely a pity that both articles are written in rather difficult language and peppered with foreign words. Shubin is in Rome; he has devoted himself entirely to his art and is considered one of the most notable and promising young sculptors. Strict purists are of the opinion that he has not made sufficient study of the ancients, that he has no 'style', and rank him with the French school; he has an enormous number of commissions from English and American clients. Just recently a great deal of fuss was occasioned by one of his Bacchantes; the Russian Count Boboshkin, a well-known plutocrat, was on the point of buying it for 1,000 scudi, but finally preferred to give 3,000 to another sculptor, a *pur sang* Frenchman, for a group depicting 'A Young Peasant Girl Expiring From Love on The Bosom of the Spirit of Spring'. Shubin occasionally exchanges letters with Uvar Ivanovich, who alone has not altered in any respect. 'Do you remember', he wrote to him recently, 'what you told me that night when the news of poor Yelena's marriage broke, when I sat on your bed and talked with you? Do you remember, I asked you then whether we shall ever have some human beings? And you replied to me: "We shall." O, power of the black earth! And now again from here, from my "splendid far-away", I ask you: well, Uvar Ivanovich, shall we?'

Uvar Ivanovich twiddled his fingers, and fixed his enigmatic gaze on the distance.

EXPLANATORY NOTES

Rudin

3 *verst*: one verst = 1.06 km.

   armyak: a Russian peasant's coat of heavy cloth.

5 *droshky*: a low, four-wheeled open carriage.

   kolomyanka: a heavy linen fabric.

6 *Yes indeed, miss*: in Russian, *tochno tak-s*. Pandalevsky makes excessive use of the particle *-s*, a mark of social deference and submission. In the translation, the lisping 'miss' is used, as a rough approximation.

8 *the plural form*: in pre-revolutionary Russia the third-person plural was often used by social inferiors when addressing and referring to persons of rank. In the translation the archaic plural form of the personal pronoun—here, *onye*—is rendered here as 'her ladyship', and similar forms.

   Zhukovsky: V. A. Zhukovsky (1783–1852), Russian poet and translator, who did much to found the basis of the modern Russian literary language.

9 *Roxolan Mediarovich Ksandryka*: apparently a reference to A. S. Sturdza (1791–1854), a political conservative and author of various religious and political works.

   Thalberg: Sigismond Thalberg (1812–71), Austrian composer and pianist.

10 *barin*: in pre-revolutionary Russia this word was used to refer to a man of the upper class, usually a landowner. The English words 'master' and 'gentleman' are near approximations.

11 *muzhik*: like the English 'peasant', the Russian word has the secondary meaning of 'lout' or 'bumpkin'.

   dressing-gown: the Russian word, *khalat*, may also mean an (eastern) robe.

12 *Rastrelli*: V. V. Rastrelli (1700–71), the Russo-Italian architect who designed many buildings in St Petersburg, including the Winter Palace.

13 *bien-trouvés*: witty remarks.

14 *gymnasium*: in pre-revolutionary Russia, a secondary school that prepared its pupils for entry to the universities.

   Dorpat: now Tartu, in Estonia. The city has an ancient and distinguished university that dates back to the period of Swedish rule in the seventeenth century.

   candidate's degree: the approximate equivalent of a Master of Arts degree.

16 *Mais . . . monsieur*: 'But what you've just said is appalling, sir.'

17 *Merci . . . Il est si distingué*: 'Thank you, it's charming... He is so refined.'

18 *Griboyedov's line*: a reference to a line from the comedy *Gore ot uma* (*Woe From Wit*) by the Russian dramatist A. S. Griboyedov (1793–1829). In the original, the word 'incurable' is used instead of 'incorrigible'.

the Oka: the River Oka, the chief tributary from the right of the River Volga.

Khokhol-land: 'Little Russia', or Ukraine. *Khokhol* is a disparaging term for a Ukrainian, derived from the frequency of the aspirated 'kh' sound in the Ukrainian language.

19 *Little Russian*: Ukrainian. Many Russians—though obviously not Basistov —tended to take a patronizing view of the Ukraine, which was thought by many not even to have a proper language of its own, but merely a comical 'dialect' of Russian. Attempts to revive and restore the Ukrainian language were generally met with disparagement in the Russian press of Turgenev's time.

Duma . . . gop: a parody of Ukrainian 'ethnic' verse style. The phrases of the 'poem', entitled 'Reflection', read, approximately: 'Oh, fate, my fate!' 'The Cossack Nalivaiko sat on a burial mound', and 'Down the green hill, hey, ho, hop, hop!'

Khramatyka ye vyskus'tvo pravyl'no chytati y pysati . . . : the same sentence, with 'Ukrainian' aspirations and vowels.

Hegel: G. W. F. Hegel (1770–1831), German idealist philosopher, whose writings had a profound influence on radical thinkers in nineteenth-century Russia.

20 *Le Baron . . . il vous entraîne*: 'The Baron is as charming as he is clever... It is truly a torrent... he sweeps you along.'

21 *Ah! . . . Rentrons!*: 'Ah, the bell for dinner... Let us return!'

quel dommage . . . conversation: 'what a pity that this charming lad has so little conversation.'

22 *kvass, du prostoï Russian kvass*: kvass is a fermented but almost non-alcoholic drink made from rye-flour or bread. *Prostoï* is a French transliteration of the Russian word *prostoy*, meaning 'plain, simple'—in the context, the juxtaposition of French and Russian has an ironic significance.

tarantass: a springless carriage.

23 *uyezd*: in Tsarist Russia, a government district.

27 *C'est un homme comme it faut*: 'He's a man as he ought to be.'

28 *C'est de Tocqueville, vous savez?*: 'It's de Tocqueville, you know him?' Alexis de Tocqueville (1805–59), the French political writer and statesman, whose political works were widely read in Russia.

29 *Kant*: Immanuel Kant (1724–1804), German philosopher.

30 *yeralash*: a Russian card game related to bridge.

31 *Schubert's 'Erlkönig'*: Franz Schubert's famous setting of Goethe's super-natural ballad of 1782. A piano transcription was made by Franz Liszt.

32 *I recall a Nordic legend*: in fact an Anglo-Saxon legend, recorded by the
    Venerable Bede (673–735) in *Historia ecclesiastica gentis anglorum*.

34 *à la Madame Récamier*: Mme Récamier (1777–1849), famous for her liter-
    ary and political salons. The well-known portrait of her by David shows
    her reclining on a couch, dressed in the 'classical' simplicity favoured in
    post-Revolutionary France.

36 *Voilà Monsieur Pigassoff enterré*: 'That's buried Mr Pigasov.'

    From a sick head... how is it again... on to a healthy one: Darya Mikhailovna,
    who from speaking and thinking mostly in French has forgotten some
    of her Russian, cannot completely recall the Russian idiom *valit's bol'noy
    golovy na zdorovuyu* (literally, 'to lay [the blame] from a sick head on to a
    healthy one'), which suggests the idea of laying one's own fault at some-
    one else's door.

    Entre nous . . . fond: 'Between ourselves... it's rather lacking in substance.'

    un parfait honnête homme: 'a perfect gentleman'.

37 *mais c'est tout comme*: 'but she's just the same'.

38 *N'est-ce pas, comme il ressemble à Canning?*: 'Don't you agree, he's the image
    of Canning?' George Canning (1770–1827), British prime minister (1827).

    vous gravez comme avec un burin: 'it's as if you are etching with a needle'.

39 *all your muzhiks are rent-payers, are they not?*: Lezhnev's peasants paid him
    a quit-rent (*obrok*) in money, rather than the feudal *barshchina*, or *corvée*
    (statute labour). They were thus better off than most of their kind.

    Vous êtes des nôtres!: 'You are one of us!'

    Diogenes in his tub: born *c*.412 BC, the cynic philosopher Diogenes was
    supposed to have lived in a tub or oil-jar.

40 *Et de deux!*: 'And a second one!'

41 *Constantin . . . secrétaire*: 'Constantine, he is my secretary'.

42 *Qu'arez vous?*: 'What's the matter?'

    mon honnête homme de fille: 'my daughter, the gentleman'.

43 *Dumas fils*: Alexandre Dumas the younger (1824–95), author of *La Dame
    aux camélias* and many other novels dealing with *le demi-monde* (a term
    he coined).

    Cambyses: Cambyses II, King of Persia (529–522 BC), who led an expedi-
    tion against Egypt, the only independent kingdom left in the Middle East
    after the conquest of Asia by his father.

47 *of honour high and true doth speak*: Lezhnev quotes Repetilov's monologue
    in Act IV of Griboyedov's *Woe From Wit*.

48 *Pechorin*: the hero of Lermontov's *A Hero of Our Time* (1841), whose
    nihilistic and cynical view of life became rather fashionable in some
    nineteenth-century Russian intellectual circles.

51 *Goethe's 'Faust'* . . . *Novalis*: the two parts of Goethe's poem *Faust* were published in 1808 and 1832; *Hoffmann*: E. T. A. Hoffmann (1776–1822), author of fantastic stories; *'Letters' of Bettina: Goethes Briefwechsel mit einem Kinde* (1835), an imaginative rehandling of her correspondance with Goethe by Bettina von Arnim (1785–1859); *Novalis*: pseudonym of the German Romantic poet Friedrich, Freiherr von Hardenberg (1772–1801).

56 *Tartuffe*: pious hypocrite in the eponymous play by Molière (1622–73).

58 *Burned . . . shrine*: the lines are Turgenev's own.

60 *Demosthenes*: Greek orator (*c.*383–322 BC), also supposedly cured a stammer by declaiming on the seashore with pebbles in his mouth.

   Bursch: in German universities, a mature student.

61 *Manfred*: dramatic poem by Byron (1817), whose hero lives among the Alps as an outcast, tortured by remorse for a mysterious crime.

63 *Paul and Virginie*: the principal characters in the novel of the same title by the French writer Bernardin de Saint-Pierre (1737–1814).

70 *La Rochefoucauld*: (1613–80), author of the *Maxims* (*Réflexions, ou Sentences et maximes morales* 1664/5), a series of penetrating epigrams analysing human motivation.

   feuilleton: article or short story.

74 *the poet Aibulat*: pseudonym of the poet K. M. Rozen—his poem *Dva voprosa* (*Two Questions*) is thought to be the source of the quotation.

82 *Lovelace*: seducer in the novel *Clarissa Harlowe* (1747–8) by Samuel Richardson.

88 *chibouk*: a long Turkish tobacco pipe.

89 *galushki*: dumplings.

   yamshchiks: coachmen, drivers.

92 *barynya*: feminine form of *barin* (see note to p. 10 above).

96 *'Freedom . . . for it!'*: from the *Second Part* of *Don Quixote* (1615), ch. 58.

97 *'Blessed is he . . . young . . .'*: see Pushkin, *Eugene Onegin*, viii. 10.

99 *'Whoe'er has felt . . . gnawed . . .'*: see Pushkin, *Eugene Onegin*, i. 46.

100 *mais elle aura moins d'abandon*: 'but she will be more restrained'.

105 *Tsarevokokshaisk or Chukhloma*: remote rural locations.

110 *guberniyas*: provinces, 'governments'.

    troika: a team of three horses.

111 *svita*: a long garment worn by Ukrainian peasants.

    A Prisoner of the Caucasus: a poem (1822) by Pushkin.

    Georges de Germany: the principal character in a French novel popular in Russia during the 1830s: *Trente ans, ou la vie d'un joueur* (1827), by Dinaux and Ducange.

115 *on familiar terms*: Lezhnev also means that they should use the familiar *ty* ('thou') when addressing each other.

120 *philology*: in Russian, *slovesnost'*—an older term, denoting the study of literature and folklore, as well as language.

122 *Koltsov*: the poet A. V. Koltsov (1809–42). The words are from his poem 'Crossroads' (1840).

   a man who is loyal: the Russian word Rudin uses is *blagonamerennyi*. Its literal meaning is 'well-intentioned', but it carries a political meaning of 'loyal to the state'.

124 *Gaudeamus igitur!*: 'Let us then rejoice!', old students' drinking-song.

126 *Tiens! . . . le Polonais*: 'Damn! The Pole's just been killed.' Many émigré Poles who had taken part in the Polish Uprising of 1830 took part in the 1848 Revolution in France. Thus, Rudin is mistaken for a Pole.

   Bigre!: 'Damn it!'

On the Eve

130 *third candidate*: a lower academic degree awarded at Russian universities between 1804 and 1884 to the students who successfully completed the university course and wrote a special dissertation. They were then able to join a not-very-elevated rank of the Russian civil service.

131 *Dantan*: Jean Pierre Dantan (1800–69), French sculptor and designer of monuments, who made satirical busts of his contemporaries.

133 *'long live Marya Petrovna!'*: Shubin sings a well-known Russian student song, to words of N. M. Yazykov.

   Vous me comprenez: 'You understand me.'

134 *Oberon's horn*: a reference to Weber's opera *Oberon* (1826).

137 *rusalkas*: in Russian folkore, water-nymphs.

   khokhols: see note to *Rudin*, p. 18.

   Stavasser: the Russian sculptor, P. A. Stavasser (1816–50).

139 *a quit-rent basis*: see note to *Rudin*, p. 39.

   yeralash: see note to *Rudin*, p. 30.

140 *frondeur*: a political rebel. *Fronde* (a word derived from *frondes*—slings—used in a boys' game), was the name given to two uprisings against the absolutism of the Crown in France during the minority of Louis XIV.

   Mein Pinselchen: 'my little simpleton' (German).

142 *La dernière pensée de Weber?*: 'The last thought of Weber?'

143 *Timofei Nikolayevich's*: a reference to Professor T. N. Granovsky (1813–55), historian and friend of Turgenev.

144 *a Schellingian*: a follower of the German philosopher Friedrich Wilhelm Joseph von Schelling (1775–1854), one of the leading exponents of idealism and of the Romantic tendency in German philosophy. His earlier work

was widely read among the Russian intelligentsia, and influenced, among others, the poet Fyodor Tyutchev.

149 *Schiller*: Friedrich Schiller (1759–1805), German poet and dramatist.

151 *Raumer's History of the Hohenstaufens*: a work by the German historian Friedrich Georg von Raumer (1781–1873).

160 *contrabombardon*: a brass musical instrument invented by the Belgian instrument-maker Adolphe Sax.

mankirovat': to show disrespect. The Russian word is derived from the French *manquer*.

161 *dans mon gros bon sens*: 'with my crude common sense'.

devant les domestiques: 'in front of the servants'.

165 *êtres sans cœur*: 'heartless beings'.

168 *the Nevsky Prospect*: the principle shopping street and thoroughfare of St Petersburg.

169 *'Self-Sleeper'*: in Russian, *Samoson*, the name of Turgenev's favourite sofa. It is nowadays housed at the Turgenev Museum in Oryol.

Illuminatus: member of the 'Illuminatenorden', a freemason-like group founded by A. Weishaupt in 1776 and suppressed by the Elector of Bavaria in 1784.

170 *the liberation of his motherland*: since the fourteenth century Bulgaria's political and cultural existence had been almost entirely wiped out by the Turkish domination of the country. During the late eighteenth and early nineteenth centuries Bulgarian nationalist movements began to develop, aiming at liberation from Turkish rule.

175 *the eastern question*: here, the Balkan question, posed by the decline of the Ottoman Empire. The 'Eastern Question' was really a kind of diplomatic shorthand, used to denote several problems related to the decline of Ottoman authority in Europe. These included not only the independence of the Balkan States, but also the control of the Bosporus Straits and the Dardanelles, and the possession of Constantinople. During the Crimean War (1853–6) these problems became very acute.

Feuerbach: Ludwig Feuerbach (1804–72), German philosopher, famous for his nationalist analysis of Christianity.

177 *the obscure but great Venelin . . . the Bulgarian King Krum, Khrum, or Khrom, who had lived very nearly in the age of Adam*: Yu. I. Venelin (1802–39), an eminent researcher of Bulgarian history, language and folklore. *Krum, Khrum, or Khrom*: king of Bulgaria from AD 802.

178 *Wer?*: 'Who?'

179 *like Max to Agatha*: characters in Weber's opera *Der Freischütz*.

181 *Step' mozdokskaya*: 'Mozdok Steppe', a Russian folk-song (about the death of a cabman in a foreign land).

183 *kasha*: a dish of cooked grain or groats.

183 *Themistocles . . . Salamis*: Athenian general (*c.*528–462 BC) who was instrumental in defeating the invading Persians, particularly at the sea-battle of Salamis.

189 *Tsaritsyno*: the remains of a palace near Moscow built for Catherine the Great, who adandoned the project in 1785.

190 *Quelle bourde!*: 'What a sham!'

192 *an Alexandrian shirt*: the shirt is made of *aleksandriyka*, a brightly coloured cotton material.

 Niedermeyer's 'Le lac': a 'romance' by the French composer Louis Niedermeyer (1802–61).

 O lac . . . carrière . . . : 'O lake! The year has just run its course...'.

196 *unabating laughter . . . heaven*: a reference to the 'unquenchable laughter' of the Gods in *Iliad*, i. 599.

217 *Trema Bisanzia!*: should be *Trema, Bisanzio!* ('Tremble, Byzantium!') A reference to Donizetti's opera *Belisario* (Act II, scene xi).

 en canaille: 'like the rabble'.

 Dantan: see note to p. 131 above.

222 *Sortez . . . je vous prie*: 'Please leave . . . And you, madame, be so good as to stay.'

224 *the Order of St Stanislas*: an Order and badge, founded by Stanislas Augustus Poniatowski, the last king of Poland, in 1765 on the eve of the Feast of St Stanislas, the patron saint of Poland. In Poland the Order was second in rank only to the Order of the White Eagle. After the Polish Insurrection of 1830 and the suppression of the Kingdom of Poland, Tsar Nicholas I incorporated the Order among the Russian orders of chivalry. Kurnatovsky's name itself sounds somewhat 'Polish' to a Russian ear.

 pères de comédie: 'theatrical fathers'.

 un vrai stoïcien: 'a true Stoic'.

 à bras ouverts: 'with open arms'.

225 *To St Petersburg and comme il faut*: 'comme il faut' was a phrase much used in nineteenth-century Russia to refer to the ways and manners of polite society, particularly in the capital city.

228 *the Prechistenka*: one of Moscow's central streets, with many literary and historical associations.

 the occupation of the Principalities by Russian forces: the occupation in 1853 by Russian troops of the Turkish principalities of Moldavia and Walachia (now Romania).

232 *Kuznetsky Bridge*: Kuznetsky Most, in Turgenev's time a fashionable Moscow shopping street with restaurants and cafés.

233 *pieniadze*: Polish for 'money'.

235 *tarmalama*: literally, 'Tarma llama'. The llama's long, coarse wool was used for making textiles.

235 *pirozhki*: Russian for 'patties', 'pasties'.

238 *aut Caesar, aut nihil*: 'either Caesar or nothing'.

 Grote: George Grote (1794–1871), the British banker, historian of Greece, and politician.

241 *Werther*: Goethe's *The Sorrows of Young Werther* (1774), whose hero commits suicide because of his love for a friend's fiancée.

250 *ces femmes . . . montre!*: 'these women—let someone show me them!'

251 *Vous revez, mon cher*: 'You are dreaming, my dear.'

 guberniyas: see note to *Rudin*, p. 110 above.

255 *the Sinope Massacre*: on 30 November 1853, after Turkish troops had crossed the Danube into Walachia, the Russian fleet sank a Turkish squadron at Sinope in the Black Sea, provoking widespread protest in Britain and France.

 this type of address: in the Russian original, Nikolai Artemyevich uses the form *vy*—equivalent to French *vous*.

256 *vous me faites mourir*: 'you are killing me'.

257 *raznochinets*: an intellectual not belonging to the gentry.

259 *the Metropolitan*: in the Orthodox Church a metropolitan bishop ranks above an archbishop and below a patriarch.

 Brutus: Marcus Brutus (*c.*85–42 BC), revered by republicans for his assassination of Julius Caesar.

261 *Diesen Insaroff vorziehen—und wem?*: 'To prefer this Insarov—to him?'

264 *yamshchik*: see note to *Rudin*, p. 89.

 'With God upon the distant road...': the first line of a poem by Pushkin, one of his 'Songs of the Western Slavs'.

268 *Aufgepasst!*: 'Look out!'

270 *cameriere*: waiter.

 frutti di mare: mussels, oysters.

 La Traviata: opera by Giuseppi Verdi, based on *La Dame aux camélias* by Dumas *fils*. The heroine, Violetta, dies of consumption.

276 *the place for Marino Faliero*: the black fund portrait—a sign of ignominy —of a Doge beheaded in 1355 (as the inscription says, 'for his crimes') after a conspiracy against the state, in the Room of the Major Council. Marino Faliero was the subject of a drama by Byron, and of an opera by Donizetti.

 Boustrapa: nickname of Napoleon III (1808–73), composed of the first three letters of the three cities in which he tried to foment insurrections— Boulogne (1840), Strasbourg (1836), and Paris (1851).

 Les Châtiments: a collection of poetry by Victor Hugo (1853). The line quoted, 'The future—God's gendarme', is the last line of a poem from Book IV, 'On loge à la nuit'.

276 *Prince Vyazemsky*: the poet and literary critic Prince P. A. Vyazemsky (1792–1878).

"Europe repeats: 'Basgedikler', her eyes on Sinope fixed.": a line from Vyazemsky's poem 'To Arms!' (1854). Basgedikler was the site of a defeat inflicted by Russian forces on the Turkish army on 19 November 1853. For Sinope, see above, note to p. 255.

Proudhon's latest book: a reference to *La Révolution sociale* (1852), a work by the French political theorist Pierre Joseph Proudhon (1809–65).

278 *the Solovets Monastery*: the fifteenth-century Russian Orthodox monastery on the Solovets Archipelago in the White Sea. Later, under Stalin, this location became the site of an enormous labour camp.

A SELECTION OF   **OXFORD WORLD'S CLASSICS**

LUDOVICO ARIOSTO	**Orlando Furioso**
GIOVANNI BOCCACCIO	**The Decameron**
MATTEO MARIA BOIARDO	**Orlando Innamorato**
LUÍS VAZ DE CAMÕES	**The Lusíads**
MIGUEL DE CERVANTES	**Don Quixote de la Mancha** **Exemplary Stories**
DANTE ALIGHIERI	**The Divine Comedy** **Vita Nuova**
BENITO PÉREZ GALDÓS	**Nazarín**
LEONARDO DA VINCI	**Selections from the Notebooks**
NICCOLÒ MACHIAVELLI	**Discourses on Livy** **The Prince**
MICHELANGELO	**Life, Letters, and Poetry**
PETRARCH	**Selections from the *Canzoniere* and** **Other Works**
GIORGIO VASARI	**The Lives of the Artists**

The Oxford World's Classics Website

www.worldsclassics.co.uk

- Information about new titles
- Explore the full range of Oxford World's Classics
- Links to other literary sites and the main OUP webpage
- Imaginative competitions, with bookish prizes
- Peruse *Compass*, the Oxford World's Classics magazine
- Articles by editors
- Extracts from Introductions
- A forum for discussion and feedback on the series
- Special information for teachers and lecturers

www.worldsclassics.co.uk

American Literature

British and Irish Literature

Children's Literature

Classics and Ancient Literature

Colonial Literature

Eastern Literature

European Literature

History

Medieval Literature

Oxford English Drama

Poetry

Philosophy

Politics

Religion

The Oxf

A complete list of Oxford Paperbacks,
OPUS, Past Masters, Oxford Authors,
and Oxford Paperback Reference, is av
Division Publicity Department, Oxford
Street, Oxford OX2 6DP.

In the USA, complete lists are availa
Manager, Oxford University Press, 198 N

Oxford Paperbacks are available from all
customers in the UK can order direct fro
Freepost, 116 High Street, Oxford OX1 4
10 per cent of published price for postage